ONE BY ONE

Snow is falling in the exclusive alpine ski resort of Saint Antoine, as the shareholders and directors of Snoop, the hottest new music app, gather for a make or break corporate retreat to decide the future of the company. At stake is a billion-dollar dot com buyout that could make them all millionaires, or leave some of them out in the cold. The clock is ticking on the offer, and with the group irrevocably split, tensions are running high. When an avalanche cuts the chalet off from help, and one board member goes missing in the snow, the group is forced to ask — would someone resort to murder to get what they want?

RUTH WARE

ONE BY ONE

Complete and Unabridged

CHARNWOOD
Leicester

First published in Great Britain in 2020 by
Harvill Secker
An imprint of Vintage
London

First Charnwood Edition
published 2020
by arrangement with
Vintage
Penguin Random House UK
London

A catalogue record for this book is available
from the British Library.

ISBN 978-1-4448-4508-2

Published by
Ulverscroft Limited
Anstey, Leicestershire

Set by Words & Graphics Ltd.
Anstey, Leicestershire
Printed and bound in Great Britain by
TJ Books Limited, Padstow, Cornwall
This book is printed on acid-free paper

To Ali, Jilly and Mark who first showed
me the Hidden Valley

From the 'about us' page of the Snoop company website

Hey. We're snoop. Come meet us, message us, snoop on us — whatever. We're pretty cool. Are you?

Topher St Clair-Bridges
Who's the daddy? Well, if anyone's got a claim, it's Toph. snoop co-founder (along with ex-girlfriend, model/artist/professional badass @evalution) it all started here. If he's not at his desk, he's probably riding the moguls in Chamonix, losing his mind in Berlin's Berghain, or just hangin'. Come find him on snoop at @xtopher or hit him up via his PA Inigo Ryder — the only dude who gets to tell Topher what to do.
Listening to: Oscar Mulero / Like a Wolf

Eva van den Berg
From Amsterdam to Sydney, New York to London, Eva's career has taken her all over the world — but right now home is Shoreditch, London, where she lives with her husband, financier Arnaud Jankovitch, and their daughter Radisson. In 2014 she co-founded snoop with her then life-partner @xtopher — their idea born of a single desire: to maintain their connection across 5,000 km of ocean. Topher and Eva have since uncoupled,

1

but their connection remains: snoop. Make your own connection with Eva on @evalution, or via her personal assistant Ani Cresswell.
Listening to: Nico / Janitor of Lunacy

Rik Adeyemi
head of beans
Rik's the money man, the bean counter, the keeper of the keys — you get the picture. He's been keepin' snoop real since the very first days, and he's known Toph for even longer. What can we say? snoop's a family affair. Rik lives with his wife, Veronique, in Highgate, London. You can snoop him at @rikshaw.
Listening to: Willie Bobo / La Descarga del Bobo

Elliot Cross
chief nerd
Music may be snoop's beating heart, but code is its DNA and Elliot is the maestro of code. Before snoop was a hot-pink logo on your phone, it was just lines of java on someone's screen — and that someone was Elliot. Best friends with Toph since before they could shave, he's cooler than any tech-head has a right to be. snoop him on @ex.
Listening to: Kraftwerk / Autobahn

Miranda Khan
friends tsar
Miranda is into killer heels, sharp fashion, and really *great* coffee. Between savouring Guatemalan carbonic maceration and surfing Net-a-Porter, she's snoop's smile to the world. Wanna write

2

us up, hit us up, haul us over the coals, or just say hi? Miranda's the place to start. snoop knows you can never have enough followers — or enough friends. Make Miranda one of yours at @miran-delicious.
Listening to: Madonna / 4 Minutes

Tiger-Blue Esposito
head of cool
The epitome of chill, Tiger keeps her trademark zen state with the help of daily yoga, mindfulness and — of course — a steady stream of snoop through her oversize headphones. When she's not pulling a Bhujapidasana or relaxing into an Anantasana (that's a side-reclining leg lift to the uninitiated), she's polishing snoop's cogs to make sure we look our very best, and getting the word out. Chill with her on @blueskythinking.
Listening to: Jai-Jagdeesh / Aad Guray Nameh

Carl Foster
law man
There's no two ways about it — Carl keeps us on the straight and narrow, making sure that wherever we snoop, we're doing it on the right side of the law. A graduate of UCL, Carl did his pupillage at Temple Square Chambers. Since then he's worked in a variety of international firms, mostly in the entertainment industry. He lives in Croydon. Snoop him on @carlfoster 1972.
Listening to: The Rolling Stones / Sympathy for the Devil

Taken from the BBC News website
Thursday 16 January

4 BRITONS DEAD IN SKI RESORT TRAGEDY

The exclusive French ski resort of St Antoine was rocked by news of a second tragedy this week, only days after an avalanche that killed six, and left much of the region without power for days.

Now, reports are emerging that in one remote ski chalet, cut off by the avalanche, a 'house of horror' situation was unfolding, leaving four Britons dead, and two hospitalised.

The alarm was only sounded when survivors trekked more than three miles through the snow to radio for help, raising questions of why the French authorities did not work to re-establish power and mobile phone coverage more quickly following Sunday's avalanche.

Local police chief Etienne Dupont refused to comment, except to say that 'an investigation is in progress', but a spokesperson at the British Embassy in Paris said, 'We can confirm that we have been informed of the deaths of four British citizens in the Savoie department of the French Alps, and that the local police are treating these incidents as a linked murder inquiry at this stage. Our sympathies are with the friends and families of the victims.'

The families of the deceased have been informed.

Eight survivors, also thought to be British, are said to be helping the police investigation.

This year has been marked by unusually heavy snowfalls. Sunday's avalanche is the sixth since the beginning of the ski season, and brings the total of fatalities in the region to twelve.

FIVE DAYS EARLIER

LIZ

Snoop ID: ANON101
Listening to: James Blunt / You're Beautiful
Snoopers: 0
Snoopscribers: 0

I keep my earbuds shoved into my ears on the minibus from Geneva airport. I ignore Topher's hopeful looks and Eva, glancing over her shoulder at me. It helps, somehow. It helps to shut out the voices in my head, *their* voices, pulling me this way and that, pummelling me with their loyalties and their arguments to and fro.

Instead I let James Blunt drown them out, telling me I'm beautiful, over and over again. The irony of the statement makes me want to laugh, but I don't. There's something comforting in the lie.

It is 1.52 p.m. Outside the window the sky is iron grey, and the snowflakes swirl hypnotically past. It's strange. Snow is so white on the ground, but when it's falling, it looks grey against the sky. It might as well be ash.

We are starting to climb now. The snow gets thicker as we gain height, no longer melting into rain when it hits the window, but sticking, sliding along the glass, the windscreen wipers swooshing it aside into rivulets of slush that run horizontally across the passenger window. I hope the bus has snow tyres.

The driver changes gear; we are approaching yet another hairpin bend. As the bus swings around the narrow curve, the ground falls away, and I have a momentary feeling that we're going to fall — a lurch of vertigo that makes my stomach heave and my head spin. I shut my eyes, blocking them all out, losing myself in the music.

And then the song stops.

And I am alone, with only one voice left in my head, and I can't shut it out. It's my own. And it's whispering a question that I've been asking myself since the plane lifted off the runway at Gatwick.

Why did I come? *Why?*

But I know the answer.

I came because I couldn't afford not to.

ERIN

Snoop ID: N/A
Listening to: N/A
Snoopscribers: N/A

The snow is *still* falling — fat white flakes drifting lazily down to lie softly over the peaks and pistes and valleys of St Antoine.

Three metres have fallen in the last couple of weeks, and there's more forecast. A snowpocalypse, Danny called it. Snowmaggeddon. Lifts have been closed, and then reopened, and then closed again. Currently almost every lift in the entire resort is closed, but the faithful little funicular that leads up to our tiny hamlet is still chugging away. It's glassed in, so even the heaviest dump doesn't affect it, the snow just lies like a blanket over the tunnel rather than clogging the rails. Which is good — because on the rare occasions it does shut, we're totally cut off. There's no road up to St Antoine 2000, not in winter, anyway. Everything, from the guests in the chalet, right through to every scrap of food for breakfast, lunch and dinner, has to come up in the funicular. Unless you've got the money for a helicopter transfer (which, believe me, is not unheard of in this place). But the helicopters won't fly in poor conditions. If a blizzard comes in, they stay safely down in the valley.

It gives me a strange feeling if I think about it too much — a kind of claustrophobia that's at odds with the wide-open vistas from the chalet. It's not just the snow, it's a hundredweight of unwelcome memories bearing down on me. If I stop for more than a minute or two, the images start to come unbidden, crowding into my mind — numb fingers scrabbling through hard-packed snow, the sheen of sunset on blue skin, the glint of frosted lashes. But fortunately I've got no time to stop today. It's gone one o'clock and I'm still cleaning the second-to-last bedroom when I hear the shuddering sound of the gong from downstairs. It's Danny. He shouts my name, and then something I can't make out.

'What?' I call down, and he shouts again, his voice clearer this time. He must have come out into the stairwell.

'I *said*, grub's up. Truffled parsnip soup. So get your lazy arse down here.'

'Yes, chef,' I shout back, mockingly. I quickly dump the contents of the bathroom bin into my black sack, change the bin liner, and then jog down the spiral stairs to the lobby, where the delicious smell of Danny's soup greets me, along with the sound of 'Venus in Furs' emanating from the kitchen.

Saturday is both the best day of the week, and the worst. Best, because it's changeover day — there are no guests, and Danny and I have the chalet to ourselves, free to laze in the pool, steam in the outdoor hot tub, and play the music we like at the volume we want.

Worst, because it's changeover day, which means nine double beds to change, nine bathrooms to clean (eleven, if you count the loo downstairs and the shower room by the pool), eighteen ski lockers to sweep and hoover, not to mention the living room, the dining room, the den, the snug and the outdoor smoking area, where I have to pick up all the disgusting butts the smokers always strew around in spite of the prominent bins and buckets. At least Danny takes care of the kitchen, though he has his own to-do list. Saturday night is always a big dinner. Got to put on a show for the new guests, don't you know.

Now, we sit down together at the big dining-room table, and I read through the information Kate emailed this morning as I spoon Danny's soup into my mouth. It's sweet and earthy and there are tiny little crunchy bits scattered over the top — shaved parsnip roasted in truffle oil, I think.

'This soup is really good,' I say. I know my job here. Danny rolls his eyes, in a *well, duh,* gesture. If there is one thing about Danny, he's not modest. But he is a great cook.

'Think they'll like it tonight?' He's fishing for more compliments of course, but I can't blame him. Danny's an unashamed diva about his food and, like any artiste, he enjoys appreciation.

'I'm sure they will. It's gorgeous, really warming and . . . um . . . complex.' I am striving to pin down the particular savoury quality that makes the soup so good. Danny likes compliments to be *specific.* 'Like autumn in a bowl.

What else are you doing?'

'I've got amuses-bouches.' Danny ticks the courses off on his fingers. 'Then the truffled soup for starter. Then venison haunch for the carnies and mushroom ravioli for the veggies. Then crème brûlée for dessert. And then the cheese.'

Danny's crème brûlée is his showstopper, and it's to die for. I've literally seen guests come to blows over a spare portion.

'Sounds perfect,' I say encouragingly.

'As long as there aren't any fucking stealth vegans this time,' he says morosely. He's still reeling from last week, when one of the guests turned out to be not just vegan, but gluten intolerant as well. I don't think he's forgiven Kate yet.

'Kate was *really* clear,' I say, cajoling. 'One lactose intolerant, one gluten-free, three veggies. No vegans. That's it.'

'It won't be,' Danny says, still enjoying his martyrdom. 'One of them will be low-carbing or something. Or a fruitarian. Or a breatharian.'

'Well, if they're a breatharian, they won't be bothering you, will they?' I say reasonably. 'They've got all the air they could want up here.'

I wave an arm at the huge window that dominates the south side of the room. It overlooks the peaks and ridges of the Alps, a panorama so breathtaking, that even though I live here now, I still find myself stopping mid-stride on certain days, almost winded by its beauty. Today the visibility is poor, the clouds are low, and there's too much snow in the air. But on a good day you can see almost to Lake Geneva. Behind us, to the north-east of the chalet, rises the Dame Blanche, the mountain that forms the highest peak of the St Antoine valley, overshadowing everything.

'Read out the names,' Danny says, around a mouthful of soup, only he says it more like *read aht the names*. His accent is pure sarf London, though I know in reality he grew up in Portsmouth. I'm never quite sure how much is all part of the act. Danny's a performer, and the more I get to know him, the more I'm fascinated by the complicated mix of identities beneath the surface. The cheeky cockney geezer he puts on for the guests is just one of them. On nights out in St Antoine I've seen him pivot from note-perfect Guy Ritchie, to a gloriously flaming RuPaul, all in the space of five minutes.

Not that I can talk. I'm putting on my own act. We all are on some level, I suppose. That's one of the joys of coming here, to a place like this, where everyone is passing through. You get to have a fresh start.

'I need to get it right this time,' he says, breaking into my thoughts. He puts a minuscule grind of fresh black pepper onto his soup and tastes it, then looks approving. 'Can't afford another fucking Madeleine. Kate'll have my guts for garters.'

Kate is the area rep, and is in charge of coordinating all the bookings and logistics for all six of the company's chalets. She likes us to greet the clients by their names right from day one. It's what marks us out from the big chain operators, she says. The personal touch. Only it's harder than it sounds, week in, week out. Last week Danny made friends with a woman called

Madeleine, only when the feedback forms came in, it turned out there was no one called Madeleine in the group. Or any woman with a name beginning with M. He's still got no idea who he was talking to all week.

I run my finger down the list Kate sent across last night.

'So it's a corporate party this time. Tech company called Snoop. Nine people, all in separate rooms. Eva van den Berg, co-founder. Topher St Clair-Bridges, co-founder. Rik Adeyemi, Head of Beans. Elliot Cross, Chief Nerd.' Danny snorts out his soup through his nose, but I carry on. 'Miranda Khan, Friends Tsar. Inigo Ryder, Topher's Boss. Ani Cresswell, Chief Evatamer. Tiger-Blue Esposito, Head of Cool. Carl Foster, Lawman.'

By the time I'm finished, Danny is actually crying with laughter and his soup has gone down the wrong way.

'Is that really what it says?' he manages, between coughs. 'Head of Beans? Tiger — what the fuck else? I didn't think Kate had a sense of humour. Where's the real list?'

'That *is* the real list,' I say, trying not to laugh at the sight of Danny's screwed-up face, shining with tears. 'Have a napkin.'

'What? Are you shitting me?' he gasps, and then sits back, fanning himself. 'Actually, I take that back. Snoop's that sort of place.'

'You've heard of them?' I'm surprised. Danny isn't normally the sort of person with his finger on the button that way. We get all types here, lots of private parties, the odd wedding or anniversary, but a surprising number of corporate

16

retreats too — I guess the price tag is easier to swallow if your company is paying. There's a lot of law firms, hedge funds and Fortune 500 companies. This is the first time Danny's heard of one of the companies and I haven't. 'What do they do?'

'Snoop?' Now it's Danny's turn to look surprised. 'Have you been living in a fucking cave, Erin?'

'No, I'm just — I've never heard of them. Are they a media company?' I don't know why I chose that. Media seems like the kind of industry that would have a Tiger-Blue Esposito.

'No, they're an app.' Danny looks at me suspiciously. 'Have you *really* not heard of them? You know — Snoop — the music app. It lets you — well, snoop on people. That's kind of it.'

'I have literally no idea what you're on about.'

'Snoop, Erin,' Danny says, more acidly this time, like if he keeps saying it, I'll smack my forehead and go *oh yeah,* that *Snoop!* He pulls out his phone and scrolls down the apps to one that looks like two eyes on a hot-pink background. Or maybe two cogs, it's hard to see on the logo. He presses it, and the screen goes bright pink, then black, blazoned with *snoop. Real people, real time, real loud* in fuchsia letters.

This time the two Os of the name are the wheels of a cassette tape.

'You like hook it up to your Spotify account or whatever,' Danny explains, scrolling through menus as he does, as if lists of random celebrities will make everything clear. 'And it makes your listening public.'

17

'Why would anyone want to do that?' I say blankly.

'It's a quid pro quo, innit?' Danny says, sounding impatient. 'The whole point is no one wants to listen to you, but if you join, you get to listen to other people. *Voyeurism for your ears* is what Snoop calls it.'

'So . . . I can see what . . . I don't know . . . Beyoncé is listening to? If she were on there.'

'Yup. And Madonna. And Jay-Z. And Justin Bieber. And whoever else. Slebs love it — it's the new Instagram. It's like, you can connect, yeah? But without actually giving away too much information.'

I nod, slowly. I can actually kind of see the attraction of that.

'So it's basically famous people's playlists?'

'Not playlists,' Danny says. 'Because the whole point is that it's real time. You get what they're listening to *right now*.'

'What if they're asleep?'

'Then you don't get anything. They don't appear in the search bar if they're not online and listening, and if you're snooping on someone and they stop listening, their feed goes dead and you get the option to shunt along to someone else.'

'So if you're snooping on someone and they pause a song to answer the phone — '

Danny nods.

'Yeah, it just cuts off.'

'That's a really terrible idea.'

He laughs and shakes his head.

'Nah, you're not getting it. The whole point is . . . ' He stops, trying to formulate something unquantifiable into words. 'The whole point is

18

the connection. You're actually listening to the same thing at the same moment as they are — beat for beat. You know that wherever she is in the world, Lady Gaga is listening to the exact same thing you are. It's like . . . ' Inspiration strikes, and his face lights up. 'It's like, you know when you're first going out with someone, and you're sharing a set of headphones, one earpiece in their ear, one earpiece in yours?'

I nod.

'Well, it's like that. You and Lady Gaga, sharing her earphones. It's really powerful. When you're lying there in bed, and they switch off, and you know that somewhere they're probably doing the exact same thing as you, rolling over, falling asleep . . . it's pretty intimate, you know? But it's not just celebrities. If you're in a long-distance relationship, say, you can snoop your bloke and listen to the same song at the same time. Assuming you know his Snoop ID of course. I keep mine locked down.'

'OK . . . ' I say slowly. 'So . . . like . . . your feed is public, but no one knows it's you?'

'Yeah, so I have like two followers, because I've not bothered to hook up any of my contact list. Mind you, some of the most popular Snoopees are totally incognito. There's this one guy in Iran, HacT, he's called. He's in the top ten Snoopees pretty much every month. Well, I say in Iran, there's no actual way of knowing. That's just what it says on his Snoop biog. He could be from Florida.'

An alert pings on his phone, and he brings it up.

'Ah, yeah, there, see? This is someone I'm subscribed to, Msaggronistic. She's this French-Canadian chick in Montreal, she listens to some really cool punk stuff. That alert was telling me she's come online and she's playing . . . ' he scrolls down the notification, 'the Slits, apparently. Not sure that's my cup of tea, but that's the thing, it might be. I just don't know.'

'Right.' I'm not sure I'm any the wiser really, but it's sort of making sense.

'Anyway,' Danny says. He gets up and starts clearing our soup plates. 'That's what I meant, these tech start-ups, you could actually imagine them calling their head of finance Chief Bean Counter or whatever the fuck he was called. They'd think it was edgy or something. Coffee?'

I look at my watch. 2.17.

'I can't. I've got a couple of rooms still to do, then the pool.'

'I'll bring you one up.'

I stand and stretch, working the kinks out of my neck and shoulders. It's physical work, cleaning. I never realised how much before I started this job. Heaving Hoovers up and down stairs, scrubbing toilets and tiles. Doing nine rooms on the trot is a workout.

★　★　★

I'm finishing the pool when Danny comes in with a cup of coffee. He's wearing his usual trunks — the smallest, tightest ones I've ever seen in real life. They are banana yellow, and when he turns round to put my coffee down on

20

the lounger, you can see that he has BAD BOI written across his butt in scarlet letters.

'Don't make *any* splashes,' I warn him, as he stands poised at the edge of the pool, his arms outstretched. 'I'm not mopping again.'

He says nothing, just sticks out his tongue, and then does a perfect, splash-free dive into the shallow end of the pool. It's not really deep enough for diving, but he skims the bottom and comes up safely at the far end.

'Come on, the bloody place is clean enough. Get in.'

I waver. I haven't hoovered the dining room, but I don't know if anyone would be able to tell.

I look at my watch. 3.15. The guests are supposed to arrive at 4 p.m. I'm cutting it fine.

'Oh all right then.'

It's our weekly ritual. A ten-minute dip after all the chores are done, like a way of reclaiming our territory, reminding ourselves who's actually in charge in this place.

My bikini is on under my clothes and I pull off my sweaty T-shirt and stained cleaning jeans, and ready myself to dive. I'm just about to push off, when I feel a hand grab my ankle and yank me forwards, and with a shriek, I pitch into the pool.

I surface, spluttering, raking hair out of my eyes. There is water *everywhere*.

'You fucking imbecile! I said no splashes!'

'Chill.' Danny is laughing uproariously, the water like jewels on his dark skin. 'I'll mop it, I swear.'

'I'll bloody kill you if you don't.'

'I'll do it! I said so, didn't I? I'll do it while you

dry your hair.' He points to his buzz-cut scalp, reminding me that he's got a head start on me in that department.

I punch him on the shoulder, but I can't stay mad at him, and for the next few minutes we swim and wrestle, and fight like puppies, until at last we're both drenched and gasping for air and have to stop to catch our breath.

Danny pulls himself out of the water, grinning and panting, and pads off to the changing room to get dressed and greet the guests.

I should follow him, I know it. There is plenty still left to do, jobs to complete, tasks to finish. But for a moment, just a moment, I let myself float, spreadeagled on the clear blue water. I touch my fingers to the scar that runs across my cheek, tracing the dented line where the skin is thin and still tender, and I gaze up at the grey sky through the glass roof above, watching as the snowflakes come spiralling down.

The sky is the *exact* colour of Will's eyes.

The clock is ticking down to the arrival of our guests, and I can hear Danny beginning to mop the changing rooms. I should get out, but I can't. I can't look away. I just lie there, my dark hair fanning out around me, floating, gazing up. Remembering.

LIZ

We are quite high in the mountains now. The minibus makes its way up through little Alpine villages that would look like picture postcards, except the sky is a threatening slate colour, not blue. The slushy rain down in the valley has turned into huge white flakes, and the driver has the windscreen wipers on full, swishing them aside as fast as they fall. Beneath us the wet black tarmac has turned into frozen grey ridges, and the tyres are making a strange rattling sound as they pass over them. Either side of the road, huge mud-spattered drifts have been thrown up by the snowplough. It feels like we are driving through a tunnel. It gives me a strange hemmed-in feeling and I look down at my phone, flicking through the apps to try to distract myself, before coming back to Snoop.

After I left the company, I deleted the app. I wanted everything about Snoop behind me, and I didn't like the idea of Topher, Eva and the others keeping tabs on me through the software. But a few weeks later, I found myself downloading it again. There is a reason it has just tipped a hundred million users: it's addictive. But this time my profile is locked down as tight as it will go, and there is a junk email address attached to the account so that even Elliot, who has access to all the behind-the-scenes information, can't know it's me. It's not that I'm paranoid. I don't imagine he sits there searching the user records for *Liz Owens* every few days. I'm just quite a private person. That's normal, isn't it?

Topher says something over his shoulder to me. I pull my earbuds out.

'Sorry, what did you say?'

'I said, drink?' He holds out an open bottle of champagne. I shake my head.

'No. Thanks.'

'Suit yourself.' He takes a swig directly from the bottle and I try not to shudder. He swallows, wipes his mouth, then says, 'I hope the weather clears up. We won't get much skiing in at this rate.'

'Can't you ski in the snow then?' I ask. He laughs, like he thinks I'm an idiot.

'Well, you can, but it's not much fun. It's like running in the rain. Have you never been skiing?'

'No.' I realise I'm chewing the dead skin at the side of my nail, and I make myself drop my hand. I have a sharp flash of my mother's worried voice. *Liz, please don't do that, you know Daddy doesn't like it.* I raise my own voice, shutting it out. 'I mean, not really. I did dry-slope skiing once at school, but I don't think it's really the same.'

'You'll love it,' Topher says, with that infuriating confidence. The truth is of course that he has no way of knowing whether I will love skiing or not. But somehow when he makes these pronouncements, you believe him. When he says, *your money will be completely safe*, or *it's an amazing investment*, or *you'll never get these terms again*, you trust him. You sign that cheque. You make that deposit. You put everything into his hands.

It is why he is who he is, I suppose. That million-dollar confidence. Ugh.

I don't say anything in response. But he's not waiting for an answer. He gives me a big, flashing grin and takes another gulp of Krug, then turns back to the driver.

'We must be almost there, is that right?'

'*Comment?*' the driver says, in French. Topher smiles with exaggerated patience, and repeats himself, more slowly this time.

'Almost. There?'

'*Presque*,' the driver says, brusquely.

'Nearly,' I translate under my breath, and then wish I had not.

'I didn't know you spoke French, Liz,' Eva says. She turns round to look at me. She is smiling. She says the words like she is handing out gold stars.

There's a lot you don't know about me, Eva, I think.

'GCSE,' I mutter instead. 'Not very good.'

'You are such a dark horse,' Eva says admiringly. I know she is trying to flatter me, but her words have a patronising edge considering English is her second language, after Dutch, and she is fluent in German and Italian as well.

Before I am expected to reply, the minibus

comes to a halt, the tyres squeaking in the snow. I look around. Instead of the chalet I was expecting, there is a dark opening into the snowy hill and a sign saying 'Le funiculaire de St Antoine'. A ski lift? Already?

I am not the only one who's puzzled. Carl, the thickset lawyer, is looking alarmed too. The driver gets down from the front and starts heaving out cases.

'Are we walking from here or what?' Carl says. 'Didn't bloody pack my snow shoes!'

'We're staying in St Antoine 2000,' Topher's assistant says. His name, I discovered on the plane, is Inigo. He is American, blond and extremely good-looking. He is speaking to Carl, but also to the rest of us. 'This is St Antoine le Lac, but there are a lot of little hamlets scattered around, some of them just a couple of chalets. The one we're staying in is at nearly 7,000 feet — I mean, 2,000 metres,' he says hurriedly, as Eva raises an eyebrow. 'It's got no road access, so we have to travel the last part of the journey in this funicular railway.' He nods at the dark opening, and as my eyes adjust, I can see a turnstile inside, and a bored-looking man in uniform playing with his phone in a little booth.

'I've got your tickets,' Inigo adds, holding up a sheaf of paper.

He hands them out as we climb down from the minibus onto the soft snow and we stand, holding them, looking up. I flex my fingers nervously inside my pockets, feeling, rather than hearing, the joints click. It is 4.07 p.m., but the clouds are so thick with snow that the entire sky

26

is dark. We each take a case, with the driver bringing up the rear, and then there is an uncomfortable wait for the funicular. It is invisible, somewhere far up the tunnel, though we can hear the thrum of the huge steel cable as it approaches.

'How are you doing, Liz?' a voice says behind me, and I turn to see Rik Adeyemi, Snoop's financial controller. He has an empty bottle of champagne under one arm. Rik is one of the few people I recognise, apart from Eva, Topher and Elliot. He grins, huffing a white cloud into the cold air, and claps me firmly on one shoulder. It hurts. I try not to wince. 'Long time no see!'

'I'm all right,' I say. My voice sounds stiff, prim. I hate myself for it, but I can't help it. It always comes out that way when I am nervous. And Rik has always made me nervous. It is partly his height. I don't relate well to men in general, particularly tall men who loom over me. But it's not just that. Rik is so . . . polished. Much more than Topher, although they both come from the same world. Literally. He, Topher and Elliot met at boarding school. Apparently Elliot was always a genius, even then. It's a long way from Campsbourne Secondary in Crawley, where I went to school. I know I am a creature from another planet to them. Weird. Awkward. *Working class*.

I clench my fingers, making the joints crack, and Rik winces and then gives an awkward laugh.

'Good old Liz,' he says. 'Still doing that old clicking thing?'

I don't reply. He shifts his weight from one foot to another, absently adjusting his silver Rolex as he does, staring up the track in the direction of the invisible carriage, lumbering towards us.

'How are you doing, anyway?' he asks, and I want to roll my eyes. *You just asked that*, I think. But I say nothing. I am learning that it's OK to do that sometimes. In fact it is quite fun to watch people's reactions.

Rik's eyes flick to me, waiting for my socially conditioned 'fine', and when it doesn't come, he shoves his free hand in his pocket, looking distinctly disconcerted.

Good. Let him wait.

ERIN

Snoop ID: LITTLEMY
Listening to:
Snoopscribers: 0

'Littlemy?' Danny says, looking over my shoulder as I type in my brand-new username. He pronounces it like two words — *litt lemy*. 'What the fuck does that mean?'

'Not Lit Lemmy. Little My. It's a character from the Moomins.'

'The moo you what?'

'The Moomins! It's a series of children's — look, never mind,' I say, seeing his baffled expression. 'What's yours?'

'I'm not telling you,' he says, affronted. 'You might snoop on me.'

'Oh, so you're allowed to know mine, but I'm not allowed to know yours?'

'Too bloody right. What are you going to listen to?'

I click a profile at random. NEVERMIND-THEHORLIX. It's someone the app suggested from my contact list, and although I don't know who it is for sure, I think it might be a girl I went to school with. 'Come and Get Your Love' by Redbone fills the room. I've never heard of the band but I know the song.

'Someone's been watching *Guardians of the Galaxy*,' Danny mutters with a touch of derision, but his hips are twitching in time to the beat as he walks across the room to peer out into the snow. He's only there for a second before he swings back round, grabbing a bottle of champagne from the cooler on the coffee table and popping the cork with a sound like gunshot.

'They're here, I can see the funicular coming up.'

I nod and shove my phone into my pocket. No time for chat now. This is action stations.

★ ★ ★

Ten minutes later I am standing in the open doorway of Chalet Perce-Neige, tray of glasses in one hand, watching a little group staggering and sliding down the path from the funicular to the porch. None of them are wearing suitable shoes, and they've not mastered how to walk in snow, with short steps, and your weight thrown forward, not back. One of them, a very good-looking black guy, is carrying what looks like — yes, it is. It's an empty bottle of Krug. Great. They're already drunk.

A tall blond man reaches me first, in his early thirties, handsome in a 'don't I know it' kind of way.

'Hi. Topher. Snoop founder,' he says grinning in a way that is clearly meant to charm the socks off me. His breath smells of alcohol, and his voice is every boarding school boy I've ever met. He looks faintly familiar although I can't place

30

the connection — but maybe it's just the fact that if you were casting for the CEO of a hip Internet start-up, he's exactly what you'd choose.

'Good to meet you,' I say. 'I'm Erin, your chalet host for the week. Champagne?'

'Well, since you insist . . .' He takes a glass of champagne off the tray and knocks it back in one. I make a mental note that next time I pre-pour drinks for this party, I'll use prosecco. There is no way they'll be able to taste the difference, throwing them back like that.

'Thanks.' He replaces the empty glass on the tray and stares around him. 'Great location, by the way.'

'Thanks, we like it,' I say. The others are coming up behind him now. A stunningly beautiful woman with caramel-tanned skin and white-blonde hair is picking her way through the snow.

'Eva van den Berg,' Topher says as she comes level with us, 'my partner in crime.'

'Hi, Eva,' I say. 'We're delighted to welcome your group to Chalet Perce-Neige. Do you want to leave your bags here and head inside to warm up?'

'Thanks, that would be great,' Eva says. When she speaks there's a tinge of something not quite English in her inflection. Behind her one of the men slips in the snow and launches into a grumbling rant under his breath and she says, quite carelessly over her shoulder, 'Do shut the fuck up, Carl.'

I blink, but Carl doesn't seem to notice

31

anything out of the ordinary, and simply rolls his eyes, picks himself up, and follows his colleagues into the warmth.

Inside the lobby, a fire is roaring in the big enamelled wood burner. The guests shake the snow off their coats and rub their hands in front of the fire. I set down the tray of glasses within easy reach and unfurl the list of guests and room numbers. I glance around the room, mentally trying to match people to names.

Eva and Topher I've got already. Carl Foster, the guy who slipped in the snow, is a stocky white man in his forties with a buzz cut and a pugnacious expression, but he's cheerfully downing champagne in a way that suggests he's not brooding on the moment outside the door. Judging by her surname, Miranda Khan is probably the very elegant Asian woman over by the stairs. She's wearing six-inch heels and she's talking to the guy with the Krug, who's swapped the empty bottle for a full glass along the way.

'Oh, Rik,' I hear her say, a touch of flirtation in her voice. 'You *would* say that.'

Rik Adeyemi. I put another mental tick on my list of names. OK, so that's five of them. The four remaining guests are more of a puzzle. There's a slim woman in her mid-twenties with ombré tips to her short hair, holding, for some reason, a rolled-up yoga mat under her arm. There's a boy in his early twenties with a strong resemblance to a young Jude Law. He seems to be American from what I heard of his accent when he took a glass of champagne. Behind him is a girl with fluffy yellow hair that cannot

32

possibly be her real shade. It's the colour of buttercups and the texture of dandelion fluff. She is wearing huge round spectacles and looking wonderingly around the lobby, and combined with her hair, the impression is of a particularly adorable baby chick. She must be either Ani or Tiger. She's about the furthest thing from a tiger I could possibly imagine, so I put her down as a probable Ani.

The ninth and last guest is a tall awkward-looking man, staring out of the window with his hands in his pockets. His stand-offishness compares strangely with the other guests, who are all chatting companionably with the easy back and forth that you only get from people who've worked or socialised together for a long time.

No, wait. There is one other guest who's standing alone. A woman, in her late twenties, standing hunched in an inconspicuous corner by the fire, as if hoping no one will speak to her. She's wearing dark clothes and she blended into the shadows so well that I didn't notice her at first. She's almost . . . the word that comes to mind is *cowering*, and although it feels too strong, it's the only one that really fits. Her uneasiness is in sharp contrast to the rest of the group, who are already laughing and refilling their glasses, in defiance of the advice about acclimatising to altitude. But it's not just her body language that sets her apart — it's everything. She's the only one wearing clothes that look more H&M than D&G, and though she's not the only one wearing glasses, the others look like they're wearing props provided by a Hollywood studio. Hers look like NHS cast-offs. She reminds me of a bird too, but not a fluffy little chick. There is nothing cute about her. This woman looks more like an owl — a hunted, panicked owl caught in the headlights of an oncoming car.

I'm about to go over to her, offer her a glass of champagne, when I realise there are none left on the tray. Did I put out the wrong number?

I look around again, counting. There are ten people in the lobby, not nine.

'Um . . . excuse me,' I say quietly to Topher, 'is one of your party staying elsewhere?'

He looks uncomprehendingly at me.

'I've only got nine guests on the list,' I explain. 'You seem to be ten? It's not a problem exactly — we can sleep up to eighteen — but there are only nine rooms so I'm just wondering . . . '

I trail off.

Topher claps a hand to his forehead and turns to Eva.

'Fuck.' His voice is very low, almost mouthing the words rather than saying them. 'We forgot Liz.'

'What?' she says, rather irritably, shaking her curtain of silky hair back. She's unwinding a long linen scarf from round her neck. 'I didn't catch what you said.'

'We forgot *Liz*,' he says, more emphatically this time. Her jaw drops, and she looks over her shoulder at the girl by the fireplace before mouthing a silent echoed *fuck* at her business partner.

Topher draws us both into a corner away from

34

the other guests, and beckons across the young Jude-Law-alike. As he comes closer the likeness fades, but the impression of startling good looks only intensifies. He has olive skin, sharp, Slavic cheekbones, and the most extraordinary topaz-blue eyes I've ever seen.

'Inigo,' Topher hisses, as the boy approaches, 'Inigo, we forgot Liz.'

Inigo looks at Topher blankly for a moment and then the words sink in, and the colour drains out of his cheeks.

'Oh my God.' His accent is American, Californian at a guess, though I'm not very good at placing Americans. He puts his hand over his mouth in horror. 'Topher, I'm — I'm such a dick.'

'It's not your fault,' Eva says acidly. 'Topher's the one who forgot her when he drew up the original list of names. But of all the people — '

'If you're so damn efficient,' Topher growls between gritted teeth, 'maybe you should have got Ani to do some of the legwork instead of leaving Inigo to do all the heavy lifting?'

'It's fine — ' I break in, hurriedly. This isn't going the way it was supposed to. The first day is supposed to be rest and relaxation — unwinding in the hot tub, drinking *vin chaud*, and appreciating Danny's cooking. Mundane reality isn't supposed to surface until later, when the PowerPoint presentations come out. 'Honestly, we can cater for more. The only issue is how we rearrange the bedrooms. We've only got nine guest rooms, which means two people will have to share.'

'Let me see the list,' Topher says, frowning.

'No, let *me* see the list,' Eva snaps. 'You've already screwed this up once, Topher.'

'Fine,' Topher says irritably, and Eva takes the piece of paper, running her finger down it. As she does, I notice there are what seem to be like burn holes in her sweater — it looks like she's been doing welding in it, but something tells me it came off the peg like this, and probably with a hefty price tag.

'Liz could share with Ani,' Inigo says helpfully, but Eva shakes her head.

'No, absolutely not. Liz can't be the one to share or it'll be obvious what happened.'

'What about Carl?' Topher mutters. 'No one gives a fuck about him. He could share with someone.'

'Who?' Eva says. 'Rik's never going to agree to share a room, is he? And as for Elliot — ' She jerks her head at the awkward-looking guy standing with his back to the others.

'Yes, OK,' Topher says hastily. 'I can see that's not going to work.'

Both their gazes travel thoughtfully to Inigo who is staring worriedly down at the list. Feeling their eyes upon him he looks up.

'Did I miss something?'

'Yes,' Eva says, briskly. 'You're sharing with Carl. Now run along and break the news to him.'

Inigo's face falls.

'I'll have to switch the rooms around,' I say, mentally running through the list of which rooms can fit a second bed. 'Liz will have to go into Inigo's old room, that's the smallest, is that OK?

36

And then Miranda can have Carl's, and then Carl and Inigo can share Miranda's old room, that's one of the few that can take an extra bed.'

'Where is Miranda?' Topher says, looking around. I glance over at the stairs. Rik is now talking to the fluffy chick — definitely Ani, I have deduced — and tall, elegant Miranda has disappeared. Eva sighs.

'Damn, she's probably already gone up to her room. Well, she won't be impressed at being downgraded, but she'll have to put up with it. Let's go and find her before she unpacks.'

'I'll come with you,' I say. 'Someone will have to move the cases.'

From somewhere, I feel a headache begin behind my eyes. Suddenly, this feels like the start of a very long week.

LIZ

Snoop ID: ANON101
Listening to: offline
Snoopscribers: 0

Something happened on arrival. I don't know what, but I saw Eva, Topher and Inigo huddled in the corner of the lobby with the chalet girl. And I heard my name, I'm certain. They were talking about me. *Whispering* about me.

All I can think about is what they were saying, and why they were glancing over their shoulders and scheming.

Oh God, I hate this.

No. That's not true. I don't hate *all* of this. This place — this incredible chalet, with its pool and its views and its sheepskin throws and velvet sofas — this place is a dream come true. I don't think I have ever set foot in anywhere so luxurious, at least not since leaving Snoop. If I was here alone, I would be perfectly happy, more than happy in fact. I would be pinching myself.

I hate *them*.

When at last I'm alone in my room, I sink onto the hand-stitched quilt, lie back on the feather-stuffed pillows, and shut my eyes.

I ought to be prowling around the room, taking in the glorious panoramic view of the mountains, testing out the spa settings on the bath, marvelling at my luck in being here. But I'm not. Instead I am lying here with my eyes closed, replaying that awful, awkward moment downstairs over and over again.

I should be used to it. Used to them forgetting about me, taking me for granted, ignoring me. I had a whole year of that at Snoop. A year of people going out for drinks after work, and not inviting me. Twelve months of 'Oh, Liz, would you reserve a table for four at Mirabelle?' and knowing that that four didn't include me. One full year of invisibility. And I was fine with that — more than fine, actually. I was quite comfortable.

Now, three years after I left, everything has changed. I am very, *very* visible. And somehow Topher and Eva's scrutiny and their efforts to charm me are worse than being ignored.

It is 5.28 p.m., French time. I have about ninety minutes before dinner. An hour and a half to wash and change and try to find *something* in my suitcase that won't make me look like a frump compared to Eva's new assistant and that Tiger girl from marketing.

I don't even consider competing with Eva and the other woman with the high heels — what was her name? Miranda. They are not just out of my league, they're out of my pay grade. Eva was a catwalk model, and even before Snoop started to take off, her budget for shoes was higher than my whole salary. I have always known that we were operating on different levels. But it would be nice if I could go down to dinner looking like I belong in the same room with the others.

I unzip my sagging wheelie case and rummage through the layers of clothes I stuffed in there early this morning. At last, halfway down, I find a dress that might do. I drag it over my head, and then I stand in front of the mirror, smoothing down the material, staring at myself. The dress is black and stretchy, and I bought it because I read some piece in *Elle* that said every woman needed a little black dress and this was the cheapest one in the feature.

But somehow it doesn't look like the dress in that photoshoot. It is crumpled from my case, and although I've only worn it two or three times, the material has gone into bobbles under the arms giving it a tired, charity-shop look. There are what look like cat hairs all over the back, even though I don't own a cat. Maybe they've come off my scarf.

I know that a girl like Tiger would probably pick this dress up in a thrift shop and accessorise it with something ridiculous like a chain-mail vest and biker boots and walk out looking like a million dollars.

If I wore a chain-mail vest, it would pinch the skin under my arms and clank when I walked and strangers would laugh and say 'Taking up jousting, love?' And it would rust where my sweat seeped into the links, and stain my clothes, and I would hate myself even more than I do already.

I am still standing there, gazing blankly at myself in the mirror, when there is a knock at the door.

My stomach flips. I can't face them. I can't face any of them.

'Who — who is it?' I call. My voice breaks on the last syllable.

'It's Erin, I'm your chalet host,' I hear, faintly through the wood. 'Just wanted to check you have everything you need?'

I open the door. The girl who greeted us earlier is standing there. I didn't get a chance to really look at her when we arrived, but now I do. She is pretty and tanned, with shiny chestnut hair, and she is wearing a neat white blouse tucked into dark blue jeans. She looks self-possessed, assured, everything I am not.

Only one thing is out of place — the thin, pink tracing of a long scar that runs across her right cheekbone, disappearing into her hair. It stretches as she smiles at me, and I'm . . . surprised, I suppose. She looks like the kind of person who would cover such a thing up with make-up. But . . . she hasn't.

I want to ask her how she got it, but it doesn't feel like the kind of question you can just blurt out. Once upon a time I would just have asked. Now I have learned the hard way, that kind of directness makes people think you are weird.

'Hi,' she says, still smiling. 'I'm Erin. I just wanted to check everything was OK with your room, and to let you know there will be pre-dinner drinks in the foyer this evening at 6.45, followed by a short presentation.'

'A presentation?' I tug at the hem of the dress. 'About the resort?'

'No, a business presentation I think. Was it not on your schedule?'

I rummage in my case and pull out the creased

and folded itinerary Inigo emailed over a few days ago. I have spent practically every spare second since poring over it, trying to figure out how this week is going to play out, so I know full well there is nothing listed for the first night, but I still need to reassure myself I'm not going crazy.

'There's nothing listed,' I say. I can't prevent a note of accusation creeping into my voice. The girl shrugs.

'Probably a last-minute addition? Your colleague — Ani, is that right? She just asked me to set up the projector in the den.'

It is on the tip of my tongue to blurt out that Ani isn't my colleague. I have never worked with her. In fact I barely know any of them apart from the four original founders, Rik, Elliot, Eva and Topher.

But I am too busy trying to figure out what this means.

Ani is Eva's assistant. So this presentation must be something Eva has hatched up. And Eva is the most strategic person I know. She would never leave anything off an agenda by accident. Which means she has done this on purpose. She is executing some kind of plan.

But what?

'Do you know what it's about?' I ask. 'The presentation?'

'No, sorry. The timing is literally all I know. Drinks at 6.45, presentation at 7.'

'And . . . what should I wear?' I don't want to ask her, but I'm starting to feel desperate.

The girl smiles, but there is puzzlement

behind her expression.

'How do you mean? We're really informal at Perce-Neige, no one dresses for dinner. Just wear whatever you feel comfortable in.'

'But that's what they always say!' The words burst from me, in spite of myself. 'They say, oh, just wear whatever you want, and then when you turn up there's some secret dress code that everyone seems to know apart from me. I go too smart and they're all in jeans and I look like I've tried way too hard, or I wear something casual and they're all in suits and dresses. It's like everyone else has the key to this and I don't!'

As soon as the words are out, I want to take them back. I feel naked, unbearably exposed. But it is too late. They cannot be unspoken.

She smiles again. Her expression is kind, but I see the pity in her eyes. I feel the blood creeping up into my cheeks, turning my face hot and red.

'It's really relaxed,' she says. 'I'm sure most people won't even change. You'll look lovely whatever you wear.'

'Thanks,' I say miserably. But I don't mean it. She is lying, and we both know it.

ERIN

Snoop ID: LITTLEMY
Listening to: Snooping XTOPHER ✔
Snoopers: 1
Snoopscribers: 1

As the various members of the party assemble in the foyer, the song that keeps running through my head is not the Chilean R&B I was listening to before they came in (yes, I was snooping on Topher), but the Beautiful South's 'Rotterdam'. OK, not everyone is blond. But everyone is most certainly beautiful. Almost absurdly so. There is Eva's assistant, cute little Ani with her heart-shaped face and buttercup hair. Topher's PA Inigo, now sporting a bronze five o'clock shadow that makes his cheekbones look like he stepped off a film set. Even Carl the lawyer, who is probably the least conventionally attractive of the party, with his bullish expression and stocky frame, has a definite magnetism. '*Thicc*,' Danny whispers appreciatively into my ear as he passes me with a tray of canapés. 'I would, wouldn't you?'

'Carl? Uh, no,' I whisper back, and Danny laughs, a deep throaty laugh, deliciously infectious.

'Who then? Coder-dude over there?'

He nods at Elliot, who is standing in the same spot he chose on arrival, deliberately not making eye contact with anyone. I laugh, and shake my head, but it's not because I find Elliot unattractive. OK, he looks rather like an awkward schoolboy, but he still manages to be sexy in a geek-chic kind of way. He has the kind of body that looks as if his bones are too big for his skin, all jutting wrists and angled cheekbones, and knobbly ankles protruding from too-short trousers. But his lips are surprisingly sensuous, and when one of his colleagues manoeuvres past him, she slips an arm around his midriff in a way that looks . . . well, it looks intimate. And Elliot doesn't flinch away as I thought he might.

'Come on,' Topher calls over the sound of voices. 'Let's get this party started. Carl, Inigo, surely one of you can figure out this speaker system? Jesus, no one would think we were a tech company.'

From nowhere, music starts up. David Bowie, 'Golden Years', filtering out of the Bluetooth speakers. I'm not sure who put it on, but it's an apt choice, almost to the point of irony. There is a definite gilded quality to this group. Nothing's going to touch them.

'Hey.' The girl who pushed past Elliot has woven her way through the group to where Danny and I are standing. She is swaying in time to the beat, and wearing a very short sweater-dress that exposes slim, toned legs, made more diminutive by her Doc Martens boots. For a minute I can't place her and I have a flutter of panic, but then I clock the ombré hair and nose ring. She is the woman who was holding the yoga mat when she arrived and the realisation enables me to remember her name. Yoga. Tiger. Tiger-Blue Esposito. Head of Cool.

'Hi, Tiger,' I say. I hold out the tray of cocktails I'm holding. 'Can I offer you a drink? This is a bramble gin martini, or on the left is a marmalade old-fashioned.'

'Actually I came over to get something to eat.' She gives me a beguiling smile, showing very white, even teeth and a dimple in her peach-soft cheek. Her voice is throaty — reminding me of a cat's purr and her odd name seems suddenly rather apt. 'Sorry, I know it's bad manners to hog the canapés straight out of the kitchen door, but the last tray were too good and I'm starving. They didn't serve any food on the plane, so all I've had since breakfast is Krug.' She pauses for a second, and then gives a surprisingly earthy laugh. 'Oh, who am I kidding? I'm just pathologically greedy.'

'Don't apologise,' Danny says. He holds out the tray, where his carefully handmade canapés stand in rows like little battalions. 'I like a girl with a good appetite. These are Gouda-filled profiteroles — ' he points to the tiny, feather-like puffs on the left of the tray — 'and these on the right are quails' eggs with smoked ricotta.'

'Are they both veggie?' Tiger asks, and Danny nods.

'Gluten-free?'

'Only the quails' eggs.'

'Great,' Tiger says. The dimple flashes again, and she picks up a quail's egg and pops it directly into her mouth, closing her eyes voluptuously as she chews. 'Oh my God,' she says as she swallows. 'That was a canapé-shaped orgasm. Can I have another?'

'Sure,' Danny says with a grin. 'But save room for your tea.'

She takes another, stuffs it into her mouth, and then says, thickly, 'OK, save me from myself, take the tray away before I go full Homer Simpson and start drooling on the floor.'

Danny gives a little mock bow and moves over towards Elliot, and Tiger looks after him, appreciatively. I can't blame her. Danny is kind, a great cook, and cute as hell. He's also single. It's just a shame he's not into girls.

'Tiger,' a clipped, monied voice says behind us, and I turn my head to see the PR woman, Miranda, stalking her way across the room. Her black hair is loose, a dark satin curtain down her back, and she's wearing a stunning black silk jumpsuit, cinched in to show an enviably tiny waist, and midnight-blue velvet stilettos. I notice with a wince that the pointed heels are leaving little divots in the polished wood floor, but I can't really say anything. Instead I hold out the tray of drinks. Miranda takes a glass without looking at me and dumps a half-eaten smoked duck skewer in the space left.

'We need to talk,' she says to Tiger. Her voice is high and sharp, her accent cut-glass, a few vowels away from full Princess Margaret.

'Sure,' Tiger says good-naturedly. She swallows and wipes her mouth. 'Hey, have you tried the quails' eggs? They're to die for.'

'Never mind that, Tigs, listen, we need to put some time aside to discuss the comms strategy on Elliot's geosnoop release. I've just had that pushy little shit from Unwired on the phone asking about it.'

'What?' Tiger looks taken aback. 'How did that get out? It's not even in beta yet, is it?'

'I have no idea, but I suspect Elliot blabbed about it. He's never been able to stick to an embargo and he's been telling anyone who'll listen how 'cool' it's going to be.' She makes air quotes as she says the word. 'I think I've shut Unwired down for the moment, but it's going to get out sooner or later and I have significant concerns about how it's going to go over in the press. I don't need to tell you that privacy on social is a big buzzword right now. I'm not sure if anyone's clocked the change in user-end permissions yet, but it's only a matter of time before they do. Christ, will someone please shut down that God-awful racket?'

She looks round at me, pressing her fingers to her temple, and I realise she's talking about the music.

'One of the guests put it on,' I say, trying not to sound defensive, 'but I'll adjust the volume.'

'I'm thinking we need two approaches,' Miranda continues as I move away in search of the remote control for the speakers. 'A plan A which assumes a deliberate timed release, i.e. marketing, PR, social buzz and so on. Basically all the stuff we'd already sketched out. But then a plan B in case of an early leak, in which case the question then is whether we bring forward aspects of the marketing campaign to support our narrative. It's absolutely *essential* we control the conversation on social.'

They launch into technicalities as the discussion fades away into the background babble. I locate the remote underneath a dirty napkin, turn the volume down a notch, and then glance at the clock on the mantelpiece. It's 6.55. They should be moving through shortly, but someone seems to be missing.

'Ah, about fucking time!' a man's voice says over my shoulder, and I turn to see Topher standing behind me. 'Bloke could die of thirst waiting for service around here.' He shakes his blond hair out of his eyes, then sweetens the rudeness with a grin that's just the right side of charming.

'So sorry!' I hold out the tray, masking my irritation with a polite smile. 'Bramble martini?' Topher takes one, and knocks it back with alarming speed. I restrain the urge to tell him that they are about 50 per cent gin. 'Carl?' I hold out the tray to his colleague, who nods heavily and takes the last old-fashioned.

'Cheers. Though I don't need any more booze if I'm being honest — it's food I'm after. Any more of them cheesy puffs going around? I'm bloody starving.'

'Cheesy puffs!' Topher scoffs. 'That's not how you maintain a ski-ready physique, Carl my dude.'

He pats Carl's ample midriff, straining beneath a plaid shirt.

'Carb-loading, mate,' Carl says, with a wink at

me. 'Essential part of my training regime.'

'Danny's circulating with the canapés, I'm sure he'll be over in just a sec,' I say, though I can see over Carl's shoulder that Danny has been cornered by Elliot who is methodically picking off the Gouda profiteroles one by one and putting them into his mouth like they are crisps. I hope there are some more in the kitchen.

Topher has seen it too, and now he leans past me to grab Elliot's shoulder.

'Elliot, my man. Stop hogging the server. Carl is carb-loading,' he says, and I take the opportunity to slip away and check on the rest of the room.

It's 7.05 according to the clock above the fire, but when I count heads, only nine guests are present. Someone is late, and I'm not the only one who has noticed. Eva is tapping her foot and looking anxiously around.

'Where the fuck is Liz?' I hear her hiss at Inigo, who whispers something apologetic under his breath. Then his face brightens, and he touches Eva's arm.

Eva looks up towards the gallery landing. I follow her gaze, to see Liz there, standing at the top of the spiral staircase. She has her arms crossed around herself, and her awkwardness makes Elliot look almost at his ease.

'Liz!' Eva calls, welcoming. 'Come down, have a drink.'

Slowly, almost reluctantly, Liz descends the stairs. She's wearing the lumpish, unflattering black dress that I saw when I encountered her in her room earlier, and my heart sinks for her. It's cut all wrong for her shape, making her look like a bunch of potatoes in a sock, and you can tell from the way she's holding herself, plucking at her VPL that she knows it. At the foot of the stairs she pauses, and flexes her finger joints, like a kind of nervous tic. It makes a crackle like wood popping on a hot fire, surprisingly unpleasant.

I am about to step forward with a drink, but to my surprise, Topher forestalls me. He grabs a bramble martini from my tray and rushes forward, holding it out towards Liz with a puppy-dog expression of eagerness on his face.

It is so out of character that I blink.

Who *is* this woman? Why are they so keen to keep her on side? It's almost like . . . I frown, wondering. It's almost like they're afraid of her.

But that's absurd.

LIZ

Snoop ID: ANON101
Listening to: offline
Snoopscribers: 0

They are all waiting, crowding around the bottom of the stairs as I reach the foyer — Eva, Topher, Inigo, Rik. Eva is wearing a long dress of white wool that I think is probably cashmere and which makes me feel like a frump. Topher is wearing jeans and an open-neck shirt. He is brandishing a martini glass in my face.

'Cocktail, Liz?' he says, flashing a smile.

'No thanks,' I say.

'Come on,' Topher says. His voice is his very best cajoling charm. 'It's a special occasion — all the gang back together!'

I should smile, but I do not feel like smiling. My dress is too tight. I wore Spanx underwear to try to make it fit better, but it is pinching and my stomach hurts. And the music is too loud.

'Thanks, but I've got a headache,' I say. I do not want to tell Topher the truth — that I do not drink alcohol any more. He might wonder why — what has changed since I left Snoop.

'Oh, you poor thing,' Topher says. 'Let me get you something, I've got some ibuprofen in my room. Inigo — '

'No thanks,' I say again. My heart is beating in a weird fluttery way that is making me feel slightly sick. 'I don't want any pain-killers. I think I need a glass of water.'

'It's probably the altitude,' Eva says solicitously. 'And the dry air. It's very easy to get dehydrated up here. You're so sensible not to drink alcohol.'

Topher frowns at Inigo and jerks his head towards the kitchen. Inigo nods, and hurries off. I suppose he has gone to get me water. This feels so wrong. It used to be me Topher barked at. And honestly, I preferred that. I preferred being invisible.

When Inigo comes back, Topher grabs the glass off him and says to the others, 'Let's give Liz some space.' Then he ushers me over to a small sofa where he gestures for me to sit down. I can't see any way out so I do. Topher sits beside me, too close, and takes one of my hands.

I feel my sense of panic rise.

I know what he's going to say.

'Liz, I just wanted to tell you,' he begins. I look around, panicked. My heart keeps skipping beats. I wonder if I might have some kind of heart defect. Topher is talking about how proud he is of having given me my start, about the way I stood out at the interview, about the contribution I made to Snoop, about our 'journey together'.

His words are drowned out by the janglingly loud background music and a weird hissing in my ears. But I don't need to listen to his words to know what he is really saying.

I stood up for you.

I gave you your chance.

You wouldn't be here without me.

You owe me.

And he's right. I know he's right. That's the worst thing. Because I'm about to betray all of that.

He's being so nice that I want to be sick. But at the same time I can smell the booze on his breath and feel the heat of his body shoved up against mine, and all I can think of is my father, lowering over me.

I am about to nervously crack the joints in my fingers, when a voice comes into my head unbidden. *If you make that disgusting sound one more time . . .*

I flinch, in spite of myself.

' . . . and that makes me so proud,' Topher is finishing.

I have no idea what to say. Before I can come up with anything, there is a high ringing noise from the far side of the foyer. It is Eva's assistant, Ani. She is wearing a silk dress that looks like it is made of two scarves tied together, and she is standing on her tiptoes and tapping two champagne flutes together. It makes a *ting ting ting* sound that echoes around the foyer.

Everyone falls quiet, apart from Elliot. He is still speaking to Rik. His deep bass monotone booms around the silent lobby.

' . . . server problems with the geosnoop roll out, if we can't — '

Rik nudges Elliot, who looks around. He breaks off mid-sentence, his face confused.

Beside me, Topher has gone completely stiff

and his expression is taken aback. This must be Eva's presentation. But it looks as if Topher knew nothing about it.

Suddenly I know what this is. I know what is happening. This is an ambush.

No. That's not the right word.

This is a coup.

ERIN

Snoop ID: LITTLEMY
Listening to: offline
Snoopscribers: 1

'Snoopers!' Eva is saying, in a high-pitched, artificially jolly voice. She is standing on the bottom step of the spiral staircase, though she doesn't need the extra height, and she looks amazing in her flawless cashmere sheath, like a tall flute of champagne. 'I know this wasn't on the agenda, but Ani and I wanted to welcome you all here, and begin the week with a few highlights from the Snoop journey, just to remind you all how amazing you are, and how far we've come, and what you, all of you, have contributed to the phenomenon that is Snoop. Will you come into the den for a few minutes? You can bring your drinks.'

There is a general shuffling, and a weird feeling of electricity in the air that I can't quite pin down.

Looking around the room, I can see from the reactions of everyone here, and the expressions on their faces, that the group divides into three camps.

First, there is Eva's little coterie — which seems to comprise Rik and Ani. They knew

56

about this, and were waiting for her cue. They were gathering round even before she made the announcement, and now that she has spoken they look tense, as if ready for battle.

Then there is a middle ground of people who are surprised, but pleasantly so, and looking forward to the diversion with a cheerful obliviousness. That group includes Tiger, Miranda and the lawyer, Carl. They are picking up their drinks, chatting away, seemingly quite unaware of the tensions flowing around them.

And finally there is Topher's little group who are also surprised — but not in a good way. His assistant, Inigo, looks like a kid who has stepped in dog mess in new shoes and is about to get shouted at by his dad. Techy Elliot is standing in the corner with his arms folded, and he looks mulish. He is tapping his foot and glaring through his glasses like he's just been bluffed in a poker game. Topher himself has risen from the couch where he was talking to Liz, and he looks positively alarmed. It's the first time I've seen his boyish charm properly ruffled, and I realise that beneath the charisma and the projected confidence, there's something else. I'm just not sure what. Is his smooth surface hiding a frightened little boy inside? Or is it something very different, more dangerous perhaps? For a minute, I think I see a flicker of anger cross his face.

Finally there is Liz. And I am not sure what camp she is in. She doesn't fit into any of them — but I think she does know what's going on. Her face is blank, her glasses reflecting the overhead light so that I can't see her expression.

But she doesn't look happy. In fact she's got her arms wrapped round herself like she's fending off a blow.

'Hold on a second, Eva — ' Topher says, with an attempt at his customary tone of command, but it's too late, Eva is ushering the others swiftly into the den, and he has no choice but to follow with Elliot, or get left behind. 'Eva, what the f — '

And then the door shuts behind them.

LIZ

Snoop ID: ANON101
Listening to: offline
Snoopscribers: 0

As Ani ushers us inside, I feel a twinge of panic. The den is small and dark. The windows are covered with blinds. The only light is coming from the doorway, and from a projection of the Snoop logo being beamed onto a blank wall. The image is bright pink, and it turns the faces of the others a strange, cooked colour, like hot gammon. I settle myself onto a sofa and as the door swings softly shut, I feel the atmosphere close around me like a fist.

It is an atmosphere I haven't felt for nearly three years.

Money. Privilege. *Ambition.*

The scent of it is as real as Topher's expensive bespoke cologne, the same brand I used to have to order in from a little Paris perfumery in the rue des Capucines, stammering through his order in my bad schoolgirl French. I can smell it now, though he is over the other side of the room.

I get a sudden wave of anxiety.

I think I might throw up.

'Tiger,' Eva says, when everyone has found a

place to sit, 'would you lead us through a short meditation?'

'Sure!' Tiger says. Her voice is slightly husky. I think she always sounds like that, but it makes me want to clear my own throat. I resist the urge to cough as she looks around the group. 'Make yourselves comfortable, everyone — whatever that means to you. That could be sitting, leaning, standing, embracing.'

I can't stop myself shuddering at the last word, but my reaction is better than the snort of derision I hear from Carl. Eva shoots him a look that could kill, and he covers it by shifting on his floor cushion. The filling inside squeaks and hisses as it resettles.

Tiger closes her eyes.

'Shut your eyes,' she whispers, 'and take a moment, everyone, to centre yourselves.'

There is silence in the room now. I shut my eyes, but it doesn't help the feeling of being trapped, in fact if anything it worsens it. I can feel the warmth of Inigo's shoulder to my left and Rik's thigh pressing against mine to the right. They can't help touching me — the sofa is too small for three — but it doesn't make me feel any less tense. I am sweating. My palms are sticky. My whole body is rigid with discomfort. I do not want to be here. I do *not* want to be here.

'Take a moment to thank yourself,' Tiger says, her voice low and soft. 'Thank your body for bringing you here, your bones for carrying you, your muscles for supporting you, your mind for freeing you.'

I don't want to thank anyone for this. I want to

60

get *out*. There is another rustle as Carl shifts uncomfortably, and suddenly I can't cope with the claustrophobia any more. I open my eyes a crack, trying to dispel some of the discomfort. I am about to shut them again when I see I'm not the only one peeking. Opposite me, Topher's eyes open for a moment. He scans the room, trying to figure out what the hell is going on. Our eyes meet. *I see you*. He raises a single eyebrow. I shut my eyes quickly.

'Take a moment to thank the universe,' Tiger-Blue continues. 'For the gift that is your being, for the gift that is your being *here*, for the gift that is this place, the majesty of the mountains shared with us for just a few days.'

Beside me I can hear Inigo's breathing. It is fast and shallow. When I glance over it looks like his teeth are gritted, and a muscle is jumping in his cheek. He is hating this as much as me, and clearly he did not know this was happening any more than Topher did. I know from my own PA days how Topher reacts to being out of the loop. Someone is going to get both barrels later. I feel sympathy for Inigo, but my main emotion is relief that it is not going to be me.

'And take a moment to thank Snoop,' Tiger intones. 'That thing that we are, and that is bigger than all of us. For all that we are — for all that we have — for bringing people into contact, and music into our lives. For the simple miracles it makes happen every day.'

Thank God I don't work for Snoop any more, is all I can think.

I don't know if she is finished or not, but there

is a short silence. I can feel a pulse beating in my throat. Just when it has stretched out to something almost unbearable, Eva speaks.

'Thank you, Tiger-Blue, that was beautiful. And it brings me to what I wanted to say, which is thank you for all coming here, and for all that you've done for me, for Topher, for Snoop and for music. Thank you for the music.'

'Hear, hear,' Topher says. Eyes snap open around the room, and he raises his glass, so that we all have to drink, whether we want to or not. I sip my water.

'Now, you'll forgive me for springing this on you, but I couldn't let the week begin without a little celebration of our triumphs, of what you've achieved over the last four years.' Eva says. She does not look at me when she says it, but it is impossible for me not to realise I am the odd one out here. I am the only person not currently employed by the company.

'Ani?' Eva says. And Ani nods, and presses something on the laptop balanced on her knees. There is a crackle from the speakers. Music begins to blast out, uncomfortably loud. Moving images begin to light up the wall opposite.

I should be watching the film — but I can't concentrate. The music is too loud. It is making my skull hurt. The images are too bright. They are zipping past too quickly. There is a kind of desperate, hectic intensity. My headache, which had been slowly fading, is back and pulsing in my temples. It feels as if a band is tightening around my forehead.

Figures and graphs flicker across the screen

— profit and loss, user profiles, expansion rate competitors. I press my fingers to my eye sockets, shutting out the flashing images, but I can't shut out the thumping music as it segues from one song to another in a frenetic sample of Snoop's greatest hits.

Eva is talking over the music. She is speaking about social media reach and key influencers. The rest of the group is silent. I can feel Topher's simmering resentment from the other side of the room, even with my eyes closed.

And then the music cuts out. I feel a weight lifted off my shoulders, like someone has stopped screaming in my ears. I open my eyes. There is a single chart on the projector, overlaying the Snoop logo. It is full of figures. Eva is taking us through each set, explaining what they mean. Percentages, projections, ongoing costs — and then I hear it. The word we have all been dancing around for almost twelve hours.

Buyout.

I feel the band around my scalp squeeze unbearably tight. I am not ready for this.

She is talking about the offer. She is explaining what it could mean in terms of company expansion, employee opportunities — but she is barely halfway down the second table of figures when Topher interrupts.

'No, no, just fucking no, Eva.'

'I beg your pardon?'

He stands up. His face obscures part of the projection so that his profile is beamed black and sharp onto the wall and the figures overlay his face like some sort of grotesque tattoo.

'This is half the story and you know it. Where would we be if we'd given up our IP to Spotify like they wanted back at the beginning? Nowhere, that's where. We'd be some other tinpot little streaming app no one's heard of and — '

'Topher, this is completely different.' Eva is standing in the shadow, away from the projector beam. Her voice sounds pissed off, but also as if she is trying her best to sound reasonable. 'You know it is.'

'Different how? I'm not going to end up like fucking Friendster.'

'If we try for another funding round we're more likely to end up like Boo.com at this rate,' Eva snaps back. Then she takes a deep breath. I can see that she's trying to rein in her anger. 'Look, Toph, you have some valid points, but I don't think now is the time or place — '

'Not the time or place?' He is crackling with anger. I feel sick. I have a violent flashback to my childhood, my father standing over my mother, his voice raised. I squeeze my eyes tighter shut. I feel myself begin to shake. 'You were the one who decided to kick off the week with your little propaganda film — '

'Guys.' There's a lurch of cushions to my right and Rik stands up. I open my eyes. He is picking his way through the cushions and glasses, to put himself physically between them. 'I think Eva was just trying — '

'I know exactly what Eva was trying to do,' Topher shouts. I fight the urge to put my hands over my ears again. 'She's trying to get her shot in first. Well, fuck that.'

'Topher.' Eva sounds close to tears, though I am not sure if she is. It's very difficult to know whether her upset is real or a strategic distraction. If she is acting, it is very convincing. 'Toph, please. This was supposed to be a celebration — '

'It was supposed to be a fucking ambush — ' Topher says.

'No, absolutely not, never.' Her words carry conviction. But she has overreached herself with that statement. Everyone in the room knows that she is lying, and there is a rustle as people shift uncomfortably, refusing to meet each other's eyes.

'Guys!' Rik says, desperately. 'Guys, please, this isn't how we should be starting this week. We need to come out of this with a result everyone's happy with.'

'Happy?' Topher rounds on him. 'Happy? At this rate we'll be lucky to come out of it with everyone alive.'

And with that he slams down his empty glass onto the coffee table and storms out of the room.

ERIN

Snoop ID: LITTLEMY
Listening to: Loyle Carner / Damselfly
Snoopers: 2
Snoopscribers: 3

I have my headphones in when Topher comes barrelling out of the den and snatches a bottle of whiskey from the honesty bar in the lobby. I'm caught unawares, laying the table, tapping my feet to the beat. I wasn't expecting them to break for another ten minutes, and as I pull the earbuds hastily out, I catch the tail end of his remark.

'— can add this to the bill of that Dutch bitch.'

Holy shit. What has gone down inside the den? For a minute I stand there, looking after Topher's retreating back, and then the rest of the group comes filing out, their expressions subdued, and I have to start showing them to their places at the table.

The big glass door in the lobby is still swinging to and fro from where Topher stormed out into the snow. Where on earth is he going? He was wearing jeans and a shirt, and it's minus 11 outside right now. There are no restaurants or bars in our little hamlet. St Antoine 2000 is not much more than a handful of chalets. People who want to eat out in the evening have to go down to St Antoine le Lac, which has all the shops, restaurants and cafes you could wish for. It's an easy ski down — a long blue run right into the centre of the village. But the only way back up at this time is the funicular, and that closes at 11 p.m.

Someone puts music onto the big main speakers in the dining room, the 1975, jangly and bright, perhaps in an attempt to raise the mood. But as I begin to serve up Danny's amuses-bouches — miniature wild mushroom gratins in little china spoons — Topher's absence is like a twinging nerve. The gratins go down well — as Danny's food always does — but I'm clearly not the only person stressing over Topher, and the atmosphere is strained. There is an empty space at the foot of the table where Topher should have been, flanked by Inigo and Miranda, who exchange worried glances every time another course comes and goes without him reappearing.

Elliot, his back to the wall, eats with his head down, talking to no one, and spooning food into his mouth like it's a race. 'Spooning' is literal. The starter is the truffled parsnip soup so the spoon makes sense, but when I try to clear the cutlery away for the main course, Elliot snatches the spoon back and glares at me, like he caught me trying to steal his watch. When the venison arrives he attacks it with the soup spoon, ignoring the fork and steak knife to either side of his plate. In between courses he sits with his head bowed, staring at the knots and whorls of the wooden table, blanking Tiger to his left, who chatters away to Miranda as if this is perfectly normal, and Carl to his right who ignores him back, pointedly angling his body away from Elliot towards Ani and Eva.

Eva, at the head of the table, picks at her food, looking at her watch and out of the window at the falling snow, her face showing all the anxiety I am trying to conceal. When Carl makes some innocuous remark to her, she snaps back with a viciousness that makes me wince, though he seems to accept it as par for the course.

Liz looks pale and frankly miserable, like a rabbit in the headlights, and refuses all offers of wine. At one point Rik tries to talk to her. I don't know what he says, I don't hear the opening, but she shakes her head violently, and when he opens his mouth again, she bursts out, 'Excuse me, I'm going to the loo,' pushing her chair back with a violence that makes it clatter against the tiled floor.

After she is gone Eva glares down the table at Rik, mouthing something that I can't quite read but which I think may have been *I told you so.*

Even Danny's crème brûlée fails to revive the evening, and after supper the group scatters, with pleas of headaches, early nights, and emails to send. As I pass through the lobby on my way to replenish the wood burner in the living room I notice that two more bottles are gone from the honesty bar.

The mystery of one at least is solved when I go through to the living room to find Rik and

Miranda huddled in the corner of the big squashy sofa, a depleted bottle of Armagnac on the table between them, and some kind of Cuban jazz filtering out of the speaker system, presumably from either Rik or Miranda's phone. Rik sees me clocking the bottle and flashes a smile.

'You don't mind, do you? We'll add it to the book at the end of the evening.'

'Not at all,' I say, truthfully. 'It's how the system is supposed to work. Can I get you anything else? Cheese? Coffee? Petits fours? Danny makes these incredibly moreish chocolate-dipped prunes that go really well with a glass of brandy.'

Rik looks at Miranda and raises one eyebrow, in a kind of wordless exchange that speaks more about their relationship than anything physical. There is something going on here. They are more than just colleagues, whether they realise that themselves or not.

It is Rik who answers for them both.

'No, we're fine, thanks.'

'No problem,' I say. 'Just let me know if you change your mind.'

I begin to stack logs into the fire, and Rik leans closer to Miranda and recommences their conversation as if I'm not there.

'Did you see the *look* she gave me when I brought up the shares to Liz? I had to check it hadn't burned a hole in my shirt.'

'I know.' Miranda puts her head in her hands. 'But, Rik, honestly, what were you thinking? Eva made it crystal clear — '

'I know, I know — ' Rik says. He rubs his hand over his short hair, shaking his head in

69

frustration. 'But I was ticked off by Eva acting like she's the fucking Liz whisperer. I've known Liz as long as she has. We got on pretty well before all this blew up.'

'What *did* happen?' Miranda says. 'It was all before my time, I've never understood.'

'You've got to understand, it was all just running on a shoe string in those days. It was a joke, those first six months. None of us were getting paid, not that Elliot gave a shit, I don't think he'd spend any money at all if Topher didn't make him. He's been like that ever since school. But the rest of us *did* mind. Eva was running through her modelling savings like no tomorrow. Topher had finally pissed his parents off so much they'd cut him off without a penny and he was sofa-surfing old school friends. I was working days at KPMG and nights at Snoop, and right at the bottom of my overdraft. And Liz was just this secretary who answered an advert online and was happy to work for a shit wage. I mean, even then, she dressed like some kind of sister-wife, but she was efficient and she didn't make a fuss about working out of a crappy rented office with no air con in South Norwood.'

'I didn't mean that, I meant how did she end up being the one casting — '

'I'm coming to that. We were about two weeks off launching, when we finally ran out of cash. We were just broke — flat broke — not a single avenue left. Credit cards, overdrafts, friends and family — we'd wrung them all dry, and we were about ten grand short of what we needed to keep the lights on. Topher had even sold his Ferrari

70

but it just wasn't enough. For about four days it looked like we were going to the wall — we had bills rolling in and contracts we'd signed and we were getting 'letters before action' and bailiff notifications left, right and centre. And then out of nowhere, little Liz pipes up that her grandmother just died and left her ten thousand pounds. And she says she'll put it into the company. Only she wants security. Not interest — she wants shares in the company. And not just any shares — but voting shares. Well, we left it to the lawyers to argue the split, but the end result was 30 per cent shares to Topher, 30 per cent to Eva, 19 to Elliot, 19 to me, and 2 per cent to Liz.'

'Two per cent?' Miranda says. 'Of a company that hadn't raised any capital and was barely solvent? It doesn't sound like much security for ten grand.'

'Some people might agree,' Rik says drily. 'But she's getting the last laugh. That ten grand will be worth around twelve million if the buyout goes ahead.'

In my shock, I drop a log. It clatters to the slate hearth, knocking over a little pottery jar that holds firelighters. The jar smashes with a noise that sounds almost absurdly loud, and I catch my breath, ready to apologise, but Rik and Miranda don't seem to have even noticed, and as I resume stacking the logs more carefully, they are still talking.

'Holy shit,' Miranda says, and she's laughing, but in a slightly shocked way, as if this is the first time she's heard the numbers. 'I mean I knew the buyout offer was good but . . . ' She looks

71

like she's doing sums in her head. 'So if Liz is getting twelve then that makes your share — '

'You can do the maths,' Rik says, and there's a grin pulling at the side of his face. 'But that's the point. *If* the buyout goes ahead. The investors are getting antsy, and I don't think they're going to stand for another round of funding. If Topher just keeps on like this and runs us all into the ground — '

'Yup. Gotcha,' Miranda says, a little bitterly. 'Back where we started, in the insolvency courts. But then, surely, it's a no-brainer for Liz, isn't it? OK, Elliot will vote with Topher, we all know that. But if Liz uses her brain and votes with you and Eva, then ka-ching.' She makes a money-rubbing gesture with her fingers.

'Yeah, it's just a pity Eva's such a fucking bitch,' Rik says, half under his breath. 'She doesn't make it easy to do the right thing, sometimes.'

I'm trying not to eavesdrop, but it's hard not to overhear what they're saying, even above the music, and by the time I have finished clearing up the pottery shards, I know more than I ever expected about Eva's bullying of the junior staff, Topher's instability, and Snoop's precarious financial position. It's almost a relief when they move on to other topics — plans for tomorrow's skiing, the crap Wi-Fi, Rik's wife, who seems to be causing him some grief. At some point one of them turns up the volume on the music, so that I can no longer hear their words clearly.

But as I stand, feeling the small of my back complain after the long day of lifting and bending, I do hear the tail end of Miranda's

72

reply, to something Rik said.

'Well, you're probably right. But in that case, we'll just have to *make* her, won't we?'

The words stay with me as I close the door quietly behind me, and move out into the lobby, to stare out at the still-falling snow.

We'll just have to *make* her.

Who are they talking about? Liz? Eva? Or someone else completely, Rik's wife, maybe?

On the face of it, there's nothing remarkable about her words. It's a phrase you might hear any day of the week. So why does the cool determination in Miranda's voice stick in my head?

LIZ

Snoop ID: ANON101
Listening to: Snooping XTOPHER ✔
Snoopers: 0
Snoopscribers: 0

It is 11.02 p.m. I am up in my room. I am in bed, in my dressing gown, but I am not asleep. I am snooping Topher. Not because I want to listen to his music, which is always weird experimental club stuff, but because I am trying to work out whether he is all right.

There is no check-in function on Snoop. As far as location goes, the only way of knowing where people live is if they choose to list their location in the brief paragraph of description attached to each username. Still, some part of me had been hoping that his music choices would give me an insight into his psyche.

I don't know what I imagined. Sad guitar solos. An infinite loop of 'All by Myself'. What he is actually playing is an endless stream of angry Spanish punk rock. Or it could be Portuguese. It sounds annoyed, but that is as much as I can tell. On the plus side he is listening to *something* and is therefore presumably alive. Though on reflection, I realise I can't even be sure of that. There's nothing to say his phone isn't just streaming to a frozen ditch. After a few minutes, I minimise the app with a sigh.

The memory of our conversation on the sofa downstairs is still with me, like a hangover. I know what Topher was trying to do. He was trying to guilt-trip me. Trying to remind me of everything I owe him.

The thought should make me feel angry, and it does, in a way. He is an arrogant public-school boy who got lucky with a great idea and, more crucially, a mummy and daddy who were prepared to bankroll him — at least for the first few years. He is everything I'm not. Rich. Entitled. Confident

But underneath my anger there are some uncomfortable facts. The fact that he took a chance on a gawky, awkward twenty-something, who no one ever looked at twice. The girl from Crawley, smelling of charity shops and hand-me-downs and desperation — he looked past all that, and saw the person inside, the *real* me, dogged, determined, prepared to give 110 per cent.

Most importantly, when I offered to put my grandmother's money into Snoop, *he* was the one who told me to stick out for shares, not repayment interest. Rik, Eva, they both tried to persuade me against it. They talked about the uncertainty of the returns — the possibility that Snoop might fold without ever making a profit. But Topher told me that shares would be in my own best interests. And he was right.

Topher is the reason I'm here today. I still do not know whether I should be grateful to him for that, or blame him. Both, maybe.

That girl — Erin — told us that the funicular stops at 11. So if he caught it, he should be here soon. But that is the question. Did he catch it?

I move restlessly to look out of the window, at the snowflakes still whirling down. The forecast was predicting lows of minus 20 tonight. People die in cold like that.

The knock at the door makes me jump. I tighten the belt on my dressing gown, and walk over. My heart is thumping as I turn the lock.

It is Eva.

'Liz,' she says. 'May I come in?' She has changed out of the white woollen dress she wore at dinner. Now she is wearing stretchy yoga pants that make her legs look extremely long. Her scent trails after her like an oil slick. It is strong and a little sickly. I think it might be Poison.

'Um . . . OK,' I say. I feel a little ambushed and resentful. I do not really want her in my room, but I am not sure how I can say that without sounding strange.

She pushes past me and goes over to the window, where she stands looking out across the valley with her back to me. I notice that my closet door is ajar, showing a rail full of dowdy, unironed clothes and my two cases. The biggest suitcase is sticking out slightly, preventing the door from shutting. I nudge it with my foot, and close the gap.

Eva turns, just as the door clicks shut.

'Are you OK?' she asks abruptly.

I am taken aback by the question, unsure what to reply. It is probably just a figure of speech, but still, I am not used to people, least of all Eva, caring what I think. It makes me feel strangely exposed. I cannot think what to say, but it doesn't matter, Eva is speaking.

'I wanted to apologise for springing that presentation on everyone, but I was afraid that if I put it on the agenda, Topher would find a way to get his side in first — '

Oh. She has come to try to persuade me again.

'Eva, please.' My headache, which had subsided after dinner, starts up again. It throbs in time with my heartbeat. 'Please, I don't want to do this now.'

'Don't worry.' She takes my hands in hers. They are cold and strong. 'I totally understand. I'd be torn in your shoes too. You feel loyalty to Topher, I get that, I do. We all do. But we both know . . . '

She trails off. She does not need to finish.

And in fact, she does not really need to make her case. The facts make it for her.

There are twelve million reasons to vote with Eva. She doesn't need to make it twelve million and one.

'I know,' I say. It's a whisper. 'Eva, I know, it's just that Topher . . . '

Topher, who gave me my first ever chance, who told me to hold out for the shares in the first place. How can I tell him I am betraying him? What will he *do?* For the first time, I realise: I am frightened.

'Liz, you *know* what you want to do, what you *need* to do . . . ' Eva says, and her voice is cajoling, like she is talking to a scared child.

'Come on, haven't I always had your back? Haven't we always taken care of each other?'

I remember Rik's question at dinner last night, the question that made me push back my chair and leave the room. *So, Liz, how are you going to spend your share bonus?* It was so brash, so bold, so full of assumptions.

Eva is more subtle. She knows that the money terrifies me in a way. Because for someone like me, who grew up having to hoard every last penny my dad didn't spend on the slots, it is an unimaginable sum. Ridiculous. Transformative. *Life*-changing.

Eva knows that the thing that will persuade me is not the money — but something else. Something much more personal, between her and me; an appeal to the past we share. I was her assistant too once, back in the days when Snoop could only afford one. In a different way, I owe as much to Eva as I do to Topher. More.

But really, she knows what Rik knows, what Carl knows, what everyone apart from Topher and Elliot seems to accept: that it is not a choice at all.

There is only one sane answer to the question in front of me. My loyalty to Topher is being weighed against not just twelve million pounds, but against something else entirely — the prospect of a very different life to the one I am used to. In the end, what is at stake is my freedom. Freedom from work, from worry, from watching every step — freedom from this.

'I know, Eva,' I say. My voice is very low. 'I know. It's just . . . it's hard.'

'I understand,' she says. She presses my hand again. Her fingers are cold against mine, and very insistent in the message her grip is conveying. 'And I know it's hard. I feel that loyalty to Toph too, of course I do. But I can count on you, yes?'

'Yes,' I say. My voice is almost inaudible, even to myself. 'Yes, you can count on me.'

'Good.' She smiles her wide, beautiful smile. It is a smile that once beamed out from a thousand billboards and catwalks all across Europe. 'Thank you, Liz, I know what that means. And you can count on me, too. We'll take care of each other, won't we?'

I nod, and she gives me a perfunctory hug and leaves the room.

When she's gone I open the window to get rid of her scent. I lean out, and I let the anxiety locked inside my chest explode into something huge and almost overwhelming. I imagine the meeting, the vote, me raising my hand in support of the buyout, and the expression on Topher's face as he registers my betrayal . . . And then I imagine what will happen if I don't, and I feel utterly sick.

Because Eva is right. There *is* only one choice. I know what I have to do. I just have to find the courage.

And once I have made up my mind, a strange kind of peace descends on me.

It will be OK. It will all be OK.

I shut the window. I climb back into bed and I switch off Snoop. Then I lie, quite still, listening instead to the whisper of the snow falling onto my balcony outside. Obliterating everything.

ERIN

When my alarm goes off, I struggle up out of a deep, disturbing dream — a nightmare of digging, digging, digging through hard-packed snow, my hands numb with cold, my muscles shaking, hot blood running down my neck. I know what I'm going to find — and I'm both yearning for it, and dreading it. But I wake up before I reach my goal.

It's a relief to open my eyes and find myself in my own little room, my phone alarm screeching into the silence, until I grope my way to the snooze button and shut it off. The clock says 6.01, and I lie there for a minute, blinking, still half asleep, and trying to throw off the uneasy feeling the dream has left.

Just because it's a weekend, it doesn't mean it's not an early start. Danny and I swap, so that one of us gets up at 6 to fire up the coffee machine, get breakfast started and clear up from the night before, while the other has what passes for a lie-in. Today it's my turn for the early shift, and I can't stop yawning as I stumble out of bed

80

and pull on my clothes. Some people find they get insomnia at altitude. Not me. If anything it's the reverse.

As I pass Topher's door I pause, trying to hear if he's inside. Did he get home OK? I didn't hear him come in, but I left the front door open, and when I came down at midnight to check, there were wet footprints in the foyer.

I stand there, holding my breath, when suddenly a huge snore rips through the silence, and I let out a shuddering laugh. *Someone* is in there at any rate, even if it's not Topher.

Downstairs is quiet, last night's log fire just glowing embers behind the wood burner's glass door. I open up the vents and stick another log on top of the ashes, and then I begin clearing up the debris of the night before.

Snoop are no worse than a lot of the other groups that stay here, but I don't know why, today I feel particularly jaded as I pour thirty-year-old brandy down the sink, and pick melted Camembert out of the dining-room rug. Someone has been smoking inside too, in defiance of the rules — there is a cigarette butt stubbed out in a dish of Danny's painstakingly made petits fours. That's what sets my teeth on edge, I think. I remember him making those miniature Florentines; mixing them, baking them, carefully dipping each one into precisely tempered chocolate, laying them out to set. Treating them like the little master-pieces they were. And now someone has used them as a makeshift ashtray.

It takes me a while to shake off the cloud of anger, but by 7 a.m. my mood has lifted a little.

81

The rooms are clean, the fire is crackling, the oven is on for sausages, and the Bircher muesli is standing in a big crystal bowl on the side, along with huge pitchers of fresh-squeezed juices and jugs of milk and cream. There is still no noise from above, which means I can afford ten minutes to sit down with a coffee and my phone. Normally I'd be checking the snow forecast, or scrolling through Twitter — but today I find myself opening up Snoop, and idly flipping through lists of my favourite artists, figuring out who's online, who's listening to what, as I sip my coffee. There are some amazing people on here, proper celebs, mixed with people who are just fascinating personalities, and Danny's right, there's something incredibly addictive about pressing play on the song they are actually listening to at this precise moment, knowing that you are beat-for-beat in sync with each other. It's midnight in NYC and lots of the people I snoop on are playing late-night, come-down music, which is not what I'm looking for at this time of day, but then I hit a cool little vein of British celebrities who all seem to be up and listening. Why are they are awake 6 a.m. UK time? Couldn't they sleep? Maybe they always get up at this time.

I'm washing up the serving bowls that are too big for the dishwasher, tapping my feet to 'Rockaway Beach' by the Ramones, when the sound begins to break up. As I'm digging my phone out of my pocket to check the headphone connection, the song drops out completely. Damn. I stare at the screen. The Wi-Fi is still showing a strong signal, but when I click on the Snoop tab a little pop-up message appears. *We can't get no satisfaction. (Please check your Internet connection.)*

I sigh, turn off the app, and begin washing up again, this time in silence, but before I have done more than a couple of plates, there's a tap on the window to my right, and I look across to see Jacques from the bakery down the valley, holding a stack of baguettes and a giant bag of croissants. I pull off my rubber gloves and open the door, breathing white into the cold morning air.

'*Salut, ma belle,*' he says around his cigarette as he hands the bread over, and then he takes a long drag of his Gitane and blows the smoke over his shoulder.

'Hi, Jacques,' I say in French. My French isn't perfect, but I can hold a conversation. 'Thanks for the bread. What do you say to the forecast?'

'Ah, well, it isn't pretty,' he says, still in French, taking another long thoughtful drag and looking up at the sky. Jacques is one of the very few people who actually grew up here. Almost everyone else is an incomer, either a tourist or a seasonal worker. Jacques has lived here all his life, his father owns the bakery in St Antoine le Lac and Jacques will be taking over for good in a few years when his dad retires.

'Do you think there will be the possibility to ski today?' I ask. Jacques shrugs.

'Perhaps, in the morning. But the afternoon . . . ' He holds his hand out and makes the rocking motion the French use to signify that something might go one way or the other.

'There's heavy snow coming. You see the colour of those clouds over La Dame?'

La Dame means La Dame Blanche — the big peak that looms over the whole valley, casting a near-permanent shadow over the chalet. Now, as I look up at the top, I see what he means. The clouds that gather up there are ugly and dark.

'But it's not just that,' Jacques says. 'It's the wind. It makes it difficult for the guys in the avalanche control teams. They can't get out to start the small falls, you know?'

I nod. I've seen them doing it on fine days, after big dumps — setting off small charges to safely release the build-up of snow on the upper slopes before it can get to critical mass. I'm not sure how they do it exactly — sometimes they seem to use helicopters, other times it looks more like some sort of gun. Either way, I can imagine that the wind makes it too hazardous and unpredictable.

'You think that there is a danger of falls?' I ask, trying to hide my uneasiness.

Jacques shrugs again.

'Serious ones? Unlikely. But there will be slopes closed this afternoon for sure, and I wouldn't plan any off-piste skiing.'

'I don't ski off-piste,' I say shortly. Well, not any more.

Jacques doesn't respond to that, he just looks thoughtfully up at the slopes, and then blows out a ring of smoke. 'Well, I must be going. See you later, Erin.'

And he crunches off through the soft-fallen snow towards the funicular. I feel my stomach shift with the lingering chill from my dream as I watch him go, and then turn back, into the warmth of the kitchen.

Inside, I am stacking the bread on the table when the sound of a croaky, sleep-hoarse voice comes from behind my shoulder, making me jump.

'Monsieur Bun the boulanger's son?'

It's Danny, leaning against the counter, squinting at the bright morning lights.

'Jesus.' I put a hand on my chest. 'You startled me. Yes, it was Jacques. He says there's going to be more snow.'

'You're shitting me.' Danny rubs a hand over his stubble. 'There's not going to be any more of the stuff left up there. Will we get any skiing in?'

'I think so. This morning he reckons. He says the runs will probably be shut in the afternoon — avalanche risk.'

'It's already on orange,' Danny says, referring to the coloured scale published by Météo-France. Orange is level three — 'considerable risk' of avalanche occurring, and means off-piste skiing is inadvisable, and some of the steeper slopes are probably going to be shut. Red is level four and is when the whole resort starts to close. Black is level five and means risk to settlements and roads. Black is like, make sure your last meal is a good one, but the control teams don't let it get to that point if they can help it.

I'm gathering up the tray of coffee cups when Danny speaks again, his voice casual.

'Who's Will?'

The question is a shock — enough to make

me stumble, and two of the cups slide off the tray and shatter on the floor. By the time Danny and I have gathered up the shards, I'm composed enough to answer.

'What do you mean? There's no one here called Will.'

'You were dreaming last night, shouting about someone called Will. I heard you through the wall. It woke me up.'

Fuck.

'Huh, weird.' I keep my voice light, and just a little puzzled. 'Sorry about that. Nightmare I guess.'

And then before he can pursue the question, I leave the room. I carry the tray through to the dining room with hands that are only slightly trembling, and begin laying out the breakfast things on the big wooden dining table. I'm setting out the last jars of preserve, when I hear the click of heels on the stairs and look up to see Eva, coming into the lobby. She looks pissed off.

'Hi,' I say.

'Hi, what's happened to the Internet?' she says without preamble. My heart sinks. Shit. I'd hoped it was a temporary thing.

'Oh God, I'm so sorry. Is it still down?'

'Yes, and the mobile reception is terrible.'

'I'm ever so sorry, it's something to do with the snow. It happens occasionally. I think it means a wire's snapped in the snow or a repeater's gone down or something. It's not uncommon after very heavy falls, and we've certainly had enough of that recently.'

I wave my hand at the window where the snow

is halfway up the glass in some parts.

'I don't need the science bit, what I want to know is when it will be back up?'

Her tone is sharp and unapologetically annoyed. It's the voice of someone used to saying 'jump' and getting the answer 'how high?' Which doesn't bother me in itself — in some ways I prefer people who are clear about their expectations, rather than smiling at you all week and then giving you a shitty write-up on their feedback forms. But in this instance I can't help, and something tells me Eva isn't going to like that fact.

'I don't know,' I say. I fold my arms. 'I'm sorry. They usually get it up and running in a few days, but I can't say with more certainty than that.'

'Fuck.' She is annoyed, and not trying to hide it, but the expression on her face is something more than that, there's a level of stress and upset here that's out of proportion.

'I'm sorry,' I say again. 'I wish I could do something more concrete. Is it a problem with work?'

'Work?' She looks up at that, and then shakes her head and gives a bitter little laugh. 'God no. All my work problems can be summed up in one word — Topher. No, this is home. It's — ' She sighs, and then runs her hand through her silky white-blonde curtain of hair. 'Oh, it probably doesn't sound like a big deal, but I always skype my daughter, Radisson, every morning when I'm away. It's our little ritual, you know? I have to travel so much, and I'm not always able to be there as much as I'd like. But the one thing I always do is say good morning to her over breakfast, and I feel like a complete shit that I can't do it today. I managed to get through on the phone to my partner, but you know, with little kids they don't really understand phones. She's only eighteen months. She needs to see a face.'

'I can understand that,' I say softly. 'It must be really hard being away from her.'

'Thanks,' Eva says shortly. She blinks, and then turns away, under the pretence of filling up a cup at the steaming tea urn. I think she is pissed off with herself for showing that she's only human, but it makes me like her a bit more. Underneath that icy facade is a person, apparently.

Then she picks up a tea bag, puts it into the cup of boiling water, and walks away back to her room without another word.

★　★　★

Topher, Rik and Carl are the next guests down, about half an hour later, and my heart does a little jump of relief at the sight of the three of them. Well — at the sight of Topher, to be more accurate. He looks bleary-eyed and hung-over, but he's here, which is as far as my responsibility to the group goes.

'So you weren't the only dirty stopout,' Carl is saying to Topher as they enter the room. 'Inigo came crawling back to our room at 5 a.m.'

'Oh Christ,' Topher says. He rolls his eyes. 'Not that again. Eva should know better.'

Eva? Her name gives me a little prickle of reaction, though I can't say why, exactly. It's none of my business after all. Perhaps it's coming straight after her obvious distress at not being able to talk to her family. Is Topher right, or just stirring up trouble?

'Hashtag cougar,' Carl says with a grin. He walks across to the breakfast buffet I have laid out, picks up a warm croissant, and dunks it straight into the glass Kilner jar containing Danny's golden home-made apricot preserve. Then takes a huge bite, grinning through the crumbs.

'Hashtag?' Rik says disdainfully. He's wearing a black merino polo neck and looks like a page ripped from a high-end men's knitwear catalogue. 'Cougar? Have I woken up in a frat house in 2005?' Then he turns to me with a deliberately charming smile that crinkles the skin at the corners of his mouth. 'I'd love an espresso, please, Erin. If that's OK.'

Carl glares at him with a force I can feel over the other side of the room.

It should have come across as a dick move — a younger, fitter, better-looking man taking the piss out of his less hip colleague. But I get the impression that Rik's issue isn't really with Carl's choice of words, but more with his choice of conversation topic. It's funny, I'm starting to like Rik more and more. There is something about the way he relates to Eva — and Miranda actually — that is very different to Carl and Topher's sniggering boys' club attitude. Much more likeable.

'So, skiing today?' The voice comes from the

top of the stairwell, and I look up to see Miranda making her way down the spiral. Her dark hair is tied back in a bun and she looks ready for business. She clocks me dispensing Rik's espresso and says, 'Good morning, Erin, mine's an almond milk cortado please. What's the forecast?'

'More snow in the afternoon,' I say. 'In fact some people are saying they expect the avalanche rating to rise, which means more closures. If you want to ski, do it this morning is my advice.'

'Eva won't be pleased,' Carl says. 'She's got this morning packed with presentations.'

'Eva will have to lump it,' Topher says sourly. He pops two white pills into his mouth and washes them down with a gulp from his stainless-steel water bottle, then massages the bridge of his nose. 'I didn't come all this way to sit in a boardroom all week listening to her bore on about investor expectations. She can push her little bits of paper around this afternoon.'

'I'm sure she won't mind rescheduling,' Miranda says mildly. 'It'll be good for everyone to blow off some steam. I certainly can't wait to get my skis on.'

She has the look of a skier. Lean but strong. Topher looks like a boarder and I'm unsurprised when he says, 'What's the off-piste like round here, Irene? Any good powder?'

It takes me a beat, then I realise he's referring to me, at the same time as Miranda hisses, 'She's called *Erin*,' in Topher's direction.

I smile, trying to convey that I don't mind. Irene, Eileen, Emma — it's all the same. When you're staff, you're not really a person. Topher would probably treat a robot with high-quality AI with the same level of polite disinterest.

'The snow must be amazing right now,' Rik says. 'Can you show us some good off-piste routes, Erin?'

I feel the blood drain from my face, and I'm trying to think what to say, when I'm saved from answering by Danny, who comes out at that moment carrying a huge platter of bacon rolls.

'Erin's too much of a wuss to go out of bounds,' he says with a grin. 'But I can show you some cool little routes if you want. Not today though.'

'Why not today?' Topher says, frowning.

'The avalanche risk is too high,' I say, trying to regain my composure. 'But it should be better later in the week when they've had the chance to set off some controlled explosions.'

In truth I have absolutely no idea whether it'll be better, but no one likes a pessimist, and they've got to get up there and clear the build-up some time.

'Well, that's a plan then,' Topher says briskly. He picks up a bacon roll and takes a bite.

'What's a plan?'

The voice comes from the direction of the living room and we all turn to see Eva standing there. She's holding a massive sheaf of files and a laptop and looks ready to go.

'Erin says that the only skiing today is likely to be in the morning,' Rik says quickly, 'so we thought we'd get the finance presentation out of the way now, and then move the rest of the stuff to the afternoon.' He speaks rather fast, and I have the impression he's attempting to head off Topher from saying the same thing, but with less diplomacy.

Eva pauses in the doorway. She looks like she's trying to decide how to feel about this, whether to make a fuss. Then she looks at her watch, and shrugs.

'Fine. It's nearly 8.30. Shall we get going on the presentation? It shouldn't take more than half an hour, so we won't be far off the first lift if we leave straight after that.'

'Sooner the better, as far as I'm concerned,' Topher says. 'We can take breakfast into the den with us. Where the fuck are the others?'

'I'm here.' It's a voice from the doorway, and we look across to see Tiger entering the room. 'Sorry, have I kept you?' She looks pale and rumpled, her short, ombré hair sticking out in all directions as if she hasn't brushed it yet this morning.

'Yes,' Topher says, at the same time as Miranda says, 'No, you're not the only one missing.'

'Ready to milk some pow, Tiger?' Topher asks. I hear a noise from the direction of the kitchen where Danny has stifled a derisive snort, and I busy myself over the espresso machine to hide my own expression.

'Sorry?' Tiger says. She rubs her eyes as if the morning light is hurting her. 'I didn't catch that.'

'Are you ready to get on your board?'

'Oh, yes, sure.'

'You look worse than Topher,' Eva says bluntly, and Tiger laughs, with an uncertain look at Topher.

'I didn't sleep well. I had awful insomnia all night.'

'It's the altitude,' Eva says. 'It affects some people that way. I always take sleeping pills for the first few nights.'

I don't hear Tiger's reply, because Topher pulls me to one side.

'Are all the hire skis here?'

'All waiting for you in the locker room,' I say. The ski shop is down in the village, so we pick up the gear for the skiers. Most people here have brought their own though. It's only Liz, Ani and Carl who have hired equipment. 'Before you go, let me show you the best route back to the chalet. It's a really great run, but it's a bit counter-intuitive, looking at the map. You actually have to cut across a little bit between two runs.'

'Is that safe?' Carl says, sounding alarmed. 'You just said it was too dangerous to go out of bounds.'

'Oh, no,' I hasten to reassure him. 'It's totally safe, it's a very well-trodden path. It's not off-piste in that sense. But it's just not shown as a route on the lift map, so unless you know to peel off through the trees, you get taken right down Blanche-Neige into St Antoine le Lac and have to come back up the funicular.'

'Is it safe for beginners?' Carl says, still looking anxious.

'The cut-through? Absolutely. It's the equivalent of a green run. Have you skied at all?'

'Yeah, but not for years.' He looks over his shoulder. Topher and the others have gone through into the den to begin the meeting, and we are alone. 'Strictly *entre nous*,' he says, rather bitterly, lowering his voice, 'I'd rather have poked my fucking eyes with cocktail sticks than gone on a skiing holiday. But this is what you get for working for a company like Snoop. Topher's a snowboarding nut, Eva's practically a pro skier, and what they say goes. The rest of us have to lump it.'

I nod, as if he's making small talk, but in truth this insight into Snoop's inner workings is weirdly fascinating. There may be five shareholders, but in day-to-day life it seems that Topher and Eva call the shots pretty autocratically.

It makes it all the more interesting that for once, the balance of power is out of their hands. One of them is *not* going to get their way over this buyout. The question is, which one?

94

LIZ

Snoop ID: ANON101
Listening to: offline
Snoopscribers: 0

'OK,' Rik says. He clicks off the PowerPoint slide, and turns on the lights. 'That's it. I think everyone can go and get into their ski gear now.'

I rub my eyes, feeling the sudden brightness searing the back of my skull. My headache is back again. I stand up, pulling my tights straight. Around me there is the rustle of beanbags and the noise of sofa springs as everyone else gets to their feet.

'Just a second,' Topher puts in. His voice is smooth. 'Can the shareholders stay back for a sec?'

I feel something in my stomach drop away. There is a murmur of assent. Ani, Inigo, Carl, Miranda and Tiger rise and begin to file out.

Within a few seconds it's just Topher, Eva, Rik, Elliot . . . and me.

Oh God. I feel my breath coming fast. Oh God, oh God, oh God . . . they're going to ask and I'm going to have to — to have to —

'Look,' Eva is saying, 'I think the cold hard reality of Rik's figures wasn't lost on any of us. It's a pretty stark picture. Our overheads — '

'I don't want to go over all that again,' Topher says dismissively, as if the profit and loss sheets Rik just took us through were totally irrelevant. 'We can all read a spreadsheet and Rik made his points very ably. Before we head out, I think it would be really helpful to take an indicative vote, so we know where we stand.'

My breath quickens. The headache behind my eyes intensifies until the edges of my vision begin to fray.

'But, Topher,' Eva is saying, 'you know perfectly well that we don't have full information yet, that's the point of this week, to weigh up all — '

'And it's why I said *indicative*,' Topher interrupts, a touch of aggression creeping into his voice. 'This is non-binding, Eva. It's just a show of hands to see where we are. It's possible we're already close to an agreement.'

Eva says nothing. She glances at me and I know what she is thinking, and I know she can't figure out how to head Topher off from this. He is like a mule when he puts his mind to something. He just pushes, and pushes, and pushes . . .

Elliot also says nothing, of course, but we all know what his silence means — support for Topher. It's what it always means. Elliot doesn't care about anything except for code. For everything else, he defers to Topher.

'Rik?' Eva says. Her tone is brittle.

'Why not?' Rik says. His acquiescence surprises me.

'So,' Topher says, in a slightly mollifying voice. 'As before, in a *non-binding* show of hands,

96

who's in favour of the buyout?'

'Me,' Rik says.

'And me,' Eva adds. There is a long silence, and I can feel the tension as they wait. When Topher speaks again, there is satisfaction in his tone, like a cat that's got the cream.

'Great, and who's against?'

'Me.' Elliot's deep monotone makes the word sound like a full stop.

'And me, obviously,' Topher says. There is another pause, and then he says, as if attempting to sound more casual than he really is, 'And . . . um, what's your vote, Liz?'

I swallow. There is something hard, stuck in my throat, and I realise that I haven't spoken since I got up this morning. No one talked to me at breakfast. No one asked my opinion at the meeting. I don't know if I can trust my voice when I speak.

'Liz?' Eva says. I can tell that she is trying not to pressure me, but at the same time, the edge in her tone shows clear.

'I — ' There is a crack in my voice, it is croaky with disuse. I swallow again, vainly forcing down the obstacle that feels like it is choking me. 'I don't know.'

'Come on, Liz,' Rik says, and though he is trying to sound jolly and supportive, there is impatience in his tone as well. 'You must have an idea of how you feel. Do you want twelve million, yes or no? It's not a hard question.'

'Or,' Topher says, and the sharpness makes me flinch, 'do you want shares worth potentially much more if we retain control and go public?'

97

'If we retain control and manage to remain *solvent*,' Rik shoots back.

'For fuck's sake, Rik — ' Topher snaps, and I feel the panic in my chest begin to explode like a slow but inexorable chemical reaction. Before it can escape, Eva stands up, holding out her hands, putting herself physically between them.

'Guys, guys, come on. We've got plenty of time to go through the question of a public offering, now's not the time. Liz, am I to take it that you can't give us an indication right now?'

I can't bring myself to speak, I just make a swing of my head that could be yes, or could be no. Eva smiles, and crosses the room to take my hand. She squeezes it reassuringly, the scent of her perfume drug-like and headily overwhelming in the small room.

'No problem. OK, well, in view of that, I suggest we all head up to our rooms to get ready, and we can go through the issues Rik raised in more detail after lunch. Agreed?'

There are nods and murmurs of assent, and then Topher, Elliot and Rik file out.

I stand up, my legs shaking, and I'm about to follow them when Eva stops me.

'Liz, hold up a second. Are you OK?'

I can't speak for a minute, and then I manage.

'I'm — I'm sorry, Eva, I know we talked about this last night and I promise, I am — I am going to do it — it's j-just — '

'Of course,' Eva says, and she puts a hand on my arm. I think it's meant to be reassuring, but the effect is to prevent me edging towards the door. 'I completely understand.'

'It's just — ' I glance out of the door, checking Topher isn't within earshot. But he is gone, thank God. 'It's just, it's hard to come out and say it, you know?'

'I get that. There's a lot of loyalty between you. And I understand what you're saying, he's going to see it as a betrayal, no matter how reasonable your decision is.'

'I'm — ' I swallow. The truth is I'm frightened, but I don't want to say that to Eva. It sounds absurdly dramatic. 'I'm just — '

Eva's looking at me with concern, and I know why. She's wondering if I will go through with our agreement. But I have made up my mind now. I grope again for that fatalistic peace that descended on me last night. I try to remember how it felt — that certainty, that calm resolve. My heart steadies a little. I can be as determined as Topher, when I make up my mind.

'You don't need to worry,' I say, and my voice is stronger. 'I'm not going to let you down. I just — I need to bite the bullet.'

Eva's face clears, and she pats my arm sympathetically, giving it a little squeeze to show that we are in this together.

'Look, he'll be pissed off,' she says. 'I can't pretend that's not the case. And I can't say I'm relishing this either. But he'll get over it. He'll understand.'

The thing is, he won't. As we file out of the little room, to change into ski clothes and get our stuff together, that's what I realise. He definitely won't understand. There is no way of seeing what I'm about to do as anything other than a huge betrayal. But I have no choice. That's what I just have to keep telling myself. I have no choice. I have to see this through.

ERIN

Snoop ID: LITTLEMY
Listening to: offline
Snoopscribers: 10

'Right,' I call to the little group standing in front of the chalet, fiddling with bindings. 'Let me explain the lay of the land a bit. The track in front of us, leading off to the left, is the one you took from the funicular railway. You can retrace your steps back up the hill, which would get you back to the funicular and the long blue run down into St Antoine.'

'Blanche-Neige, right?' Topher puts in, and I nod.

'That's right. It's a really nice run. *However,* getting back up there would require a fair amount of sidestepping uphill, so assuming you want to ski out, the only downhill route is this path down through the woods.' I indicate a little path that winds along the side of the chalet and disappears through the pines behind us. 'It leads onto the bottom of the green run, Atchoum, and from there to the Reine telecabine.'

'Telecabine?' Inigo asks, and I remember the Americans use different terms.

'Oh, sorry, the what do you call it. The bubble lift. Are there any complete beginners here?'

'M-me!' Liz calls nervously. 'I've only skied once before. Dry slope. I wasn't very good.'

'OK, well, don't worry, the path is a little bit steep for the first few metres but then it levels out and really all you've got to do is point your skis forward and slide the whole way. You can snowplough the first section if you want, but I wouldn't recommend it, you want a bit of speed for the flat. I suggest the experienced skiers go first, then the snowboarders, you're going to have a bit of trouble on the flat section, and then I'll bring up the rear with anyone who's slightly less confident. After the flat part the path joins the green piste and there's a very gentle descent to the lift.'

'Give us a tow,' Topher says to Eva, with a grin, and she rolls her eyes and sticks a pole out behind her. I point them in the right direction and watch as they schuss off along the little narrow path between the trees. When they get to the flat Eva breaks out into a beautiful skating motion, pulling Topher along behind her, and I watch her as she goes, her scarlet ski jacket flickering in between the trees. Whoever it was described her as practically an Olympian is right, she's a very good skier. Better than me, and I'm no slouch. Topher, from the way he handled the steep little descent at the beginning, not easy on a board, is evidently in his element.

Rik goes next, he's clearly an experienced skier, even if he lacks Eva's flair. Then Miranda, who snowploughs the first steep section in defiance of my advice, grinds to a halt on the flat, and has to stump along looking embarrassed. I would guess she's competent rather than excellent, probably knows the basics but is a little too cautious to be really good. Next comes Inigo in a grass-green jacket that somehow makes his azure eyes look even bluer. He swooshes down with an elegant economy and passes Miranda, kindly putting a hand in the small of her back to help her regain her momentum. He's obviously been skiing since childhood, no mistaking that relaxed grace. Then Tiger, who turns out to be a very good snowboarder. She doesn't have Topher's advantage of a pull from Eva, but she makes it look easy.

Carl shoots off with a look of grim determination on his cherry-pink face that says, *fuck it, might as well be hung for a sheep as a lamb.* He manages to get one ski stuck in a soft bank almost at once and falls over with a painful-sounding crunch, but he hauls himself up uncomplainingly, gets himself back in position, and this time makes it without incident. Next up is Ani. She is wearing a bright blue jacket and white salopettes that look fresh off the peg, and her buttercup hair is sticking out around her hood. The effect is somewhere between adorable toddler and children's TV presenter. She gives me a wry smile.

'I maybe should have put my hand up as a complete beginner,' she says apologetically. 'I'm really not very good!'

'Don't worry,' I say, encouragingly. 'There's literally nothing that can go wrong on this bit, and the advantage of a heavy dump of snow is that at least it's soft when you fall over.'

She grins at me, shoves off with her poles,

giving a little squeak of alarm as the path falls away and she almost tips backwards in surprise, wheeling with her poles. But she regains her balance somehow, and with a laugh she's off through the trees to where the others are waiting, just out of sight.

Finally it's just me and Liz. In contrast to Ani's game enthusiasm she looks hot and stressed, and overdressed — she's clearly wearing far too many layers for such a nice day, and is already visibly sweating. I'm annoyed with myself for not checking the gear of the inexperienced skiers, but it's probably better for her to be overdressed rather than under-, and in any case, it's too late to tell her to take some off. I'm just about to give her a pep talk when something strikes me.

'Hang on, where's Elliot?'

'Oh.' Liz looks embarrassed. 'Didn't Topher tell you? He doesn't really . . . join in.'

'Oh.' I'm surprised somehow. I kind of had the idea that Snoop was one of those companies where joining in wasn't exactly optional. Carl certainly gave that impression. Liz must have read my expression.

'I know . . . he's not the only person who'd rather be in their room, but somehow he's the only one who gets away with it. But that's what you get for being Topher's best friend, I guess.'

'Have they known each other long?'

'They were at boarding school together,' Liz says. The talk is helping, I realise. She's lost the look of pinched anticipation. 'Along with Rik.'

'Christ, talk about the old boys' network,' I

104

say, before I can help myself, and then blush. Out here, in my salopettes, it's harder to remember I'm Erin the ski chalet host, not just Erin the skier. But Liz doesn't seem offended. She even gives me a very small smile.

'I know, right?' she says. Then she reddens, as if she's been unspeakably daring.

Encouraged by her unbending slightly, I decide it's time to go.

'OK, well, we'd better catch up with the others. Are you ready? I'll go in front, so don't worry, you're never going to get out of control — if you do, you'll just slide gently into me.'

'I still . . . ' Her face looks pinched again, staring at the narrow path with something like dread. 'It just looks so *steep*.'

God, she really isn't a natural skier. I make up my mind.

'I tell you what, give me your poles.'

She hands them over, obediently like a child, and I clamp them under one arm and stick my own out behind me.

'Now hold on to these, OK? Got it? One in each hand.'

She nods, and I push us off, very gently, using my thigh muscles to slow our descent.

With Liz's weight behind me, pressing on my poles, the easy little schuss is much harder work than usual, but we make it to the flat, and I follow Eva's example, skating along, pulling Liz behind me, listening to her panting breath.

At last we come out of the trees and glide down the slope to the bubble lift, where the others are waiting for us, standing just outside the turnstiles, underneath a painted wooden sign reading LA REINE TC.

'This lift is easy,' I say to Liz, reassuringly, under my breath. 'No skiing on or off to worry about, you take your skis off and walk on.'

'Oh . . . phew.' Her expression clears a little bit, and then she glances up at the top of the mountain where the clouds are gathering. 'What's the run down like?'

'There's two stations. If you get off at the first station, it's easy. You're halfway up the mountain and you can pick either the green run, Atchoum, back down to the bottom of the lift, or the blue which peels off down to St Antoine le Lac. If you stay on the lift it goes right up to the top of the mountain. There are amazing views when it's sunny but, well.' I wave my arm at the clouds that are already closing in. 'Anyway, from the top station you have the choice of two runs, La Sorcière, which is a black run off to the left that follows the path of the lift, or the top part of Blanche-Neige. That's a blue, but in poor conditions it can feel a bit more like a red. If you're not very experienced then I'd recommend sticking to the first station, just until you get the feel of your skis, anyway. You could always have a go at the second station after lunch.'

'OK,' Liz says, and she looks up at the mountain, but I can feel her doubt from here. 'Will you be with us all day?'

'Just for the first couple of runs, I'll show you the way back to the chalet, and then I'm afraid I've got to go and help Danny with lunch.'

Liz says nothing at that, but from the way she

clutches her ski poles like grim death, I can tell she's not keen on being abandoned.

'It'll be fine,' I tell her, with more assurance than I actually feel. 'You're not the only beginner, Ani isn't very good, nor is Carl. And even Miranda doesn't look very confident.'

Liz says nothing. She just unclips her bindings and pulls off her skis. But the look on her face is anything but happy.

LIZ

It is almost noon. We have been skiing all morning. The wind is mounting. Erin disappeared back to the chalet long ago, leaving me alone with Topher and Eva and the other adrenaline junkies. We have done the green run, Atchoum, back to the bottom of the bubble twice, and a long blue down into St Antoine, then back up the funicular. My legs feel like jelly with being continually on edge. My face is stinging with cold and my armpits are damp with sweat inside my many layers. My breath comes fast, misting my scarf with wetness, and I am simultaneously freezing and much too hot.

We gather, panting at the bottom of the Reine lift and I can hear the relief in Ani's voice when she whispers, 'Yay! Lunch!'

And then Topher says, as I *knew* he would, 'Come on, time for one more before we break for the afternoon. Let's go up to the top of La Dame. Second stop on the bubble lift. Which of you pussies is with me?'

My heart begins thumping in my chest.

'Wouldn't it be better to stop before we're all

too tired?' Miranda says. I can tell she does not want to do this, but she also doesn't want to be the party pooper. 'I mean, it's the first day, and we've got all week to get skiing in.'

'I agree,' Ani says. She lifts her ski goggles. Beneath, her face is red and blotchy with a mixture of cold and exertion. She looks tired. 'Plus, I just, like, really think it's too big a run for me?'

'It's a fucking blue,' Topher says dismissively. 'Come on! It'll be fun. There's a black that peels off from the top, La Sorcière, and the blue is just the top section of that run we did before, Blanche-Neige. We can split into two groups and take whichever one you fancy. Blue for the babies, black for the big boys and girls.'

'Topher,' Eva says, wagging her finger, but her annoyance is pretend. She looks in her element, tall and slim on her improbably long skis. She is wearing a bright red ski jacket — scarlet silk, that looks like a splash of blood against the white snow, and the sight gives me a weird pang, because I remember buying that jacket for her, back when I was her assistant. I got sent out to Harrods with her credit card and instructions to pick it up. I remember it so clearly, like it was yesterday.

I think, suddenly, of the fairy tale for which the blue run is named — Blanche-Neige — Snow White. Skin as white as snow, lips as red as blood, hair as black as ebony. The hair is wrong. Eva's hair is almost as white as snow too. But today it is tucked into a black beanie, making the comparison almost spookily accurate.

'Come on . . . ' Topher cajoles. 'We can't get

109

back from here to the chalet anyway, it's all uphill, so unless you want an hour of sidestepping, we might as well go to the middle station. Just a little bit further doesn't make much difference . . . does it?' He lifts his goggles, and turns the full force of his charm on Ani. 'Ani? Give this old man one last wish?'

Ani gives a little sigh. Then she caves like wet snow.

'Oh . . . OK. I suppose you only live once. You'll make sure I get down in one piece, won't you, Inigo?'

He smiles and nods.

'Miranda?' Topher says, smiling at her with all his considerable persuasive force. When he turns it on, it is not hard to understand how he got where he did. There's something about Topher that is very, very hard to say no to. 'Miraaaanda . . . ?'

'Fine,' Miranda says, rather grumpily. 'If we've got to go up anyway, I suppose it won't make much difference.'

And then Topher turns to me.

'Liz?'

So here it is then. Why do I always seem to end up being this person — the person everyone else's fun hinges on, the person who's required to make a decision? I can feel myself shrinking beneath their gaze — but I have no choice.

'Fine,' I say, but my voice sounds strained and tense, even to me.

'OK!' Eva says briskly. 'Right, let's regroup at the top, and if anyone gets lost, we'll meet at the shortcut back to the chalet — does everyone

110

remember where the path splits off? That big pine Erin showed us, the one with the fluorescent padding.'

There are nods and murmurs of assent.

And then it is happening. People are unclipping their bindings and shuffling forward in stiff heavy ski boots, clutching poles and skis, shoving through the turnstile barrier. There is no queue at all. The weather is too poor for that. All the sensible French are huddled in cafes having *vin chaud* and raclette, and we are the only people heading up the mountain, on this lift at least. I feel my heart do that sickening skipping rhythm as the bubble looms nearer and I shuffle ahead, pushing past Ani with an assertiveness that's out of character for me. I cannot afford to get left behind.

The bubble glides down the last part of the track, slowing dramatically as it enters the shelter of the lift terminal, and our little group surges forward and begins to clamber in as the plexiglas doors slide back. There are four seats inside each bubble and I watch, counting under my breath as Topher, Rik and Miranda climb in — and then it's my chance. The lift is almost at the barrier where the door will start to close, but I go for it, lumbering towards the doors with my boots clomping on the rubber tiles. I shove my skis roughly in the pigeon holes outside, their bindings tangling with Topher's snowboard — the doors are closing.

'Come on, Liz!' Miranda shouts encouragingly, and I scramble through the gap, sitting down, panting as the doors glide shut and the bubble shoots away up the mountain. Yes. I have done it. I am over the first hurdle.

I squeeze in beside Miranda, crushing my bulky jacket into the narrow gap and she laughs.

'Liz, how many layers are you wearing? You look like the Michelin Man.'

Topher gives a grin.

'Don't knock it, Miranda. Liz might have the last laugh when we get to the top.'

He nods at the window, and I realise he is right. As the lift climbs, you can literally feel the weather getting colder. The condensation on the inside of the bubble begins to bead, and then freeze, spreading into beautiful frost flowers as the lift climbs, and climbs, past the midway station, where the doors slide open invitingly, but no one moves.

Then out again, and up, past the treeline, and up, up, into the clouds. I can feel the little bubble being buffeted by the wind, feel it swaying on its wire, and I have a sudden thrill of fear at what is awaiting us at the top. Oh God, am I *really* going to do this? Can I really go through with it? Suddenly I am not sure if I can. My stomach is sick and clenching with nerves. I have never felt so scared in my life of what I'm about to do. But I have to go through with it. I *have* to.

And then the doors are sliding back and we are stumbling out into a cold so profound that it strikes right through all my layers, even inside the relative shelter of the lift terminal.

We clip on our skis and slide out — into a white wilderness.

It is snowing — hard. The wind is fierce and

112

vicious, driving the snow into our eyes and noses, making everyone fumble to pull down their goggles and pull up their scarves. Between that and the cloud that has descended to wreathe the mountain, the visibility is not the miles the brochures promised, it is metres.

I know that there should be two runs coming off here. To the left is the black run Topher wants to do, La Sorcière. To the right is the top part of the blue run, Blanche-Neige. They meet at the second station of the bubble lift, but Blanche-Neige takes its time, curving round the mountain in gentle loops. La Sorcière, on the other hand, follows a more direct route, zigzagging down the mountain beneath the bubble lift. Direct is an understatement. We passed over the run in the lift a few minutes ago, and it looked like a sheer sheet of ice, like the side of a hill, even seen from forty feet up in the air.

I push off, wobbling as I clear the ice from my goggles with my mittens. Ahead is a snow-covered sign that might once have been two arrows, but is now nothing but an indistinct white lump. To the left there is a kind of tennis net thing cutting off the access. By the time I see this, I'm sliding towards it.

'Help!' I shout. There is nothing any of the others can do, and I ricochet into the net, feeling its springiness catch me across the middle. I flail for a moment, my poles pinwheeling, and then I teeter ungracefully to the ground in a clatter of skis.

Rik comes sliding across, laughing, and helps me up.

'You were lucky,' he yells in my ear, over the shriek of the wind, pointing to the snow-blasted *piste fermée* sign tacked over the net. 'That's La Sorcière. You could have been skiing your first black if they hadn't closed the piste! Or worse.'

He is right. Beyond the net is a steep run, dropping almost vertically away. It curves around the mountain and beyond the edge of the curve is . . . nothing. If I had shot off the edge at speed, there would have been nothing anyone could do. I could have been plummeting to my death in the valley a thousand feet below before anyone had a chance to stop me. The thought of that fall makes my stomach lurch with nerves at the thought of what I'm about to do.

I am too out of breath to reply, but I let him haul me to my feet and then guide me back to the others who are standing in a little huddle at the top of the blue piste.

'They've closed La Sorcière,' Rik calls across to Topher, who nods bitterly.

'I saw. Fucking pussies.'

'Should we wait?' I hear Miranda shout. Her voice is barely audible beneath the howling of the storm. 'It's fucking freezing!'

'I think we have to,' Rik says. 'We can't go without Ani and Carl, they're not very experienced.'

'They've got the others to babysit them,' Topher grumbles, but Rik shakes his head.

'What if they come up separately and try to follow? Look.' He points down the mountain where a bubble lift is emerging from the clouds, a single figure inside, or maybe two sitting close

114

together. It's impossible to make out at this distance. It might not even be one of our party. It is so far below that the figure looks absurdly small.

I am shaking. My heart is pounding. I can't go through with this. But I have to. This might be my last chance — I have to say something. Now. *Now*.

'I can't do this,' I force out. Topher looks across at me, as if surprised I've spoken.

'What did you say?'

'I can't do this,' I say louder. I am breathing very fast, and my voice is high and squeaky with a barely contained fear. My pulse is going a mile a minute. 'I can't. I just can't. I'm not going to ski down. I *can't*, Topher.'

'Well, how do you plan to get to the bottom,' Topher says sarcastically. 'Toboggan?'

'Hey, hey.' Rik has been trying to consult his phone, but now he looks up. 'What's going on here?'

'I can't do it,' I say desperately, as if, if I just keep repeating this one phrase, everything will slot into place. Maybe it still will. Maybe it will all be OK. 'I can't. I can't ski down in this. I'm going to die, I know I will. You can't make me do it.'

'Liz, it'll be fine.' Rik puts a hand on my arm. 'I'll take care of you, I promise. Look, you can snowplough all the way down if you want to, I'll guide you, you can hold my sticks.'

'I. Can't. Do. It,' I repeat doggedly. If I keep reciting this mantra, it will be OK. They can't *make* me ski with them. I *know* Topher. He's not a patient man. Very soon he will get pissed off with trying to persuade me and give up.

'Fuck,' Topher says irritably. He wipes the snow from his goggles and looks at Rik. 'So what then?'

'Liz — ' Rik begins, and I feel that hard thing rise up in my throat, choking me, like it did at the meeting. The bubble with the single figure in it reaches the terminal. I think I am going to be sick. It's now or never.

'I can't do it!' I scream, and suddenly, out of nowhere, I am crying. The noise astonishes me — great ugly sobs, racking me. I lift up my goggles to scrub at my eyes with my frozen gloves, and the wind is so cold I can feel the tears running down my nose freezing as they reach the tip. I swipe away the frozen drops, feeling them crackle against my skin. 'I can't fucking do it!'

'OK, OK!' Rik says hastily. 'Liz, don't panic, it'll be fine. Look, we'll sort this out.'

There is a schussing sound behind us and we turn to see a figure skiing down the slope towards us. It is Inigo, his green jacket unmistakable even with his goggles down and his scarf pulled up. Behind him, Tiger has shuffled out onto the bank immediately outside the lift. She is sitting on the snow, fastening her snowboard bindings.

'I'm going back,' I say, gulping down my sobs. I point down the mountain, where the empty bubble lift Inigo came up in is returning back to the valley. 'I'm going to talk to the lift attendant, make him let me back in. I'll explain I can't do it, that it's all been a mistake.'

'Liz, this is fucking ridiculous,' Topher explodes.

'What's the matter?' Inigo's voice is muffled from behind his scarf, barely recognisable.

'It's Liz,' Topher says angrily. 'She's having some kind of existential crisis.'

But I'm not. I'm calm now. There is another bubble lift coming up the mountain, with another figure inside it. I can do this. I know what I need to do, and no one can stop me. I begin to sidestep up the slope.

'Liz,' Rik calls, 'are you sure?'

'Yes,' I yell back, though I'm not even certain they can hear me over the wind now. 'I'm quite sure. I'll meet you back at the chalet.'

And as I step inside the terminal building and the bubble lift doors open, a sense of peace enfolds me. I know what I have to do, and it's going to be OK. Everything's going to be OK.

ERIN

Snoop ID: LITTLEMY
Listening to: offline
Snoopscribers: 10

It's nearly half past one. They said they'd be back by one at the latest, and Danny is shouting expletives from the kitchen as the minutes tick past and his risotto clogs.

At 1.45 he sticks his head out the door with a face like thunder, and I shake my head.

'There's only one thing I hate more than fucking stealth vegans, and that's wankers,' he growls, and disappears, the swing door clacking behind him.

And then, suddenly, there's the clatter of ski boots on tiles, and I hurry into the lobby to hear noises from the ski entrance, the unmistakable sounds of people clumping along a hard floor, clanging open the heated ski lockers that line the corridor.

'Eva?' someone calls irritably. 'Eva, where the fuck are you?'

No answer.

Then the insulated door to the lobby swings open and Topher comes in wearing ski gear and thick socks, looking pissed off.

'Oh, it's you,' he says shortly, when he sees

118

me. 'Where the fuck is Eva?'

'Eva?' A retort about his rudeness hovers on the tip of my tongue but I swallow it back. 'Sorry, Topher, I have no idea.'

He stops, halfway to the stairs.

'You mean she's not here?'

'No, you're the first back.'

He stands there, quite still, the expression on his face wavering between irritation and concern. Then he calls over his shoulder.

'Miranda, she's not here.'

'You're kidding.' Miranda is the next out of the door. Her face is bright pink, with the painful flush that always follows extreme cold. 'Huh. Well . . . I guess at least that means we didn't freeze our arses off for no reason. But what do you think could have happened?'

'Maybe the lift closed before she could get on, and she skied back down into St Antoine to get the funicular?' Topher says, but Carl has come out now and is shaking his head.

'She got on before me, mate. She was on that lift, I'd swear to it.'

'And I saw her,' Ani says. They gather in the lobby, sweaty and confused, melting snow dripping from their jackets. 'I told you, Carl and I were coming up in the lift and I *saw* her skiing down.'

'What's the matter?' Rik says, coming through in his turn, shaking the snow off his black salopettes. Miranda turns to him, and now her face is definitely worried.

'Eva's not here.'

'She's not here?' Rik's expression is blank.

'But — but that's not possible. There's nowhere else she could be.'

They all begin talking at once, offering up different theories, many of them totally impossible based on the geography of the resort.

'Hold up, hold up,' I say, and amazingly they all fall silent. Somehow, they want leadership, and I am the closest thing to it. 'Start from the beginning. When was the last time you were all together as a group?'

'At the bottom of the Reine ski lift,' Ani says promptly. 'We had a discussion about whether to break for lunch there, or do one last run. Topher made the point that it was uphill from the ski lift to the chalet, so we had to do a run, and we agreed to go up to the top station and do either La Sorcière or Blanche-Neige, depending on ability.'

I bite back my reply to this. La Sorcière is a bitch of a run. I've been skiing all my life, and there's no *way* I'd do it in this weather. Even Blanche-Neige with this visibility is no joke for inexperienced skiers. Not for the first time it strikes me that Topher is kind of a jerk.

'But when we got up there Liz had some kind of breakdown,' Topher says bitterly.

'Toph,' Rik says sharply, with a jerk of his head towards the ski door, and I look over Topher's shoulder to see Liz plodding wearily across from the boot room. She is covered in snow and looks utterly exhausted, even more so than the others.

'When we got to the top the weather was pretty extreme, and Liz decided to take the lift back down,' Miranda says smoothly, but looking

120

at Topher's mutinous face I can well imagine the discussion that decision must have entailed. Part of me is amazed at Liz's strength of mind, that she didn't let herself be bullied into trying the run. But fear can make people amazingly resilient.

'The rest of us waited up there for the others,' Topher says. 'But Eva never came.'

'But she *did*,' Ani puts in. 'We saw her, Carl and I. Didn't we?' She nudges Carl, who nods.

'Yeah, no doubt about it, mate. We saw her get on the bubble a few lifts ahead of us.'

'A few?' Topher says. 'How's that? There was no queue at all.'

Carl reddens.

'Well, look, there's no point in beating about the bush. I — well, I fluffed getting on the bubble if you must know. Ani and I were supposed to be getting in after Eva, but I tripped over my bindings. Fell over, and the lift doors closed and Eva went up with my skis still stuck in the rack. It took me a few minutes to get myself sorted again, and then Ani and I caught the next lift after that.'

'Could she have got confused and got off at the first station?' Miranda says with a frown, but Ani shakes her head.

'No, that's what I'm trying to tell you. I saw her, when we were coming up in the bubble. It goes right over that black piste — the really steep one that Topher wanted to do.'

'La Sorcière,' I put in, and Ani nods.

'That's the one. And I saw a skier coming down it. She stopped for a second on the ridge

121

and kind of raised her hand, waving at me. And I realised, it was Eva.'

'How could you tell at that distance?' Rik says sceptically. 'It could have been anyone.'

'I recognised her red jacket. It's, like, really distinctive. No one else here has one like it, and we were the only people on that lift.'

I look around the circle, and she's right. Topher is in mustard and khaki, Rik and Carl are both in black. Miranda is in a kind of purple jumpsuit. Inigo has a green jacket and black salopettes. Tiger is wearing kind of shabby surfer chic that looks like an eighties denim bomber jacket and cargo pants, but I suspect is actually pretty expensive snowboard gear. Liz is wearing a faded navy-blue all-in-one that's too big for her and looks as though it was borrowed from a friend. And Ani herself is wearing the bright sea-blue jacket and white salopettes that I noticed earlier. None of them could possibly be mistaken for Eva.

'When we got off at the top my skis were waiting,' Carl says. 'She must have taken them off the lift and then skied off.'

'Didn't you notice she wasn't at the top?' I ask, and Rik shakes his head, looking rueful.

'No, the visibility was really poor and well . . . look, if you must know there was a bit of . . . well, argy-bargy at the top.'

Argy-bargy? What the hell does that mean? I'm about to ask, when Miranda butts in.

'You might as well say it plainly, Rik. The lift attendant came out to tell us the avalanche warning had gone up to red, and they were closing the whole mountain, but half the party ignored the warning and deliberately skied off before they could get the nets out.'

'I'm so sorry.' Inigo at least has the grace to look embarrassed. 'It was a total misunderstanding. I thought he was saying now or never, so I, uh, pushed off.'

'So wait, some of you skied home,' I say slowly, 'and some of you took the bubble back down?'

Nods all round the circle.

'Naturally we stopped for a bit at the big pine by the shortcut back to the chalet to see if anyone was catching up, but when we saw people travelling back down in the bubble, we skied down to the bottom of the lift,' Topher says. 'So we waited there for another twenty minutes, only for the bastards in charge of the resort to close *that* lift too. At that point we concluded Eva had fucked off back to the chalet, but since we were now downhill from the chalet with no functioning lift, we had no choice but to ski down to St Antoine and get the funicular back up.'

'OK . . . OK . . . ' I say, trying to make sense of it. 'So the last time anyone is absolutely certain they saw her, she was skiing La Sorcière?'

Ani nods, turning to Carl for confirmation, who says, 'That's the size of it.'

'But La Sorcière was closed,' Topher explodes. 'That was the whole fucking problem.'

The whole fucking problem is that your colleague and co-founder is missing in extreme weather conditions, I think, but I don't say it. I am thinking about La Sorcière, about its

123

treacherous, icy slopes, and the way the loose powder builds up on the sheet ice beneath, making every turn a throw of the dice between a painful skid and a mini avalanche. I'm thinking of its brutal moguls, hidden by the drifting snow between, and the impossibility of even seeing the icy hummocks beneath their blanket of snow, let alone judging those knee-juddering turns in bad visibility.

Most of all, I'm thinking of the sheer drop at the side of the run. A precipice lies just metres from the side of the piste in places; in conditions like this, you could simply sail off the edge into nothingness. *That* is why they shut La Sorcière first, out of all the runs in the resort. Not because they're risk-averse, or health and safety nuts, or don't trust experienced skiers to navigate it. But because the twists and turns are a death trap in low visibility. But then I remind myself that the worst section of the drop is right at the start of the run, and Ani saw her skiing further down. It's small comfort, but I'll take whatever comfort I can get right now.

'Has anyone tried her mobile?' I say. Inigo nods.

'Several times. There's no reception.'

Danny comes out of the kitchen at that point, looking royally pissed off. *What about my fucking risotto?* he mouths at me over the heads of the guests, and I hurry across to him.

'Eva's missing,' I tell him in a low voice, and his expression switches instantly from irritation to concern.

'What, really missing? Not just gone AWOL?'

124

'I don't know, it's hard to tell. They've all acted like complete fuckwits. They split up, no one kept track of who was in which party, and Eva seems to have gone off by herself to ski La Sorcière.'

'Alone?' Danny's jaw drops. 'But, there's a red avalanche warning. Why the hell didn't the *pisteurs* shut the run?'

'Apparently they did. She must have ducked under the netting or something, or somehow got lost and traversed across to the wrong run.' Though I can't think quite how that could have happened. There is no obvious interconnection between Blanche-Neige and La Sorcière. That's part of the problem with the black run. It is hemmed in by a sheer cliff on one side, and a sheer drop on the other. There is no way out once you're going down, it's all twists and turns. 'I don't know. But Ani is pretty convinced she and Carl saw Eva skiing down it. I mean, I know she's good, but that's just foolhardy in weather like this.'

Danny's face is really grave now.

'And no one's seen her since?'

I shake my head.

'Do you think we should call the PGHM?' I ask. This is the specialist branch of mountain police who operate in the higher mountain ranges — a combination of gendarmes and mountain rescue.

'I dunno,' Danny says. He pushes his bandanna up his forehead and rubs fretfully at the furrow between his brows, trying to think. 'It's not impossible she's just got lost and gone

125

down the wrong route. With the lifts shut it'd take her a while to get back. I reckon they'll tell us to give it a few hours before we panic. Should we try the ski pass office first? Maybe they can tell us if her pass has been used on any lifts?'

I want to kiss him. It's not just a good idea, it's a great one. But when I go to the phone in the lobby and dial the number on the back of the lift pass, I get only the insistent beep-beep signal of a busy line.

I go back to the little group huddled in the lobby, who are looking hot in their ski gear, and increasingly worried.

'We think the best thing is to check in with the lift pass office and see if Eva's used her pass anywhere. I've tried phoning, but the line's engaged, so rather than hanging around here, I think I'm going to hop down on the funicular and talk to the office in person.'

'I'll go,' Topher says immediately.

'Do you speak French?'

I know the answer before I ask the question, and his face changes to chagrin as he shakes his head.

'I totally get why you want to help,' I say, trying to be gentle, 'but I think it would be better for someone who speaks French to go. If she's not used her pass, that's probably the point where we need to report her missing to the police and we'll definitely need a fluent speaker for that. You should all change into dry clothes and get some food into you, and I'll be back really soon. Meantime, keep trying her number.'

They all nod, soberly.

'I'd better tell Elliot,' Topher mutters, and I remember with a shock of surprise that Elliot was the only member of the group not skiing. He is still holed up in his room, presumably working on his coding update, or whatever he's doing up there alone.

They all disperse, talking quietly under their breath to each other, and I grab my coat from the locker and hurry back to Danny to explain the plan.

'So you'll have to serve up alone, is that OK?'

He nods.

'Yeah, of course.'

He disappears into the kitchen to begin plating up.

I put my coat on and open the front door.

LIZ

Snoop **ID**: ANON101
Listening to: offline
Snoopscribers: 0

I am upstairs in my room, changing out of my skiing clothes when it happens. At first it is just a noise, and then I feel the ground begin to shake, like an earthquake.

I turn to look out of the window. I see what looks like a wall of snow coming down the valley towards us. But not a wall — that implies something solid. This is something else. A boiling mass that is air and ice and earth all rolled together.

I scream. I do the only thing I can, even though it is stupid. I fall to my knees with my arms over my head, as if that pathetic gesture might protect me.

I stay there shaking for a long time, before I dare to get up, my legs trembling. Did it miss us? Did it stop?

From far away I can hear other voices, shouts, screams, cries.

Somehow, I force my legs to work, and I stumble out into the corridor.

'Jesus Christ!' Topher is shouting. He is running towards the stairs. 'What the hell just happened?'

'Erin!' I hear from below. It is a bellow of fear from a voice I don't recognise, and then I realise — it is the chef, Danny, calling for his friend. 'Erin!'

The corridor is full of terrified people. There is a smoke alarm going off, shouts of panic.

Down in the lobby the chef is struggling with the front door which has cracked and bowed beneath the weight of packed snow pressed up against it.

'Don't open the bloody door!' Topher yells. 'You'll let all the snow in!'

Danny turns on him. His face is full of fury.

'My fucking friend is out there,' he spits over the scream of the alarm. 'So if you want to stop me, mate, come and try.'

He shoves again. The door gives with a shriek of protest, and a mass of snow and ice comes skittering into the lobby. The doorway is still blocked four feet deep, but Danny clambers up the bank and over the top, sinking into the debris. The last I see of him is his legs as he staggers off into the storm.

'Oh my God,' Miranda is saying. She is holding on to Rik like she is drowning. 'Oh my God. Oh my God. What if Eva's still out there?'

There is no answer. I don't think anyone can bring themselves to say what they are thinking — which is that if Eva is still out there, she is dead. She must be.

And maybe Erin too.

'Is the building safe?' Rik says, with sudden practicality. 'We don't want to stay here if it's about to collapse.'

'I'll go and turn off that alarm,' Tiger says, and she disappears into the kitchen. I hear her dragging a chair across tiles, and then the alarm stops. There is a sudden, shocking silence.

'OK,' Topher says. His voice is shaking, but it is so natural for him to take charge that he slips into the role. 'Um, we should — we should check. We should check the building.'

'The kitchen side isn't too bad,' Tiger says as she comes back into the lobby. 'I looked out of the window. There's a couple of windows broken in the den but the snow isn't particularly high. It'll be the living-room side that's suffered, and the pool extension.'

'We should go upstairs,' Topher says. 'Get an overview.'

Tiger nods, and we all troop upstairs to look out of one of the upper windows. What we see makes my knees go weak. We have been *extremely* lucky.

The long single-storey building to the rear of the chalet, which housed the swimming pool, has been crushed and obliterated. The roof has caved in like an empty eggshell. Beams and planks are sticking out of the huge snowdrift that has engulfed the extension. But the chalet itself is still standing. There is a mass of snow, sticks and rubble piled up against the north side, but the structure has held firm. Just a few metres more, and Perce-Neige would have been matchsticks, like the swimming pool building. I can't see any of the other chalets. The path to the funicular is covered with fallen trees and rumpled snow. The funicular itself is out of sight in the gusting snow.

Erin is nowhere to be seen.

And then I notice a movement around the side of the building. It is Erin. She is holding on to Danny, the chef, and they are limping over the uneven, debris-covered surface, stumbling on the hard-packed lumps of snow scattered across what used to be the track to the funicular.

They go out of sight beneath the shadow of the building. From downstairs I hear the screech of the buckled front door scraping against the tiles, and Erin's sob of pain as she squeezes over the drift and down, inside the house.

'Is it broken?' I hear Danny saying, breathlessly. As if instructed, we all file down the spiral stairs to stand in a concerned circle around Erin.

'Is she OK?' Miranda asks, frowning.

'What do you think?' Danny snaps. Erin doesn't seem able to speak, but she holds up her hand. I'm not sure what she means, but her signal clearly conveys something to Danny, and he shakes his head angrily and stamps off to the kitchen.

'I'm gonna get you some ice,' he calls back over his shoulder. 'See if we can get the swelling down.'

'I've got some arnica in my bag,' Tiger calls after him. I cannot hear Danny's reply. It does not sound complimentary.

'I don't think arnica is going to cut it, Tig,' Rik says quietly.

Erin is slumped on the floor of the lobby. Her face is grey. She looks like she is going into shock.

'What happened?' Tiger crouches beside her, putting her hand on her arm. Erin looks up at her. She blinks dazedly. She looks like she is unsure why she is here.

'Erin? Are you OK?'

'I don't know,' Erin manages. Her voice is shaking. 'I was walking towards the f-funicular and I heard this n-noise and then it was like — it was like the mountain just came and *swallowed* the lift.'

'You mean — the funicular is gone?'

There is horror in Tiger's voice, but her tone only echoes the shock I can see reverberating around the room.

'Not gone,' Danny says, coming back with a bag of frozen peas. He scowls around the group. 'But . . . yeah, buried. A big chunk of glass has been stove in. *Shit*. There might have been people in there.'

'We should, like, call 999?' Ani says, and Topher nods emphatically.

'17,' Erin says tiredly.

'What?'

'17,' Danny echoes. 'That's the French number for the police. But I reckon you should try 112. That's the international number, they'll have English speakers.'

Ani takes out her phone, and then frowns.

'I've got no reception.'

'Transmitter's probably down,' Danny says shortly. He is pressing the peas very gently onto Erin's ankle. Her face has gone a strange yellow-ish white and her eyes are closed. 'Try the phone on the desk.'

Ani nods, and goes across to the landline phone on the desk next to the stairs, but when

132

she picks up the receiver her face falls.

'There's no dial tone.'

'Fuck.' Carl speaks for the first time. His broad face is red. He looks angry. 'Fucking hell, that's all we need. Avalanche took the line out, I guess. Has *anyone* got any reception? Anything at all?'

There's a momentary shuffle. Everyone feels for their phones. I get out mine too. The reception bars are greyed out.

'Nothing,' Topher says. Others are shaking their heads.

'No, wait.' It's Inigo, his voice cracking with excitement. 'I just got a bar! I've got one bar!'

He dials and then waits, holding up his hand for silence. We all stay totally still, listening.

'Hello?' he says. And then, 'Hello? Hello? Shit, they can't hear me!'

'Go upstairs,' Miranda says sharply. 'You might get better reception with the extra height.'

Obediently Inigo climbs the spiral staircase and goes to stand at the end of the corridor, at the long window that overlooks the valley, as if the visibility might somehow translate into better reception.

'Hello?' We can hear him saying and then, 'Yes,' and 'OK,' and 'Chalet Blanche-Neige,' followed by some information about our situation. There are long pauses, and many times when he says 'Can you repeat that? I'm sorry, the reception is really poor, you're breaking up. Hello? Hello?'

At last he comes back down looking grave.

'I lost reception in the end, but I spoke to the

police operator and I think I managed to give them all the details before I got cut off.'

'Did you tell them about Eva?' Topher shoves in, and Inigo nods.

'Yes, I told them that we lost our friend right before the avalanche and we don't know if she's still out on the mountain.'

'Is someone coming to rescue us?'

'I don't know,' Inigo says, and he looks for a minute like what he is — a PA who has failed to get the result his boss wanted. 'They said they're under enormous strain, there are people trapped on lifts and stuff. I'm not sure — ' His voice falters a little at Topher's expression. 'I'm not sure that people with food and shelter are their priority right now. They've got my number. They said they'd be in touch as soon as possible with more information.'

'You mean we're fucking stranded?' Topher explodes. 'The fucking funicular's down, Eva's missing, and we're trapped in this godforsaken chalet with an injured woman — ' He indicates Erin. 'We should be their top priority!'

Inigo says nothing, he just shrugs helplessly.

'Could one of us ski down?' Rik says, but Inigo shakes his head.

'No, they were really clear about that. We should stay where we are. There could be more falls.'

'Well, we can't just stay here,' Topher says angrily.

'You won't be skiing on that piste, mate,' Danny says, looking up from where he's tending Erin.

'I'll have you know,' Topher says, 'I'm a boarder and a damn good one.'

'You could be Shaun White, mate, you still wouldn't be going down there. You didn't see it — it looked like a boulder field. There's no piste left.'

'So we're stuck?' Topher says, furious disbelief in his tone. 'And they're doing nothing at all, while Eva could be out there under a thousand tonnes of snow?'

No one answers. No one wants to say the fact that is obvious to all of us — if that is the case, there's nothing he or any of us can do.

ERIN

Snoop ID: LITTLEMY
Listening to: offline
Snoopscribers: 10

I'm sitting in the kitchen, shaking. Danny has gone to get the first-aid kit, and in truth I'm grateful to be alone for a few minutes. It gives me time to get myself back together.

That noise — that horrific, deafeningly soft roar that has haunted my dreams for three years — for a moment I thought it was some kind of flashback, like PTSD. And then I glanced over my shoulder and it was real. A wall of white engulfing the valley.

And the strange thing was, I felt nothing but peace, as it came towards me. It felt like justice. It felt like retribution. It felt completely right.

For a moment I thought about opening my arms and letting it swallow me. Only it didn't. It didn't swallow me. It spat me back out. To this.

'I'm gonna fucking kill them all.' The swing door bangs back, and it's Danny, stomping in with the first-aid box in his hand. 'Fucking wankers, every last one of them. You could've been killed and he's busy worrying about when his airlift is coming. You know he's out there

136

right now trying to get through to a private helicopter firm?'

'They won't do anything, even if he gets through,' I say. I change my position on the makeshift footrest Danny has set up in the corner of the kitchen, trying to ignore the pain shooting up and down my leg as I move it. 'They can't — not in this weather. Look at it.'

I wave a hand at the window, where the wind has picked up into a full-blown blizzard.

'Get those peas off your ankle,' Danny says brusquely, 'they've defrosted anyway.' I hold out my leg meekly as he lifts off the soggy bag of peas and straps an icepack sleeve around my throbbing ankle. It hurts, but in a weird kind of way, I welcome the pain. It anchors me, reminding me that I'm here, alive.

Danny has found an old FM radio and while he cooks, I sit quietly, listening to the accounts of the rescue attempts. The realisation that keeps shivering up and down my spine is how incredibly lucky we have been — all of us. At least eight buildings have been totally crushed by the avalanche. Four were lift stations that were confirmed empty, since the lifts had been closed earlier that day. Two were cafes that are believed to have been closed at the time the avalanche hit. The remaining three were chalets. One, much further down near St Antoine le Lac, has been evacuated. Minor injuries, no fatalities. No one knows about the other two. Amid questions about responsibility and whether the resort authorities should have acted earlier, the newscaster emphasises again and again how fortunate it was that so many pistes and lifts were shut. Even the funicular had only four people in it, and they have been safely evacuated down the smashed, glassed-in tunnel, but the announcer has already said, ominously, that it is going to take 'many days to assess the repairs'. Not even complete the repairs, assess them.

Given that, a mangled swimming pool seems like getting off pretty lightly. If it wasn't for Eva, we would be counting our blessings. But the knowledge that she's still missing is like a dark, spreading poison, gnawing at the edge of everything. When I shut my eyes, I can see her — buried in darkness, growing colder and colder with every moment that passes, wondering if anyone is coming. If she's lucky, the close-packed snow will suffocate her quickly. If she's not . . .

The thought makes me feel suddenly weak with fear.

'How much food have we got?' I ask Danny, trying to distract myself from my thoughts, and he shakes his head dismissively.

'Plenty. Don't worry about that. Tony Stark down there might have to go without fresh milk for a few days, but the store cupboard's got enough in it for a siege.'

There's always the possibility that Eva got bored of waiting for everyone, skied down into St Antoine hours ago, and is absolutely fine, just unable to contact us. But as the hours tick on, that's starting to look more and more unlikely. The landline and the Internet are still both down, and the mobile reception has only worsened since the avalanche, the remaining masts presumably buckled beneath a hundred-weight of snow, but Inigo's phone continues to get a few erratic bars every now and again. He's had a text from home — just one — and managed to reply saying he was OK. Wouldn't Eva have texted to say she was all right when all this kicked off? Wouldn't she have found a way, *somehow*, to get word through?

LIZ

Snoop ID: ANON101
Listening to: offline
Snoopscribers: 0

It is 3.11 p.m. when the electricity dies. I am sitting up in my room, trying to shut out the noises from downstairs, when the room is suddenly plunged into darkness. I fumble for my phone, wondering if a bulb has blown. Then I hear shouts of annoyance coming from up and down the corridor. It is not just me.

'Did your electricity just go off?' It is Topher's voice, right outside my bedroom. For a moment I think he's talking to me, but then I hear an answering deep rumble: Elliot. 'Fuck,' Topher says, in answer. 'That's all we need.'

I open the door to find the rest of the group congregating on the landing, discussing what to do by the light of their mobile phone torches. In the end, we traipse downstairs to consult Erin and Danny. I hang back as Topher knocks irritably on the kitchen door. He is grumbling under his breath about fucking arse end of nowhere.

'What?' Danny answers. His expression is belligerent.

'Hello,' Topher says, abruptly changing his

tone. He is out to charm now. He is not stupid. He knows he has got to get these people on his side. The effect is impressive. It is like a switch being flipped. 'So sorry to disturb, but our electricity's gone out.'

'You and me both, mate,' Danny says shortly.

'And, is there anything one can do?' Topher asks. He's stressed, and I can tell because his accent has become indefinably more monied.

'Not really. The backup generator was in the pool house.' Danny waves a hand at the debris just visible from the kitchen window. Topher swears. His charm is slipping.

'So we just wait and freeze to death?'

'Not freeze,' Danny says. 'We've got plenty of wood. You can start by putting a log on the living-room fire.'

Topher opens his mouth like he is about to say something. Then he seems to think better of it and closes it again. He turns, and walks slowly back through to the darkened living room. The rest of us follow.

In the lounge, Topher flings himself onto the sofa while Miranda lights candles. Rik opens up the stove, stirs the embers, and puts another two logs on top.

'Great,' Carl says. 'Bloody great. This is all we need. We're gonna be fucking ice cubes by the time they find us.'

'We'll be fine,' Miranda says shortly, her voice clipped and annoyed. 'It's Eva we need to worry about.'

Eva. In all the commotion I had almost succeeded in forgetting about her. My stomach crunches with mingled guilt and anxiety.

There is a long, horrible pause while no one asks the questions that are running in their heads. What has happened to her? Was she caught up in that avalanche? Is she dead?

'Wouldn't she have, like, phoned, if she were OK?' Ani says at last, breaking the silence. Her usual diffidence is even more pronounced. 'I know there's not much signal, but just . . . like . . . a text, even?'

'She might not have been able to get through,' Miranda says, but I can tell she is trying to persuade herself, more than convinced by her own argument.

Elliot is standing in the corner of the room, looking out at the darkening snow, and then he says something to Topher in his deep, abrupt voice, and leaves. Topher gets up from the sofa and follows him without a word.

I frown, watching them go, watching their shadows leap and flicker in the light from the guttering candles. Where are they going? There is something in Topher's expression I don't like. A sense of sudden purpose. And it gives me a jolt of unease.

Erin

Snoop ID: LITTLEMY
Listening to: offline
Snoopscribers: 10

'This is bad, Erin.' Danny is rummaging through tins at the back of the darkened kitchen. As I watch him, he straightens up, running his hands over his close-cropped hair. 'This is very, very bad.'

'It'll be OK,' I say, but the truth is, I'm lying and I know it. My ankle has puffed up to twice its usual size and still won't bear my weight properly. We have no lighting, and the only heat is from the wood stoves. Danny can't even microwave a frozen curry for dinner. And Eva — but I can't think about that now. I push the image of her white, cold face away from me, locking it behind the door in my mind where I keep images like that, frozen in ice. I have to hold on to the possibility that she's OK, that she made it down into the village and just hasn't been able to get through on the phone. God knows, the reception is bad enough.

'Your foot could be broken for all we know,' Danny says, but I shake my head, with a confidence I don't feel.

'I don't think it's broken. I think it's just badly sprained.'

'How the fuck would you know?' Danny asks, and then holds up a hand. 'Never mind, I forgot you're a bloody doctor. Tell me again what you're doing cleaning up after posh wankers for minimum wage?'

I could give about eight different answers to this. I could remind him that I'm not a doctor, I'm a medical school dropout. I could tell him the truth about what brought me to St Antoine. I could give him a lecture on greenstick fractures. But I don't need to say any of this because he's gone back to looking through the tins.

'I could heat up soup or something on the wood burner,' he's saying, his brow furrowed as he tries to read a label with the aid of his mobile phone. 'Jesus, what a carve-up.'

The knock makes us both jump, and we stare at each other, and then Danny goes to the door. It's Topher again, but he's wearing a very different expression to the ingratiating one he used to ask us to magically fix the lights. He looks . . . I'm not sure. I don't know him well enough to tell. He could be pissed off, or gravely worried.

'Yes?' Danny says abruptly, but I heave myself to my feet and hobble past him. There is a reason Danny doesn't deal much with front of house. He's got no tact and no patience. But the fact is that however bad the situation is, Topher and Snoop are still our guests and we still need to behave like we're representing the company.

'Topher,' I say, and then I see Elliot hovering behind him. 'Elliot, how can I help?'

'Elliot thinks he's found Eva,' Topher says without preamble.

144

'*What?*' It's the last thing I'd expected. Questions jumbled through my mind. Where? *How?* 'Is she OK?'

'We don't know.' Topher pushes past me and Danny and unfolds a laptop, putting it down on the stainless-steel kitchen worktop. It lights up the circle of faces with an unearthly glow as he taps in a password. A screen of garbled code comes up. It means nothing to me.

'To be precise — ' it's Elliot's deep monotone — 'we know the location of her phone.'

'Her phone?'

'One of the reasons I didn't want to agree to the buyout,' Topher begins, 'is because Elliot's been working on a major update to help monetise Snoop. We're calling it geosnooping in beta, but that probably won't be the final name. As you may know, Snoop is as anonymous as you want it to be at the moment — you can't tell where someone is, all you've got to go on is what they declare in their profile.'

'Right,' I say slowly.

'But Elliot's been working on an upgrade that will allow people to view other Snoopers within a fifty-metre radius. You won't know exactly where they are, but you'll know they're close to you.'

'OK, I get that.'

'It hasn't gone live yet. But as part of the preparations for rolling it out we changed the permissions Snoop requires to give the app access to your location. Basically Snoop knows that information whether or not you choose to display it — it's part of the data profile we share with stakeholders to create income.'

145

'Right . . . ' I say again, trying to get him to cut to the chase. I don't care about the inner workings of Snoop, and I think I know where this is going. 'Are you saying you used this information to find out Eva's location?'

'Yes. Elliot's been able to hack into the back end and get the GPS coordinates of Eva's phone.'

'It's here,' Elliot says, pulling up a GPS map, where a red flag shows the location of the coordinates he's tapped into the search bar.

As soon as I see the pin, my heart sinks down into my stomach, and I feel myself going cold with dread.

'Where is it exactly?' Topher is saying, but his voice sounds very far away now. Danny suddenly puts a hand to his mouth, and I know that he has just figured out what I already knew.

The pistes are marked on Elliot's maps, but not the elevations, and without the simplified three-dimensional rendering of the resort's official piste map, it's not very easy to put together the geography of the peaks and valleys. Eva's little dot is showing very close to La Sorcière run. So close in fact that she could almost be on the run.

But she's not. Because if you've skied the run, as I have, many times, what you know is that there is a sheer drop to the side of La Sorcière. A drop that falls hundreds, maybe thousands of feet into a deep, inaccessible valley. Somehow, in the blinding snow, Eva must have done exactly what I feared in the first place — she has skied over the edge.

146

'If we can give these coordinates to search and rescue — ' Topher is saying, with the kind of blithe confidence that only the CEO of a major international company could muster, but I interrupt.

'I'm sorry, Topher, I'm so sorry — '

'What do you mean?'

'This — ' I swallow. I try to find a way of putting the news that's not too brutal. 'This dot, it's off the side of the piste.'

'Eva's an excellent skier,' Topher says confidently. 'Off-piste, even in this weather — '

'No, you don't understand. I'm not talking about a bit of loose snow. I mean she's skied *off* the piste. Off the edge. La Sorcière — ' I swallow. There is no way of saying this nicely. 'That section of La Sorcière runs alongside a sheer drop. A very steep one.'

Topher looks at me blankly, unable, or unwilling, to understand what I'm trying to tell him.

'What do you mean?' he says at last.

'Topher, if Eva is really where that dot is showing, she's dead.'

I regret the starkness as soon as the words have left my mouth, but they are said, and they can't be unsaid.

Topher's face goes white. Then he turns to Elliot.

'How accurate is this positioning?'

'GPS is typically accurate to about five metres,' Elliot says. He looks . . . God, I don't know. Unperturbed almost? Can that be possible? Surely not. No one could be that callous. Even if they were, wouldn't they at least try to feign some kind of concern? 'But you can get interference — bounced signals and so on. I'm not totally sure how the mountains would affect it. It's not impossible it's a few metres off.'

'So, what, ten metres? She could be on the piste,' Topher says desperately, but we can all see, looking at the map's scale, that that's not possible. Even fifty metres wouldn't put her back on the run. 'Or — or she could have dropped her phone skiing down.'

'If she'd dropped it, I think it would be on the run,' I say very quietly.

'She could have thrown it off the edge, for fuck's sake!' Topher cries.

No one responds to this. It's true of course, but the obvious response is *why*, and no one can bring themselves to say it, not even Elliot, who simply nods in acceptance of the fact that Topher's remark is essentially correct. All we have found is Eva's phone. It's just very hard to work out how it could have got where it is now without Eva.

'Fuck,' Topher says. He gropes his way to the footrest I was using to prop up my injured foot and sits, as though his legs will no longer hold him up. '*Fuck.*'

'If she's dead,' Elliot says flatly, 'what does that mean for Snoop? Is Eva's husband a shareholder now? Will he get a vote on the buyout?'

'Fuck!' Topher looks wild-eyed, as if he can't believe what's happened. 'Arnaud? I — I don't know! Jesus, Elliot, how can you — '

He breaks off . . . I can see his brain ticking.

148

Even now, below his grief, he is still Snoop's founder as much as, if not more than, he is Eva's friend.

'I suppose — I remember now, when we set it up. There was something about this. It was supposed to stop the company passing out of control of the original shareholders without their agreement. I'm pretty sure that shareholders can't sell or give away their shares — they can only offer them for sale to Eva and me. I mean — '

He stops. Swallows.

'To me.'

LIZ

Snoop ID: ANON101
Listening to: offline
Snoopscribers: 0

Eva is dead.

I don't know how the word gets out, but once the whispers start they are like frost creeping across a window. Soon everyone knows. In the living room Miranda and Tiger are exchanging urgent whispers.

'I know,' I hear Miranda hiss. 'But we have to figure out *some* kind of announcement for when we're back online, Tiger. There's no way we can keep a lid on news this big, and if it leaks, it'll be worse in the long run.'

'I can't believe it.' Ani comes to sit beside me on the couch. Her face is swollen and blotched, even in the dim light from the stove and candles. 'Have you heard?'

I nod. I don't trust my voice. In spite of everything, in spite of all that's happened and all the years since I left Snoop, my feelings are still too raw.

'I can't believe it!' Ani repeats desperately. 'Oh God, this is awful. Poor, poor Eva. Rik says they may not even be able to recover a body. Oh God, poor *Arnaud*. And he doesn't even know. How will he tell Radisson? How do you explain to a child of that age that Mummy's never coming home?'

Radisson. The name stabs me like a knife. I had almost forgotten that Eva had had a child in the years since we worked together.

'I don't know,' I say hoarsely.

'Fuck knows what this means for the buyout,' Carl says morosely from the other end of the room, and Ani rounds on him.

'Carl! How can you even *think* about that?'

'I know.' Carl holds up his hands. 'Look, I'm not being selfish here, *I* won't be getting any million-dollar payouts, will I? I'm not talking about the money, I'm talking about the safety of the company. I'm still chief legal officer at Snoop and I have to think about this stuff. Snoop doesn't poof out of existence because Eva's had an accident. All our employees don't go away. I've got a duty to them and to the company. I'd be saying the same if it was me skied off a cliff. Well, I mean, assuming I could still talk.'

'Carl's right.' Rik comes up behind us unexpectedly, looming out of the shadows, and puts his hand on his colleague's shoulder. His face, in the candlelight, looks uneasy. 'However crassly he's phrased it. Eva's death is a tragedy — there's absolutely no doubt about that — but in the coldest possible way, it's got very little to do with Snoop. The company is a completely separate entity to any of us — even Eva and Topher. The buyout offer is still on the table. The clock's still ticking. We still have to come up with an answer. Eva's death doesn't change that.'

151

'Well . . . it does change one thing, doesn't it, mate?' Carl says. There is something in his voice I don't quite like. It is a kind of grimness. Rik looks puzzled.

'Sorry, I'm not sure what you're getting at. Eva's shares, you mean? They'll go to her husband I assume.'

'Except they won't,' Carl says flatly.

'What? I don't understand what you mean. Even if Eva's intestate, Arnaud would still stand to get everything, and he'll certainly want to accept the buyout now, won't he?'

'Shareholders agreement,' Carl says. When Rik still looks blank, he spells it out. 'When the company was set up there was a clause in the original paperwork to say that no one could pass their shares to an outsider. You're a shareholder, mate, didn't you know this?'

'*What?*' Rik says, more forcefully. 'No I didn't know this! Why the fuck would anyone think that was a good idea?'

'It's quite common,' Carl says with a shrug. 'In fact I'd go as far as saying it's good practice. Stops the company passing into the hands of twats and plonkers. Means the original founders can't be forced out without their consent, that kind of thing. Topher and Eva set it up that way so this sort of thing couldn't happen — you know, if someone gets divorced and has to give up half their assets, you don't necessarily want their loony ex to have voting rights.'

'So what the fuck are you saying?' Rik says. He looks horrified. 'Eva's shares disappear on her death?'

152

'Nah, they still exist. But Arnaud has to sell them to Topher.'

'To *Topher?* Why not to the rest of us?'

'Because this agreement pre-dates you and Elliot coming on board,' Carl says shortly. 'This is how they set it up back when it was just the two of them. It was never updated when they issued more shares.'

'So . . . Topher will have to buy out Arnaud?' Miranda says. She comes to sit beside Rik, her brow furrowed. 'Except, well . . . ' She stops, significantly, and exchanges a look with Rik.

'Except he can't,' Rik says bluntly. 'He doesn't have enough liquidity. I don't think that's any big secret, is it? So what does that mean?'

'There's an insurance policy to cover the cost. At least there should be, assuming they kept up the payments. They'll have to be independently valued, and Arnaud'll get whatever the valuers thresh out, I imagine. No idea how they'll take the buyout into consideration. That's for the insurers to decide, I suppose.'

'So wait, what you're saying is . . . ' Rik looks thunderstruck. 'What you're telling me — '

'Is Topher's voting share just got increased to 60 per cent. Yup, that's about the size of it,' Carl agrees.

There is deathly silence in the room.

Miranda looks stricken.

Rik turns and walks out the door.

ERIN

The news of Eva's death is like a pebble thrown into a pond. No, not a pebble — a rock. First there is the God-awful bone-shaking impact, and then the ripples of reaction, radiating out from that original catastrophe, and then rebounding, interacting, magnifying and negating each other.

As Danny and I serve out soup to the guests in the silent, candlelit dining room, I can't help watching them, the way they're trying to make sense of Eva's disappearance in their own individual ways.

Some of them are in deep denial. Inigo, for instance, refuses to believe the GPS evidence. 'She could still be down in St Antoine,' he keeps repeating. 'GPS is wrong all the time, and anyway, even if her phone is somewhere — what does that prove?'

Some of them seem to have been struck dumb by the tragedy. Tiger hardly eats. She just sits, head bowed over her untouched soup, letting the noise of the group wash over her as if the others aren't even there.

Some of them look stunned. Ani seems only

154

half aware of what's going on, she crumbles her bread and makes inane remarks to no one in particular. Liz looks white and shocked, and barely speaks.

But some of them don't seem to be affected at all. Elliot, for instance, is spooning his soup with a poker face and much gusto, as if the tragedy had never happened. His lack of reaction is almost disturbing, though when Ani bursts out, 'Elliot, don't you care?' he looks genuinely surprised.

'Of course I care,' he says. 'I still have to eat dinner.'

It's Topher that my gaze keeps returning to. Topher, who has lost a partner, and gained a company.

For Snoop is now in Topher's complete control, that seems pretty clear, and for all his wild-eyed grief in the kitchen earlier, he doesn't seem that shaken by the news that he is now the majority shareholder in a billion-dollar company. In fact, he seems to have taken it in his stride, feeding on it almost, as if his personality has expanded to fill the vacuum left by Eva's absence. As I clear the soup bowls and refill the wine glasses — at least wine doesn't need cooking or refrigeration — he picks up his glass and downs it, laughing wildly as he does. He has been drinking a lot, throwing back glass after glass as he regales the silent Tiger with some tale of his and Eva's exploits when they first started the company. And the thing is, I can see it — I see the reason why they made this man CEO. I see the confidence that led him to think he could take a wild, improbable idea in a crowded market — and make it into a billion-dollar proposition. Something I never quite understood before — *how* someone would have the chutzpah to do this, and all before their thirtieth birthday — is suddenly plain.

Rik on the other hand seems to have shrunk. He looks bewildered, punch-drunk, like a man who's lost everything which, in a sense, I suppose he has. With Topher in charge, that billion-dollar buyout is melting away, leaving him with . . . what? Shares in a company he tried to sell out from under the founder? A position under a leader he doesn't trust? I can't see him surviving much longer in his post when they get back to the UK, best friend or no best friend. Topher doesn't strike me as the kind of man who would forgive or forget the kind of coup Rik and Eva were attempting to pull.

What's more impressive is that Carl and Miranda, who might easily have switched loyalties when they saw which way the wind was blowing, have instead both rallied around Rik. Do they really believe Snoop is doomed, without Eva at the helm? Either way, they are not siding with Topher, that much is plain. Instead they sit, either side of Rik, like chess pieces guarding their king.

But it feels like the match is over. They have lost their queen. For once more there is a space at the table, an empty place. Not Topher's this time, but Eva's, her empty chair a constant painful reminder of what has happened, not letting anyone forget, even for a second, what has occurred.

156

The chalet is still relatively warm, in spite of the power cut and the temperature drop outside. Its thermal insulation and triple glazing means that the heat from earlier in the day is still enough to make the bedrooms bearable, while the two log burners downstairs keep the living room and dining room toasty.

Nevertheless, I distribute extra blankets and duvets before bed, limping from door to door with a torch clamped under my elbow, clutching armfuls of the spare bedding we keep for emergencies, along with Thermos flasks of hot chocolate.

I'm about to knock at the last door but one when Danny, trailing behind me with a stack of blankets, says, 'Erin, mate — ' with a warning note in his voice.

And I stop. It's Eva's door.

And somehow that one simple thing catches me like a blow to the stomach, a reminder of the reality of what has happened here. An avalanche. A *death*. Will Perce-Neige ever recover from these twin disasters? It's hard to imagine people reading news like this in their Sunday paper and then turning to book a holiday, but then, St. Antoine isn't the first Alpine resort to experience tragedy in the form of an avalanche. It happens almost every year, in fact there was another, similar fall just up the road earlier in the season.

'Mate?' Danny says, and I realise I have stopped stock-still, lost in thought.

'Sorry,' I say stupidly. 'I — I wasn't keeping track — I — '

'You all right?' Danny asks uneasily. 'You

should be sitting down, I'm not happy about you walking on that ankle.'

'I'm fine,' I say shortly. The truth is that my ankle is hurting. A lot. Danny's probably right and I shouldn't be putting weight on it. But I can't bear to sit alone and silent in the darkness of the staff quarters, feeling it throb, thinking about what's happened and what's going to happen. I'm better off working; somehow the endless tasks keep my thoughts at bay. Plus, more practically, guest interaction isn't Danny's strong suit. They've forgiven him for his tactlessness in the wake of the avalanche, at least I hope they have, but our roles are firmly back in place now. We're here to be polite, good hosts, even in these circumstances. Perhaps *especially* in these circumstances. It feels like everything is crumbling — and our ordained roles are the only things we have left to hang on to. Danny and I *must* remain in charge. If we don't keep that authority, if we let Topher take over — well, I don't like to think about how the situation could play out.

There's just one door left. Topher's. And I hitch my armful of blankets a little higher before I knock.

He's drunk, I can tell that when the door opens. He's wearing a robe, open to the waist in spite of the cold, and holding a bottle. And he's not alone. With the overhead light out, I can't see who's inside but I've got a horrible feeling it might be little Ani, who didn't open her door when I knocked a few minutes ago. I want to tell her the answer to her distress over Eva doesn't lie in Topher's bed — but I can't. It's none of my business. She's the same age as me, she's a guest, not a friend, and I have no right to tell her what to do, even if I think she's making a fairly huge mistake.

'Ellen,' he slurs. 'Why hello. What brings you to my room at this late hour? It's a bit late to be tucking people in.'

'Extra blankets,' I say with my best cheerful smile. 'Just in case the temperature drops overnight. Can't have you all freezing to death on my watch.'

'I'll tell you a secret . . . ' Topher leans in, confidentially, his robe gaping to show a smattering of dark blond chest hair. 'The best survival kit is a naked woman.'

Oh ffs.

I can feel my smile thin.

'Well, I'm afraid the service doesn't extend to that.'

'I've already got that part sorted,' he says, but he reaches for the blankets I'm holding out, swaying slightly as he does.

I'm about to turn and leave when he says, out of the blue, 'Don't I know you?'

'I don't think so,' I say firmly.

'No I do . . . I've seen you somewhere before. Did you waitress in London before you came here?'

'Sadly, no.'

'I do,' he persists. 'I *know* you. I've thought it since I first arrived.'

'Mate, she said she doesn't know you, and you're pissed,' Danny breaks in, pushing past my

159

shoulder to stand in front of me. Topher steps forward too, his expression turning ugly in less time than it takes for me to think *oh shit*.

Danny bunches his fists, the tendons in his neck standing out like cords, and for a minute the two men just stand there, chest to chest. I feel my heart thudding. Danny *cannot* hit Topher. He will get fired.

But Topher knows when he's on thin ice, and it's he who steps back, with a laugh that's just the right side of ingratiating.

'My mistake. *Mate*.'

And then he closes the door, and Danny and I are left standing, looking at each other, wondering how much longer this can go on, before the ice cracks.

LIZ

Snoop ID: ANON101
Listening to: offline
Snoopscribers: 1

When I wake up, it is *cold*. That is the first thing I notice. It is a sharp contrast to yesterday, when I woke with a dry mouth and the feeling of having slept all night in a room a few degrees warmer than my bedroom at home.

I reach out and take a sip of the water on my bedside table. It is chilled, as if it has been in the fridge.

Under the extra duvets Erin dropped off I am still relatively comfortable, but I am not looking forward to getting dressed. In the end I reach out and grab the complimentary towelling robe off the end of the bed, dragging it under the covers with me to warm up before I put it on. I remember doing the same thing in my childhood bedroom when I was growing up, pulling my school uniform under the covers to get dressed. The room was in a badly converted loft, and in winter it was almost like sleeping outdoors. When I woke in the morning and breathed out, there would be a cloud of white hanging in the air. At night the moisture used to condense on the sloping ceiling and then freeze, so that I would wake to little runnels of ice on the wall above me. This is not as bad as that. I am in a luxurious chalet, not a Victorian terrace in Crawley, for a start. But as far as temperature goes, it is still painfully chilly.

I pick up my phone and peer at the screen. It is 7.19. The battery is down to 15 per cent but I barely have time to worry about that fact, because I am distracted by something.

I have a notification.

At some point in the night my phone has managed to connect to the Internet. The reception is gone now, the bars greyed out to zero, but that notification is still there, proving that at least for a moment, there was a flicker of connection.

The second surprise is that it is from Snoop. I never get notifications from Snoop. You only get a notification if you get a new subscriber to your feed, and I never do.

Only . . . now I have. At some point in the night, someone snooped me. I'm not even sure how, since I wasn't listening to anything. I had no idea that was possible. Although maybe when the Wi-Fi connected it somehow restarted my stream where I left off, just for a minute?

The realisation gives me an odd feeling. There is no way to know who it was — you can only see who is snooping you in real time; once they log off the connection is severed, only the number remains. Then I dismiss the issue from my mind. In all probability it was a bot or a server glitch, or someone mistyping the ID of someone they actually wanted to follow.

Downstairs the rooms are quiet but considerably warmer, and there's a pile of what I imagine must be yesterday's croissants keeping warm by the wood burner in the lobby, and two big Thermos flasks sitting on the hearth.

I pick up a croissant, and go through to the living room to warm my hands at the fire while I eat it. I assume I am alone. But then something catches my eye and I turn to see Elliot, seated in an armchair, bent over his laptop. The sight surprises me for two reasons — one, his laptop is on and seems to be plugged in. And two, Elliot almost never comes out of his room except for meals. In fact, when I was working at Snoop, he didn't even leave his office for those. He got whoever was doing work experience to bring him takeout — the same thing every day, black coffee and three Pret cheese-and-bacon croissants. It must have been very inconvenient when they stopped serving croissants all day and moved them to the breakfast menu. I find myself wondering what he did. Changed his lunch? Somehow I can't imagine that. Maybe he started sending the work experience person out at 10 a.m.

I don't normally talk to Elliot. He is very hard to make conversation with, though perhaps that is not my fault. Eva once told me that he divides women into ones he would like to sleep with and ones that are not of interest to him. I am definitely in the latter category. But now I pluck up my courage.

'Hi, Elliot'

'Hello, Liz.' He says it flatly, but I know him well enough to know that's not a measure of his enthusiasm. He greets everyone like that, even Topher, who is probably his favourite human being out of anyone.

'How come your laptop is working?'

'I always carry a battery pack.' He holds it up, a chunky thing the size of a brick that is plugged into the power port of his computer. Of course. How like Elliot to leave nothing to chance.

'But you've got no Internet, right?'

'No,' he agrees. 'But I don't need it for coding.'

'What are you working on?'

'The geosnoop update.' His normally pale face flushes with excitement a little bit, and he launches off into a long explanation I don't completely follow about geotracking, ad partners, information storage, GDPR and the technical challenges of making all those elements work with the law and the existing Snoop interface. I nod along, feigning more interest than I really feel. The only thing I really care about is the fact that he used this technology to find Eva. Somehow that seems unbearably poignant — that her own app may be what leads search and rescue to her body.

'I see,' I say at last, as Elliot grinds to a halt. 'It sounds very . . . exciting.' I try to make my voice sound convincing, but Elliot doesn't really seem to care. It's not like he ever shows much expression of his own feelings.

'Now if you don't mind, I need to work,' he

says abruptly, with the directness that is so disconcerting.

'Sorry,' I say. 'I thought maybe you came down to chat.'

'I came down because it's too cold to type in my room,' he says, and then he puts his headphones on, and his fingers begin to clatter across the keyboard once more.

I should be offended. I feel like I ought to be. But I'm not. He may be direct to the point of rudeness, but right now, there is something reassuring about that. With Elliot, there are no secret codes to unravel, no hidden meanings, no weight of expectation. If he wants you to know something, he says it. If he wants something to happen, he tells you. Just at the moment, there is something comforting about it, in contrast to the smoke-and-mirror world of Topher and Eva, where you never know quite where you stand. Sometimes, back in the early days at Snoop, they would remind me of my parents — the way it would all be sweetness and light in front of visitors, and then screaming and threats when the company had left. At least when Elliot says 'Have you got a problem with that?' you know he genuinely wants an answer.

When my father said it, there was only one answer you were allowed to give: *no, Daddy.* And then get out of the way as fast as possible, before the blow landed.

I'm nibbling on the edge of the croissant, staring into the flames of the wood burner, when a noise behind me makes me jump. The croissant falls to the floor in a shower of crumbs. I pick it

165

up. Then I turn to see Rik and Miranda coming into the room. Rik looks like he hasn't slept.

'How are you?' he says to me abruptly, as he sits beside me. I'm taken aback, not sure what to answer. It's the perfect illustration of the difference between Rik and Elliot. If Elliot were asking I would know what he meant — only Elliot would likely never ask, because he would understand the impossibility of the question. But when Rik asks, it becomes a puzzle to decode. What does he mean? Does he want to know how I feel about Eva's death? How can I sum that up in a simple answer? Or is he just asking in the meaningless way that people do, only wanting the answer *fine?*

'I'm . . . I'm OK,' I say cautiously. 'Considering.'

'Really?' Rik looks at me, surprised. 'You're a bigger person than me.' He glances across at Elliot and then lowers his voice, though Elliot is still wearing his big noise-cancelling headphones, and I doubt he can hear a thing. 'Having that kind of money dangled under your nose and then snatched away . . .'

Suddenly the real meaning of his question is clear. He wants to talk about Topher. About what this shift in power means for the buyout.

'I . . . I hadn't really thought about it,' I say, and it's the truth . . . in a way. I would be lying if I claimed I hadn't wondered what would happen now Topher controls the company. But somehow the money never felt that real to me. I never felt I had earned it. It doesn't feel like I had anything taken away — just like I had a strange dream, and then woke up to reality. Only, this — the avalanche, Eva's death, this doesn't feel like reality either. More like waking from a dream to find yourself in an equally surreal nightmare.

'But hadn't you made plans? Banked on the money?'

'Not really,' I say slowly. 'To be honest, I hadn't really come to terms with the idea that it was going to happen anyway.'

'Jesus,' Rik says. He looks annoyed. I think I've said the wrong thing, but I don't know how. A sense of panic sets in. It is the same sense I always got with my father. That I would do or say the wrong thing. That he would take it out on my mother. 'Could you cut the Mother Teresa act, Liz? We've lost everything. Don't you get that?'

'W-we haven't lost everything though, surely? I mean, we've still got the shares.'

'The shares!' Rik gives a short, barking laugh. 'Liz, did you listen to the P&L figures I gave out yesterday? We'll be lucky if Snoop makes it to the year end at the rate Topher's going, and without Eva to reassure investors, that's only going to get worse.'

'But, the update,' I say, although I know I am scrabbling for reassurance now. 'Elliot's geo-snooping thing — isn't the whole point of that to make Snoop more profitable?'

'From a revenue point of view, we've already got that information, we've had it since the permissions changed last year. How Elliot integrates it into the app may make a difference to the user experience, but user satisfaction has never been our problem, the issue has always been monetising that. From an investor perspective rolling out the geosnoop update won't make a difference — all the added value is already there. And anyway — ' he glances over his shoulder at Elliot who is still typing away — 'I've got concerns about that update. I don't think people realise how much information Snoop is gathering on them. I think when this update makes the level of tracking visible, we might have a backlash on our hands.'

'One of Snoop's USPs has always been its light touch,' Miranda says, coming in from the lobby with a cup of coffee in her hand. She takes a sip and makes a face. I think it is the taste of the coffee that she is reacting to. Though it could be the prospect of the update. 'People like the fact that you can be as anonymous as you want, it's part of what keeps celebrities coming back. I'm not sure how many people clocked the change in permissions and really realised what it meant, because nothing changed at the user end. But this update is going to make it very obvious. Users will see exactly how much Snoop knows about their movements. I told Topher and Elliot at the time that there was a big PR risk with all of this, but they're both so focused on the cool techy side of it — '

She stops and glances again at Elliot. He is still head down, tapping away with his earphones on.

'Anyway, never mind. This probably isn't the time or place to have this discussion. It's too . . . soon.' She sits beside me and Rik and takes another sip of coffee, then puts the cup aside.

'How *are* you?' she says to me. I can hardly prevent myself from rolling my eyes. It seems like everyone is asking that question, when what they really want to know is, *what are you thinking?*

I am saved from answering by Elliot, who stands unexpectedly, clicking his laptop closed, and pulling off his headphones. He looks . . . tense. Which is unusual. He doesn't show emotion easily.

'OK, Elliot?' Miranda says brightly. I can tell she is wondering how much Elliot heard of our conversation. 'Erin's put out coffee in the lobby if you want it,' she adds, but he ignores the remark.

'Do you know where Toph is? I need to speak to him.'

'He's still in his room, I think,' Rik says. He is frowning. I can imagine him running over our conversation in his head, trying to work out if he said anything incriminating, and what Elliot might be about to pass back to Topher. 'But wait,' he adds, as Elliot heads purposefully towards the stairs. 'I wouldn't go up there, I think he's got . . . company — '

But it is too late. Either Elliot didn't hear, or he doesn't care. He doesn't reply to Rik's warning. The last we hear of him is his heavy footsteps, thumping up the spiral staircase towards the bedrooms.

169

ERIN

Snoop ID: LITTLEMY
Listening to: offline
Snoopscribers: 10

'Oh, hey, Erin.'

I'm putting out another Thermos of coffee, when Ani trails into the dining room, smiling. She looks like she's not slept a lot. *I hope you know what you're doing*, I want to tell her, but I don't.

'Morning, Ani. Can I get you coffee? The espresso machine isn't working, but Danny's managed to rig up a kettle on the wood burner so we've got hot French press.'

'Ooh, yes please,' Ani says. 'Could you take a cup up to Topher?'

'Sure.'

'Oh, I mean, unless . . . how's your ankle?' she adds, flustered at having slipped so easily back into guest and server mode. 'I can take it up if you're not — '

She stops. Everyone has been thrown off-kilter by the strangeness of our set-up here. Are we fellow survivors, or still holiday-makers and staff? I don't know myself, but I do know that it's going to be easier for everyone if we stick to the normal protocols. Someone needs to be in

170

charge, and to be perfectly honest, I'd prefer it if that someone were me, not Topher.

'It's loads better, thanks,' I lie. 'I can manage the stairs no problem.'

'But you shouldn't have to,' Ani says, making up her mind. 'I'll take it up.'

'Are you sure?'

'Yes, totally. I'll take one for Elliot too. He must be freezing up there.'

She pours out three cupfuls and carries them carefully up the spiral staircase to the bedrooms.

★ ★ ★

By 10 a.m. everyone is awake, and Danny and I make the decision to summon all the guests into the lobby for a meeting. There's no real news, and the weather is still too unpredictable for a helicopter to land on our narrow slice of mountain-side, but local radio reports have been saying that search and rescue for casualties is ongoing, and that EDF are working on restoring power to outlying hamlets. We are not the only people trapped without electricity, by the sound of it. In fact we're considerably better off than some. But it feels like a good idea to reassure everyone that progress is being made, and to stress that we have enough food and water to see us through until they either restore the funicular or get a helicopter up to airlift us out.

We also have to discuss the elephant in the room — Eva's death. Although the rumour has gone around the group and everyone seems to have learned of Elliot's conclusions, neither

Danny nor I have formally acknowledged the issue. I've been putting it off, unable to face the reality of what has happened, but the time has come that we really *have* to make an announcement, make it clear that we're trying our best to contact the authorities and alert them to what's happened, but at the same time put to rest any false hopes, dispel any fantasies that she's going to come limping over the horizon at any moment.

Danny beats the gong in the lobby, sending its deafening crescendo ringing around the rafters and when at last everyone is gathered I tap a spoon against a coffee cup and wait for silence.

'Hi, um, hi, everyone. Sorry for dragging you out of your rooms like this, but Danny and I just wanted to give you an update into our situation. Danny spent the morning trekking out to our two closest chalets, which unfortunately — or perhaps fortunately, for the inhabitants — seem to be unoccupied. One is very badly damaged but it doesn't look like anyone was there at the time of the avalanche. The other one was out of the path of the fall so is fine, but again, there's no one home. We were hoping to find someone with a two-way radio or a satellite phone, but it's not looking good so far. There's one more chalet up at this level but it's about three miles away, so Danny's going to wait until the weather clears before he heads out to check on that one.'

'And have you managed to make contact with search and rescue?' Rik says.

'Yes and no,' I say. 'As you know, Inigo made contact yesterday and told them about our

172

situation, but we haven't been able to get through since, and without access to a satellite phone, I don't think that's going to happen until the power is restored. The power cut seems to have wiped out the remaining cell phone reception. But the key thing is that they *do* know we're here. We know from what Inigo said that we're on their list, we just have to be patient while they work through the more critical rescues.'

'Do they know about Eva though?' The question comes from Tiger, her voice even more husky than usual, as if she is holding back a strong emotion, and a silence falls over the room as I try to answer it.

'Inigo told them that's she's missing, yes. But they don't know the latest. However — '

I stop and swallow. I knew this would be hard but this is ridiculously hard. I see Liz's eyes, luminous with distress, reflecting back at me from the other side of the room, Topher's anguished face, Ani shading her eyes with a hand to hide the sudden tears that Tiger's question has provoked. I take a breath, steady myself on the arm of a chair, trying to take the weight off my ankle, give myself space to find the right words. What I want to try to tell them is that even if we *can* get Elliot's information to the search and rescue team, it's not going to help. Eva's already dead, and now she's probably under thousands of tonnes of snow as well. There is no chance of anyone rescuing her alive, in fact there's not even any certainty that they will be able to recover her body. Some of the high passes never melt, even

173

in summer. If Eva is buried at the bottom of one of the steep ravines, well, that's it. There aren't enough resources and money in the world to make that recovery.

'The position she's in — ' I stop, swallow again, but before I can find words to go on, Carl is interrupting.

'How do we know she's definitely there though?' His expression is truculent. 'I mean this whole place has shit phone reception. How can Elliot say those coordinates are right?'

I look around for Elliot. Where is he?

'My understanding is that GPS doesn't rely on phone reception,' I fumble, still desperately scanning the room for his face, willing him to step in and explain the technicalities of how Snoop gets its geolocation information. I am way out of my depth here. 'I mean, obviously you have to relay the positioning, you can't do that without some kind of information exchange, but the GPS coordinates themselves don't rely on mobile towers for accuracy, they're . . . satellite I think? Is that right, Elliot?' But I can't see him. 'Where *is* Elliot?'

Other people are looking around now, asking themselves the same question.

'He was up in his room when I last saw him,' Ani says, frowning. 'He was working on something. He's probably got his headphones on, didn't hear the gong. I'll go and get him.'

She turns and runs lightly up the spiral staircase and we hear her footsteps receding down the corridor towards Elliot's room, and the rat-a-tat on his door.

No answer. She knocks again, more loudly, and then calls 'Elliot?' through the wood.

There is a pause. I imagine her cautiously opening the door, venturing forward to tap Elliot on the shoulder . . . but my mental picture is broken into shards by a scream. And not just a little shriek of surprise, either. This is a full-throated panic-cry.

With my injured ankle, I'm not first up the stairs. Topher, Rik, Danny and Miranda are ahead of me, and Liz and Carl both jostle past me halfway up. By the time I reach the first floor I can hear Ani's sobbing cries of 'Oh God, he's dead, he's dead!' and Topher's brusque, impatient, 'Stop being hysterical.'

When I finally make it to the end of the corridor and push my way into Elliot's room, everything looks completely normal, except for two things.

Elliot is lying slumped across the little desk by the window. He is face down in a pool of black coffee, spilled from a cup tipped on its side.

Next to his desk, on a towel on the floor, is his computer, and it has been smashed to pieces.

LIZ

Snoop ID: ANON101
Listening to: offline
Snoopscribers: 1

Elliot is dead. You can tell that without even touching him. There is something about the unnatural way he is slumped, one arm hanging limp, the spilled coffee pooling around his face and in his eyes.

But it is not only that. It is what has happened to his computer that makes it clear. Elliot would have died before he let anyone touch that computer.

It has been — wrecked doesn't seem the right word. It has been *obliterated*. The keyboard has been ripped off, revealing the inner workings of the device. The screen has cracked and a dark stain is spreading across the LCD. And finally, the hard drive has been pulled out, cracked open, and bent and twisted beyond all recognition.

'What — 'Topher's face is white and stark. He looks more frightened than I have ever seen him. 'What's happened? Oh my God, oh God, oh Jesus — he wanted to tell me something and I didn't — I wouldn't let — oh God . . . '

He stumbles from the room. He looks like he might be sick.

Ani appears struck completely dumb by the discovery. She simply stands there, gaping, tears streaming silently down her face, until Tiger takes her arm and leads her away.

It is Erin who speaks.

'Everyone, out.'

'What?' Carl says it stupidly. He looks like a boxer who has taken too many blows to the head.

'Out. Out of the room. This is a crime scene.'

She goes across to Elliot, puts two fingers to his neck, pulls Elliot's eyelids back, and then shakes her head very slightly at Danny.

'Well, what are you waiting for?' Danny says to the rest of the room. He sounds almost angry. 'Didn't you hear what she said? Get out.'

We file out. Erin takes a staff key from her pocket and locks the door behind us. Her face is outwardly calm, but I think underneath it she is holding down panic.

'Inigo,' she says, 'I know I don't need to tell you this, but please keep checking for reception with your phone. It's absolutely imperative that we get hold of the police, now.'

'Uh, yes, of course.' Inigo looks as stunned as Carl. 'I'll go now, and check. I left it downstairs.'

'What can we do?' Miranda says blankly to Erin. 'What can we do?'

'Nothing,' Erin says. Her face is grim now. 'There is nothing we can do. Try to keep it together until the search and rescue come.'

177

ERIN

Snoop ID: LITTLEMY
Listening to: offline
Snoopscribers: 10

In the kitchen, Danny stands with his back to the door as if his weight can shut out the reality of what we left behind us, and he stares at me with an expression of horror.

'Fuck,' he says. And I can't think of anything to say in reply. Because what else is there to say? This is . . . this is bad. This is beyond bad. And I can't make sense of it.

'Danny, what the hell is going on?'

'I have no fucking clue, mate. Did he commit suicide?'

'Maybe.' I realise how little we know about these people — any of them. After all, Elliot could have been under any kind of pressure, and Danny and I would never have known. But that's the thing — we *don't* know. We have no idea what is happening here.

I put my hands to my head as if I can forcibly keep it together with the pressure of flesh on bone. Oh God, it feels like everything is falling apart.

'He wasn't hurt,' I say, trying to figure it out as I speak. 'I mean, I couldn't see any physical injuries, it didn't look like anyone had attacked him. Which means . . . I suppose he must have taken something. Don't you think?'

'Drugs? Injectables? Pills?'

'I don't know. I don't *know*. Holy fuck. Danny, what do we do?' The reality — if you can call it that — of our predicament is sinking in. We are stuck here — very stuck, in my case, with my wrenched ankle — in a chalet with a group of people we barely know, and two of them have died in the last twenty-four hours. Eva — Eva's death was a tragic accident. One of those horrible, awful lightning strikes that can occur in even the most tranquil places. But Elliot — surely there is no way his death can be anything but murder or suicide. A brain aneurysm — a massive stroke — a heart attack — any of those might kill near enough instantly. But they don't explain the smashed-up computer.

'Was he *definitely* dead?' Danny asks.

'Definitely.' I can't suppress a shudder as I think of it.

'Are you sure?' Danny is grasping at straws and I think he knows it, but he can't stop himself asking. 'Are you absolutely certain, mate?'

'Danny, I may have dropped out of med school without a degree, but I've seen enough dead bodies to know one. I promise you, he was dead. Dilated pupils, absent pulse, the works.' I don't mention the puddle of piss under the chair. Danny doesn't need to know about that.

'But how?' Danny says. He looks like he might be sick. 'How the fuck did someone get to him, if

179

that's what happened? Something in the coffee?'

'Maybe, I don't know.'

'Should we go and, you know . . . check?'

'I don't *know*,' I say again, more forcefully this time. My head is spinning, trying to figure out the right course of action. 'The police will want to — I mean, we shouldn't disturb the scene. But maybe if we knew what it was — '

I look down at the key in my hand and make up my mind.

'We'll go and check. We won't touch anything, we'll just look.'

Danny nods, and together we make our way quietly up the service stairs to the first floor, trying not to let the others see where we're heading.

We don't discuss our decision to stick together, but I know we are both thinking the same thing. If Elliot didn't commit suicide, then someone in this group is a murderer. And that is a very scary idea indeed. Could one of those sleek, monied hipsters downstairs *really* have murdered someone? I try to imagine gentle Tiger with her slim hands around Elliot's neck, or Topher whacking him with an empty bottle of whiskey — and I feel suddenly sick.

The staff key grates in Elliot's locked door, and then turns, and Danny and I tiptoe inside the room. It is very cold, and it smells of spilled coffee, and something else, more acrid: that stench of urine, which I recognise from my hospital days.

Danny hangs back, by the door, as if he can't bring himself to come any closer to Elliot's body.

180

So it's clearly up to me. I swallow. Very, very cautiously, trying not to disturb anything, I move forward towards the desk. Elliot is still lying in the same slumped, unnatural position, his face in the puddle of cold black coffee. I already moved him slightly to check for signs of life, but I want to avoid disturbing the scene any further. So without touching him, or anything else, I lean over, and try to peer inside the empty, fallen cup. It's difficult, without moving it, the angle is all wrong. I go round to the other side of the desk — and suddenly, there, I can see it.

Shit. Danny was right.

'There's something in the cup,' I tell Danny, who is not coming any closer than he can help. 'Something white.'

'Sugar?'

'No, definitely not. It's . . . chalky.'

'Fuck.'

I straighten up and Danny and I look at each other, trying to figure out what this means. His black eyes are very, very worried.

'I think this rules out suicide,' I say, with immense reluctance. I am keeping my voice low. I don't want anyone but Danny to know I'm in here.

'Do you think?' Danny looks like he is desperate for an alternative. I can't blame him. 'What if he was really bad at taking pills — don't you think someone might crush them?'

I shake my head.

'You didn't see him eating, Danny.' I think of Elliot at dinner, spooning down his venison with concentrated ferocity, swallowing great gulps of it while barely chewing. 'But it's not just the pills. Look at the computer.'

'What do you mean? He could have smashed it up himself, couldn't he?'

I shake my head, pointing to the wreckage, strewn across one of the chalet's thick, fluffy white bath towels.

'Someone wrapped it in a towel before they destroyed it. Which means, they didn't want to be heard. If it was Elliot smashing up his own laptop in a fit of frustration, he wouldn't have bothered to keep the noise down. And if he was trying to cover something up covertly, he'd just have reformatted the hard drive — why take the risk of smashing it up if you can just rewrite all the data? No, this was done by someone who couldn't log in. Someone who couldn't afford to be overheard.'

We both stand, contemplating the smashed screen and broken pieces of hard drive. Danny doesn't say anything. I'm not sure there is anything he can say.

Then something else occurs to me.

'Were they *his* pills, do you think? Did he take any medication?'

'We'll have to ask the others.' Danny looks like he's relishing the prospect about as much as a slug enema. 'Jesus. How do we have that conversation?'

How do we discuss any of this? *Hey, guys, listen, there's a strong chance one of your colleagues is a murderer.*

But why? Why would anyone want to kill Elliot? His shares? His support for Topher? With

Eva dead, is it possible someone is trying to undermine Topher's support?

None of that would explain the destruction of Elliot's computer, though. It is the computer that I keep coming back to. That vicious, efficient, stealthy act of destruction. That could not have been an accident. And I don't for a second believe it was Elliot.

There is only one plausible reason for this action — to hide something on the computer itself. Something Elliot knew. Something that got him killed.

I think of Topher's anguished wail, when we found Elliot's body: *oh God, oh Jesus — he wanted to tell me something . . .*

I swallow.

'Danny, what if Eva's death wasn't an accident?'

LIZ

Snoop ID: ANON101
Listening to: offline
Snoopscribers: 1

We sit, all of us, huddled around the wood burner in the living room. Except it is *not* all of us, that is the problem.

Now we are ten.

Now we are nine.

Now we are eight.

The words chant inside my head, a kind of gruesome countdown, edging closer to zero, one by one.

Suddenly I think I might vomit.

'Was it . . . ' Tiger speaks. Her voice is cracked and rough, as if she has been crying. 'Was it . . . suicide?'

'No!' Topher's answer comes as quick as a gunshot. He stands up. He begins to pace. 'Fuck no. Elliot? Never.'

'So what?' Rik stands too, squaring up to Topher as if he is about to punch him. 'What are you saying?'

Topher looks at him. I think he genuinely does not understand Rik's question.

'Use your head, Toph. If it's not suicide — ' Rik's voice has an edge I have never heard before. He sounds . . . dangerous. 'Then it's *murder*. Is that what you're saying, Topher? Is it?'

Topher's mouth falls open. Then he sits abruptly. He looks winded, almost as if Rik really had punched him.

'God. You're right. Oh my God.' His face is ashen. 'Elliot,' he says brokenly. And then he begins to cry.

It is awful, watching him. None of us knows what to do. Rik looks at Miranda, whose face is aghast. Carl puts his hands up in a *don't look at me, mate* gesture of repudiation. Inigo's expression is pure panic.

It is Tiger who steps up. She goes to sit beside Topher. She puts her hand on his arm.

'Topher,' she says. Her voice is gentle. 'We all feel his loss, but it must be incalculable for you, more than any of us. Coming on top of Eva's death — '

She stops. Not even Tiger can spin this as *what will be, will be*.

'Why?' Topher's mouth is square and ugly, tears running down his cheeks. He looks so far from the polished, urbane sophisticate I used to know, I am not sure if I can bear it. 'Why would anyone do this to him? Why would they hurt Elliot?'

That, of course, is the $64,000 question.

We all look at each other. No one is sure what to say.

'Come on.' Tiger takes Topher gently by the hand. She leads him from the room. 'Let's go and splash your face with water.'

185

As they leave, a sigh of released tension ripples round the room.

'Jesus,' Carl says gruffly.

'But he's right,' Rik says. 'Why *would* anyone hurt Elliot? I mean Eva, OK. But Elliot? It makes no sense at all. I know Topher doesn't want to hear it, but maybe he *did* commit suicide, uncomfortable as it is for all of us to face? I mean Eva's disappearance and then on top of that the shock of the avalanche — he was quite a — ' He stops. I think he is trying to work out how to phrase it without giving offence. 'He was quite a quirky personality.'

'I think that's a pretty offensive stretch, Rik,' Miranda says wearily. 'Yes, he had his eccentricities — we all do. But to go from that to — '

'No,' Rik says defensively, 'that's not what I meant. Jesus, I *liked* him. We were at school together, for goodness' sake. I'm just saying — look, he was very hard to read. Still waters run deep and all that. There could have been a lot going on underneath.'

'And what do you mean, you could understand someone wanting to hurt Eva?' Carl says suddenly. Rik winces. He knows that he has made a misstep, not once, but twice.

'I didn't mean that either. Oh bloody hell, I'm putting my foot in it all over the fucking shop.'

'So what *did* you mean?' It is Inigo. His voice is bitter, almost accusing. His interjection is so uncharacteristic that we all turn and stare at him.

Rik flushes.

'All I meant,' he says carefully. I can tell he is

186

picking his words now. 'All I meant was Eva's death . . . it changed stuff.'

'What *stuff*?'

Rik does not want to spell it out. I can see that he doesn't.

It is Carl who says it for him.

'Eva's death gave control of Snoop over to Topher, isn't that what you mean, mate?'

Rik cannot bring himself to reply, but he gives a small, tight nod.

There is a moment's long shocked silence, as what he is saying sinks in around the circle.

Rik has joined the first two dots, but no one wants to go any further. They can already see the pattern that is forming.

Several people here had a powerful financial motive for Eva's death. Specifically, Topher and Elliot. Plus anyone else who was opposed to the buyout for their own private reasons.

Which means . . .

It means —

I feel the blood rush to my face. Suddenly I can't go on with this, can't sit here thinking the thoughts that are threatening to overwhelm me. I have to get out — get away.

I stand, and I run out of the room.

ERIN

Snoop ID: LITTLEMY
Listening to: offline
Snoopscribers: 10

Danny and I are still standing outside Elliot's room when I hear the sound of running feet, and I turn to see Liz hurrying along the corridor. For a minute I think she is running towards us, and I tense, bracing myself for whatever has happened, but she stops halfway along the corridor, opens her bedroom door, and slams it behind her. I hear the key scrape in the lock from the inside, and then nothing.

'Jeez,' Danny says. He looks taken aback. 'What's eating her?'

'Do you need to ask?' I whisper it. The doors here are thick, but you can hear through them if your room is quiet.

'Do you think she heard?' Danny lowers his voice too. 'You know. What we were saying before.' He doesn't repeat it, but the words I uttered just before Liz came barrelling towards us still hang in the air between us. *Maybe Eva's death wasn't an accident.*

'I don't know,' I mutter. 'Let's get out of here. We can't talk here, and I need to think this through.'

188

As we make our way down the corridor to the staff part of the building, where Danny and I have our private rooms, my mind is racing, ticking through possibilities. But it's only when we're safely in my little bedroom, the door closed behind us, that I feel able to voice them.

'What I just said — '

'Eva's death?' Danny looks troubled, but sceptical. 'Yeah, how d'you make that out? Elliot, sure. There's some kind of hanky-panky there. But Eva? She skied a black run in a fucking blizzard and fell off the edge. It's a tragedy, but I can't see how it's anyone's fault.'

'Listen,' I say. I'm speaking very low, even though we're behind two sets of doors. Somehow it feels like I need to get these suspicions out in the open, like it might even be dangerous to keep quiet right now. Because if I'm right, it was Elliot's silence that killed him. 'Listen, we're missing the important thing here. Whoever killed Elliot — '

'If he was killed,' Danny breaks in.

'If he was killed,' I echo impatiently, brushing his words away like irritating flies. 'But the point is if he was killed, whoever killed him didn't just get rid of him, they got rid of his computer. Why would they do that? It's really hard work to destroy a hard drive — it takes a while, and they must have risked someone noticing their absence or hearing them do it.'

'So . . . you're saying . . . he was killed for something on his computer?'

'Yes. He was killed for something he knew, but it must have been something he'd figured out from his computer data.'

'Something about Snoop?'

'Maybe. Kind of. Look at the timing. Elliot is coding this geo-location update, whatever they're calling it. Then he realises that the information he's got can lead him to Eva. That much we know. But what if he began to track back from that? What if he was looking at her movements before she died? What if there was something fishy about them, like perhaps she didn't shoot off the edge, but stopped for a chat with someone, and was pushed?'

'Holy fuck.' Danny's face is stricken. 'You're saying . . . someone in that group got rid of Eva and then killed Elliot to cover their tracks?'

'I don't want to believe it, but . . . I can't see what else makes sense.' I feel sick even saying the words. 'There is one other possibility, but I don't know if it's much better.'

'Which is?'

'Well, Elliot is the only person without any kind of alibi the day Eva died. He was supposed to be here, working on his code, but there's no corroboration of that. It's not impossible he had something to do with her death. Maybe . . . maybe he couldn't live with that knowledge any longer.'

'You're saying he topped himself out of guilt?'

'I'm saying it's a possibility.'

'OK, yeah, but even supposing he killed Eva to help Topher then had an attack of conscience, why would he destroy his computer? If he's dead, why would he care about the evidence?'

I swallow. This is why this possibility isn't

190

really any more comforting than the others.

'Because whatever was on there, implicates someone else. Someone he's trying to protect.'

'Flaming Nora.' The words should sound funny, coming in Danny's deep, matter-of-fact voice. In fact, they're anything but. Actually I think I want to be sick.

'So you think I'm right?'

'I think . . . ' I can see Danny's brain processing furiously, trying to find holes in my logic and failing. He pulls off his bandanna irritably, scrubs his face with it. 'Fucking hell. I don't know. I think you could be, and that's enough to give me the cold heaves. What do we do? We gotta tell someone, right?'

'Who can we tell? And what could they do even if we did?' I wave a hand at the window, where the vicious wind is whipping the snow past the glass with the scouring force of a sandstorm. No one can go out in that, let alone fly a helicopter. You'd be mad to try.

'FUCK!' Danny bellows it, standing up and running his hands over his short hair like he can cudgel an idea out of his head.

'Shh!' I say frantically. 'Be quiet! The others'll hear.'

'But we have to tell them!' he says. 'Don't we? I mean, what's the alternative, we keep quiet and let some homicidal prick pick them off one by one?'

'We can't tell them!' My voice is a screaming whisper now. 'Are you mad? Tell whoever's responsible for this that we might be on to them?'

'We can't *not* tell them!' Danny takes my arms, and for a minute I think he's going to shake me, like an actor in an old movie dealing with a hysterical woman, and I feel a desperate urge to laugh in spite of the predicament we're in, but he doesn't, he just stares into my face, his dark eyes very wide and as scared as I feel. But somehow seeing my own fear reflected back at myself, the realisation that Danny's as terrified as me, and that we're in this together, it anchors me. I take a deep, shuddering breath, and Danny says quietly, 'Erin, I'm shitting myself as much as you are. But I don't think I'm going to be able to go down there and act normal, knowing that one of those hipster wankers might be an honest-to-God murderer. Look at me — ' He holds out a trembling hand. 'I'm shaking like a bloody leaf. Whoever's done this, they're going to figure out that we *know* something, and if we haven't told anyone what we know, we'll end up the same way as Elliot. The best way to make ourselves safe is to *not* keep this a secret.'

His words silence me. There is a kind of horrible logic in that.

'And besides,' he adds, 'I reckon we owe the others the chance to protect themselves. What if they know something they don't realise? What if they're the next people drinking coffee with a kick?'

I swallow. But his words have an undeniable truth behind them. Put like that, it's hard to justify not warning the seven innocent people in the chalet, even if that means giving the murderer a heads up.

Murderer. The very word, hanging unspoken in my mouth, feels unreal. Is this actually happening? Are we really going to do this?

'OK,' I say at last. I look out of the window, at the storm, a sinking feeling beginning to churn in my gut at the thought of the meeting to come. 'OK . . . maybe you're right. So . . . what? How do we tell them? *What* do we tell them?'

'We tell them the truth,' Danny says. His expression is set and grim now. 'We say we think Eva's death may not have been an accident after all, and that Elliot might've been killed for whatever he was about to tell Topher. We tell 'em to stay in pairs at all times, make their own drinks, eat nothing but stuff you and I serve them. We're the only people who can't possibly be suspected. We didn't know any of them before they came here. We weren't up on that mountain. We've got no connection to any of that group.'

I nod. Only . . . and I can't bring myself to say this to Danny, not now . . . the problem is, in my case, it's not quite true.

LIZ

Snoop ID: ANON101
Listening to: offline
Snoopscribers: 1

I am up in my room with my head in my hands, trying to block out the reality of what is happening, when I hear the sound of the gong in the foyer being struck.

My head jerks up.

I open my door, cautiously. Erin's voice comes floating up the stairwell.

' . . . you could all come and gather in the lobby for a second. This won't take long, and then we'll serve lunch.'

I am not ready to face the others. But whatever is going on down there, I have to know. Maybe the police have been in contact. Maybe we are about to be airlifted out.

I take a deep breath. I flex my fingers. I open the door of my room and walk downstairs.

The others are all waiting in the foyer, huddled around the wood stove. It has got noticeably colder now. The warmth left over from yesterday's central heating has dispersed, and now only the two stoves downstairs are keeping the place from slowly freezing.

Erin is standing a few steps up on the spiral

staircase. Her face is very white, and her scar looks more shocking than ever, a livid slash against her pale skin. Danny is at her shoulder like a lieutenant. I have to push past them to get to the ground floor. There are puddles on the wood in the foyer, where the piled-up snow is leaking in through the bowed front door, spoiling the polish.

When we are all gathered in front of them, looking up expectantly, Erin clears her throat.

'OK, is everyone here?' She's counting heads, and I realise with a shudder that she is thinking of our abortive meeting this morning, that ended with the realisation that Elliot was missing. I taste blood, and I realise I am chewing my cuticle again. *Disgusting little girl.* I flinch. I shove my hands in my pockets.

'We're going to serve lunch in the living room if that's OK — the dining room is starting to feel quite cold. It's salad — I know that's not the most appropriate, but without electricity Danny is very limited on what he can cook, and we need to finish up the fresh vegetables, now that the fridge is off.'

There's a mild grumble from Topher, but Miranda glares at him, and everyone else nods. We know we are not in a position to complain.

'But . . . the real reason we asked you all here — ' Erin stops. She looks a little bit sick. Like she is working herself up to say something she really doesn't want to say. Suddenly, I do not want to hear what she is about to say. 'Danny and I, we . . . '

She looks over her shoulder at Danny. He

195

gives her a look back. I am not sure if it is encouragement or impatience, but it seems to spur Erin on.

'We have some concerns,' she finishes, in a rush, 'about the manner of Elliot's death. We're pretty sure that he — that he was poisoned.'

Little gasps come from all around the room. It is what they have all been thinking, but there is something horrifying about hearing the words spoken aloud.

'There are traces of crushed pills in his coffee,' Erin says, 'and while he may have taken an overdose deliberately, the sabotaged computer makes it at least possible — '

Danny mutters something. His voice is too low for me to hear, but Erin sighs. She tightens her fists at her sides.

'Maybe even *probable*, that Elliot was murdered. And that leads backwards to the possibility that Eva was killed too, and Elliot was murdered because of what he knew.'

There is another ripple of reaction around the room, but it is not really surprise. She is only voicing what most people here had already begun to suspect. It is more like a kind of horror: these are no longer paranoid fears, but a potential reality.

'Danny and I debated this announcement long and hard,' Erin continues, 'because ultimately it's only speculation — we have no proof of any of this. It's still possible that Eva's death was an accident and Elliot's was suicide or an accidental overdose. However, the fact remains that two deaths have occurred and that is . . . well,

196

concerning doesn't really cover it. So even while we hope this is overk — '

She stops. I realise that the word she was going to use was 'overkill', but that she has thought better of it.

'Even while we hope this is overly cautious,' she rephrases, 'we would still urge everyone here to take precautions. If you know something that may endanger you, come and tell me and Danny as quickly as possible. Stay in pairs or groups at all times. That includes sleeping. Prepare your own drinks and don't leave them lying around. Only accept food from Danny or me. There's no need to be paranoid but — '

Carl breaks in. His short laugh sounds like the bark of a dog.

'No need to be paranoid? Are you having a giraffe?'

'I realise this is all — ' Erin begins, but he cuts her off again.

'You're telling us there's a homicidal fucking maniac running around and the answer is to make our own coffee?'

'I'm not telling you anything of the kind,' Erin says. Her voice is very level. 'I am simply stating the facts of what's happened. Whether you concur with my conclusions and follow my advice is up to you.'

'This is a fucking shitshow,' Carl says angrily. 'And I should sue the arse off you. Thousands of pounds to stay in a tinpot little shithole with a psycho on — '

'Oi,' Danny breaks in. He steps forward so he is close to Carl's face. 'That's enough of that, mate. Erin and me are not responsible if you brought some psychotic fucker with you from the airport.'

'Are you accusing Snoop employees of this?' Carl is practically shouting now. He and Danny are squaring up. 'Because that, *mate*, is slander and I'll see you in court.'

'I'm not accusing Snoop employees of anything,' Danny snarls, 'I'm saying that we've hosted a hundred fucking holidays and it wasn't until you lot turned up — '

'Hey.' Erin steps forward. She is speaking to both of them, but it is Danny's arm she takes. She shakes it gently. '*Hey*. This isn't helping.'

'Carl.' Tiger puts her hand on Carl's shoulder. 'Come on, Erin's right. It's completely under- standable that you're angry, but you need to channel that energy into a more positive place. Erin and Danny aren't at fault here. They're trying to help. C'mon. Deep breaths.'

Carl is still muttering as he stalks to the other side of the room. He slumps on the sofa, arms folded, but I can see he knows Tiger is right.

'Inigo,' Erin says now, 'have you had *any* more luck with mobile reception?'

Inigo shakes his head.

'Nothing, sorry. And now I'm down to 12 per cent battery, so I'm trying just to turn it on occasionally to check.'

'Anyone else?' Erin says. There is an edge of desperation in her voice. There are headshakes all around the room. Most people must be out of battery now, anyway. I turned my phone off when it got to 4 per cent.

'And what did they say when you spoke to them?' Erin asks, turning back to Inigo. He frowns.

'What do you mean?'

'I mean, did they give any timescales at all? Any indication of how they proposed to get to us? I know they didn't know the full extent of it then, but they knew we had someone missing, right? I would have thought we'd have been quite high up the list of priorities.'

'I . . . ' Inigo is frowning, as if he is trying to remember. 'Yes, I mean, I told them Eva was missing and that we were trapped in our chalet at the top of the funicular. And I said . . . I told them about your ankle. And they just asked some questions about supplies and then said they would come out to us as quickly as possible.'

'That was it? No timings at all?'

'N-no . . . ' Inigo sounds uncertain. 'I mean, the reception was really bad. I'm trying to remember but I don't think it was mentioned.'

'OK,' Erin says. There is an edge of frustration in her voice that her calm politeness doesn't quite mask. 'That's understandable. Well, we'll just sit tight, I guess. OK, well, that's it, everyone. If you go through to the living room, Danny and I will bring lunch along very shortly.'

Everyone begins to disperse. Carl is still muttering angrily. Tiger is talking to him soothingly. Miranda and Rik are the last to leave the lobby. I am directly in front of them. I can hear their low conversation as we file slowly into the lounge.

'I suppose Inigo did actually phone the

police?' Rik speaks. His voice is barely above a mutter.

'What do you mean?' Miranda sounds surprised.

'Well . . . I mean . . . Erin seemed pretty concerned that we hadn't heard anything. And I can see her point. You'd have thought they'd have got *someone* up here, right? Even if it was just a scout.'

'But we heard him, Rik, we heard him calling them.'

'We heard his end of the conversation, yes. But how do we know he actually made the call? I mean it's a bit suspicious full stop that he managed to get reception when none of the rest of us did. What was that all about?'

Miranda doesn't answer that. But I notice that when we are all gathered in the living room, she takes the seat furthest away from Inigo, and she doesn't meet his eyes.

ERIN

Snoop ID: LITTLEMY
Listening to: offline
Snoopscribers: 10

'Bollocks.' I'm standing in the kitchen, watching Danny put the finishing touches to big bowls of salad. He's done an amazing job with tins and jars, but there is no way of masking the fact that the bread is stale, and the lettuce has seen better days. Twenty-four hours without electricity is starting to take its toll on the freshness of the chilled food.

'What do you mean, bollocks?' Danny doesn't look up. He's crumbling crushed walnuts over a big plate of ripe, sliced pears and slightly overripe Bleu d'Auvergne cheese.

'I just . . . I feel like that didn't go so well?'

Danny tastes the dressing, and then shrugs.

'I dunno. You were telling them something they didn't want to hear. What did you expect them to do — applaud?'

I shrug. I am not sure what to say.

At last Danny is ready and we each pick up a couple of bowls and carry them out. As I limp after Danny, through the empty lobby, I see croissant crumbs from earlier today scattered across the thick sheepskin rug. There's not much

I can do without any electricity for the Hoover, but in my current mood it feels like a sign of the way things are fraying at the edges, falling apart, while Danny and I desperately try to keep the wheels on.

In the living room, the silence is deafening. There's no longer any friendly backdrop of music to mask the tensions in the group, only the soft roar of the log burner, and the patter of snow against the window. Rik and Miranda are sitting together, their arms touching. They seem to have abandoned all pretence of not being a couple and as I draw closer I see that their hands are entwined in Miranda's lap.

Tiger is still talking to Carl in a low voice, as if she can calm him down.

Liz is sitting awkwardly on the edge of her seat. Her fingers are in her mouth, chewing at her nails, but as I enter the room she takes them out and flexes her hands nervously, cracking her knuckles. The little volley of clicks is very loud in the quiet room, and Ani, sitting between Liz and Topher, makes an involuntary grimace at the sound.

Only Inigo is by himself, and when I offer him the last bowl of salad, he waves it away with one hand.

'Thanks, but I'm not hungry.'

'You've got to eat, Inigo,' I say, but the look on his face worries me more than his appetite The last thing we need is someone sinking into a depression.

'I'm not hungry.' He says it with more force and I put my hands up.

'OK, OK. Not trying to strong-arm anyone. I'll leave it here, OK? If you don't want it, no pressure.'

I am turning to go back to the kitchen when I hear his voice, very low.

'I feel like everyone is blaming me.'

'Blaming you?' I say in surprise. 'Why on earth would they do that?'

'Because of what you said before — about not being able to get through to the police. I heard them.' His voice drops to a whisper, and I have to bend closer to find out what's being said. 'I heard Rik and Miranda, they were saying — ' He stops, swallowing heroically, and I see there are tears in his eyes. 'I think they think I was making it up. That I didn't talk to the police, or if I did that I didn't stress the urgency of the situation enough. But why?' He looks up, his extraordinary blue eyes swimming with tears. 'Why would I do that? Unless I'd — unless I'd k- k-'

But he can't say it. *Unless I'd killed her.*

'I loved her,' he says, his voice cracking on the last syllable. 'That's what none of them understand. I *loved* her.'

Oh shit. I remember the rumours of the first morning, Inigo coming to bed late, Topher's drawling, *Not that again. Eva should know better.*

'I loved her!' Inigo repeats, and I very, very much want to tell him to shut up. Because he seems to believe that this confession will exonerate him. But if anything, it's the reverse. Because you need a pretty powerful motive to kill someone — and one of those motives is money, that's the one we've all been assuming was at the bottom of this. And Inigo has no financial motive to kill Eva. Only Topher and Elliot fall into that camp, as far as we know. But the other thing that provokes people to kill, is love. And Inigo's just put himself forward as the only candidate for that category.

'I'm sure you did,' I say quietly, and then I watch as he stands and walks out of the room, unable to hold it together in front of his colleagues any more.

In the kitchen I sink into my chair, prop my aching foot on Danny's makeshift footrest, and wait for him to come in through the service door.

'What was all that about with Inigo?' he asks, and I explain.

'Bloody hell.' He runs his hand through his hair. 'What a stupid little prick. What with Eva shagging Inigo and Topher getting his end away with Ani — haven't they heard of Me Too? You can't go around bonking your employees any more. It's not right.'

'It gives him a motive though, doesn't it?' I say reluctantly, and Danny shrugs.

'I dunno. I mean, we could probably give them all motives if we needed to. Miranda could be madly in love with Inigo herself. Rik might have been a raging incel who hated having a female boss. Who the fuck knows. I could come up with some old bollocks against all of them if I had to. If you ask me it's alibis we should be looking at. There must be some of them we can rule out.'

'Not for Elliot's death. That could be anyone.

We were all here — everyone was coming and going from the living room.'

'Ani took him the coffee. And we all know she's got the hots for Topher.'

'She took him *a* coffee, but we don't know if it was the same cup that killed him. You'd have to be pretty stupid to announce to the world you were taking up coffee to someone you were about to poison.'

'Could be a double bluff,' Danny says a little feebly, but I can tell he's only playing devil's advocate. 'But OK, sorting out alibis for Elliot's gonna be tricky, I can see that. What about Eva though? If we're accepting that Elliot was killed because he knew something about what happened to Eva . . . '

'Well . . . ' I'm trying to think back, remember what everyone said about their whereabouts when we were discussing Eva's disappearance. 'Ani and Carl saw Eva safe and sound halfway down La Sorcière. So if someone did kill her, they must have been on the mountain before Ani and Carl. *And* they must have been a good enough skier to intercept Eva halfway down that run. Right?'

'Riiight . . . ' Danny echoes, slightly doubtfully. 'Although . . . if it comes to that, Carl never actually said he saw her. It was only ever Ani's word for it.'

'OK, but she *did* see her, she must have done. This was before Elliot's GPS information came out. Ani had no way of knowing that Eva had gone down La Sorcière otherwise, surely? If she were lying, she'd have said that Eva went down

Blanche-Neige, which is what you'd assume, and what anyone would say if they were trying to throw someone off the scent.'

'OK, I can buy that. So Ani and Carl are in the clear, is that your point?'

'Yes, and Liz, because she'd already gone down in the bubble lift. She left before Eva even arrived at the top. We're looking at the people who were at the top of the run before Eva — which means Topher, Rik, Tiger, Inigo and Miranda.'

'Not Miranda,' Danny says unexpectedly, and I frown.

'Why not?'

'Well, if we're accepting Ani's sighting, Eva was killed about halfway down La Sorcière. Which means we're looking for someone who's good enough to ski that run.'

I nod slowly. He's right. Which means . . . well, it's actually a pretty small group of people in that case. Tiger. Inigo. *Maybe* Rik, though I'm not certain about that. He's good, but you wouldn't need to be just good, you'd need to be very good indeed. And Topher.

We keep coming back to Topher. Which is hardly surprising, because Topher has the strongest motive out of anyone here. And now he has opportunity as well.

'They got separated at the top, didn't they?' I say, thinking aloud. 'When the *pisteurs* closed Blanche-Neige. Some of them went back down in the bubble, and some of them skied it anyway. The people who took the bubble back down can't have had anything to do with it. Who was that?'

206

'I don't think they ever said.' Danny's frowning now. 'I know Topher and Inigo skied it, but I'm not sure about the others. Want me to ask?'

I nod, a little reluctantly. I should go out there myself, really. Danny's manner with the group is getting more and more terse. He was close to squaring off with Carl earlier which is — well, it's just unthinkable. The last thing we need is a fight, added to this powder keg of grief and tension. But my ankle is hurting. A lot. And I can't bring myself to put weight on it right now.

When the door swings shut behind Danny, I feel in my pocket for the blister pack of ibuprofen and count the hours since I've had my last dose. Three. I should really wait another hour. Instead, quickly, before Danny comes back, I crack the foil and swallow down two more pills.

As I wash it down with a gulp of cold tea, the door swings open.

'Topher, Inigo, Tiger and Rik skied Blanche-Neige,' Danny says. 'The rest of them went down in the bubble and met up with Liz, who was already waiting at the bottom.'

'OK. Well . . . if someone hung back they could probably have sidestepped back up to the top of the run and skied La Sorcière instead. But they'd have had to be quick. Very quick. Eva was a fast skier and she was already halfway down the run when Ani saw her. That doesn't give someone much time to intercept her before she got to the bottom.'

'Unless . . . unless . . . ' Danny says. He's

speaking slowly, I can almost see him figuring out the possibilities. 'What if she'd fallen? What if they caught up with her, she's hurt herself or something, they're pretending to help her with her bindings and instead . . . '

I nod. There's a definite possibility in what he's saying. If this were opportunistic rather than planned . . . but then an objection occurs to me, and it's a big one.

'There's no drop on the bottom section of the run,' I say. 'There's no way someone could have pushed her off the edge.'

'No, but if she was incapacitated somehow they could kill her and leave her body in the trees. Elliot said himself that he wasn't sure how the mountains'd affect the GPS signal. Maybe that's what he discovered — that she wasn't in the valley at all. Someone killed her on the piste.'

'Maybe . . . ' But Danny's comment has tipped off something in my mind. 'But just a second, there's one other problem with all of this.'

'What? I thought we was doing pretty well.'

'It all hangs together except for one thing. How did anyone *know* Eva was skiing La Sorcière? We're talking as if someone went after her deliberately in the hopes of catching up with her. But no one saw her leave. No one knew she was skiing that run.'

'Fuck, you're right.' Danny frowns again, his dark brows knitting together. 'How the fuck did they know to go after her?'

'The only person . . . ' I'm thinking, putting two and two together. 'The only person who *knew* she was on that run was Ani. What if she told someone what she saw?'

'If she told someone . . . ' Danny says slowly, but when he finishes his sentence, it's not what I expected him to say. 'If she told someone, she could be in a fuck of a lot of danger. We have to find out who she told. And quick.'

LIZ

'Fucking hell.'

Topher is in my room. *Topher* is in my room. He is pacing, back and forth, back and forth, between me and the door. He looks demented. I don't know what to do. My room has always been my refuge — the one place I could close the door and shut everyone else out — the smell of beer, the sound of my mother's sobs, my father's bellowing voice. *Go to your room, Elizabeth.* He meant it as a punishment. Instead it was an escape.

Now my room has been invaded and my escape has been cut off.

'Fucking hell, Liz, this is a nightmare. They're all looking at me. They all think it's me!'

'Topher — '

I try to think what Tiger would do in this situation. Would she put her hand on his arm? Give him a hug? The latter makes me feel a bit ill, but I could try the arm.

I stick out my hand, awkwardly, but Topher is pacing. He just brushes straight past it like I was hailing a taxi and he was a driver with a passenger. I am not sure he even sees it. I go to chew my cuticles, then I shove my hand in my pocket to stop myself.

'God, I think I'm going mad. Oh Jesus, Eva. Eva!'

Topher stops, and slumps onto my bed. He puts his face in his hands, and then to my horror, he begins to sob.

At least he's stationary now. I put my hand out, trying to remember how Tiger calmed Carl down. I let it drop onto his shoulder.

But then he gives a huge wrenching sob, almost like he's about to be sick, and I snatch it away.

'Topher,' I whisper. 'Let me — ' I look around the room, searching for inspiration. My eye falls upon the empty water glass by my bed. 'Let me get you a glass of water.'

I'm not sure if he hears me as I tiptoe into the corridor. I shut the door, leaning against it, breathing hard.

Oh God, this is not what I am good at.

I am good at filing, and taking notes, and making sure everything adds up. I am good at tidying up loose ends and keeping everything straight. I am task-oriented and time-conscious and detail-focused. And I am very, very good at making myself invisible.

In short, I was a perfect PA. But I am not cut out for this.

ERIN

Danny and I should be washing up from lunch — it's no joke, with no dishwasher. The only hot water now comes from kettles we boil on the wood-burning stove, and it's becoming a full-time task just to keep enough clean crockery to serve meals. The greasy crockery from lunch is piled high on the draining board, and cutlery is soaking in lukewarm water that's fast losing its heat. But important as it is to keep the guests fed, keeping them alive is more crucial, and neither of us wants to leave the other on their own so there is no discussion over who will go and who will stay, when I propose talking to Ani. That we will both tackle her is without question. The only thing in doubt is where and how.

'Now,' Danny says firmly. 'If she talked to the murderer, told them where Eva was, it's only a matter of time before they figure that out. And when they do . . . '

He trails off. I swallow. I know he's right.

'But, what if she's with one of the others?' I ask. 'What's our excuse for talking to her alone?'

Danny shakes his head.

'No, we talk to her in front of everyone. It's better to get it on the table. If everyone knows the truth, great They can't kill *all* of us.'

He says it almost glibly, and a part of me finds myself wanting to laugh hysterically. How has it come to this, that we're discussing murder like some kind of parlour game? But he's right. There's no sense in keeping whatever Ani has to say under wraps. The more people who know the truth, the better.

We don't have far to go to find her. We exit the kitchen and make our way through the chilly dining room, and there she is — sitting in the lobby in front of the wood burner, playing cards with Carl, Rik and Miranda, her huge glasses pushed up on her forehead as she stares down at her hand.

'Three of a kind,' Carl is saying smugly, as he lays down three kings.

'Hi,' Danny says, a little brusquely, positioning himself in front of the group. 'Can we talk for a moment?'

'Sure,' Miranda says with a sigh, stacking her cards. 'Carl's whipping our arses anyway, so please come and save us from another defeat.' She runs a hand through her long dark hair, and then makes a face. I know how she is feeling. No hot water means no showers, and everyone is looking a little limp and grubby around the edges, including me and Danny. 'Have you got news?'

The hope on her face gives me a momentary stab of guilt, as I realise what our purposeful entry must have looked like. I shake my head.

'No, I'm so sorry. Still nothing.'

'Bloody hell,' Rik says. 'Still? Isn't this getting a little bit . . . concerning?'

'Well, I must admit, I would have hoped they'd be here by now.'

I look out of the tall windows that span the double-height lobby. It's the middle of the afternoon, but the air is so dark with whirling snow that it looks like twilight, and I can't see the lights of St Antoine le Lac below, let alone the far-off mountain ranges. But then, the thought occurs to me uncomfortably, maybe they are without power down in le Lac too. The batteries in Danny's radio have died, and we have no idea now what's happening down there. It could be much worse than we're imagining.

'It's more than twenty-four hours since the avalanche,' Rik presses. 'Shouldn't *someone* have been in contact by now?'

'I don't know,' I say. His concern is making me increasingly uneasy. Maybe he's right. Maybe there *is* something wrong. 'They're very stretched, I imagine.'

'What are you getting at, mate?' Carl says, sharply, looking across at his colleague. 'You got a point to make, spit it out.'

Rik exchanges a look with Miranda and then says, almost reluctantly, 'Look, this isn't an accusation, please don't think that. But I'm just saying that it's . . . well, it's *unfortunate* that no one else managed to talk to the police, apart from Inigo.'

'What do you mean?' Carl says, taken aback.

'I'm just saying . . . it would be nice to have

214

corroboration of what went down. We only heard his side of the conversation. And it does seem a little . . . strange that he's the only person who managed to get any reception.'

'Are you saying he didn't call them?' Carl's eyebrows go up to his shaven hairline.

Rik says nothing, but he gives a little shrugging wince that could be yes or no, but functions effectively as an acknowledgement of the possibility.

'Fuck,' Carl says. He breathes it out like some kind of prayer. 'Faaaark.'

Danny shoots me a startled, worried look, and I realise that I never told him about my conversation with Inigo, and Rik's suspicions, perhaps because I never really believed they were true. Now I feel frighteningly naive. What if Rik's right? What if *no one* is coming?

'What did you want to talk to us about?' Miranda says, bringing us back to our original mission, and I drag my mind back to the task in hand with an effort.

'Oh. Yes. Well, it was actually Ani we wanted to speak to — we had a quick question.'

'Oh?' Ani looks up from her hand. 'Yeah! I mean, sure, anything I can help with?'

'You want a bit of privacy?' Carl says, and he makes to half rise, but Danny shakes his head.

'Stay. Better to keep all our cards on the table, if you know what I mean.'

Carl considers for a second, then sees the wisdom of what Danny's saying and gives a short nod, and sits again.

'Ani,' I say, trying to think how to put this,

215

without causing undue alarm, but being as clear as possible about what I mean. 'You saw Eva skiing La Sorcière when you were coming up in the lift, is that right?'

'Yes,' Ani says. 'Definitely. I, like, already said that though?'

'Yes, but what I wanted to ask is, did you *tell* anyone at the time?'

'Oh . . . ' She frowns, trying to think. 'I don't remember. I might have said something to Carl? Like, *oh hey, there's Eva.* Do you remember, Carl?'

'To be quite honest, I don't,' Carl says flatly. 'I don't think you said anything but hand on heart, I couldn't swear to it either way.'

'Oh!' Ani says suddenly. She's flushing pink, and she looks like a child who's pleased they've come up with the answer you were prompting for. I realise, with a disquieting shift, that Ani thinks we are testing *her*, checking up on her story, and she's pleased she can give us corroboration. 'Wait, I *did* tell someone. We came off the lift at the top, and Topher was talking about setting off, and Inigo said, but, like, we can't, because of waiting for Eva, and I said, gosh no, didn't she tell you? She's already left. I saw her skiing down the black run. I'm not sure if Topher heard me, but Inigo *definitely* did. He can back me up.'

He can back me up.

She's looking at me with wide, shining eyes, and her trust makes a lump come to my throat.

But Carl . . . Carl is looking at her with a kind of horror, and I know that he has joined the dots that Danny and I had already figured out.

'Bollocks to backing you up,' he says abruptly. 'Don't you get it?'

'Get what?' Ani says. She looks surprised, like we've taken away her gold star. She can't understand why Carl isn't pleased for her, happy that her story has checked out.

'Inigo *knew*,' Carl says. 'He knew where she was skiing. Eva. You told him how to find her.'

'Oh my God,' Ani says, and the colour drains out of her face, leaving her translucent skin bone white, the blue of her veins showing through at the temple. 'Oh my God, you're saying — you're saying — '

'I'm saying, someone went down that run and killed Eva. So question is, who knew she was skiing it?'

'Not Inigo!' Ani says, and her voice is a cry of anguish. 'Not Inigo, no, he was — he and Eva — '

She stops, her hand over her mouth, as if she's said too much.

'Eva was shagging him,' Carl says brutally. 'Come on, love, we all know that. You don't have to be Sherlock bloody Holmes to get that far. But shagging someone isn't an alibi, you know that.'

'No!' Ani stands up. The colour has come back to her face and she looks pink and furious. 'No. I'm not having this! Eva's death — it was an accident. And Elliot — I just — no! I won't — I *can't* think like this. I can't!'

She lets the cards flutter from her hand, and stumbles from the room.

LIZ

Snoop ID: ANON101
Listening to: offline
Snoopscribers: 1

I am standing outside my bedroom door, my back pressed to the wood, when someone comes up the stairs. I can't see who it is at first. With the lights out, the corridor is too dark. But as she comes closer, I see that it is Ani. She looks as if she has been crying.

My first instinct is to duck back inside my room — but I can't. Topher is in there. I am trapped. She is walking towards me. I am going to have to interact with her.

'Are you OK?' I say.

'They're — they're saying awful things,' she gulps. 'About Inigo. I don't believe it, Liz, I won't!'

'What kind of things?' There is a cold feeling in the pit of my stomach.

'That he — ' She gulps again, and forces herself on. 'That he *killed* Eva. That he didn't call the police.'

'He didn't call the *police*? Are you saying no one's coming?'

'But he did!' Ani wails. 'We saw him! It's completely unfair they're saying this stuff and

218

not giving him the chance to defend himself. I've worked side by side with him for two years, for God's sake. I know him!' She pushes past me and bangs on his door.

Carl has pursued Ani up the stairs. The others are following. I see Rik, Danny, holding a torch, Miranda, last of all Erin, still limping.

'Ani, wait,' Carl says. Just as he says it, my bedroom door opens so suddenly that I nearly fall backwards, because my weight is still resting against the wood. Topher shoves past me into the corridor. His face is still blotched from earlier but he is no longer crying.

'What's going on?' he asks abruptly.

'Inigo!' Ani is still banging on his door. There is no answer. 'Where is he?'

'Oh God,' Rik says. He looks at Miranda, and then at Erin. 'You don't think — '

'Oh no, no,' Danny says quickly. 'We're not having another body. Not on my watch.' He elbows past Ani, takes a staff key out of his pocket, and opens the door. Then he shines the torch into the room.

There is no one inside.

Over his shoulder I can see Carl's belongings, thrown untidily around, and Inigo's camp bed, the covers neatly smoothed and tucked.

In the centre of the pillow is a folded piece of paper.

No one seems to know what to do, but then Erin hobbles past Danny into the room and picks it up.

'It's a note,' she says, scanning it in the torchlight. Then her face goes blank. 'Oh . . . fuck.'

219

It is the first time I have heard her swear in front of us. Danny has lost it a few times but Erin has always been completely professional. Now her face is white. She looks up at Danny and mouths something I can't decipher.

'What does it say?' Topher says authoritatively. Apart from a slight croakiness in his voice, you would never know he had been sobbing his heart out in my room a few minutes ago. 'I have a right to know, I'm still CEO of this company.'

He pulls the note from Erin's fingers. She does not resist. He reads it aloud.

' 'Dear everyone, I have made a terrible mistake. I have gone to try to put it right. Please don't come after me. Inigo.' '

'Oh fuck,' Miranda says, echoing Erin. 'The idiot.' She is standing in the doorway. Now she turns and looks out of the long window at the end of the corridor, the window Inigo stood at to try to get reception. It is almost completely dark now. The snow is beating on the glass as if it is trying to get in. I cannot help an involuntary shiver at the sight. 'I mean — look at it out there. He's going to kill himself.'

'What does it actually mean though?' Erin asks. She looks bewildered. 'The note I mean. Is he saying he *didn't* call the police but now he's gone to fetch them? Or has he gone after Eva?'

'Fuck knows,' Carl says brusquely. 'Stupid little plonker. Has he actually left already?'

'Good question,' Danny says. 'I'll check.' He turns and walks quickly down the corridor, taking the torch with him. The shadows close around us as he disappears. We hear him clattering on the spiral staircase, and then the bang of the door into the service part of the building where the ski lockers are. When he returns, he is walking more slowly, and his face is set. 'Yes, he's left,' he says as he comes closer to our group. 'His skis are gone. So's his jacket.'

'*Shit*,' Carl says angrily. 'Bloody little idiot. When did he go? Who saw him last?'

There are shrugs all round the group.

'I saw him at lunch,' Miranda volunteers, and several other people nod.

'I saw him at lunch too,' Erin says heavily. 'He was . . . he didn't eat. He wasn't in a good state. He went off, I assumed to his room but he might have gone to the ski lockers. Did anyone see him after lunch?'

Everyone shakes their head. Then Erin frowns. 'What about Tiger?'

We all look around at each other, and I can see a sinking dread mirrored on the face of the others. Where *is* Tiger?

Without saying anything, Danny sets off in the direction of her room. We all follow him, like a flock of anxious sheep.

At the door he knocks. Nothing. I can feel the tension rising.

'Bollocks to this,' Danny says roughly, and he sticks his staff key in the lock. The door springs open — and everyone crowds inside, jostling to see. I am at the back, my view blocked by Topher's broad shoulders. I hear Ani's anxious, 'Tiger?'

And then I hear a sleepy voice saying, 'Hey, what's happened?'

221

There's an audible exhalation, a mixture of relief and exasperation.

'Jesus, Tiger!' It's Miranda. Her accent is usually an upper-class drawl. Now she sounds sharp and annoyed. 'Don't do that to us! Didn't you hear Erin's speech? Stick together!'

'I locked my door,' Tiger says. Her normally unruffled voice sounds a little bit less serene than normal. 'What's the matter?'

'Inigo's gone,' Miranda says. And then, to my astonishment, something in her polished facade seems to crack, and she begins to cry.

ERIN

Snoop ID: LITTLEMY
Listening to: offline
Snoopscribers: 10

We all go to bed very early, exhausted by a hideous, hideous day. Some people pair up, making sure everyone knows who they're with. Miranda and Rik aren't pretending any more. After Miranda's breakdown outside Tiger's room earlier, they have been inseparable. Now, Rik simply says, bluntly, 'I'll be sleeping in Miranda's room tonight,' and there is not even a ripple of surprise.

What is perhaps more surprising is that Tiger and Ani pair up, leaving Carl and Topher as the two remaining single men. I had thought that Ani and Topher would have gone off together too . . . but something has changed between them since Elliot's death. What I can't figure out is who initiated the reserve. Elliot died having tried to tell Topher something, something Topher never gave him the chance to say. You don't have to be a genius to figure out that maybe there was a reason Topher didn't want him airing those suspicions.

But on the other hand, it was the fact that Topher was in bed with Ani that prevented Elliot from talking to Topher. It wouldn't be surprising if Topher, on some level, however irrationally, resented that fact. And Ani was, undeniably, the person who took up that coffee. Or at least a coffee, I remind myself. Though it was Topher who asked her to do it, from what she said to me in the kitchen. Assuming she was telling the truth. Jesus. I am talking myself in circles here.

It's Miranda who raises the question we'd all overlooked.

'What about Liz?'

There is an awkward silence as we all realise that, once again, everyone has forgotten about Liz. All eyes turn to her, and she seems to shrink into herself, wrapping her arms around herself as if she can protect herself from our stares.

'Do you want to, like, share with me and Tiger?' Ani says brightly, but Liz shakes her head.

'No thanks, I'll be fine alone.'

'Liz, no,' Miranda says, with some concern, 'I really *don't* think that's a good idea. Erin's right — we should stay together.'

'Honestly,' Liz says. There is something obstinate, mulish almost in her face. 'I don't like sharing a room. I'll lock the door.'

'Full disclosure,' Danny says bluntly, 'Erin and me, we've got staff keys. We can get in everywhere. Now, I'm not saying we're gonna come and bump you off in the night, but these doors ain't exactly Fort Knox, if you know what I'm saying.'

'I'll put a chair under the doorknob,' Liz says. She folds her arms, and I exchange a glance with

224

Danny, and a minute shrug. We can't *make* her take our advice.

'All right,' Danny says at last. 'Your funeral.'

It's only after the words are spoken that he realises how they sound.

LIZ

Snoop ID: ANON101
Listening to: offline
Snoopscribers: 1

I know what they are thinking as we trail slowly off to our separate rooms. They are thinking I am mad. Perhaps they are right. As I shut and lock the door behind me, I can't help wondering if this is a terrible, dangerous idea, making myself the odd one out like this. What if it gives someone ideas?

But I cannot explain to them how much the thought of sharing a room with Tiger and Ani fills me with dread. It has been bad enough during the day, jostling with these faces from the past, hemmed into a nightmare with people I barely know.

I need my refuge. I need to be able to close the door behind me. The idea of spending the night on a mattress on Tiger's floor, listening to her soft breathing, and Ani shifting in her sleep — it makes me want to shudder.

I push a chair under the handle of the door, then get into bed, fully dressed. It is too cold to change. I am lying there, with my eyes closed, trying to relax my stiff muscles, trying to tell myself it's safe to fall into unconsciousness,

226

when there is a noise at the door. I raise my head. Instantly my heart is racing at 150 beats a minute.

'Wh-who is it?' My voice is shaky with adrenaline.

I can barely hear the whisper through the thick wood.

'It's me, Ani.'

'Hang on.' I swing my legs out of bed and make my way over to the door, pulling away the chair. Then I open it cautiously.

Ani is standing outside. She is dressed in a thick pink sweater that comes almost down to her knees. Her eyes are huge in the darkness.

'Ani, what are you doing? You nearly gave me a heart attack.'

'I'm sorry,' she whispers. 'I couldn't sleep, you know? I kept worrying about you, and I think Erin's right. We should, like, stick together? Please come in with me and Tiger.'

'No, honestly, I'm fine,' I say. Ani stands there in the dark corridor, twisting her fingers together. She is looking at me in a way I don't like. Her eyes are very wide and very worried. 'I'm *fine*,' I say more forcefully. 'Go — Tiger will be wondering where you are.'

'Tiger's already asleep,' she says with a tremulous little laugh. 'Out like a light and snoring. I don't know how she does it — she's so Zen. And I just kept thinking about things, turning stuff over in my mind.'

'I think she took a pill,' I say. 'She was talking about it at breakfast. But — what do you mean, thinking about stuff?'

'Oh . . . nothing.' She gives that little shaky laugh again, but there is something in her eyes. It is pleading and concerned. I get a sudden lurch of apprehension.

'Ani, do you know something you've not told anyone?'

She shakes her head, but it's not really a decisive shake, it's more of a worried *don't know*.

'Listen to me,' I say. My voice is an urgent whisper. It is not like me to be so forceful, but I am very worried. 'You heard what Erin said, if you know something *tell* someone. Keeping secrets is the most dangerous thing you can do. Did you see something? Was it when Elliot came to Topher's room? Something about Inigo?'

'No, I didn't — ' she says, with a catch in her voice. 'I just — I keep feeling like there's something wrong . . . something I saw . . . I just — like, can't put my finger on it?'

Oh God. My stomach is churning with unease. I have a horrible feeling that what Ani can't remember might be very, very important. It might be the clue to the killer's identity. It might be the one thing that gives them away.

'Ani, *tell* me,' I plead. 'Don't keep this to yourself.'

Our eyes lock, and I see something there. Something that she *knows*. And suddenly I am very, very frightened.

'Ani, *please*,' I say. I am begging, I know I am, and I no longer care. But she just shakes her head, her eyes as wide and as scared as I feel.

'I can't,' she whispers. 'I have to . . . I have to *think* . . . '

Then she disappears into the shadows, leaving me standing in the corridor, watching with foreboding as Tiger's door closes softly behind her. I wait, just to make sure, and then I hear the click as she turns the key in the lock, and I turn back to my room. There is nothing else I can do.

ERIN

'Shit.' Danny is lying on a mattress he's dragged into my room, his hands over his face. 'Why did I say that about the bloody funeral? I'm so bleeding tactless! Their mates have just *died* and they probably think I'm making cracks about it.'

'Honestly, Danny, I truly think that's the last thing anyone is worrying about.'

I am so tired my eyes are scratching with it, and I'm sure Danny must feel the same, but I also know that there's no way I'm going to be able to fall asleep. Everything is too wrong. Danny's presence, comforting as it is, is too strange. The room is too cold. The situation is too dire. And I'm worried that if I do fall asleep, I'm going to have my recurring dream about digging through snow, that I'll wake up Danny, that he'll ask questions I can't answer.

Most of all I just feel incredibly scared.

It doesn't help that my foot is hurting again. A *lot*. I am starting to worry that maybe something is broken after all.

'Someone should have come,' Danny says into the silence, and I know what he's talking about.

230

'We don't *know* Inigo didn't phone.'

'What did he mean then, about making a huge mistake?'

'I don't know, but it makes no sense, Danny. Why on earth wouldn't he phone? The only reason would be if he'd killed Eva, and if that's the case, we're safer without him, aren't we?'

'Maybe he did. Maybe he's getting a head start on the police. We don't know, do we?'

Danny's remark stops me in my tracks, and I can't honestly think what to say in reply. The truth is that I just don't think Inigo is a killer. He seemed gentle, and desperate, and genuinely sad about Eva. But then I think of all the newspaper pieces I've ever read about 'perfectly nice guys' who killed their kids or their partners or a complete stranger. And I am forced to remind myself of what Danny was trying to get at — these people are strangers to us. Whatever odd intimacy this situation has created, it's illusory. We have known Inigo, like the rest of them, for less than three days.

There's another long silence, and for a while I think maybe Danny has drifted off to sleep, but then he gives a great sigh.

'Shit, what are we going to do, Erin?'

'I don't *know*.' The three words encompass all the desperation I've been building up since Eva's disappearance. This is just unimaginably awful. First Eva, then Elliot, now Inigo. Our guests are disappearing one by one, like some bad horror movie. 'If Inigo really has gone to get help — '

'I don't believe it,' Danny says, with finality. 'If he called the police like he claimed, then there's no need for him to go and get them. And if he *didn't* call them, why go and become the knight in shining armour all of a sudden? It doesn't make sense. He's not gone for the police. He's scarpered, and this is his way of covering it up.'

His words make my stomach sink, but there's no denying the logic of what he said. The truth is, whether Inigo has disappeared or not, it doesn't change our predicament. We are stuck here, and we have no way of knowing whether Inigo will succeed in getting help — or even if he'll try. All the complicated analysis in the world can't change that. All we can do is sit, and wait. Then, suddenly, an idea comes to me.

'Wait, there's one thing we could do.'

'What?'

'You could go. You could walk to Haut Montagne. Raise the alarm.'

There's a long silence. Then Danny says, flatly, 'No.'

'I know it's dangerous but I can't go with my ank — '

'Fuck the danger,' Danny breaks in. 'I don't care about the bloody danger. But you're right — you can't go, and I'm not leaving you here with a bunch of psychopaths.'

'We don't know anyone here is a psychopath — if it's true that Inigo — '

'I'm not leaving you,' Danny says, and something about his tone makes it very clear, that's going to be his last word on the subject. I hear a rustle of covers as he turns sharply over in bed. 'And that's that. Now go to sleep.'

But it's a very long time before I do.

232

LIZ

Snoop ID: ANON101
Listening to: offline
Snoopscribers: 1

I climb back into bed. I am so tense that I am not sure I will get to sleep, but when at last I do drift off, it is into the deep, dreamless sleep of complete exhaustion. When I wake up it is bitterly cold, and although my clothes feel crumpled and sweaty, I am grateful that I never took them off. Getting up would have been too painful. Even with my clothes on, it is too cold to face getting out of bed, and I shut my eyes and just lie there. My phone has died completely, so I have no idea what the time is.

It is then that the scream rips through the quiet. It is a long, loud one, that goes on, and on.

I sit bolt upright, my heart thumping, and then I swing my legs out of bed and stand. The movement is much too fast. I feel the blood drain away from my head, and then return with a prickling rush. My heart is still pounding with adrenaline.

Out in the corridor I can hear doors banging. Voices are calling out in panic.

'It's coming from Tiger's room,' I hear someone shout.

My hands are shaking as I fumble for my glasses and shove them onto my nose. It is so cold that my breath huffs white as I undo the door lock.

In the corridor Rik, Miranda, Topher and Carl are crowded around Tiger's door. Miranda is wearing a beanie hat and gloves.

'Open up!' Topher is shouting. 'What's the matter? Ani? Tiger? Open the door!'

The screaming has died into a low sobbing. It is impossible to tell who is making the sound.

I hear running feet, and then Danny the chef comes skidding round the corner of the corridor, wearing jogging pants and a crumpled sweat-shirt.

'What the fuck's going on? What's all the shouting?'

'We heard screaming,' Rik says tersely. 'From Tiger and Ani's room. We can't get them to open the door.'

'Stand aside,' Danny says, reaching into his pocket for his pass key. His hand comes out empty. 'Fuck, must have left it in my other trousers. Oi!' He bangs on the door. 'Open up! We can't help you unless you open the door!'

There is a click. The door swings open.

With so many people in the way, I can't see who it is. But then I hear Miranda's startled voice say, 'Tiger! What on earth is the matter?!'

Tiger is sobbing so hard she can hardly get the words out.

'Ani, oh God, p-please help me. It's Ani. I think she's d-dead.'

234

ERIN

Snoop ID: LITTLEMY
Listening to: offline
Snoopscribers: 10

It takes me painfully long to hobble along the corridor. My ankle has puffed up overnight and it hurts to put weight on it. As I round the corner the sound of voices swells into a panicked hub-bub.

'What's going on?' I ask, but no one's listening, they're crowding around Tiger and Ani's door. Tiger is crouched in the corridor, her arms wrapped around her head, sobbing hysterically. Liz is standing over her looking terrified, and occasionally placing a hand gingerly on Tiger's hair, like it's about to burst into flames.

'What's going on?' I say again, and this time Danny appears out of Tiger's room, his face grey.

'Fucking hell,' he says. 'They've got Ani.'

'They've *got* her? Who's got her? What do you mean?' I can feel fear rising inside me.

'I mean, I'm pretty sure she's dead.'

Oh God. Dread twists at my guts, as I push past the others and into the room.

Ani is lying on a mattress on the floor. She's face down, but when I pull her shoulder to turn her over, she comes all of a piece, like a

235

mannequin, her joints locked with rigor mortis. I don't need to feel her cold, waxen face to know that she's very, very dead.

Suddenly my legs won't hold me and I stagger to Tiger's bed, still warm and rumpled. The room swims in and out of focus and I put my head between my knees, trying to hold it together.

'That can't have been Inigo,' Danny says hoarsely. I shake my head in agreement. That much is clear. Oh God, what is this living nightmare we've found ourselves in?

'And then we were six,' says a little voice from the doorway, and I look up to see Liz, her face a white mask of horror as she gazes at Ani's prone form.

'What?' Danny says. He looks bewildered, as if he didn't hear her right.

'Nothing,' Liz says. She gives a shaking, tremulous laugh. It sounds like she's on the verge of hysterics. I know how she feels. And then she turns and disappears. I hear her door slam, and the lock grind into place. I don't blame her. A strong part of me would like to do the same. But I can't. I have to . . .

I stand, go over to the body, and very gently turn it again, this time forcing myself to look down at Ani's dead face.

She looks almost like she died in her sleep. *Almost.* Not quite. There's a tiny staining of blood on her lip where she must have bitten her tongue. And on her face, a few minute red dots. I know what they are, or rather, I know what they mean, but it takes a few minutes cudgelling my memory before my brain can come up with the medical term. *Petechiae*. First-year medical students don't come across much homicide — but I've seen enough textbook photographs to recognise it.

There are no marks on her neck, and no other wounds that I can see, apart from the tiny specks of blood on her lips. When I bend to lower her gently back to the position I found her, face down, I see it has flecked the pillow too. A line sings in my head: *Lips as red as blood, skin as white as snow.*

'I think she was smothered,' I say quietly to Danny. 'Whoever did it either pressed her face down into the pillow, or held something over her face and then turned her over afterwards. There's not much bruising and no defensive marks that I can see — she was probably asleep.'

'Oh my God.' Danny's face crumples into horror. He looks like a man decades older than his twenty-five years. 'But, you're not telling me — Tiger?'

I shake my head, but I'm not disagreeing with him — I just have no idea what to say. I can't believe that gentle, Zen-like Tiger could possibly have done this. But on the other hand — the door was locked. And could someone really have crept in and smothered Ani in her sleep without Tiger waking? I think back to her yoga-toned body, those slim, strong hands. The world seems to tilt and shift on its axis.

★   ★   ★

Out in the corridor, the others are waiting, pale and worried. Tiger has sobbed herself silent and is still crouched against the wall, Miranda's arm protectively around her. Liz is still locked in her room. Carl and Rik are standing with grim, drawn faces either side of the door like sentries. Topher is pacing, and he looks like a man possessed by demons. There is an expression on his face that frightens me.

'What. The. Fuck,' he spits as Danny and I leave the room, closing the door behind us.

'Oi, mate.' Danny puts up his hands, but I shush him. Five of these people are scared and grieving. One — but I can't think about that. It's too surreal, too horrible.

'Come down to the living room,' I say. 'I think we all need a drink.'

It's barely 9 a.m., but downstairs I pour us all stiff whiskeys, and everyone drinks them without a murmur, except for Tiger, who is lying on the sofa, shivering, in a state of what I can only call near-catatonic shock.

'So,' Rik says, as he puts his glass down. 'What happened?'

'Just a second,' Miranda says. 'Where's Liz?'

I feel a wash of panic, followed by a wave of rationality. There is no way anyone can have killed Liz while we were all standing out in the corridor.

'I think she's in her room,' I say. 'I'll go and get her.'

'Not alone you won't,' Danny growls, and he follows me upstairs like a watchdog as I make my painful, limping way along the corridor to knock at Liz's door.

'Wh-who is it?' I hear through the wood. She sounds as scared as I feel.

'It's me, Erin,' I say. 'And Danny. We — we need to talk about this, Liz. About what happened. We need to try to figure out what to do next. Can you come out?'

There is a scraping noise, and the door opens, very slowly, until Liz is standing there, white-faced and hollow-eyed. She looks terrified, like there is nothing in the world she would less rather do than go downstairs and face her fellow guests — and I can't blame her. I feel the same way. But we have to do it.

By the time we get downstairs, Miranda has built up the fire and Rik has poured everyone another round of very generous whiskeys. I want to say something about the advisability of adding more alcohol to this mix, but since I was the one who suggested a drink in the first place, I don't feel like I have the right to object.

'So, what happened?' Rik says again as he hands Liz a glass. His voice teeters on the edge of what sounds like aggression, but I think it's actually fear. 'Don't tell me she just died in her sleep.'

'She didn't,' I say, very quietly, but they all fall instantly silent. 'She had something called petechial haemorrhaging. Do you know what that means?'

There are head shakes all around the circle, apart from Carl, who nods.

'Little red dots, right? Yeah, I watch *CSI*. Shoot me.'

'Exactly. Little red dots where blood vessels have broken in the skin. It usually means someone has died of some form of asphyxiation

239

— choking or hanging. In this case, given there weren't any marks around her neck, I think Ani was probably smothered in her sleep.'

'Oh my God.' It's a long groan from Miranda. She puts her hands over her face.

'She — she knew something.' It's Liz. She speaks very low, and I have to shush the others to hear what she's saying. 'She came to my room last night, to try to persuade me not to sleep alone. When I asked why she was still awake, she said she had something on her mind, something she'd seen — I begged her to tell me — ' She breaks off, her voice cracking. It's virtually the longest speech I've ever heard her make, and she looks like she's shrinking as all the eyes of the room turn to her.

'Oh bloody hell.' Danny's voice is angry, and he stands up, as if he can't contain his feelings. 'What did Erin fucking say? If you know something *tell someone.*'

'I know!' Liz says, her voice like a sob. 'I begged her to say something, I really did — but she said she wasn't sure — '

'Tiger.' Miranda is shaking Tiger now, gently. 'Tiger, did Ani say *anything* to you last night, before she fell asleep?'

'I was asleep.' Tiger's voice is broken, and very hoarse. It's hard to understand what she's saying, the words are cracked and fractured. I make out, 'I'm so sorry . . . asleep . . . took a sleeping pill . . . '

'Wait, you take sleeping pills?' I say. I glance at Danny, who raises an eyebrow back, and I know he is thinking, as I am, of the crushed pills in

240

Elliot's coffee. Tiger gives a huge sob.

'Not normally, but I couldn't sleep, I haven't been able to since I got here. It started the f-first day. Eva said it was the altitude. She gave me some of her pills.'

'It's true,' Miranda says. She glances round the circle, looking for support. 'It was after breakfast that first morning, I remember the conversation. Rik, you heard her, didn't you?'

'I'm sorry,' Rik says with a shrug. His voice is defensive. 'I'm sure you're right, but I don't remember.'

'Everyone was there,' Miranda persists. 'It was right before we went into the meeting room. Eva said to Tiger, you look like you haven't slept, and Tiger said, I actually didn't. And Eva said, it's the altitude. Remind me to give you some of my sleeping pills. Carl was there too, and Liz. And Topher.'

'I don't remember either. I expect I was too busy thinking about the presentation,' Topher says rather brusquely. 'What are you trying to say?'

He looks ruffled, like he thinks Miranda is trying to pin something on him. But I know why Miranda is pushing this. She knows that Tiger is the number one suspect for Ani's death. Tiger was in the room when Ani was smothered, and she slept through it. Which is pretty unlikely — unless you know that she was taking sleeping pills. Miranda is trying to show that everyone knew that fact. That anyone could have taken advantage of Tiger's drugged state to sneak in and kill Ani while Tiger slept. I admire her for it, in a way — she's standing by her colleague in the face of some pretty horrible evidence.

But there is still the question of the locked door.

'Who got to Ani's room first?' I ask.

'I did,' Topher says. He is standing propped against the mantelpiece. Now he folds his arms. 'But it was locked. You saw that.' He nods at Danny, who shrugs with corroboration.

'I tried the door, yeah. It was locked.'

'So how did someone get in?' Topher demands, 'Staff key? How many of those things are there?'

'Just two,' I say. I hold up mine. 'I had mine with me all night. I'm certain of it. Danny?'

But Danny is frowning, patting his pockets.

'I thought mine was in here. These were the clothes I was wearing yesterday. I thought . . . Hang on.'

And without waiting for anyone else to accompany him, he jumps up, and leaves the room.

'Danny!' I shout after him, but he calls back: 'I'll only be a sec.'

There's a long silence. I find my heart beating uncomfortably fast, even though I know it's irrational. Everyone is in here. I'm looking at them right now. But this is starting to feel like *Lord of the Flies*.

When Danny comes back, his face is very grave, and the look he shoots at me tells me he's not relishing what he's about to say.

'Well, there ain't no point in sugar-coating this,' he says. 'My key's gone. Someone's half-inched it.'

'Fuck.' It's Rik, the word sounding like gun-shot in the ensuing silence. '*Fuck.* You're saying someone has access to every room in the place now? None of us can lock our doors?'

'That's about the size of it,' Danny says grimly.

'You,' Topher spits, 'are a fucking irresponsible *wanker*, you had a duty of care to us and — '

Danny stands up, putting himself on the same level as Topher, almost squaring up to him.

'Don't take that tone with me, mate.'

'This is bloody convenient for you, isn't it? Before, if anyone managed to get access to any of the rooms, you and Erin were prime suspect, now you've contrived — '

'I haven't contrived anything,' Danny snarls back. 'And don't you bring me and Erin into it. We ain't done nothing, and we never had any trouble until you lot turned up and started bumping each other off. We don't know any of you from Adam. So the fact that one of your employees nicked my key — '

'Well, that's another thing,' Topher says angrily. 'Who exactly *is* Erin anyway, because she seems to be a little overqualified for a chalet girl if you ask me. Petrifical fucking whatever it was — is that part of the ski chalet training?'

Shit. I knew this was coming. I sigh, and stand up too, favouring my good leg.

'No. No it's not. The truth is . . . ' I glance at Danny, wondering what I can get away with. 'The truth is, I went to medical school before I came here. I dropped out, but that's how I know about the petechiae.'

'But that's not all, is it?' Topher prods. 'It's

been bothering me since I got here. I *know* you. I know I do.'

Fuck. *Fuck.*

There is no point in beating around the bush any longer.

'Yes, you probably do know me. My surname is FitzClarence. My friends all call me Erin, but that's my middle name.'

'I fucking knew it!' Topher's voice is a shout of triumph. 'I *knew* I knew you. Dorothea Fitz-Clarence. I was at school with your brother, Alex — the one who — '

He breaks off, and I nod, reluctantly, because there is nothing else I can do.

'*What?*' Danny says. He looks thunderstruck. 'Erin, what is this bullshit? Dorothea — you what?'

'Let me introduce you,' Topher says, with great malice, 'to Lady Dorothea de Plessis Fitz-Clarence, youngest daughter of the Marquess of Cardale.'

LIZ

Snoop ID: ANON101
Listening to: offline
Snoopscribers: 1

Looking around the circle of frowning faces, it is clear that I am not the only person who is very confused. Erin looks stricken. Topher looks delighted. But everyone else looks as baffled as I feel. What has just happened? What has this got to do with Ani's death?

There is no time to find out. Danny turns round so abruptly that he knocks over a chair. It falls with a clatter, smashing a whiskey glass.

'Danny,' Erin says desperately.

'You fucking liar,' he shoots over his shoulder. Then he leaves the room.

Erin gives a furious look at Topher.

'Thanks a bunch,' she says, and then she is gone, hobbling after Danny.

'Ha,' Topher says, sitting down in an armchair. There is a look of grim satisfaction on his face.

'Topher,' Miranda says, bewildered. 'What on earth was all that about? Ani is *dead* for good-ness' sakes. Have you forgotten that?'

'No,' Topher says, defensively, though I think the truth is that he had, just for a minute or two. 'No, not at all. That's very hurtful of you to imply that, Miranda. But I'd had enough of that chippy chef throwing around accusations. We're not the only people hiding stuff.'

'Speak for yourself, mate!' Carl splutters. 'I'm not hiding anything! What the hell has it got to do with anything if Erin's a bit posher than she's been letting on?'

'Because she's got skin in this game too,' Topher hisses angrily. 'I'm fed up of them both acting so high and mighty.'

'I remember Alex FitzClarence,' Rik says slowly. 'He was a couple of years below us. Didn't . . . didn't he die a few years ago?'

'That's him,' Topher says. 'He was a really good bloke actually. That wasn't my point — my point was simply that Erin is a bit more entangled in this than she's letting on. And what happened to Alex — ' He stops. Suddenly his expression changes and he grips Rik's arm, so hard that Rik gives a little wince. He looks as if he has been given a very generous Christmas present. 'Hang on a second. Alex died in an avalanche. With his best mate.'

'What are you saying?' Rik is looking wary.

'I remember reading about it in the alumnae newsletter. Alex FitzClarence died in an avalanche in the Alps with his best friend Will Hamilton. The only survivor was Will's girlfriend *Erin Fitz-Clarence*.'

'Topher.' Miranda is looking as alarmed as Rik now. 'Topher, what are you getting at?'

'I'm saying, this isn't the first time our little Erin has been involved in a fatal skiing accident.'

ERIN

Snoop ID: LITTLEMY
Listening to: offline
Snoopscribers: 10

'Danny!' There is no answer, but I know he's in there. 'Danny, please, I'm sorry. Please let me explain.' I bang on his door for maybe the twentieth or thirtieth time, but without much hope now. It's clear he doesn't want to open up.

Only then he does.

'This had better be good,' he says, and his expression makes me quail, it's so angry.

'Danny, I'm sorry,' I say again, desperately.

'You said you were going to explain.' He folds his arms, his fury barely contained. 'So go on then. Explain. Explain why you lied to me.'

'I didn't lie to you — '

He begins to shut the door in my face.

'Hey!' I cry, and instinctively I shove my foot in the gap, forgetting that it's my bad ankle. The door crunches on it and I let out a scream of pure agony. Danny claps his hands to his mouth.

'Holy shit, Erin, I'm sorry — I'm so so sorry — it's fine!' he bellows, knowing that the others are probably jumping up in panic, attuned to the worst-case scenario. 'Erin's fine, she just knocked her ankle.'

'I'm fine,' I call croakily, blinking away the sudden tears of pain that have started into my eyes, and whether they believe us, or they can't hear anything through the staff door, no one comes running.

Either way, something has broken in the deadlock between us, because Danny opens the door wider and jerks his head at his bed.

'You better come in. Take the weight off.'

I hobble meekly inside and sit down.

There is a long silence.

'So?' Danny says at last. Every muscle in his body screams antagonism, but at least I've been offered the chance to explain.

'You're right,' I say. 'Even if I didn't lie to you, I didn't exactly tell you the truth.'

'I thought we were friends,' Danny says, and although the anger is fading from his kind, crumpled face, what's left is worse — bewildered hurt. 'I thought — I thought you and me was on the same side.'

'We were — we *are*,' I say, desperately. 'This doesn't change anything. Everything I told you — about me, about dropping out of uni — it's all true. I just didn't tell you why.'

'Why then?' Danny says. He folds his arms and leans back against his little chest of drawers, letting me know with his body language that this isn't going to be that easy. I've got a hole to dig myself out of.

I swallow. I haven't talked to anyone about this — not since the nightmare days and weeks after the accident. But I owe Danny the truth.

'It's true my dad's a marquess,' I say. 'But

honestly, Danny, it sounds a hell of a lot grander than it is. He doesn't live in a castle. My family aren't particularly well off. Alex went to boarding school, but I went to the local comprehensive because my parents couldn't afford two sets of fees, I'm no different from you.'

He gives me a look at that, as if to say, *fuck off are you*, and I wince, knowing he's right. Danny grew up on a council estate on the outskirts of Portsmouth, the only child of a single mum who struggled for years to make ends meet. He has pulled himself up by his bootstraps, with no help from anyone. However far the FitzClarence fortunes have fallen, our upbringings *were* different, and that's the truth. To pretend otherwise is pretty insulting.

'OK, I'm sorry, that — that was clumsy. It's not what I meant. I just meant — I'm trying to explain — '

I stop. I put my head in my hands. This is all I need. Danny was the one person on my side, the one person I felt I could rely on. Have I really screwed all that up, thanks to Topher?

'When I was nineteen,' I begin again, more slowly this time, 'I went on a skiing holiday with my boyfriend, Will, and my brother, Alex, Will's best friend. We were skiing off-piste, and we were stupid. We got caught in a — ' I swallow. I don't know how to talk about this, how to explain the horror of what happened. Words aren't enough. 'We got caught in an avalanche,' I say at last, forcing the word out. 'We triggered it. We were all wearing avalanche packs, but Alex didn't manage to set his off. Will's deployed, but it didn't save him, he was buried too deep, and I couldn't dig him out fast enough. I was the only person who survived.'

I stop. I can't go on. I can't describe those nightmarish hours on the mountain, sobbing as I dug with numb bleeding hands through the hard-packed drifts to try to reach Will, trapped head down beneath a hundredweight of snow and ice. I dug and I wept, and I wept and I dug, using anything I could find in my pack — my lift pass, my water bottle, anything that could form a makeshift pick, for my poles and skis were long gone, ripped away from me somewhere far up the slope.

It was too late. I knew that. I had known it even before I began to dig, I think, and as the hours wore on, and snow lay all around in unmoving silence, I somehow found the strength to accept it. But still I dug. Not just for Will, but for my own survival. Because Will had the GPS locator beacon in his pack. And if I didn't activate it, I would die along with him.

The search and rescue eventually found us. Or rather, they found me. By the time they arrived I was hypothermic, cradling Will's dead body. Alex was not recovered until the following spring.

'I — I couldn't go back,' I say very quietly. 'Do you understand that? I couldn't go back to my old life. It was completely meaningless. I went home to bury Will, and then I came back to the mountains — at first because I couldn't bear to leave without Alex, and then afterwards because . . . '

I stop. The truth is, I don't know why I stayed.

250

Only that I couldn't stand to be at home, with the pity of all my friends suffocating me, and my parents' awful, crushing grief. And it seemed like a kind of penance to stay here, among the terrible austere beauty of the Alps, to keep forcing myself to look at the mountains that had killed Will and Alex.

'That's why you don't ski off-piste,' Danny says hoarsely. He is looking at me very differently now. The anger has gone. There is only a kind of . . . pity left. It hurts to see it in his face, and I turn away, nodding.

'Yes, that's why. I still love skiing — which is perverse, I know. My parents think I'm crazy. My dad called me a masochist when I took this job. But I can't seem to bring myself to leave the mountains, and you can't live here year-round without skiing. But I don't think I'll ever go off-piste again.'

'Fuck, Erin. Why didn't you tell me?' Danny asks, but he doesn't say it like he's expecting an answer. I think he knows that it wasn't that I didn't want to tell him — it was that I couldn't bear to say it. I couldn't bear to become a victim to him, too.

There is a silence, and then he folds me in his arms, and I rest my face against his warm, muscled shoulder and I close my eyes and breathe in the good, Danny smell of him. I feel the tears soak into the worn softness of his sweater.

'So you're proper posh, eh?' he says with a rumbling chuckle, and I give a shaky answering laugh, and lift my head, wiping the tears off my nose with my sleeve. 'You belong down there, with that lot, not up here in the servants' quarters, with the hoi polloi.'

'No I *don't*.' I say it more emphatically than I meant to, and Danny laughs again, but I'm serious. 'No, I mean it, Danny, I don't belong with them any more. I'm not sure I ever did. What they stand for — '

I stop, thinking of Topher and his cushioned, moneyed existence — the way he has had everything handed to him on a plate, the way he's never had to scrap for anything, never had to swallow a snub from a boss, or pick up a stranger's dirty underwear, or do any of the myriad demeaning, boring jobs the rest of us take for granted.

They are arrogant, that's what I realise — maybe not Liz and Carl quite so much, but all of them to *some* degree. They are protected by the magic of their shares and their status and their IP. They think that life can't touch them — just like I used to do.

Only now it has. Now life has them by the throat. And it won't let go.

LIZ

'You're saying Erin is behind this?' Miranda's face is sceptical. She folds her arms, looking at Topher with narrowed dark eyes. Topher's expression is defensive.

'No. No, that's not what I said — I simply — '

'It's what you implied though,' Miranda says. I realise something — Miranda does not like Topher. I don't know why I didn't notice this until now — perhaps it is the fact that she is so formal and polite. Now she is not bothering to hide her opinion.

'I'm just saying, once is bad luck, twice is a *hell* of a coincidence. How many skiing deaths can one person be involved in?'

'Oh, why don't we stop beating around the bush?' Miranda says bitingly. 'We all know why you're desperate to throw suspicion on other people.'

'What are you suggesting?' Topher says, and his voice is suddenly dangerous.

'I'm not *suggesting* anything,' Miranda says. She steps up to him. Even without her heels, they are almost exactly the same height. 'I'm stating facts. Most people in this room stood to

253

gain a lot of money before Eva died. Very few people had a motive for wanting her out of the way. You were one of those few.'

Rik and Carl exchange an uneasy look. Neither of them jumps in to defend Topher.

'One, that is fucking slander, and two, you are talking about my *best friend*,' Topher begins furiously, but then Tiger lifts her head and says something. It's an almost inaudible croak, but all heads turn to her, and Topher stops midsentence.

'What did you say?' Miranda swings round, and Tiger struggles upright, brushing her hair away from her forehead. Her face is blotched red and white.

'She said something,' she repeats, her voice still hoarse with tears.

'Who?' Rik comes and kneels beside them. His face urgent, and he grabs Tiger's arm. His gesture seems to have been harder than he intended, because she winces a little. 'Who said what?'

'Last night, Ani. I just remembered. She said something. She tried to wake me up, but I was — ' She gulps, forcing back sobs. 'She said, *I didn't see her*. If only I'd been able to wake up properly, if only I hadn't taken that sleeping pill — ' She breaks off. Two huge tears roll down her face.

'Tiger,' Miranda says uneasily. She crouches beside Rik. 'Tiger, are you *sure* about this? Before you were saying you didn't wake up.'

'I know, I know I said that, but I was wrong, I remember now. I remember her shaking me. I remember the words.'

Miranda shoots a questioning look at Rik and he gives a minute shrug back.

'Well,' Topher says. There's a touch of triumph in his voice. 'Well, well, well. I didn't see *her*. Now who's got a reason to start slinging mud, Ms Khan? After all, that sounds like it rules out half of the room, doesn't it?'

'What does?' says a deep voice from the direction of the lobby.

We all look round. Danny and Erin are standing in the doorway, side by side. Erin looks as if she has been crying. I am not sure if they have made up completely, but it looks like they have patched their differences enough to put up a united front. Topher looks slightly annoyed.

'Tiger claims — ' Miranda begins, but Tiger interrupts with an angry sob.

'I don't *claim* anything. I *heard* her, I'm sure of it. Ani tried to tell me something last night — she shook my shoulder and she said *I didn't see her*. Only I couldn't wake up properly. But it fits — it fits with what Liz said, that Ani had something she was trying to figure out, something she wasn't sure of.'

'*I didn't see her*,' Erin repeats slowly. 'Are you sure of that, Tiger?'

'Yes,' Tiger says, more emphatically this time. 'Yes, I was lying on the sofa just now trying to think back to last night, think whether I'd heard anything, and I remembered suddenly Ani coming over to me and shaking my shoulder. It was like a flashback.'

'Which implies,' Topher says smugly, 'that we're looking for a woman. No? *Her*, that's what

255

Tiger said. Ani was trying to figure something out about one of the women in the party.'

He glares at Miranda.

'Not necessarily . . . ' Danny says slowly. He is frowning. He scratches his head, thinking. 'Maybe she wasn't talking about the killer. Ani was the only person who saw Eva on the slope. Isn't that right? Carl was the only other person on the bubble, and he didn't see her. Right?'

'Right,' Carl says shortly. 'But what are you saying?'

'I'm saying, what if Ani realised she'd made a mistake? What if Eva never skied that slope after all?'

'But she *did*,' Miranda says with exasperation. 'Elliot's geo-targeting proves that.'

'It proves her phone is there,' Danny says. 'But the only evidence we ever had that Eva was with her phone on that slope was Ani's sighting. What if she realised she was wrong? What if . . . here, what about this — what if Eva faked her own death?'

That last suggestion causes a little excited ripple around the circle. Faces brighten. People want to believe this. Danny's suggestion is a solution that doesn't require a murderer, and everybody would desperately like that to be true.

But there is a problem. Two problems in fact. It is a solution that doesn't explain Elliot's or Ani's deaths. It does not hold up for a minute. As they would realise if they thought about it. But I can see they are *not* thinking.

Speaking up in front of the others makes my stomach curdle, but I have to say something. I can't not.

'Eva *was* on that slope,' I say reluctantly. 'I saw her too.'

Every pair of eyes in the room turns to me. It feels like they are boring into me. My cheeks flush. I want to sink through the floor.

'What did you say?' It is Miranda, her voice almost accusing.

'I said, I saw Eva too. I was in the bubble lift on the way down, and I saw her skiing as well — further up the slope than Ani did, but I saw her. She was on La Sorcière. Ani wasn't mistaken. She must have been talking about something else.'

'And you didn't think to mention this before?'

'I didn't — it didn't . . . ' I trail off.

'Not something else. Someone else,' Danny says flatly, and there is a moment's silence. Everyone's gaze travels around the room, going from one person to another. We are all realising the same thing. If Tiger is right, there are very few people Ani could have been talking about. Topher folds his arms. *Your move*, his expression says to Miranda.

'Tiger, are you *sure?*' Miranda says. Now there is a note of desperation in her voice. 'Are you absolutely certain Ani said her?'

'I'm sure,' Tiger says stubbornly.

There is a long, long silence. Miranda stands up and walks out of the room.

'I don't care,' she shoots over her shoulder as she leaves. 'I don't *care* what Ani said. There is one person in this room who had a motive for Eva's death. *One person.* Stop pretending that isn't the case!'

And then there's nothing but silence, and the

clack-clack of her heels on the spiral staircase as she runs up to her room.

After she has gone, there is an extremely awkward silence. Topher is leaning against the mantelpiece, angry and flushed. Rik looks like a man being ripped in half. Tiger is slumped, with her hand over her face. Erin and Danny look intensely uncomfortable. Carl breaks the silence.

'Yeah, but she's right, isn't she?'

His voice seems to break some kind of spell, and Topher pushes himself upright and turns for the door.

'Fuck this,' he says. 'I'm not doing this any more.'

'What do you mean?' Rik turns to stare at him, puzzled. 'You're not doing what?'

'*This*. I'm not sitting here like fucking frogs in a pressure cooker. I *didn't* kill Eva, no matter what Miranda and Carl want to believe, and I certainly didn't fucking kill my best friend or our PA. And I'm not hanging around waiting to prove it by being the next person killed. I'm out of here. I'm going to cross-country it down to St Antoine le Lac.'

'You're mad,' Rik says instantly. 'The piste is ripped to shreds, there's trees and rocks everywhere. And look at the weather for God's sake! You'll freeze to death.'

Topher shrugs.

There is a short pause.

'You're mad!' Rik repeats desperately. And then, 'I'm coming with you.'

ERIN

Snoop ID: LITTLEMY
Listening to: offline
Snoopscribers: 10

It's almost midday, and the group has spent the past hour or more discussing Topher's decision and going back and forth over the stupidity — or not — of the idea. Topher, for his part, is packing determinedly. So far he's got an avalanche pack, water, a torch, some energy bars, a rope, and he's looking for a shovel, though I'm not sure how he imagines he's going to use it. If there's another avalanche, a shovel in his pack isn't going to save him. But if he doesn't manage to get down to St Antoine before nightfall, he's going to need some kind of shelter, so maybe it's not such a bad idea. There's worse survival tactics than a snow shelter.

Above all though, he seems set on simply getting away — no matter how stupid or risky the plan. Miranda's statement has unleashed something people were refusing to face before — Topher *is* the person who has benefited most from Eva's death. He's just been handed everything he wanted — sole control of Snoop. Rik and Liz, on the other hand, stand to lose millions of pounds if the buy-out doesn't go through, and I can't imagine Miranda and Carl will survive this holiday with their posts intact. Whatever the facts, it's difficult to believe they can continue working for Topher after basically accusing their boss of murder. There are some things you don't come back from.

So I can understand why he feels he can't stay here — just as Inigo felt he had no choice but to leave when the group turned on him. What's more surprising is that Rik seems set on going too — though I don't honestly know how Topher feels about this. He has tried to dissuade Rik, but it's hard to deny that two people will stand a better chance than one. It's treacherous going out there, and if one person sprains an ankle, they'd be pretty much dead without a mobile phone. At least with two, you have a chance of sending for help.

By 12.15, Rik and Topher are standing in the foyer, looking at the large-scale map of the resort that we have pinned to one of the walls and discussing potential routes, when Tiger comes down the spiral stairs. She's wearing her snowboarding gear, and she's looking determined.

'I'm coming with you too,' she says without preamble.

Topher frowns.

'Tiger — '

'No, don't try to stop me. I'm as good a boarder as you — and I'm better than Rik.' She says it with no false modesty. 'And I can't stay here after what — ' She gulps, stops, tries again. 'After wh-what happened — '

But she can't finish. I can see that beneath her

oversized jacket her small fists are clenched.

Rik and Topher look at each other, and I'm not sure what they're thinking. Tiger is still the person who had the best opportunity for killing Ani, that part is undeniable. The two of them were locked in a room together, and one of them didn't wake up. But she was also pretty firm about Ani's final words, words that deflected suspicion from Topher, which seems like strange behaviour for a murderer. Plus Rik and Topher are two big strapping blokes, each of them probably weighing almost twice as much as Tiger by themselves. If Tiger *were* the killer, it seems unlikely she could overpower one of them, let alone both. On the other hand, and I can almost see Rik and Topher calculating this in their heads, if one of *them* is a murderer, isn't it better to have a third party witness?

The surrealness of this reasoning strikes me again, and I stifle a short, hysterical laugh, and then clap my hand over my mouth.

'What did you say?' Rik says, turning to me, frowning, and I shake my head. Tears are leaking out of my eyes, but I can't tell why.

'Nothing, I'm sorry. Ignore me.'

'Fine, you can come,' Topher says brusquely to Tiger, making up his mind.

'Rik.' We all turn at the voice from above, and see Miranda coming down the spiral staircase too. Her expression is pale, but set. Rik's face falls. He knows what's coming, and he's already shaking his head.

'Rik, you can't do this,' Miranda says. Her brittle voice seems to crack. She takes his arm,

261

her fingers digging into his jacket. 'This is incredibly stupid.'

'Miranda, I'm sorry,' Rik says. His deep voice is very quiet, he's trying to keep this between the two of them, but it's impossible, with the rest of us just feet away. 'I don't want to go — but we can't stay here and get picked off one by one like this. I think Topher's right. We *have* to get to the police.'

'But not with him.' She's whispering, but the acoustics in this room are excellent. I can hear her, so I'm pretty sure Topher can. 'Please, please, I'm begging you. Don't go with *him*. I'm frightened you won't come back.'

'Mir — '

'We'll go together. I'll get my skis on — '

'You're not a strong enough skier,' he whispers back. 'Please, darling, believe me, I would if I could but it's just too — '

'I won't stay here without you!'

'Oi, what about the other chalet?' We all turn to see Carl, standing in the living-room doorway, his hands in his pockets. Miranda frowns, thrown off course.

'What other chalet?'

'That chef, Danny, wasn't he going to hike out to some chalet earlier? Before all this started.'

I nod.

'He was,' I say. 'Chalet Haut Montagne. It's a big chain chalet and much more likely to be occupied than the two closer ones, but it's a trek — a good three or four miles up the valley. That's why he left it until last.'

'See?' Carl says triumphantly. 'Three or four

262

miles, that's nothing. You could walk that in a morning.'

'I wouldn't call it nothing,' I say cautiously. 'For a start, you wouldn't be walking it, you'd have to snowshoe, and that's a really different skill. What with the avalanche, not to mention almost a week of uncleared snow . . . I'd say you'd be looking at a good three hours snowshoeing. Maybe more if you'd never done it.'

'I reckon it's a better bet than the resort,' Carl says flatly. 'I mean, what's that, fifteen miles? And steep as fuck. You lose a ski on that boulder field, you're fucked.'

'I'm not going to lose a ski,' Topher snarls. 'For a start, I'm a boarder, not a skier. Second, I'm halfway competent. And anyway — what happens if we get to the chalet and it's shut up? We're back to square fucking one. At least we *know* the resort has people who can help us. No, I've made my choice and I'm sticking to it.'

His irritation doesn't rub off on Carl, who just gives a shrug.

'Maybe it's not a choice.'

There's a long, puzzled silence.

'What are you saying?' Rik asks at last.

'I'm saying, it's not an either/or situation. Look, the strong skiers, that's you, Toph and Tiger, try to make it to the village and raise the alarm there. The rest of us'll try for the chalet. Whoever makes it through, we'll send a party to rescue the other lot.'

It's . . . it's actually not a bad plan. I can see Topher and Rik looking at each other, thinking it over, coming to the same conclusion. At last Topher nods, like Carl was asking him for permission, though I don't think he was. We are long past the point where Topher has that kind of authority.

'Yeah, OK,' he says, a little sulkily, acceding to the inevitable.

'Miranda?' Rik says, and she gives an unhappy shrug.

'I — I guess. If you won't take me with you it's better than sitting here.'

'Liz?' Carl says. 'How about it?'

For a second, Liz just blinks, like she is startled to be referred to by name. For a moment she does nothing at all — like a frightened animal frozen, in the headlamp-beam of Carl's attention.

Then she cracks the tiniest smile, and gives a shaky, uncertain nod.

For the first time in a few days, I feel a flare of hope inside my chest.

Maybe it will be ok.

Maybe it will really all be ok.

LIZ

Snoop ID: ANON101
Listening to: offline
Snoopscribers: 1

After so many days reacting to events, it feels good to have a plan. Up in my room I struggle into my faded blue jumpsuit and pull on ski socks and gloves. My helmet and goggles are down in the locker room. I will put those on when we are ready to go outside. One glance out of the window tells me that sunglasses won't be needed. It's midday, but almost dark. The sun is barely filtering through the clouds, and the wind is howling like something trying to get in.

When I am dressed, I feel, for the first time in a couple of days, hot and puffed out. It is strange to feel too warm again, after the growing chill of the chalet. I let myself sink to the bed and catch my breath for a few moments.

Now that it is almost over, I can look back on the living nightmare of the last few days. How has it come to this? *How?* Of all the ways I was expecting this week to go, I never imagined this unfolding horror.

In my mind I tick them off, a macabre school roll-call.

Eva — dead.

Elliot — dead.

Inigo — gone, and goodness knows what has happened to him. Did he make it to St Antoine? Or is he lying, frozen with hypothermia, in some isolated shack, far from the piste?

Ani — dead.

There's just six of us left. Me, Rik, Miranda, Carl, Tiger and Topher.

Topher. It always comes back to him somehow. Because it is true what Miranda said — however much people try to ignore the fact, Topher has a very strong motive for Eva's death. In fact he has the best motive out of everyone here.

The thought should make my heart hurt. Topher — who hired me out of a pool of slick, skinny graduates, and gave me my first chance. Topher — who stood up for me, stood by me, made sure I got those shares that have hung around my neck like an albatross ever since. Topher — the reason I am here.

And maybe it's because of that last one — but my heart doesn't hurt. I feel nothing — nothing at all.

Because Topher is the reason I have been dragged into this, into something I never wanted and never asked for. Topher and Eva between them, pushing me, pulling me, manipulating me like a chess piece in their battle for control of Snoop.

I know what Topher thought, when he gave me those shares. He thought that he was handing over 2 per cent of the company to someone he could control. I was his insurance policy, in case

Eva and Rik ever ganged up on him. A way to tip the balance in his favour.

Topher thought I would be like putty in his hands. Soft. Malleable. Pliant. He thought that because of the kind of person he saw — someone meek and quiet, dressed in bad clothes, who never said boo to a goose.

In Topher's world, people are hard, polished shells, their shiny exterior hiding the inadequacies and anxieties inside.

But Topher made a mistake. He didn't understand that some people are the other way round. But Eva . . . I think Eva did understand that. And perhaps it's what killed her in the end.

ERIN

Snoop ID: LITTLEMY
Listening to: offline
Snoopscribers: 10

It is one o'clock. Everyone apart from Liz is gathered in the lobby wearing their ski gear. Topher's party is holding snowboards, skis and poles. Miranda and Carl are equipped with a pair of snowshoes each. And my heart is thumping. Thumping because . . . maybe this is it. Maybe this long nightmare is finally over. Surely one group will be successful?

'What on earth is Liz doing?' Miranda says irritably. She has been on edge ever since Rik told her she couldn't go with him down to the village. The two-party idea makes sense, and she knows it does, but she would still prefer to be with Rik, and I can see the way her gaze keeps stealing across to him.

'I'm here,' says a timid voice from the top of the stairs, and we all look up to see Liz standing at the top of the spiral staircase. She is wearing the outsize blue jumpsuit she had on the first day, and is clutching her ski poles in one mittened hand. A bobble hat is balanced on top of her head and her glasses are misted. She looks hot and sweaty, but, like the rest of us, relieved to

268

be finally doing something.

She starts down the stairs, and then it happens. Something — pole? a trailing strap? — catches in the bannisters, and she stumbles. Her socked feet go out from under her. One hand grabs for the handrail, but the mitten has no grip and the wooden rail simply slides out from under the plasticky fabric.

As we watch, helpless, Liz tumbles forwards down the spiral staircase with a series of sickening thumps. And then she lands at the bottom, ominously quiet.

LIZ

Snoop ID: ANON101
Listening to: offline
Snoopscribers: 1

I can't breathe.

I lie there, panic pulsing through me, trying to inhale and failing. I can hear myself making little strange gasps, like a fish stranded out of water.

'Liz!' It is Erin. She comes hobbling over. Her face is white. She crouches beside me. 'Liz! Oh God, are you OK?'

I can't answer. I can't get my breath enough to say a word. I make a motion, half nodding, half shaking my head. Am I OK? I am not sure.

'Fucking hell.' Carl falls to his knees next to me. 'Liz?' He turns to the others. 'Well, she's alive at least. Can you speak, Liz?' He says it very loudly, like I am hard of hearing.

'I think she's just very badly winded,' Erin says. She strokes my forehead. I resist the urge to pull away. I am not sure if I could, anyway. 'It's OK, don't fight it. Just try to breathe slowly. I'll count with you. One, two, three, four, five . . . and in. And now one, two, three, four, five, and out.'

With Erin counting, slowly and rhythmically, I

270

manage to take a breath. Then another. At last, shakily, I sit up.

'Are you OK?' Erin asks again. 'Does anything hurt?'

'My knee,' I manage. I pull up the leg of my jumpsuit, but I had forgotten my leggings underneath. You can't see anything, but my knee feels hot. When Erin squeezes it gently, a pulse of pain flares up my leg and I flinch.

'Fucking hell,' Rik says shakily. 'I thought for a minute there — '

He stops. He does not need to spell it out. I know exactly what he thought. I thought it too for a second. For a moment, we were almost five.

Erin helps me to stand up. I find I am shaking.

'Can you walk?' Erin asks. I nod and hobble a few steps. Behind me Carl's face is grim.

'Well, you can't manage four miles in snow, can you,' he says. It's not a question.

'So, we go alone?' Miranda says. Now it is Rik's turn to look uneasy. I know what he is thinking. Three people should be safe together. But if Carl is the murderer, he is sending Miranda out into the snow alone with a killer.

'I don't know — ' he says, but Erin cuts in.

'Danny will go.'

ERIN

'Danny will go.'

The words are out of my mouth before I have time to consider them, but as soon as I've said them, I know they make sense. It's not just about the maths of sending two people out into the snow together. Danny knows the way. Carl and Miranda don't.

'What?' The voice comes from behind me, and I turn round to see Danny standing there, looking mightily pissed off with me. 'Erin, could we have a word please?' he says tightly. 'In the kitchen?'

With a glance at Liz, who is white as a sheet and looks like she might keel over at any second, I follow him, and when the screen door swings shut behind us, Danny lets rip.

'Are you out of your fucking mind? We went over this. I am *not* leaving you here with a broken ankle and a psycho on the loose.'

'I didn't mean just you,' I say, trying to keep my voice low. It feels weird to be articulating our suspicions like this, within earshot of the group. 'I meant the three of you should go. It's obvious

272

— isn't it? I can't believe we didn't think of it before. Carl and Miranda have no idea where they're going — even with a map, the routes are covered up by the avalanche, it's more likely than not they'll end up wandering off into the forest and get lost. You know where the chalet is. You can speak French. And you know how to snowshoe. It makes complete sense. They stand a much better chance of getting there and back if you're with them. I'd be seriously worried about them setting out alone.'

'Huh.' Danny looks taken aback at this. He can see the logic in my argument. 'So . . . what, you and that Liz bird stay here by yourselves?'

'That's right. I mean, think about it, Danny. She's not going anywhere with that twisted knee, she's as lame as I am. And she was never really a realistic prospect for the killer anyway. She can't ski, we know she was stuck on the bubble lift when Eva actually died, and out of everyone here, she has one of the strongest motives for *not* wanting Eva dead. I mean, who knows what might have happened to everyone else in a buyout situation — they were probably going to lose their jobs at the very least. But Liz had no job to lose — and she stood to gain several million quid if the deal went through. That's a pretty strong counter-argument.'

'Yeah . . . I can see that . . . ' Danny says slowly.

'Please,' I say. I put my hand on his arm. 'Danny, *please*. Get Miranda and Carl to that chalet and get word to the police about what's happening. We can't afford another death, and I

273

don't trust Carl and Miranda by themselves.'

'All right,' Danny says, making up his mind. 'You're probably right. I'll go and get my gear. But you lock up when we're gone, and don't answer the door to *anyone* except me or the gendarmes. You got that? I don't care if Topher comes crawling back with a sob story of Rik leaving him in the snow. I don't care if Tiger snaps a binding. You don't let them in. Any of them. And fuck knows what happened to Inigo, but I don't like the idea that he might be prowling around out there in the snow waiting for everyone else to leave.'

His words are like an unwelcome splash of cold water in the face. Inigo. We had assumed — *I* had assumed — that Inigo was out of the picture now. What if he's not?

Uneasiness shifts in my belly, but I put my chin up.

'We'll be fine. Even if someone does show up — which I doubt — there's two of us, and one of them. And they'll be outside in the snow, freezing their tits off.'

'Yeah, well,' Danny says darkly. 'Just you stick to that, OK? I know you. Someone'll turn up, claim he's crawled eight miles through the snow with frostbite, and you'll open the door because you're soft. Don't be starting up with the bleeding heart crap. Put yourself first.'

I feel a sharp twinge of guilt — even though I haven't done anything — because Danny's right. That is exactly the kind of thing I would do. I try to imagine myself sitting in the warm, dry chalet while Inigo, or Topher, or even a complete stranger died slowly outside the front door, begging to be let in, and I just can't see it happening. I *would* crack. I *would* let them in. I know I would.

'We'll be fine,' I say again, though my voice is a little bit less convincing, even to myself. 'Just go and get back as fast as you can.'

LIZ

Snoop ID: ANON101
Listening to: offline
Snoopscribers: 1

After the others are gone, Erin locks and bolts the front door. She fixes it in place as securely as she can, but it is not perfect. It has been warped by the avalanche so that the bottom lock doesn't fasten properly and melted snow is leaking through the gap, but the lock at the top works. Then she checks the ski entrance, which is still buried by snow, and the door that used to lead out to the swimming pool.

'All safe and sound,' she reports as she comes back into the lobby. Her smile is bright and slightly artificial. There is something a little bit oppressive about the silence now. It weighs heavy and feels like it is pressing in on us. 'How are you feeling?'

'Uh — OK, I think.' I rub the back of my head where I hit it on the bannister and touch my knee gingerly through the padded salopettes. I wrenched it, but it is not as bad as I feared. Now that the first shock is wearing off, I can put my weight on it. 'Still a bit wobbly, but I think it was mostly shock.'

'What a pair,' Erin says. She grins at me, the

276

scar on her cheek twisting with the movement. 'Me with my ankle, you with your knee. Couple of lame ducks.'

'I know.' I try for a laugh, but it doesn't sound quite right.

'I reckon it'll take Danny's party about six hours to get to Haut Montagne and back. And who knows about Topher's lot. I have no idea how badly bashed up the piste is. If it's not easily skiable, they could be days.'

I nod. Clambering through waist-deep snow in ski boots is no joke. I know that.

'So I think we have at least six hours before we need to start worrying,' Erin says. 'The question is, how are we going to kill the time?'

ERIN

Snoop ID: LITTLEMY
Listening to: offline
Snoopscribers: 10

It's gone three. After the others left, Liz and I ate a meagre lunch of lukewarm tinned soup — the bread was almost inedibly stale, but dipping it in the soup made it soft enough to chew — and we have been playing cards ever since. The chalet is completely, eerily silent. I never realised before how stifling silence could be, perhaps because Perce-Neige is so rarely quiet — it's always full of the noise of guest footsteps, playing children in the school holidays, the clatter of skis, the sound of Danny in the kitchen. While Topher and the others were here there was the constant jangle of someone playing music, and later the babble of conversation. Even on changeover days, there is the hum of the Hoover and the noise of Danny's radio.

Now, there is no music. Our phones are long since dead. The TV and radio sit silent with no electricity to power them. There is no sound at all apart from the crackle of the logs in the burner. Even the patter of snow outside is virtually silent, behind the triple glazing.

Every few minutes I glance out of the window,

checking the weather. It . . . isn't great. There's no point in sugar-coating that. It's not as bad as it could have been. The wind has dropped at least. But the snow is still falling, and cloud has come rolling down the mountain, enveloping the chalet in a thick, frozen grey blur, so that visibility is down to a few feet. I am profoundly relieved that Danny is with Miranda and Carl, and knows where he's going. Even so, I'm starting to wonder whether he will be able to make it to Haut Montagne and back again before night falls in earnest. Maybe Liz and I will be stuck here alone overnight. It's not a completely comfortable thought.

As if echoing my unease, Liz flexes her fingers nervously *crack, crack, crack*. The noise is like gunshots in the silence, and it puts my teeth on edge.

'How did you get involved with Snoop anyway?' I ask. I pitch my voice slightly too loud, trying to cover up the sound. Liz shifts in her chair. I can't tell if her knee is hurting her, or if it's the question that's made her uncomfortable.

'I just applied for a job. They were a start-up at the time — just Topher, Eva, Elliot and Rik. I was their first . . . secretary, I suppose you'd call it. PA, maybe. They didn't have the weird job titles in those days.'

She falls silent again, as if the uncharacteristically long speech has exhausted her. I'm about to ask another question when to my surprise, she speaks again.

'I miss it. I miss them. It was fun . . . for a while.'

'What made you leave?' I ask, but that's when the shutters come down again. Her face turns blank and unreadable.

'No reason,' she says, looking down at her cards. 'I just wanted a change.'

In the silence I pick up a card, and put down a king. Liz picks it up, frowning. I have put my foot in it, but I'm not quite sure how. I think of Danny's remark about the incestuous nature of Snoop's workforce, Eva sleeping with Inigo, Topher with Ani. *Haven't they heard of Me Too?* Did something happen between Liz and Topher? Something she is running from? But no, I don't think it's that. Of all the people in the company, Liz actually seems to get on best with Topher. And Topher, for all his faults, doesn't seem like the kind of man to pressurise an employee into something sexual. Whatever was between him and Ani, I got the impression it was consensual.

But Ani ended up dead . . .

The words are a whisper in my ear, an uncomfortable reminder of the fact that Liz and I are not alone in this chalet — there are two bodies upstairs with us. And somewhere out there in the frozen peaks there is a third, Eva, and maybe a fourth, because who knows what happened to Inigo after he stumbled away into the snow. It feels like death is closing around us. It feels like Liz and I could be next.

But no. I shake myself. This is morbid — ridiculously so.

'Your turn,' Liz says, and I look down and realise I have no idea when she made her move.

280

I pick up a card from the draw pile at random and discard without really thinking about strategy. 'Rummy,' Liz says, and she lays out a run of four spades, and three kings. I force a smile.

'Well done.'

Liz picks up the cards and deals again. I pick up my hand. It's a good one — three of a kind straight off. But I can't keep my mind on the cards.

'Eva's death . . . ' I say cautiously, and Liz looks up. She's still wearing her oversized blue jumpsuit and I can't really blame her. Even with the wood stove, the chalet is now painfully cold, and I can see my breath when I speak. 'That . . . it must have been quite a shock. I suppose the buyout won't go through now? How did it feel — having all that money, and then having it snatched away?'

I'm half expecting Liz to tell me that it's none of my business — and it's true, it's not. But we've gone long past the point of guest and chalet girl, and we both know it.

'It felt . . . strange . . . ' Liz says slowly. The firelight is reflecting off her glasses, making her expression even harder to read than usual, but I can see her forehead crinkle as she frowns.

'Did you resent Topher?' I ask. 'For quashing the sale? I think I would have.'

But Liz is shaking her head.

'I never really wanted the money, to be honest. It never felt like mine. It was such a stupid sum, and for what?'

'Being in the right place at the right time, I

281

guess?' I say with a laugh, but Liz doesn't smile back. She shakes her head again, although I'm not sure what she's denying. I can't blame her though. Whatever place we have ended up in, all of us, it's definitely not the right one.

Silence falls again. I look at my watch. Ten minutes to four. God, could this day pass any slower? Suddenly I can't sit any longer, and I stand, putting my weight carefully on my swollen ankle, and make my way over to the long window, overlooking the valley.

It is almost completely dark outside now, but the chalet is dark too, and so I don't need to cup my hands to my eyes as I look out across the snow, wondering where Danny and the others are. Have they made it to Haut Montagne yet? And what about Topher and his party? I wish, harder than I've ever wished for anything before, that I had a phone with just a single bar of reception. Or a two-way radio. Or anything — *some* way of communicating with the outside world.

'Four aces,' says Liz, over my shoulder, and I sigh, and turn back to the darkening room.

LIZ

Snoop ID: ANON101
Listening to: offline
Snoopscribers: 1

It is 3.58. We are on our — I don't know. Twentieth game of rummy, perhaps. I have not been counting. Thoughts are chasing around my brain like rats. Questions like, what is going to happen? When will they come? What will happen when the police get here?

Erin glances up at the clock on the mantelpiece above the stove. I can tell that she is feeling the same way I am.

'One more round,' she says, 'and then I'll figure out something for supper. They should be there by now.'

If they made it.

The words hang, unspoken, in the air, as Erin begins to deal.

It is more to drive the unsaid doubts away than because I really want to know that I say it.

'Topher said you were in an avalanche. What was it like?'

Erin looks up. I have caught her by surprise, and for a second her face is unguarded, horribly vulnerable. She looks like I have punched her. For a moment, I regret asking her. Then she composes herself. She deals out the last few cards before she speaks.

'I was. Three years ago. It was — ' She stops, looks down at the remainder of the deck in her hand. 'It was the worst thing that's ever happened to me.'

'I'm sorry,' I say. Then something occurs to me. 'Even counting this weekend?'

She gives a laugh at that, a shaky mirthless one, and nods.

'Yes, unbelievably. Even counting this weekend. I can't explain how awful it was. The noise, the shock, the sense of powerlessness — ' She falters, as if she is struggling to find the words. 'I thought . . . I thought that it would have made it worse, you know? Being caught up in the same horror all over again. But in a strange way I . . . I think I've been expecting it to happen. Like I escaped the mountain once, so it would come back for me.'

She stares into the darkness. She is facing me, so it should feel like she is staring at me, but I have the odd feeling that she is not, that she is looking *through* me, as if I am not there. It gives me a strange sensation. As if I am already gone.

'Is that when you — when you got your — ' I can't say it. I just touch my face with my fingers, and she nods.

'Yes. I cut my face on something in the fall, probably my own ski.'

'And is that why you left uni?' I ask, and she nods, very slowly.

'Yes. I can't really explain why, even now. I just — I felt like I'd become a different person, do

284

you know what I mean?'

I nod too. I know exactly what she means. I have the impression that she is talking about this, perhaps for the very first time.

'I had to dig him out.' Her voice is barely above a whisper. I have to strain to hear it. 'I wasn't carrying a GPS locator. I had to dig out my boyfriend to activate his beacon, knowing he was already dead.'

She looks down, cuts the pack, deals the first card into the pickup pile, moving mechanically all the while.

Suddenly I do not want to talk about this any more. I wish I had never asked the question. After all, I have my own secrets, my own subjects I do not want to discuss. What if Erin asks me about my past in return? What if she brings up Snoop again? About why I left? What if she asks about the friends I don't have, the schoolmates who bullied me for fourteen years, about the family I have cut myself off from?

I hear again my father's slurring voice, my mother's sobs . . . I taste blood. I am chewing my cuticles again. I stick my hands in the pockets of my jumpsuit.

But Erin does not ask about any of these things. She seems to be somewhere else completely, somewhere very far away. When she speaks, her voice has a strange quality to it. It is like a confession.

'It was my fault, you see,' she says. She picks up her cards. Her hands are trembling a little. 'I suggested we went off-piste skiing. I was the one who wanted to do it. I killed them.' She

285

swallows. 'That changes a person.'

She looks up at me, as if expecting me to understand. I have the most peculiar urge to take her hand, and tell her that I know how she feels.

But that would be crazy. So I don't. Instead I look down at my own cards. I pick up a three of hearts and discard a jack.

'Your move,' I say.

ERIN

Snoop ID: LITTLEMY
Listening to: offline
Snoopscribers: 10

I don't know what made me spill my past to Liz like that. It was the strangest thing. I've never talked to anyone about that time — not my parents, not Will's parents; even the coroner and the search and rescue team only wanted the bare facts, not to hear about my bewilderment and grief.

It's not that I didn't have the chance — my mother urged me to see a therapist, and I lost count of the number of friends who called me up, saying *if you need to talk, I'm only a phone call away.* But I didn't want to talk. I didn't want to be that person. An object of pity. A victim.

Because I know how Topher and the others must feel, in a way. For I felt it too. And that's the thing I have never told anyone — that in the minutes and hours I spent searching for Will and Alex after the avalanche, it wasn't terror or fear that was uppermost in my mind but a kind of shocked disbelief, that this had happened to *me*, to *us*. I was not this person. I was not the person terrible things happened to. That was other people, other families. I was golden, slipping

287

through life on a charm, insulated by the security of my family, my own good looks, and the luck of having found Will's love.

Because yes, that was luck. All of it. And I knew it. But it was also how it was supposed to be, because I was supposed to be *lucky*.

And now suddenly that luck had turned.

And after it did, I found that I couldn't stand to be there with the people still walking in that perpetual golden sun while I lived in a place that was black with guilt and grief. I couldn't stand to see the pity in their eyes.

It's almost completely dark in the living room now, and when I walk across to the clock over the mantelpiece, I see that it's getting on for 6 p.m. Danny and the others should have been at Haut Montagne about two hours ago. It's possible they could be starting back. It's possible they have managed to contact the police, and a chopper is on its way.

Possible. Not certain. Possible.

It's equally possible the road is trashed and they are still trudging across icy rubble, or Haut Montagne was empty and shut up.

God, the possibilities are going to send me mad.

I don't know why, but with Danny and the others gone, it feels like the atmosphere of the chalet is closing around me and Liz. I can feel the weight of the snow pressing against the roof and the walls, feel the tonnes and tonnes still resting on the mountainside, waiting for another trigger. I can feel the darkness seeping through the rooms and corridors.

I know what the edge of endurance feels like,

because I passed it once before — sitting frozen on a cold mountainside with the dead body of my lover, not knowing whether help was going to come. I passed it, and I survived. I came back. Back to safety. Back to normality.

But there are times when I feel myself being dragged back across that line into a place where nothing matters any more, where every heartbeat drags you closer to the edge, and I think I am going to fall into the abyss again, and this time I won't be able to claw my way out.

When I shut my eyes I can see his face, Will's face, cold and white as marble, and peaceful, so terribly peaceful.

'Erin.' The voice comes from very far away. I shake my head. *'Erin.'*

I open my eyes. Liz is standing in front of me, looking anxious.

'Erin, are you OK? Should we get something to eat?'

I force myself to smile.

'Yes. Sure. Come through to the kitchen and we'll see what we can find.'

I lead the way, limping, and Liz follows me into the chilly darkened cavern of the kitchen, looking around her wonderingly as we enter, as if it's an Aladdin's cave, rather than a very ordinary professional kitchen.

'There's a t-tin of cassoulet here,' I say, trying to read the label in the dim light. It's extremely cold away from the fire, and my teeth are trying to chatter. 'At least I think it's c-cassoulet, it could be confit du canard. It's hard to tell. Will that do?'

289

'Sure,' Liz says. She's still looking at me like she's concerned. 'Are you all right, Erin?'

'I'm fine, I just — I'm just worried about D-Danny. I keep hoping we'll hear something.'

Liz nods, and I realise she must be as worried as me, she's just hiding it better, under that calm, stolid exterior. I find myself wondering what she's thinking, and when the tin (it *was* cassoulet) is decanted into a pan and warming on top of the wood-burning stove in the living room, I pluck up my courage to ask her the question I've been pondering, but not quite daring to ask.

'Liz, what do you think happened? To Eva, I mean?'

Her face crumples and I realise, she is holding back the unthinkable just as hard as I am.

'I don't know. I've been thinking and thinking — I just — I can't believe any of it is true. It doesn't seem real. I keep wondering if Eva was just in an accident, but then what about Elliot and Ani?'

What indeed.

'What do you think Ani meant?' I say, stirring the beans slowly, feeling the heat of the fire at my face and the chill cold of the room at my back. 'When she said *she wasn't there.*' Or was it *I didn't see her?* I can't remember now, and that fact bothers me. I hear the rustle of waterproof fabric as Liz shrugs.

'I don't know. I keep going over and over it in my head. I thought at first she must have been talking about Eva, but it makes no sense. She was there, on the slope, I saw her too.'

'Could it have been someone at the top?' I'm struggling to remember the exact wording now. Fuck. This could be important and I can't remember. 'I'm wondering . . . when she got to the top of the bubble lift. Was someone already missing, someone other than Eva? Someone who had already skied after her?'

'But who?' Liz says. 'There weren't that many women left at the top. I'd already gone down in the bubble. The two women left at the top were Tiger — in which case it seems very odd that she would report what Ani said — and Miranda. But she had no opportunity to go after Eva. She went down in the bubble with Ani.'

'Maybe she didn't.' My heart is suddenly thumping. 'Maybe that's what Ani remembered. That Miranda *wasn't* in the lift. It's easy to get confused after all — there's a shuffle of bodies at the top, people heading for one telecabine, it's full, they go for another. Maybe that's what Ani realised, that Miranda never got on the lift?'

'What are you saying?' Liz looks uneasy. Her brows, behind the thick glasses, are knitted together and in the darkness I hear the *crack, crack, crack* of her knuckles as she nervously flexes her fingers.

'Maybe she's a better skier than she's letting on. It's quite easy to pretend to be worse than you are. Maybe she peeled off when everyone else was getting on the lift, and instead of going down in the bubble, she followed Eva down La Sorcière.'

'I . . . I guess . . . ' Liz says slowly. She looks troubled.

I'm ladling the cassoulet out into two bowls, when I realise something. If it's true, if what I'm guessing is correct, then I've sent Danny off with a killer. And my heart clutches like someone has put it in a vice.

Because yes, it's true, there are two of them and one of her. But the path to Haut Montagne passes along some pretty treacherous stretches. How hard would it be to wait until someone was close to the edge, and then give a little shove?

I have no proof of any of this, I remind myself desperately. It's just a theory. It's *just* a theory.

But my throat is constricted, and my stomach is closed and sick, and suddenly I can't face eating the fast-cooling mess of beans and meat in front of me. I feel ill with the force of what I may have done.

Because I told him to go. With my instinct to organise, my certainty that I know what's best for others, I *told* Danny to go out into the snow alone with Miranda and Carl.

Is it true?

Have I sent another friend to his death?

LIZ

Snoop ID: ANON101
Listening to: offline
Snoopscribers: 1

Erin hardly touches her supper. She has gone from being professional and friendly to something quite different in the space of about half an hour. I am at a loss to understand it. When I ask her about it she just mutters something about being worried about Danny but I am not sure if that is completely true.

I eat most of her portion as well as my own. Then I get up and grope my way through to the kitchen to rinse the bowls under the cold tap. There is no point in trying to wash up. We are past things like that. This is starting to feel like survival. But when I turn the tap nothing happens. I try the other. Still nothing.

When I get back into the living room, Erin is hunched over, staring into the fire. I sit beside her, gingerly flexing my knee, though it's feeling a lot better than it was.

'We've got a problem,' I say.

She looks up, as if startled at the sound of my voice.

'What? What did you say?'

'We've got a problem,' I repeat. 'The water

isn't working. I think the pipes have frozen.'

'Fuck.' She closes her eyes and rubs her face as if she is trying to wake herself from a nightmare, which I suppose in a way she is. 'Well, there's nothing we can do except sit tight. Danny and the others *must* be there by now. We just have to make it until morning. If we can manage that without freezing to death.'

Her words are unsettling, the more so because I realise that even with my snowsuit on, the chalet is almost unbearably cold now. My breath in the kitchen was a cloud of white. Upstairs must be sub-zero.

'Maybe . . . should we sleep down here?' I ask.

'I — I guess. Yes. I suppose it makes sense.'

'I'll go and get my bedding,' I say, making up my mind. Erin nods.

'I'll make the sofas up into beds. They fold out.'

I'm almost out of the room when she says:

'Liz?'

And I look back, expectantly, wondering what she's about to say.

'Yes?'

'Liz, I just wanted to say — thanks. Thanks for staying here with me. And I'm sorry it turned out like this.'

'It's OK,' I say, but somehow the words are hard to say. There is something in my throat — an unexpected kind of lump. 'It's OK. It's not your fault.'

And then I turn and hobble into the lobby and up the spiral stairs, before she can see the tears in my eyes.

ERIN

Snoop ID: LITTLEMY
Listening to: offline
Snoopscribers: 10

When Liz's footsteps disappear along the corridor, I slump back in my seat with a sigh, and run my hand over my face. *I'm sorry.* I don't know what possessed me to say that, except that out of everyone here, it's Liz I feel most sorry for. I'm not even sure why exactly — maybe because it was so plain, right from the start, that she never wanted to be here. Topher, Eva, however awful this weekend has turned out to be for both of them, they brought it on themselves in a way — choosing to come here, brandishing their money, pushing people around like little chess pieces in their battle for control of Snoop.

But Liz — Liz is just a pawn, like me, caught up in something she never asked for, never wanted.

And yet not once has she complained. Where Topher has grumbled about the crap food, and Carl has stamped and roared and threatened legal action, and Rik has blustered about health and safety and corporate responsibility, and Miranda has made accusations — Liz has just trudged on, putting up with it all, even though

295

under her self-effacing manner I'm sure she was as scared as anyone.

My ankle throbs as I force myself to standing, and I begin to move aside the sofa cushions, ready to pull out the mattress hidden inside the frame. But as I pick up the last cushion, I see something lying underneath it, right where Liz and I were sitting. It glitters in the firelight, and for a second I think it's a brooch or a piece of jewellery — but when I pick it up, I realise, it's a key. A very familiar one.

It's a staff key.

Automatically I feel in my pocket, assuming it must have slid out of my jeans when I sat down, but mine is still there, hard and reassuring against my backside.

Only . . . it's not reassuring at all.

Because if my key is in my pocket it means . . . oh God, it means . . . this is Danny's key.

Danny's key that was stolen.

The key that was taken by the killer.

I stand there for a very long time, completely frozen, just looking down at the key in the palm of my hand and trying to cudgel my brain into figuring this out. Somehow, someone got hold of this key — probably during the kerfuffle over getting entry to Tiger's room, after Inigo's disappearance. It's not hard to imagine someone slipping it surreptitiously out of the lock while we were all preoccupied with checking Tiger was OK. Whoever took it used it to gain entry to that same room in the middle of the night, and kill Ani. And then at some point after that, presumably this morning while we were all distracted by talking about the plan to ski down to the village, it slipped out of their pocket and fell between the sofa cushions.

The only question is who took it. Who was sitting on that space on the sofa this morning? Because I cannot for the life of me remember.

I shut my eyes, trying to picture the scene — Tiger lying on the sofa, sobbing, Miranda trying to comfort her, Rik handing out whiskeys . . . I need to place all the characters in the room, one by one, figure this out.

Danny and I were standing. I remember that clearly. Topher . . . Topher was leaning up against the mantelpiece. Miranda was kneeling on the floor by the coffee table. Liz was in one of the armchairs by the fire. Rik and Carl . . . they were on a sofa, but which one? I squeeze my eyes shut harder, and have a sudden vision of Rik leaning forward, filling up the whiskey glass at the far end of the table. It was the other sofa, the one beneath the window. Which means . . . I open my eyes.

It means Tiger was lying on the sofa where I found the key, her hip right on the point where the cushions join. It would make complete sense — the key could so easily have slid out of her pocket while she was lying there crying. Except . . . it makes no sense at all. Tiger is the only person who didn't need a key to kill Ani. She was already in the room. And if she wanted an alibi, she could have simply said she forgot to lock the door.

But no one else occupied that seat after the key went missing, apart from me . . .

. . . and Liz.

As if hypnotised, my gaze drifts upwards, to the ceiling, where on the floor above Liz is moving around her room, gathering up duvets and pillows. I can hear the faint creak of the floor joists, and then the sound of her door shutting.

I hear the shush, shush as she drags the duvet along the corridor.

Then I hear the halting noise of her feet on the spiral stairs, going carefully this time, she does not want to slip again.

Then she appears in the doorway of the living room, her hands full of bedcovers, her face unreadable in the dim light, the firelight flickering off her big, owl-like glasses, and with a funny little pang I remember that very first day, the way she reminded me of an owl, paralysed by the lights of an oncoming car.

She still looks like an owl, but suddenly the resemblance seems very different, and quite another kind of chill comes over me as I realise I was right all along — but so very, very wrong.

Because here is the thing. We think we know owls. They are the soft, friendly, blinking creatures of children's rhymes and stories. They may be wise, but they are also slow, and easily confused.

The problem is, none of that is true. Owls are not slow. They are fast — lightning fast. And they are not confused. In their own element — the dark — they are swift and merciless hunters.

Owls are raptors. Predators.

That was what I saw in Liz, right back on that very first day. I was just too blinded by my own preconceptions to recognise it.

In the dark, owls are not the hunted, but the hunter. And right now, it is dark.

'Hi,' Liz says, and she smiles, an unreadable smile behind those blank, flickering lenses. 'Are you all right?'

LIZ

Snoop ID: ANON101
Listening to: offline
Snoopscribers: 1

When I come back down, my arms full of duvets and pillows, Erin is standing stock-still in the middle of the room, one hand on the sofa-bed frame, as if a thought has just occurred to her.

'Hi,' I say. I throw the bedding into the armchair. Then, when she still doesn't move, I add, 'Are you all right?' I don't know why I say that, except that she looks really odd. 'Is the sofa bed stuck?'

'What?' She seems to shake herself. Then she gives a smile and a short laugh. 'No, sorry. Just thinking. I was — I was thinking about Danny. They must be there by now. I was wondering if we'd hear from them tonight'

I glance up at the clock on the mantelpiece. It is so dark now that the hands are almost unreadable, but I think I can make out that it's nearly eight o'clock.

'I guess you're right. How long did you say it would take to get there?'

'I thought about three hours. But given Miranda and Carl have never snowshoed before, it might take longer. Still, they left just after one.

Even allowing for rests and stuff, they ought to be at Haut Montagne easily by now. Maybe even on their way back, though I don't know if they'll snowshoe in the dark.'

She gives the metal frame a tug. The sofa bed unfurls with a screech.

'I hope you're right.' I move my pillows onto the mattress and then help Erin take the cushions off the other sofa and unfold the bed. 'Losing the water feels like the last straw.'

'We'll have to melt snow,' Erin says. Her face looks white and strained in the dim light, but it's not surprising really. 'I can't believe it's only been two days since the avalanche. It feels like forever.'

'Two days?' For a second I don't believe her, and then I count up in my head, and I realise she's right. Two days and four hours. It feels like a lifetime ago. It *does* feel like we've been trapped here forever. And now it is almost over. The strange thing is, I am not sure I'm ready to face reality again. It is just dawning on me that what felt like captivity might actually be a kind of idyllic tranquillity. Perce-Neige is a crime scene. And we are suspects. When we get back to the real world, we are going to have to face the full glare of publicity. There will be a police investigation, reporters, news stories. Interviews. I can see the headlines now: CHALET OF DEATH.

All sorts of things are going to come out of the woodwork.

Now it is my turn to stand, stock-still, staring into the darkness, thinking.

301

'I'll go and get my bedding,' Erin says, into the silence. 'Can you put another log in the stove?'

'Sure,' I say, shaking myself back to the here and now. I watch her as she picks up a torch and passes through into the lobby, the thin beam spiralling around as she makes her way up the stairs, her hand going *click, click, click* on the bannister as something hard, a ring perhaps, strikes against the metal.

Click. Click. Click.

I hear again my mother's breathless, nervous *oh, Liz, you know Daddy doesn't like that . . .*

Tick. Tick. Tick. Disappearing into the darkness.

Perhaps it is the thought of the police, and everything that is going to come crashing down, but suddenly, I don't know why, it sounds like a clock, ticking down to zero.

ERIN

My heart is hammering as I walk along the corridor to the staff section, and let myself into my bedroom. The room is totally dark, lit only by the narrow beam of the torch, but I don't want to risk the batteries giving way so I switch it off, and in the darkness I sink down onto my bed. I need to *think*.

My fist is clenched around the key, hard against my palm, like a physical reminder of the craziness of this situation, and now as I sit there, trying desperately to make myself understand this conundrum, I find that I'm holding it so hard that it's biting into my fingers, leaving dents I can still feel when I force my hand open.

What does it mean? What does it *mean*?

If Liz took that key . . . is she the killer? But *how*?

I cast my mind back, reliving the scrum in the corridor when Danny broke into Tiger's room. Liz was there, I'm certain. But I remember that while everyone else surged forward into the room, she hung back. I thought at the time it was because of her natural reserve — it seemed so in

303

character, compared to the way everyone else thrust themselves forwards, pushing to see what was going on. But now I wonder. Was she hanging back so that she could pocket the key, unobserved?

But *why*, that's what I can't understand. Liz cannot have killed Eva. Motive aside, she's one of the few people, along with Ani and Carl, who had no opportunity at all. She was stuck on the bubble lift going back down to the bottom of Blanche-Neige, when Eva was seen skiing La Sorcière.

But the key. The key that is hard and jagged and incontrovertible in my hand, as if refusing to allow me to forget its evidence.

What about the key?

I rub my hand over my face, feeling the shiny scar tissue, the ever-present reminder of what I did, the price I paid for being too sure of myself, and I'm suddenly aware that I have been sitting here for — I'm not sure how long, but a long time. Too long. Suspiciously long. I have to get back downstairs, or Liz will know something is wrong.

I switch the torch back on and gather up an armful of duvets, and then, holding the torch in my teeth, balanced on top of the stack of pillows, I open the door with my free hand.

Liz is standing right outside, almost nose-to-nose with me, the torchlight reflecting off her glasses.

I scream, and the torch bounces off the pillows and falls to the floor with a thump, where it goes out.

My heart is hammering in my chest like a pneumatic drill.

'Jesus,' I manage, my voice shaking. 'Liz, you scared me.'

I set the duvets down with trembling hands, and grope for the torch.

'Sorry,' she says. It sounds like she's smiling, but I can't be sure in the darkness. There is something so flat about her voice, so hard to read. 'You took so long. I got worried.'

'I — ' Oh fuck, what can I say? What excuse can I give? 'I was just changing my top.'

What? Why on *earth* did I say this? She'll be able to see I'm wearing the same clothes I was before. What a *stupid* lie.

I feel sick with nerves. I am a terrible liar. Even at school I could never do the two-faced 'oh, you look so lovely! I look like trash!' thing that the other girls did. The only time I can dissemble is when I'm in staff mode. Then I'm polite and cheerful to everyone, no matter how I really feel — not because I like them, but because they are guests, and I'm staff, and that's my job.

The thought calms me.

It's my job. I can do this. Liz is a guest, and it's my job to be sympathetic to her. I just have to channel that thought.

I switch on the torch, and I make myself smile.

'Shall we head down? It's really cold up here.'

And Liz nods, and turns for the stairs.

LIZ

Snoop ID: ANON101
Listening to: offline
Snoopscribers: 1

There is something wrong with Erin. I am not sure what. She said she was worried about Danny, but if that's the case, I don't know why her fears came on so suddenly. She was quite cheerful until about two hours ago. Then she got nervous and edgy.

We have been lying in the darkness for perhaps an hour or more, but she is not asleep. It's not just that she's not snoring — out of the corner of my gaze I can see her eyes are still open, reflecting the light from the fire's embers as she blinks. She is lying there in the darkness, silently watching me. She is thinking about something. But I do not know what.

What is she thinking?

I squeeze my eyes shut, trying to look as normal as possible.

A few minutes later I hear the creak of the mattress springs. Erin is cautiously swinging her legs out of bed.

'Where are you going?' I ask.

She jumps like a criminal caught in the middle of something, and puts her hand to her heart.

'God! Liz, you scared me.'

'Sorry.' I don't say anything else. From my experience, if you keep quiet, people get nervous. They talk. They fill the silence with their own conversation. You can find out a lot that way. Sure enough, after a pause, Erin answers my question without me having to restate it.

'I didn't mean to wake you. I couldn't sleep. I'm going to the t-toilet.' She is shivering. I can hear her teeth beginning to chatter. It is very, very cold in the room now. The fire has died down to glowing ash.

'OK.' I roll over, pulling the covers up to my chin. 'Don't forget the pipes are frozen.'

'I kn-now.' She opens the stove to put in another log. 'I'll use one of the upstairs bathrooms. I think we've flushed both the d-downstairs loos already.'

I don't say anything. I just watch her as she wraps her coat more tightly around her, and then pads up the stairs. Then I turn over and feel in my pocket for the key.

It is gone.

ERIN

Snoop ID: LITTLEMY
Listening to: offline
Snoopscribers: 10

Bloody hell. My heart is pounding as I tiptoe up the staircase. I don't know where that lie about the toilets came from, but I've never been so thankful for frozen pipes. They have given me exactly what I needed — an excuse to go upstairs.

I have no idea what the truth is about the key. *Did* Liz take it? I don't dare to ask. Maybe someone else sat on that sofa when I wasn't around. Or maybe Liz found the key and picked it up, but has been too scared to tell anyone in case they suspected her. There could be a dozen innocent explanations. Or there could be one, very damning one.

Either way, I could not lie there in the darkness listening to her soft, regular breathing a second more. I had to *do* something. And at last my subconscious overrode my racing thoughts to prod me about something I had totally forgotten.

Elliot's charging block. The giant external battery he was using to power his laptop, before he died and his computer was destroyed. If I can get to that battery and plug my dead phone in, maybe I can get a sliver of connection. It's worth a try. It's also not something Liz could possibly object to. And yet, for reasons I can't face examining, I don't want to tell her.

Why not? my brain whispers as I tiptoe along the corridor, in time with my steps. *Why not?*

Because I don't trust her.

Why not?

Because . . . I swallow, hearing the dry click of my jaw in the eerie silence. Because in my heart of hearts, I do think she could have killed Eva. I don't know *how*, but my fear over these last two hours has shown me something I would not have believed before tonight: I do think Liz has it in her to kill. It's not just the key — though that is concerning enough. The panic I felt when I opened the door of my room and saw her standing there, smiling blankly at me, her face hidden behind those silvery lenses — there was something deep and true and real about that panic. It told me something I had not admitted to myself before: I am afraid of Liz. She may be meek and quiet and almost painfully reserved, but behind that meekness, I believe there is steel, and yes, I think she could kill someone. I believe that in a way that I never believed it of Inigo, or even Topher, despite all the evidence piled up against him.

Out of everyone here, I believe Liz could kill in cold blood, and conceal that fact from us all. No one pays attention to her. And for a killer, that's a kind of superpower.

I am almost at Elliot's door. I am walking as silently as I can now, remembering the way Liz's steps along the corridor were audible in the room below. I take the pass keys out of my pocket, and choosing one, I insert it gently into the lock, turn it, and open Elliot's door, very, very quietly.

It creaks, just a little bit, and I hold my breath, hoping Liz didn't hear. But there is no sound from below. If she came up, I would have no excuse for being down this end of the building. The natural thing would be for me to use the staff bathroom, up the far end. Or, if I couldn't be bothered to walk that far, to access one of the guest bedrooms closer to the stairs. Not Elliot's. Not a room with a —

The smell hits me as I open the door. It's a smell I remember from the teaching hospital.

There is a dead body in this room — beneath the reek of urine and the incongruously homely smell of spilled coffee, it smells of death. Not badly, the room is too cold for that, but unmistakably. A fetid, animal kind of smell.

There is no way you would choose to use this room for anything, if you had another option.

The smell makes me gag, but I push the urge down, and edge across the room to the far side of Elliot's desk. And there it is — sitting like a breeze block on the floor, a single red LED piercing the gloom. My heart gives a thump of relief. And almost at the same time I notice two things. The first is that a phone is plugged into the charging block, and it's switched on, and fully charged. Elliot left his phone charging. Of *course* he did.

But the second thing I see is that he has an

android, and mine is an iPhone. My phone is in my pocket, but I can't use his charger.

I want to kick myself. I should have collected my own charger first — that was incredibly stupid of me. Do I have time? Ordinarily it would take me less than a minute to run to the other end of the corridor, slam through the staff doors, and grab my charger from beside my bed. But now, I can't run. I can't slam through the doors. I can't afford to make a sound.

I make up my mind. I will try Elliot's phone first. You can dial some emergency numbers from the lock screen — I just have no idea whether 112 or 17 are among them.

I pick it up and the screen jumps into life, but with a lurch of disappointment I see there is still no reception — just an x by the greyed-out scale. I can't call anyone.

Still, there are a bunch of app notifications on the lock screen, and it's with a flicker of hope that I scroll down them, trying to figure out if the phone has connected at all during the past twenty-four hours. If it's getting even tiny blips of reception, that might be enough. If I can get into the phone I could send a text, which would just sit there in the outbox until the phone connected. I wouldn't have to do anything. Just wait for it to send.

And there it is. A WhatsApp from six hours ago. And below that, a notification from Snoop. *Anon101 is geoclose*, whatever that means. Geoclose? I've never had a notification like that on my Snoop account.

I have no time to worry about that now,

though. The question is how I get into the phone. I have three tries before it locks out, and then I'll have no choice but to go back and get my charger, and wait while my own phone powers up, which will take long enough to make Liz wonder where I am.

I'm racking my brains, trying to remember if Kate ever told me Elliot's date of birth, and if so whether to try the year, or the day and month, but when I bring up the lock screen, I come up short. It's not a pin pad, it's a thumb scanner.

My stomach drops with disappointment, but then I realise what this means, and I experience a different kind of lurch, this one of nauseated horror, as it dawns on me what I have to do next. Oh God. Can I do it? And if I can, what kind of person does that make me?

I glance across at the desk. I force myself to look at the shape I have been trying to ignore, let my eyes skitter across: Elliot. Elliot's body.

His hand is stretched out across the desk, and I feel my cheeks go hot and then cold and then hot again with a kind of deep piercing shame at what I am about to do. But I *have* to get inside that phone.

I stand up. I unplug the phone from the block, and I take a step across the room, closer to where Elliot is sprawled. And then another. And then I am standing by his desk, reaching for his hand — his cold, firm hand.

It is a little clammy, though that is mostly due to how cold the room is, and his arm is surprisingly heavy to manoeuvre, but the rigor has worn off, and it is without too much difficulty that I unfurl his fingers, and hold his long, bony thumb between mine, chill and firm as a joint of meat.

'I'm sorry,' I whisper to him. 'I'm so, so sorry.'

And then I press the tip against the lock screen.

For a minute nothing happens and I feel a piercing, shooting sense of disappointment. Can the phone somehow tell? Does it work off body warmth? Does it know that this is a dead man, not a living owner?

There is only one way to find out. Feeling even sicker, I put down the phone and rub the cold, clammy tip of Elliot's thumb between my palms, chafing it roughly, trying to get a little of my own body heat into Elliot's skin.

It's surprisingly hard. My hands are cold too, and for a long time, all I can feel is the bone-deep chill of dead flesh against mine. But I persist, huffing on his thumb to try and warm him with my breath, and at last there does seem to be some perceptible difference in temperature. Before it can dissipate, I pick up the phone and press it quickly against the tip, holding my breath.

And then the display lights up, with the hot pink of the Snoop app's home screen. And I'm inside Elliot's phone.

I'm about to minimise Snoop and navigate to the text message app, when I stop. There is something really odd about Elliot's Snoop app.

He is being followed by 1.2 million people. Which is not that surprising, I guess. He's known to be one of the co-founders of the company, and his Snoop ID is public.

But the weird thing is that he's following only two people. One of them is Topher — I remember his avatar and ID from when I followed him myself — Xtopher and a photo of him balancing a spoon on his nose, with a little tick to show he's verified. *Snooping Xtopher for 3 years*, says the text beside his name. That's not the weird part.

The weird part is that the other person he's subscribed to is a totally anonymous user, Anon101. Anon has no picture, and when I click on the blank space where their avatar would have been, to take me through to their profile, there is nothing in their bio either. *Go away* is the only line they've put in the *about* field, which maybe explains why they have only one follower. That's it.

But under *location*, there *is* an entry. A string of GPS coordinates and a tiny logo saying 'beta' in brackets.

This must be the update Elliot was working on before he died — the geosnooping update that he and Topher were so excited about, the one that let them locate Eva. But who *is* Anon101 and why is Elliot following them? Is Anon Eva? But, no, that's ridiculous, not with one follower. And besides, I've snooped Eva. I can't remember what her ID was, but I remember her avatar — a snow leopard wearing Ray-Bans.

I click back to the previous screen.

Snooping Anon101 for 2 days, says the text beside their name.

Elliot followed Anon101 right before he died.

My stomach is fluttering now, and my thumb hovers above the geosnoop (beta) tab at the top of the menu. I remember that notification on the home screen now — the notification that I swiped aside so carelessly. *Anon101 is geoclose.*

I press the geosnoop tab.

In your area: says the text at the top of the menu. And then, underneath, there is a list of just two people:

Littlemy

Anon101

I am Littlemy. Which means . . . Anon101 must be . . . Liz.

LIZ

Snoop ID: ANON101
Listening to: offline
Snoopscribers: 1

There is something wrong. Erin has not come back from her trip to the toilet. She has been gone a long time, but more than that, I can't hear anything at all. No doors opening. No footsteps on the stairs. No sound of water flushing. Has something happened? Has she fallen asleep?

I lie there chewing my lip, trying to work out what to do. I went after her last time. I was worried when she took so long over changing her top, but now I am not sure if that was a good idea. The panic on her face when she opened the bedroom door and saw me standing there, just about to knock, made me think I had made a mistake. And now I wonder, is that when her manner changed? Maybe she is frightened of me. Perhaps she thinks I'm a stalker.

People have a habit of pulling away from me. It is something I have noticed over the years. It started with the girls at school — they would be friendly at first, and I'd try to make overtures back, and then they would start to cool, for reasons I could never put my finger on. So I would try harder. Make more effort. But the more I tried, the more they seemed to grow cold, until at last everything I did just seemed to make them hate me more.

At primary school, the other girls weren't subtle about it. *Go away, Liz, you're so weird.* I heard it again and again. As we got older, the girls in my class pretended to be kinder, but underneath they were thinking the same things, beneath their 'oh, so sorry, we're saving this seat' or 'my mum says I can only have three girls to the sleepover, really sorry, Liz'.

The girls were bad. The boys were worse. The worst of all was Kevin.

Even his name makes me shudder.

I *liked* Kevin. I thought that he might like me too. He had acne and his breath was a little stale, and he wasn't particularly handsome. He didn't seem as unattainable as some of the other boys. I got a book out of the library on how to make boys like you, but it was confusing and contradictory. *Laugh at his jokes*, it said. So I did. But then Kevin would look at me as if I were crazy and say, 'What are you laughing at?'

Give him something to remind him of you. I gave him a pair of mittens I had knitted. I left them in his locker, but he never wore them. Later I found them in lost property.

Engineer chance meetings. I followed him around. I made sure that I was there, leaning against the lockers when he came out of the boys' toilets. I waited by his bus stop. One day I followed him home.

It was November and almost dusk. I didn't

think he had noticed me, but he had. We had walked nearly two miles when he turned on me. 'What do you want, you fucking weirdo?' he said, his voice cracking and breaking on the last word. Only he didn't say it. He came right up into my face and screamed it. I could smell his stale breath, and feel his spit hitting me as he shouted.

It was dark. Rain had begun to fall. We were in a lonely part of the park. A small part of me wanted to kill him. But I didn't. Instead I cowered away from him, cringing from his anger, and then, when he pushed me and yelled, 'Are you fucking desperate or what?' I ran. I was crying and shaking.

By the time I was hired at Snoop, I had learned my lesson. I kept myself to myself. I didn't try to make friends. I didn't trust anyone.

But Erin . . . somehow Erin seemed different. She was so friendly when we first arrived. I remember her sympathy when I asked her advice about the dress code, her kindness as she towed me to the ski lift that first day. She really seemed to like me. Now I am not so sure. What if she was pretending all along?

I want to go up there and ask her what she thinks of me, whether she is scared of me, what she is *doing* up there in the dark. But I don't know how she would feel about that. Maybe I could say I was worried about her? After all, three people have died. It's what a good friend would do. Look out for her. Check she was OK.

But would she see it that way? Would she *know* I was just being a good friend? Or would she give me that look again — that panicked,

318

terrified look that I saw in Kevin's eyes when he turned on me? The one I saw in Erin's eyes when she opened the door last time. The look that says *you weirdo*. The look that says *I'm scared*.

I am still dithering ten minutes later. At last I can't take the silence any more. I *have* to know what she is doing.

I swing my legs out of bed and stand up. I'm still wearing my ski suit, so I'm not that cold. My knee still hurts but I can put my weight on it now. Really I am very glad not to be snowshoeing to the other chalet. I mean, I would never have fallen down the stairs deliberately, that would be a really stupid idea, I could have been killed. But it worked out well.

Still, I go carefully on the stairs, holding the handrail. The wood is slippy beneath my socks, the treads themselves are hard to see in the darkness, and I definitely don't want another fall.

At the top of the stairs I pause, holding my breath, trying to listen. *Where* is she? In the staff quarters? I'm just about to turn left, to see if she's down that end of the corridor, when I hear a noise. It's a very slight one, but it is coming from the opposite direction — from the direction of the corridor that holds Miranda's, Elliot's and my room. What would she be doing down there?

But before I can find out, I hear another noise from the same direction — this time unmistakable. It's the sound of a toilet flushing. The door to Miranda's room opens, and Erin comes out. She doesn't look that surprised to see me this time, instead she just smiles.

'Hi, Liz.' Her voice is slightly breathless. 'Sorry, were you worried?'

'A bit.' I frown at her. 'What were you doing in Miranda's room?'

'I already flushed the staff toilet. I didn't think Miranda would mind, and it was the closest. Um, Liz, fair warning — ' It's hard to tell in the darkness, but it looks like her face is a bit flushed. 'Sorry, this is TMI, but I had a bit of an upset stomach. I think maybe the cassoulet wasn't heated through properly. That's why I — well, that's why it took me a bit longer.'

'Oh!' I'm not sure what to say to that. Should I laugh? No, that would seem strange. I arrange my features into what I hope is a sympathetic smile. Then I worry that it might just look like a smile, so I frown instead. 'Oh, gosh, poor you.'

'I realise you probably didn't want to know that, but I thought I should warn you in case — well, I mean, we had the same supper — '

'Oh, I've been fine,' I say hastily. It's the truth. I haven't had so much as a twinge. But then I've always had a really good digestion.

'Oh, good,' she says. There's relief in her face. 'I'd hate to have given you food poisoning on top of everything else.' She gives a shaky laugh, and then says, 'Well, shall we?'

For a minute, I'm not sure what she's referring to, but then she nods at the stairs, and I understand what she's saying.

'Sure,' I say. But then something stops me. 'Actually, you head down. I need the toilet as well.'

She nods, and begins to limp her way down

the spiral staircase. I watch her go for a moment, and then I head down the corridor towards my own room. I unlock the door and slip inside, and go over to the built-in closet in the corner of my room. The door is ajar, which is how I left it. But, is it my imagination, or is it very slightly wider than it was before?

I stand stock-still for a long moment, looking at the door. It's cracked open maybe two inches. It looks like a lot. It looks like a wider gap than before. But I can't be sure.

Making up my mind, I open the door and pull out my suitcase, and then I unzip the lining. Inside, pressed flat against the base of the suitcase, behind the silky lining and a piece of card, should be a scarlet ski jacket. It's too dark to really see, and I left my torch downstairs, but when I poke my fingers through the narrow gap, I can feel it is there — its downy softness reassuring. I let out a sigh of relief and sit back on my heels.

Then I zip up the lining and replace the case inside the cupboard, and I stand painfully, and go through to the bathroom. I might as well make my story convincing while I'm here.

But it's only when I'm halfway through peeling off my ski suit that something strikes me, something that stops me in my tracks.

That suitcase was on top of the stack, on *top* of my little wheelie cabin bag.

I left it the other way around. I am absolutely certain of it.

Someone has been inside my closet.

Erin? Or someone else?

My heart is thumping.

Slowly, very slowly, I pull up the zip of my jumpsuit, thinking hard, trying to figure out what to do.

Then I flush the toilet and walk back downstairs to try to figure out how much Erin knows.

ERIN

Snoop ID: LITTLEMY
Listening to: offline
Snoopscribers: 10

From up above I hear Liz's toilet flush, and I hunker down underneath the duvet, hoping I can pretend to be asleep when she comes back. My mind is racing, trying to figure out what can possibly have happened.

Thank God I heard her coming up the stairs and was able to leave Elliot's room and nip two doors down to Miranda's. If she had found me coming out of Elliot's, I would have had to come clean. And the truth is, I am much too scared to do that.

What the hell does it all mean? Is Liz the killer? But *how?* Never mind motive, she has a cast-iron alibi. She was on the bubble lift going down the valley when Eva was killed.

Except . . .

Except no one actually *saw* her get on the lift.

I try to think back to that final run down the mountain as everyone described it. Eva was coming up in the Reine bubble lift. Carl had fallen over at the bottom, trying to get on, and Ani was helping him. Everyone else standing at the top of the blue run, Blanche-Neige, huddled in the screaming wind, waiting for Eva, Carl and Ani to arrive.

Then came Liz's refusal to ski, and Topher's bullying attempt to force her to do it.

Everyone agreed what happened next — Liz tore off her skis and walked back up the slope to the lift, to get on the bubble back down to the chalet.

But, what if she hadn't? What if she had gone through the little shack housing the lift, and straight out the other side, towards the black run, La Sorcière. Then, at the top of the run, right by the steepest part of the piste, she stood and waited.

I try to imagine how Liz could have lured Eva across. Maybe she pretended she had slid helplessly down the black run, towards the sheer drop. Maybe she faked a problem with her boot or her ski. Either way, she must have called to Eva, and then, when Eva was very close to her, and off guard, she pushed her off the precipice.

That would have been the riskiest part. Not the risk of being seen — the visibility was too bad for that, and the lift building would have been between them and the skiers standing on Blanche-Neige. But the risk of failing to push Eva over the edge. If Eva had managed to save herself, or worse, if she had grabbed hold of her attacker and taken her over the edge as well, everything would have been finished. But it worked. It must have done. And now Liz just had to give herself an alibi — by ensuring that Eva was seen to be safe and well *after* Liz was supposed to have gone back down in the lift.

I remember that huge, bulky ski suit, the way Liz was sweating, just standing around at the base of the lift. I even remember thinking that she was clearly wearing far too many layers, and wondering why, on such a nice day. Now I *know* why. It wasn't inexperience at all. It was planned.

It would not have been very hard to have a second ski jacket on, underneath the first. It would have taken seconds to unzip the baggy blue jumpsuit, take off the scarlet ski jacket beneath, and put it on over the top. With her helmet, goggles and dark-coloured ski pants, anyone seeing her at a distance would take it for granted that she was Eva.

And so she set off to ski La Sorcière, stopping just to make sure that one person at least — faithful little Ani, far above her in the bubble lift — would be able to back up her story.

I think of Ani's last words to Tiger, her puzzled *I didn't see her.*

We all thought she was talking about Eva.

But what if . . . what if she were talking about Liz? Liz, who was supposed to be on the bubble going down the mountain, at the same time Ani was coming up. What if *that* was what Ani realised, that Liz never passed them going back down? That she never took the lift at all?

It is plausible. It is all horribly plausible. And it would very likely have worked if it weren't for one thing. Elliot's geosnooping app, covertly gathering data on everyone in the party.

Because Elliot wasn't stupid. As soon as he figured out that Eva had died, he would have looked at the movements of everyone else on the mountain that day. He would have known that the person who skied La Sorcière was not Eva, but Anon101. Only even with all the info at his disposal, he could not be certain who Anon101 was.

So he followed Anon on Snoop. And he set about figuring it out by process of elimination. But he was killed before he could share his suspicions with Topher.

This theory explains almost everything. It explains why Elliot had to die, why his computer, with all the geosnooping data, was smashed up. It explains why Ani was killed.

There's only one thing it doesn't explain. *Why.*

Why Eva was killed in the first place.

Because Liz still doesn't have a motive.

Still, I remember Danny's words. *I dunno. We could probably give them all motives if we needed to.*

He's right. Alibi is the key, not motive. And I have just smashed Liz's alibi to pieces. There is just one problem — if I'm right, that fact puts me next in line to be killed.

I am alone in an isolated chalet with a murderer, and there's nothing I can do.

LIZ

Snoop ID: ANON101
Listening to: offline
Snoopscribers: 1

Who moved my suitcase?

The question gnaws at me like a rat as I walk slowly back downstairs. When I enter the living room I can see Erin is huddled under the duvet. Her eyes are closed, and she's breathing softly and rhythmically. But it seems to me — and I can't tell if I'm being paranoid here — that there is something a little fake about the way she is lying. Does anyone really look that composed in sleep?

'Erin,' I whisper very softly. She stirs, her eyelids flickering momentarily, but she doesn't appear to wake.

I sit on the sofa bed beside her, and try to think.

I *am* completely sure about the suitcase. At least I think I am. But I have not looked in that cupboard since Sunday. Anyone could have moved my case. Even if they moved it, that doesn't mean they looked inside the lining. It could have been Elliot — gathering information before he took his suspicions to Topher. It could even have been something completely innocent.

I could kill Erin. That is not the issue. I could put a pillow over her face, just like I did with Ani, but here is the problem: if I kill Erin, everyone will know it was me. There is no one here for miles around. I would have no hope of persuading anyone that an unknown intruder broke in and smothered her in her sleep.

I killed Elliot and Ani because I had to. I acted quickly, on the spur of the moment, working with what I had to hand. With Elliot, that was Eva's sleeping pills, crushed into a cup of black coffee. He never suspected a thing when I offered him a refill. I guess that's all I ever was to him: someone to fetch the coffee.

For Ani, it was her own pillow, pressed over her nose and mouth. She died quietly, her struggles muffled by the thick duvet wrapped around her. I felt . . . well, I would like to say that I felt guilty for them both, but the truth is, I didn't really. Elliot brought it on himself, with his snooping and his prying. I did feel sorry for Ani. But she was in the wrong place at the wrong time. What I saw in her eyes when she stood, frozen in my doorway that night, was the sudden realisation of what she had seen. What she had *not* seen. The empty glass spheres of the bubble lift, returning back down to the station, when one of them should have contained me.

She realised what it meant. I could tell that straight away, from the moment our eyes locked and hers filled with sudden fear. She hurried back to her room, locking the door behind her. She probably felt safe. She didn't know I had a pass key.

But I don't feel guilty, even about Ani, because it's not my fault, any of this. *I* was in the wrong place at the wrong time too. I never asked for any of this. I was caught up in something I couldn't help, caught up in Topher and Eva's own personal game of thrones — not even one of the major players, just a pawn for Eva to play against Topher when the time was right, my own past leveraged against me.

Because here's the thing — I am a *good* person. I never wanted any of this. I certainly don't want to kill anyone if I don't have to. If Erin didn't look inside that case, if she hasn't figured this out, well, I don't want to hurt her.

I don't need to act quickly. I have time to think about this. There is no way help can get here before morning. I can take my time to work out if she knows something, and if so, what I can do about it. It would have to be an accident, or look like an accident. Another slip on the stairs, maybe? A carbon monoxide leak with the stove? Though I am not sure how I would engineer that.

Slowly, I take off my glasses and lie down, but I don't shut my eyes. I lie there, facing Erin, watching her. Watching her sleep.

ERIN

Snoop ID: LITTLEMY
Listening to: offline
Snoopscribers: 10

Liz is watching me. I don't dare to open my eyes more than a sliver, but under cover of tossing in my sleep I move my head a little, letting my eyelids flicker, and I can see her, lying there, staring unblinkingly into the darkness.

With her glasses off she looks quite different. The owlish, impenetrable look is gone, and she looks younger, but at the same time there is something even more unsettling about her blank, unwavering stare. When I close my eyes and settle back down with a little fake snore, I can sense her gaze boring into me.

I feel light-headed with fear. What am I going to do?

I try to force myself to breathe slowly — to think this through clearly. Am I in danger? Immediate danger? I don't know. If I am right, Liz has killed three people — but I don't think she is killing for fun. I still have no idea why Eva had to die, but Ani and Elliot were only killed when they had concrete information about Liz's guilt. If I can keep my suspicions under wraps until morning, I may be OK.

330

I squeeze my eyes shut, and I think about Elliot's phone, plugged back into the battery upstairs, with the text message I sent to Danny in the outbox, waiting for a thread of connection. *SOS, please send help. IT'S LIZ.* A message I composed with trembling fingers, trying to walk the fine line between a message Danny would understand, a message that would act as a clue if something happens to me before morning, and a message that I could plausibly explain away if Liz somehow stumbles upon it.

I don't *think* she has access to Elliot's phone. But I don't know. That's the problem, I don't know anything. She was doing something up there when she claimed to be going to the toilet. She spent much too long in her room, and I could hear her pacing around, opening and closing doors. She walked into the loo and immediately flushed it, without even closing the door as far as I could tell, let alone sitting on the toilet.

She knows something. She suspects *something*. I just don't know what. All I know is that Ani was killed in her sleep, and so I don't dare to let myself drift off.

LIZ

Snoop ID: ANON101
Listening to: offline
Snoopscribers: 1

Erin knows.

I was not sure at first, but as the time stretches out into what feels increasingly like an endless night, I am sure of it.

Because in spite of what I first assumed, she is *not* asleep. She is pretending to be asleep, but she is not. She is lying there with her eyes closed, and every now and again, when she thinks I am not watching, she opens her eyes just the smallest slit, to check if I am still awake. I see the glint of moonlight between her lashes, and then she squeezes them shut again and does a little fake snore.

It's so unfair. *God* it's so unfair!

I never asked for this. I never wanted any of it. I just wanted to be left *alone*.

It is all I've ever wanted. It's all I wanted from the girls at school, with their bitching and their teasing and their prying.

It's all I wanted at uni, with people badgering me to join up to clubs and attend freshers' formals.

It's all I wanted at Snoop. And at first they did

— they left me alone, and you know what? It was fine!

And then it wasn't. It all unravelled. And that's why I hate them so much.

I hate Topher for dragging me into this, for saddling me with these shares like a millstone around my neck.

I hate Eva for meddling and meddling and meddling when she should have left well enough alone. I hated her 'are you OK?' and 'is there anything I can do?' and 'we'll make this right, Liz, I swear'.

I hate Elliot for poking and prying and being too clever by half.

I hate Rik for just — for just being one of *them*. So entitled. So slick. Swimming with sharks and never getting hurt because he's one of *them*. Because he's a man, and a public-school boy, and so very, very charming.

And now I hate Erin too.

Lying there, with her fake little snores, and her half-smile, when all the time she has been putting two and two together . . .

Only it is too late. What can I do? If only I had been sure of this earlier — I still have eight of Eva's sleeping tablets in my pocket. It would have been possible — not easy, but possible — to slip them into the cassoulet. I could have swapped our plates when Erin wasn't looking. Now it is too late. Though perhaps that has already occurred to her. Perhaps that was what she was really doing in the toilet, when she took so long and came up with that transparent food poisoning story. Perhaps she was making herself sick.

Could I stage a break-in? Perhaps I could pretend that Inigo came back for us? It could work — but not if Inigo himself has an alibi. And the problem is that if Inigo *does* have an alibi and if Erin *doesn't* suspect me, then I would be exposing myself for no reason. I would be shooting myself in the foot.

I have to be very, very careful. I cannot afford a mistake.

But I have to know. I have to know what she knows.

'Erin,' I whisper very quietly. There is complete silence, but it is not quite the silence of someone fully asleep. It is more like the silence of someone thinking it over.

At last there is a sigh, and Erin says, 'Yes?'

'You're still awake?'

'I can't sleep. I keep thinking about the others, wondering where they are.'

It could be true. But then I think about that little slit of her eye, glinting at me in the dark. I don't think it is. I don't think that is what is keeping her awake. I play along.

'Are you worried about Danny?'

There is another long pause. I think she is trying to work out what to say. She is trying to figure out whether she needs to pretend to suspect someone else.

'A bit,' she says at last. 'I hoped he'd come back tonight, you know?'

I am about to say something else, I'm not sure what, something meaningless about being sure Danny is OK.

Only then, in the silence as I formulate my

334

words, there is a double beep. Very faint, and coming from upstairs, but completely unmistakable.

It is a sound that sets my pulse racing even before I have pinned down what it is.

It is the sound of a text message coming through.

ERIN

Snoop ID: LITTLEMY
Listening to: offline
Snoopscribers: 10

I can tell at once that Liz has heard. Her whole body goes stiff and alert and she pushes herself up on her elbow, listening intently.

Fuck.

'What was that?' she says.

My heart is racing. I know bloody well what it was. It was Danny replying to Elliot's text message. It must be. Elliot's is the only phone in the house that still has any charge left on it. There must have been a blip of reception — the same sliver that allowed the notification from Snoop to come through.

But I keep my face carefully neutral.

'I have no idea — it sounded like a phone, don't you think? But that can't be right.'

Liz is staring at me, like she's trying to figure out what's going on behind my face. Oh my God, she *knows*. She definitely knows. She just isn't sure enough to act on her suspicions. I have to be very, very careful.

'It sounded like it was coming from upstairs,' Liz says. She grabs her glasses and swings one leg out of bed.

'Yeah . . . ' I say it slowly, my mind racing. At all costs, I can't let her get into Elliot's room. If she sees that message, I am in big trouble. She already suspects me. It would be very hard to explain that message away. 'Yeah, it did.'

Could she kill me? I don't know. Her knee is as screwed as my ankle. Could she out-hobble me if it came to trying to get away? I am trying to think of a plan. Could I lure her outside somehow? Lock the door? But then I think of Danny's words, about Inigo turning up, begging to be let in, and I know he was right. I could never stand there and watch another human being freeze to death inches away, only a pane of glass separating us. I just couldn't. Not even Liz.

But I can't let her find that text message.

My mind is racing, trying to remember what I could see on Elliot's lock screen before I cleared it. Some people have their text messages show up in their entirety. Others only have the ID of the sender, or just 'you have a text'. Which is Elliot? Why didn't I *check* before I unlocked the phone and cleared his notifications? Of course, if it occurs to Liz to use Elliot's dead body to unlock the phone like I did, none of this matters.

'It sounds like it came from Miranda's room,' I say slowly, trying to think how to put her off track.

'You think?' Liz says. Her face is sceptical. 'I thought it sounded more like Elliot's. It'd be just like him to have some kind of super-long charge battery.'

My stomach flips. Of course. Of course she's right. She *knows* these people. And now I realise

I'm trapped. I can't suggest we split up and *I* check Elliot's room, when I already said I think the sound came from Miranda's. I will have to go along with her suggestion.

'Should we . . . go and check?' I try to look doubtful. 'It seems a bit disrespectful. Maybe we should rule out the other rooms first?'

Liz swings the other leg out of bed. She looks decisive.

'I think it's more important that we get to the phone while it still has reception,' she says reasonably, and I can't find a way of contradicting her because the thing is, she's right. That's exactly what I'd be saying too, if I hadn't sent that fucking text. 'I understand if you don't want to come,' she adds.

I waver. It's tempting. But I can't let her go up there alone. That would be worse. There may be some way I can get to the phone before she does, delete Danny's reply.

'Of course,' I say instead, like I'm steeling myself to do something necessary. 'Of course, you're right, I was just being squeamish. It's more important to get word out. Anyway, the door will be locked. You'll need my key.'

'Of course,' she echoes, and for a second, just a second, her hand strays towards her pocket, where the missing pass key must have been hidden, in a totally involuntary gesture that I would have missed if I hadn't been watching her every move. She catches herself before her hand makes contact, so that it just looks like she's adjusting her ski suit. But I know what she was thinking.

As we make our way up the stairs, I have a sharp, piercing sense of déjà vu, the number of times we have crept up these stairs in daylight or in darkness, to some horrible discovery. Only this time, I know what lies at the top of them, and I am the one who is fearing exposure.

My heart is racing as we approach Elliot's door, and when I reach into my pocket for the pass key, I find my hand is shaking.

'Are you OK?' Liz says. She has put her glasses back on, and they glitter in the darkness. 'You don't have to come in if you don't want.'

'I'm fine,' I say, through gritted teeth. 'Just cold.'

And then I turn the key and we are inside Elliot's room, the stench of death somehow even worse than before, though I know, logically, that cannot be the case, not in the few hours since I was last here.

Liz gags, and puts her hand over her mouth, and her action gives me an excuse.

The battery block is down the side of the desk, hidden from the door. If I can get her to concentrate on the far side of the room . . .

'The smell's pretty bad,' I say. 'If you want to concentrate on the bed side of the room, I can take the desk.'

She nods, and moves over to the other side of the room. I am busy going through the motions, opening drawers, pretending to search for a phone I know full well is just out of sight, when I hear something.

And then —

'Erin.'

I look up, look towards the bed, but she's not there. She has come up behind me. And she has found the phone.

My heart starts beating so loudly I am sure that Liz will be able to hear.

Run, run, run, a voice in my ear is screaming. But I don't. I hold very still. Maybe I can still talk my way out of this. What does it say? What does it say?

I wish I could see the lock screen, but I can't. Liz is holding the phone in her hand, angling it towards her, so that all I can see is the light from the screen reflecting off her glasses.

'That sound . . . ' she says, very slowly. She looks up at me, a frown furrowed between the lenses of her spectacles. 'It *was* a text message. And it was to you.'

LIZ

Snoop ID: ANON101
Listening to: offline
Snoopscribers: 1

I stare down at the screen, and then up at Erin's blank face.

This doesn't make sense. Or does it?

Messages: says the lock screen, and then a little preview pane showing the first line of the message. *Fuck. Erin is that you?*

Erin is looking at me like a rabbit in a snare.

Elliot's phone is a thumb lock. It makes what I have to do next very easy.

I reach out, and grab his cold, heavy hand.

'No!' Erin yelps, and she reaches for the phone, but it is too late. I am in.

SOS, I read, feeling fury begin to kindle inside me, making my cheeks hot. *Please send help. IT'S LIZ.*

I stare up at Erin, looking her right in the eye, feeling my jaw fall open with shocked betrayal.

That bitch. That total bitch.

ERIN

I see Liz's face change as she reads it and I know, instantly, there is no way of explaining my way out of this.

Her face goes white, and she stays very, very still, but I don't think it's fear that's paralysing her. I think . . . I think it might be something else. I think it might be anger.

'You don't understand,' I say weakly, but my voice is croaky, and I know there is no point in this. I don't know how I ever thought that text was ambiguous. Seeing Liz's face, I understand now, there is only one way for her to take it.

'You know,' she says, and her voice is horribly calm. I want her to scream and shout — *anything* would be better than this icy chill.

But there's a kind of relief in her words, because now I can stop pretending. I can stop this horrible dance of *does she know I know she knows*, and just face up to the truth.

'Yes, I know,' I say quietly. And then I take a step backwards, and I sink down on Elliot's bed and put my face in my hands. Partly because my ankle is killing me, and the pain is starting to make me feel sick, and partly because my legs are shaking so hard I can't keep upright any more.

She stands there, looking down at me, her face blank and unreadable behind those huge glasses. The light from Elliot's phone gives her face an eerie, up-lit glow. Behind her Elliot, the man she killed, lies sprawled across his desk — a terrifyingly immediate reminder of what she has done to protect her secret. The secret I now have. Oh God, what have I done? Danny, where are you?

'God, he *stinks*,' she says at last, wrinkling up her face. She cracks her knuckles, click, click, click, but it no longer sounds nervy. It sounds like someone limbering up for a fight. 'Let's get out of here. Come downstairs and we can talk this through.'

As if in a dream — or maybe a nightmare — I follow her out of the room. She holds the phone out in front of her like a candle, illuminating the corridor, and when we get to the top of the stairs she says, 'After you.'

I hesitate.

I don't want to make her angry — but at the same time, there is no way I am going down that slippery, precarious staircase with her at my back. I'm just not.

Liz sees my hesitation and gives a mirthless laugh.

'OK, I don't blame you. I'll go first. But you keep a step back, OK? I'm not having you pushing me down the steps either.'

I nod. I don't mind keeping my distance. It

would be almost as easy for her to snatch my ankle out from underneath me as it would be for me to kick her in the small of the back.

God, this is surreal.

I watch her as she makes her way carefully down the stairs, holding the handrail, the phone guiding the way like a faint will-o'-the-wisp.

Downstairs, she moves away from the foot of the stairs and feeds another log into the burner, making it flare so that the room is bright with its glow, and I hurry down while her back is turned, my heart beating quicker until I am on solid ground. Then she straightens up and shuts the glass door of the stove.

I am alone with a murderer. I am alone with a *murderer*. Maybe if I keep repeating the words to myself it will start to feel real?

LIZ

In a way, it is a relief to have it out in the open. I could tell there was something wrong, and I have always hated trying to read between the lines, second-guessing myself, attempting to parse a frown or a blank look or a pause that might be something or might be nothing.

Now we both know where we are. Which is a relief. But it is also a problem. Because I liked Erin. No, that's wrong. I shouldn't be using the past tense. Not yet.

I like her. I actually do really like her. I don't want to have to do this. But she did something really, *really* stupid when she sent that text, and now I have no choice. She's forced my hand, really. If anything this is *her* fault.

The sense of injustice boils up again. This is so un*fair*.

'I never wanted any of this, you know,' I say to her as she sinks down onto one of the chairs, staring into the flames. She is shaking. I'm not sure if it's cold, or shock.

'What?'

She looks up, and I feel anger bubble up inside

345

me, and then push it back down. Has she even been listening?

'I *said*, I never wanted this.' I sink down into the armchair opposite her. I stare at the fire, feeling its heat on my face. 'I would never have killed any of them if I could help it. *I'm* just as much of a victim here.'

She blinks — and for a minute it looks like she's going to say something, but then she seems to think better of it.

'Tell me about it,' she says. And so I do.

ERIN

Snoop ID: LITTLEMY
Listening to: offline
Snoopscribers: 10

I am lost in thought as Liz sits down opposite me, and it takes me a moment to realise she is talking. What she is saying doesn't make sense — some nonsense about *her* being the real victim in all of this.

I look up, and I meet her eyes, and I am overwhelmed with the urge to slap her, to shake her, to scream '*You?* Are you kidding me? What about Eva? What about Elliot? What about fucking *Ani* who never harmed a fly?'

But I don't.

Because I suddenly know what I have to do here.

I have to humour her. I have to keep her talking long enough for Danny to get back here with reinforcements. He has seen the text. He knows what it means. He will be doing everything he can to help me. I don't know what time it is, but it must be way after midnight. If I can just keep Liz talking long enough, I may be able to survive this. I may even be able to get justice for all the people she has killed.

Because I am a survivor, that's what Liz

347

doesn't know about me. She sees a soft, posh girl from the same background as Topher and Eva, someone who has never had to work for her living, to scrap for survival.

But that's not true. Not in my case. In spite of my family name, I *didn't* grow up with a silver spoon in my mouth, not in the way Topher and Eva did. I've always known that I was second-best, and that I would have to fight for myself. I know what it's like to clean up other people's mess for a living.

But more than that, the most important thing about me, something Liz will never understand, *could* never understand, unless she had stood in my shoes: I looked death in the face once, and I turned him away.

I can do it again.

'Tell me about it,' I say. There is a catch in my throat, and my voice is shaking with the effort of keeping it calm, when I feel anything but. But Liz doesn't seem to notice. Instead, she smiles. Incredibly, unbelievably, she smiles.

And she begins to speak.

LIZ

Snoop ID: ANON101
Listening to: offline
Snoopscribers: 1

'You don't know what it was like, starting at Snoop,' I say. It is easier not to look at Erin while I'm telling her this, so I look away again, into the fire, remembering that first day — opening the office door, and seeing them all, lounging around inside, laughing, bantering, so effortlessly, searingly cool. 'It was like walking into a different world. Like something off the TV, where people were sleek and beautiful and witty. They were like a different species, and I wanted to be them so much. School — school was so horrible. I can't explain it. I knew I was different from the other girls in my class, I knew they all laughed at me. But somehow I thought when I got to my real life it would be different. I thought that maybe I was just an ugly duckling.'

I swallow. It is strange saying all of this — unwrapping secrets I have carried for three years.

'But when I got to Snoop I realised that wasn't true — I wasn't going to magically grow into a swan overnight. Eva and Topher, even Elliot and Rik in a way, they had been different and special

349

and beautiful right from the day they were born. And I wasn't. I was never going to be a swan. I had to accept that. But the thing is, I *was* good at my job. Really good. And Snoop was doing well. And I cared about it — about them. So when the firm had problems raising money just before the launch, I offered Topher and Eva my grandmother's money. I still remember the shock on their faces when I made the suggestion.' I laugh, remembering Topher's expression when I spoke up in that meeting — as if his office chair had piped up, offering a solution to their finances. 'I think they realised then that they'd underestimated me — that the girl who brought the coffee and took the minutes was a real human being who could understand a profit and loss sheet, and figure out when the company was in trouble. It was like they really *looked* at me for the first time. Eva offered to pay me back with interest, and it was a good rate too. I would have got back almost half as much again by the time it was all paid back. But Topher — Topher took me aside into his office and told me I should ask for shares, and hang out until I got them.

'I knew it was a risk. Rik spelled it out really carefully — I wouldn't see my money back for a long time, and if the firm went under, I'd lose everything. But Topher — you don't know what he's like. He's so charismatic. He makes you feel that you're *everything*, that he will take care of you, that your money could not be in safer hands. So that's what I went for in the end. I thought at the time that Topher was being generous. I thought he was looking out for me.' I stare into the flames, feeling the brightness burning into my retinas, as if it can burn away the memories I have carried with me for years. 'I didn't know then what I know now — that he had seen how it would pan out in the event of a disagreement, and thought I was someone he could pressure in the event of a split.'

I stop. Suddenly this feels hard in a way I didn't think it would. It is good to spill all of this. Erin is a good listener in some ways, and it feels a little like lancing a boil — letting out all the poison that has festered away since that night. But it hurts too. And when I swallow against the pain, my throat is dry. The sensation gives me an idea.

'Shall I make some tea?' I ask.

'Sorry?' Erin says. There is an incredulous note in her voice. I can't quite blame her — the question must have sounded slightly surreal in the midst of all this.

'Tea,' I say. 'I don't know about you, but I'm really thirsty.'

'Tea?' Erin echoes, like someone speaking in a foreign language, and then she gives a shaky laugh. 'Tea . . . would actually be great. It's exactly what I need right now.'

We get up, and limp together into the kitchen, where I find two cups, and Erin fetches the stove-top kettle and a packet of tea bags.

'There's no milk I'm afraid,' she says as she puts the kettle under the tap. 'It went off yesterday.'

We both stand there, waiting for the kettle to fill, but there is no sound of rushing water. And then I remember. I can see from the sudden look of comprehension on Erin's face that she has remembered too.

'The pipes,' she says unnecessarily. I nod.

'Should we get snow?' I ask.

'I . . . guess?' Erin says, but I can hear from the hesitation in her voice that she doesn't want to go outside. I can't say I exactly blame her. I don't really want to go out either. We both know that stepping outside the chalet would give the other person the chance to lock us out, where we would very likely freeze to death. But the snow is piled up against the front door, so if we do this right, neither of us needs to go outside.

'If you open the front door,' I say, 'and stand there with the kettle, I can chip bits off the drift by the door.'

She nods, and I can see from her expression that she is grateful that I have taken on the more precarious role. The snow is piled up so high that you have to climb over the drift to get out, so it's fairly unlikely someone could just push you out of the door, but it is still possible.

'Thanks,' she says, and together we troop through into the foyer, where Erin unlocks the bowing front door. I begin to dig at the hard-packed snow with a spoon, chipping off lumps, and putting them into the kettle Erin is holding out. At last we are both shivering with cold, but the kettle is full, and we shut the door and return to the living room, and the blazing fire, where Erin balances the kettle on the edge of the wood stove, and we both warm up our hands at the glass.

'You were saying,' she prompts, as the kettle begins to hiss and sigh. 'The shares?' Her words bring me back with a bump to our present reality. I finger the empty packet of sleeping pills in my pocket. I think about what I have to do.

ERIN

Snoop ID: LITTLEMY
Listening to: offline
Snoopscribers: 10

Finding the kettle, getting the snow, all the little mundane practicalities of making the tea have let me push our situation to the back of my mind for a moment, but as the silence closes around us, I feel fear settle like a weight on the back of my neck. Liz is silent, her face blank and unreadable, her hands stuck out to the blaze, and somehow her silence is more terrifying than any speech. I find myself trying to work out what is going through her mind — is she figuring a way out of this? Or just thinking about what she has done?

The kettle hisses softly. Liz just sits there, staring at the kettle, one hand held out to the blaze, the other in her pocket, and suddenly I can't take it any more.

'You were saying?' I blurt out.

Liz looks up. She looks at me appraisingly, in a way I don't like. She is crunching a piece of plastic in her pocket. The noise is loud in the silence, and I think if she doesn't say something, I might scream.

And then she swallows and picks up her story again.

'The shares. Yes. So yes, there I am, twenty-two, a shareholder in this up-and-coming app — and Topher and Eva start treating me a bit more like a human being, now that I'm invested in the business. I mean, I've only got 2 per cent. Even Elliot and Rik dwarf my share. But I *am* a shareholder. And one night, a few days after we signed the papers, there's this drinks party in this flashy London bar — I can't remember why, I think they were after a partnership with some streaming company, some kind of quid pro quo.'

She stops. Something is coming, I can tell. I don't know what exactly, but it feels like Liz is gearing herself up for something, forcing herself on to a part of the story she doesn't want to spell out.

'They had an argument, over whether I should go. I remember Rik saying *Do you think this is the image we want to project?* He didn't know I was listening of course. They were in Eva's office, and I was listening in via the intercom. And Eva said *For fuck's sake, Rik, it's not rocket science, I can make her presentable. And she's one of us on paper now, thanks to Toph, so she might as well look the part.* Then she paused and said, *Besides, Norland likes her type. He likes them young.* So I knew what was going on when Eva got me to come over to her house before the party and offered to lend me a dress, because she knew I was on a budget after pouring all my money into Snoop. When she said it like that it sounded perfectly reasonable, kind, even, but I knew the truth.

'Well, you've seen Eva. You know what she's

like. There's probably only about three women in London who could squeeze into her jeans. But we found something, somehow, and Eva made up my face, and when we arrived at the bar and were introduced to the executives from the other company — I don't know — I actually started to feel like a real Snooper. Eva introduced me not as her PA, but as *Liz, who is a minority shareholder*, and they talked to me with respect, and as the evening wore on I really started to believe this was it — this was the life I had been waiting for. I don't normally drink much, but I drank that night. I drank a lot — a lot of cocktails, and — '

She stops. The kettle is hissing and bubbling, and she picks it up gingerly by the handle and fills each of the cups, then drops a tea bag in the top.

I take the one she hands to me, looking down into it surreptitiously. I don't want to aggravate her suspicions, but given how Elliot died, it would be stupid of me not to check. The melted snow is a little cloudy, and the tea is starting to leach out of the bag and colour the hot water, but I can still see the bottom of the cup and there's definitely nothing there. No pills, anyway.

'And?' I prompt, very gently, and then when she looks away, I say, 'I'm sorry. I don't want to pry. If this is too painful — '

'No,' she says with a rush. 'It's OK, honestly. I — it helps in a weird way, talking about it. I just haven't thought about it in so long. We all got very, very drunk. And somehow — I can't remember how — I ended up going with Eva

. . . with one of the executives from the bar. It was just the three of us. Topher had been going to come, I remember that, because he was in the taxi, but then at the last minute he bailed out and asked the driver to drop him off. We arrived at this house in Pimlico, and my God, it was amazing — it was so beautiful, this Georgian building, storeys high, with a balcony right at the top overlooking the river . . . ' She is staring past me now, as if she is looking at something I can't quite see. 'He took us upstairs, and we went out onto the balcony, and he gave us champagne and we chatted for a while, and then Eva excused herself and went to the bathroom.'

She breaks off. But I don't think it's because she can't go on. Not quite. It's because she is trying to work out what to say, *how* to say it.

'He tried to assault me,' she says at last, bluntly. 'He had his hands down my top, I was trying to push him away. And I — I — '

She stops, she puts her hands to her face.

'I pushed him. I pushed him hard. I pushed him off the balcony.'

'Oh my God,' I say. Whatever I expected, it was not this. 'Liz, I'm — I'm so sorry. I — '

The implications are buzzing in my head, even as I stammer out my pathetically inadequate attempts at sympathy.

She killed a man.

But it was self-defence.

But Liz is still talking, ignoring me, rushing on, as if she wants to be past this part of the narrative.

'I broke down when I realised what I'd done.

357

But Eva — she — she was amazing. She came running, and when she saw what had happened she didn't ask any questions, she just got us both out of there, and when it came out in the paper, it was written up as a tragic accident. There were drugs and alcohol in his system, and people, they just assumed that he fell, I suppose, or that he threw himself over. No one ever mentioned that Eva and I were even there. It just goes to show what money and influence can buy, I guess.'

She looks away at that, and then buries her face in her tea so that her glasses mist with steam.

'I couldn't stay after that,' she says very quietly. 'I left Snoop — and I never looked back. I went to work somewhere completely different, a banking call centre. It became like this horrible nightmarish episode in my life that was done and gone. Until the buyout happened. And I was dragged back into all of this.'

'I'm so sorry,' I say again, and it's true. I am sorry. Sorry for that poor kid dragged into a world she didn't understand.

But I still don't completely understand. She was assaulted. She was trying to get away from an attacker. And even if Liz didn't trust the court to believe that, and I can see why she wouldn't, why did Eva have to die? She kept Liz's secret.

And then, in a horrible, blinding flash, I get it.

Topher was the one who gave Liz those shares, on the tacit understanding that she would back him up if it ever came to a crunch like this. She owed him everything.

But Eva — Eva knew something about Liz

that could ruin her. At the very least, she would be embroiled in a messy, public court case, and I know enough about Liz to know that that would be torture to her. At the worst, she might be looking at a man-slaughter charge, and prison.

Whether she articulated it or not, Eva was the one who covered up what happened. She held that evidence in her hands. And she must have been holding that fact over Liz's head all these years.

No wonder Liz could never find the courage to say how she was planning to vote.

She could vote to betray her mentor, the man who hired her, stuck up for her, got her the shares in the first place.

Or she could vote against the person who held her life in her hands. The person who could send her to prison to rot.

When the realisation comes, it's with a twisted lurch of sympathy for Liz.

I think of that poor young girl, fresh out of university, swimming in waters far too strange and dangerous for her to navigate. Because Liz was the victim not of one horrible situation — but of two. Eva had helped her out of one nightmare, only to create another of her own making — blackmailing the girl she had professed to help.

Of course Liz did the sensible thing. She told Eva that she was voting with her. But what about next time? And the time after that? How could she live her life knowing that Eva had this secret to hold over her head any time she needed something Liz was unwilling to give?

No. She needed to make herself safe forever. She needed to get rid of the person who had started all this, the only person who knew her secret.

She needed to kill Eva.

LIZ

Snoop ID: ANON101
Listening to: offline
Snoopscribers: 1

'So that's it,' I say at last. I put my tea to my lips for a long time, pretending to gulp it thirstily down.

Erin is staring at me, but I can't tell what her expression is. It looks slightly horrified — but that could be sympathetic horror at what I've been through. Does she believe me? I can't decide.

Don't you want to drink your tea? I want to ask, but I can't say that. It would sound suspicious. Instead I raise my cup to my lips again, hoping to convey the message by subliminal suggestion. To my delight, it works. Erin picks up the cup. I see the muscles of her throat work as she swallows.

'So you had no choice,' she says faintly, and I try to arrange my face in the expression I think she will expect to see. A kind of . . . pained regret. And it's true — I do regret this. That night, most of all.

'I never wanted any of this,' I say. 'I just feel like I've been swept up in something awful and horrible.'

Erin shakes her head, but not like she is telling me she doesn't believe me. More like she's condemning whatever brought us here. She is staring down into her cup. I can't see her face very well. That bothers me, but then she takes another sip of tea, and I begin to feel more relaxed.

I put my own cup to my lips too, in order not to seem suspicious. I'm careful not to actually swallow any of the liquid inside.

'I've worked out what you did,' Erin says, as she puts the cup on her knees, nursing it with her hands. I can see from where I'm sitting that it's half empty, and I begin to feel more confident. 'It was very clever. You had a ski jacket like Eva's. You met her at the top of the lift — '

She pauses, and I know why. She is trying not to spell out what I did, as if it will offend me in some strange way. But it's OK. I have to live with what happened, there is no point in not facing up to it.

I was waiting at the top of the lift when Eva got off, right by the barrier where I had pretended to lose control and almost ski over the edge with Rik, earlier that day. Of course, I didn't lose control at all. It was a deliberate slide to give myself the chance to check out the edge up there. I wanted to see if it was as close as I remembered, to see if the barrier had been raised since my last visit, two years ago.

Nothing had changed. It was perfect.

The irony is, I'm a very good skier. But Topher and Rik and the others were too willing to believe that a girl from a Crawley comprehensive wouldn't know one end of a ski pole from the other. The truth, had they ever bothered to ask me, is that I loved skiing — right from the first time I went on a school trip, age fifteen. I had never set foot on a ski slope before, but I remember the teacher saying admiringly, 'You're a natural, Liz!'

And I was. I am not sporty, as a rule. I don't do well with anything that requires teamwork, or running in circles. I disliked getting red-faced and sweaty, everything jiggling unpleasantly under a sticky T-shirt, while girls shouted at me to pass the ball, no not that way, oh for God's sake, Liz! Until I wanted to run away and hide from them all.

But skiing was different. Skiing is solo — and it is strategic. You have to think on your feet, making split-second decisions that could save your life or send you hurtling down a sheer slope at a hundred kilometres an hour.

I loved it.

I managed to go back again during my A levels, and twice at university — the very cheapest trips I could manage: coach to Bulgaria, to stay in a Soviet-era concrete monolith; Ryanair to Romania, to a self-catering Airbnb with hot air vents that smelled of ham. But it was worth it. It was worth the scrimping and the saving and the long nights spent crunched into economy coach seats, barrelling down German autobahns in the middle of the night.

They did a corporate ski trip when I was at Snoop, wooing investors. Of course, they didn't invite me. But since I left Snoop, since I have been earning my own money, I have been back to the Alps every year, sometimes twice. And I have become a very, very good skier. Not quite as good as Eva, who has been skiing every year since she was a toddler. But almost. And I have been to St Antoine twice. I know La Sorcière very well indeed.

When she got off the lift, I was over by the barrier. I called out to her, pretending that I was in some kind of difficulty, and when she skied over I waited until she was right next to me, bending over, looking at the binding of my boot, and then I gave her an almighty push, toppling her backwards over the shallow safety barrier.

The barrier caught her in the back of her knees and she went down like a skittle and landed in the thick, untouched snow, right on the edge of the precipice, her skis windmilling in the air. For a minute I didn't think it had worked. I thought she was going to stay sprawled on the narrow ledge of snow, crawl her way back to the barrier, ask me what the hell I was playing at.

But then there was an imperceptible sound — like a sigh. The snow ledge began to shift and tilt, and a crack appeared at the top. For a second I saw Eva, frozen in horror, looking up at me, holding out her arms like I was going to be her saviour — and then the whole ledge gave way, and she was gone.

I waited for a moment, and then I unzipped my jumpsuit and pulled out the scarlet jacket I was wearing underneath. I put it on over the top of my navy-blue ski suit, pulled my scarf up, and settled my goggles over my face. Then turned my skis to face down the run, and I began to ski La Sorcière.

I would be lying if I said it wasn't difficult. It was. It twists and turns, full of sheer drops, heart-stopping hairpin bends and vertical ice sheets where I couldn't do anything but a kind of controlled fall. If I hadn't known the run well, I think it would have killed me. But I have never skied better.

I stopped halfway down to catch my breath and wait for the trembling in my legs to subside, and it was then that I saw Carl and Ani, travelling high above in the bubble. I looked up, safe in the knowledge that my goggles were pulled up and my hat was pulled down, and that no one could possibly tell who was wearing the distinctive, scarlet ski jacket. And I waved my ski pole, establishing my alibi, and Ani saw me, and waved back.

It was just my luck that she saw something else too: the empty bubble lifts making their way back to the valley floor. The bubble lifts that should have been taking *me* back to St Antoine.

I saw the recognition in her eyes that night when she came to my room. I saw her literally put two and two together standing there in the doorway, the puzzlement changing to horror as she made her excuses. Suddenly she didn't want to speak to me any more. She wanted to get away — figure out what to do, and short of putting a hand over her mouth and dragging her into my room, I couldn't think of any other alternative. So I let her go.

I knew then what I had to do. I thanked my lucky stars for Tiger's insomnia, and the instinct that had prompted me to pocket the pass key when Danny left it in the door earlier that day.

Although that wasn't luck really, was it? The truth is, I am not a lucky person. Yes, the Tiger thing went my way — but so much else has gone against me. And the pass key — that wasn't luck. That was *me*. A split-second decision that looked like it was about to save my skin.

Because the thing is, I may not be lucky. But I *am* good at thinking on my feet. Perhaps that is why I like skiing so much. It is the same skills, the same twisting and turning, the same heart-pounding excitement. The same drop in your stomach when you realise you've made a stupid mistake, and then the same lift of excitement when you realise you can manoeuvre your way out of it.

I felt bad about Ani though. Bad in a way that I didn't about Elliot. Elliot deserved what happened to him. He didn't have to poke and pry. That was his choice. Ani's choice was no choice at all — she was in the wrong place at the wrong time, just like me. And that is a tragedy. But it's not my fault. I have to remember that. None of this is my fault.

'Wh-what did you say?' Erin asks me, and I realise I must have muttered some of those words aloud. I'm about to answer, when I look at Erin more carefully. She appears almost . . . drunk. She is listing to one side.

'Nothing, don't worry. Are you tired?' I ask. I am trying not to sound too hopeful. She nods.

'Yes I feel — ' Her voice is slurred, and when she blinks, it is as if her facial muscles are moving in slow motion. 'I feel really sh-strange.'

'You must be exhausted,' I say. I try to sound soothing, but my heart is beating faster with excitement. I put my untouched tea down on the table, and wipe the dregs off my mouth, and I peer into Erin's cup. It is all but empty. 'Why don't you lie down?'

'I feel strange . . . ' she says again, but her voice tails off. She lets me help her to lie horizontally on the sofa. Her body is heavy. I have no idea how many pills she has drunk. Three or four, maybe? I had eight left and I put them all into the kettle, trusting to the boiling water to dissolve them. I had no idea whether the heat would damage the chemicals, but I knew that Erin would be on the lookout for me tampering with her cup, and I was right — she watched me like a hawk as I put in the tea bag and poured out the water.

The kettle was my only chance — slipping the pills in one by one as I packed in the snow, relying on the white snow to camouflage the white pills, and the strong, unfamiliar taste of milkless tea to mask any odd taste. And, almost unbelievably, it seems to have worked. Erin has drunk the whole cup. Elliot had five, ground up in his cup, and it killed him. Erin is smaller and lighter, and she had about half the water, which means approximately four pills. Four should be enough, assuming the heat of the water hasn't degraded the active ingredient. I will have to make sure of that. I can't take her silence for granted. But first there is something I have to do. Something quite urgent.

With a sideways glance at Erin, lying sprawled on the sofa, drool coming out of the side of her mouth, I leave the living room. I run as quickly as I dare up the stairs to Elliot's room. The door is unlocked, and I open his phone again. Then I navigate to the text messaging app, and Erin's message to Danny. *SOS. Please send help. IT'S LIZ.*

His reply is still there. *Fuck. Erin is that you?*

The precipice is in front of me — and expertly, I swerve to avoid it.

No, I type. *I already told you — this is LIZ. Erin has just confessed everything — and she's talking about killing herself PLEASE COME NOW.*

And then I press send.

368

ERIN

Snoop ID: LITTLEMY
Listening to: offline
Snoopscribers: 10

I lie completely still, listening as Liz peers into my cup and then stands over me, breathing heavily. Then she seems to make up her mind, and I hear the soft sound of her socked feet retreating into the lobby and the creak as she begins to make her way up the stairs.

I hold still for as long as I can bear, and then I sit upright, wincing at every rustle of fabric, every squeak of the sofa springs.

My arm and thigh are drenched with tea — but thank God, Liz didn't seem to notice the spreading dampness on the sofa, only the empty cup.

The pills were in the kettle. I suspected as soon as I tasted the first gulp of tea — there was a strange, chemical acridity, and a very faint sweetness that must have come from the sugar coating. And when I saw Liz putting the cup to her lips but only pretending to drink, I was certain of it. After that, I knew what I had to do. I had to pretend to drink too — taking advantage of the cover of darkness to slop the tea down my arm, onto the sofa, every time Liz turned away.

369

I had no way of knowing how long the pills should take to work — but I had to gamble on Liz's ignorance too. She would have no way of knowing exactly what concentration I had taken, or how quickly it would take effect. Ten minutes? Fifteen? Whichever, she seemed to buy my performance of slipping into incoherence, and then unconsciousness.

Everything hinges now on whether she gave me enough to kill me. If she thinks she's given me a fatal dose, I'll be safe for a little while longer — at least until she comes back and notices I'm still breathing. But if she's only given me enough to knock me out, she'll be coming back very soon to finish me off. Will it be a pillow over the face like Ani, or a blow to the head, covered up as a fall down the stairs? Or something completely different?

Either way, I don't want to find out. I *have* to get away, and the sooner the better.

Holding my breath, listening out for any sound from above, I hobble as swiftly and quietly as I can through the lobby, to the door behind the stairs, the one that leads to the ski lockers. My own ski clothes are up in my room, and I can't risk trying to get to it, but my boots and skis are down in the storage lockers, and there should be enough spare clothing strewn around for me to put together an outfit that will at least keep me warm enough to ski in. I don't have nearly enough layers to survive a night in the open, and I can't walk on this ankle. I will *have* to get down to St Antoine. But how? Skiing is the only option, and hope to God that the ski boot gives my ankle enough support to do it.

The door to the locker room opens with the gentle click, and I slide through, and close it with infinite care, my heart beating hard. It's very dark inside, the moonlight filtering faintly through a window almost completely blocked with snow, but my eyes are used to the darkness, and I'm able to pick out the vague shapes of jackets and ski pants hanging from pegs, and boots drying on their heated poles. Hastily, my heart thumping in my throat, I yank on a pair of salopettes. It's only when I look down at myself that I realise — they belonged to Ani. The thought that I'm literally stepping into a dead girl's clothes makes my stomach lurch with guilt. But I can't let myself get sentimental about this. Ani is gone — I can't save her. But maybe I can bring her killer to justice.

As I struggle into someone's ski jacket — Elliot's, I think, judging by the size — I remember Liz's self-pitying whine as she told me about everything that had happened. And the thing is, I could *almost* have bought it. I don't know for sure what happened on that balcony — but I could believe that part of it, the frightened girl, the desperate shove. And I could believe, too, her cornered fear as she realised that Eva had her trapped — and her terrified reaction.

But Elliot — no. And most of all Ani. Poor little Ani, killed as she slept for nothing more than having seen something Liz didn't want her to see.

Whatever Liz thinks about Eva, and that

unnamed investor, and maybe even Elliot — Ani, out of everyone, *didn't* deserve this. She couldn't have.

Only a monster could have killed Ani.

It's Ani's face that I see before me now as I pull on wet ski socks, and search around for mittens.

Ani's face, speckled with the scarlet dots that give the lie to Liz's story.

Because Liz says that she never wanted Ani to die — but I know that's not true. Ani must have fought. She fought for every breath, so hard that blood vessels broke in her skin.

And Liz stood there, and pressed the pillow down over her face, all that long, long time.

You have to *want* someone to die to kill them by suffocation. You have to want it a *lot*.

It's Ani I'm thinking of as I open up my ski boot as wide as it will go. Ani, as I shove my foot inside, gritting my teeth as the pain in my ankle flares suddenly, bright and hot.

My breath is whimpering between my teeth, little sobs of pain coming in spite of the need for silence as I force my foot around the curve of the boot, hearing the bones in my feet click and grind in protest, feeling the swollen flesh squeezing against the hard plastic shell. But I have to do this. I *have* to.

Ani. Ani. Ani.

And then with a crunch, my foot slides into place. I'm sweating and shaking with the pain, cold perspiration on my upper lip. But my foot is in. And, miraculously, when I try to stand, the pain isn't as bad as I thought it would be, the top

372

of the boot is tight enough that I'm taking some of my weight on my shin rather than my ankle. I ratchet the boot clips as tight as I can, praying that the support will keep the joint stable for long enough to make it down the valley. If I have broken a bone, I may end up lame for good after this — but it's better than dead.

Hastily, I shove my other foot into its boot and clip it up.

And then I hear a noise from the stairs.

My heart seems to stop. It's Liz coming down the spiral staircase.

For a second I freeze. I have everything I need — but can I get out the back entrance? The ski door faces the same way as the swimming pool, and it will have been blocked by the avalanche.

It opens inwards. At least . . . I'm pretty certain it does. I press my hands to my temples, trying to remember. Does it? If it opens outwards I'm screwed, regardless. But I'm sure it opens inwards. The question is whether I can dig my way out.

And then my eyes go to the narrow little window above the ski lockers. It's letter-box-shaped, and although it's certainly long enough, it's probably only twelve inches high, less when you take into account the frame and the hinges. But it might be my best bet.

Wincing at every sound, I climb up onto the wooden bench, and from there I lean over the ski lockers and open the window. A freezing blast scours my face, but I can see that the aperture isn't blocked — the snow obscuring the glass was just drifting flakes sticking to the pane. There is a drift almost up to the top of the lockers — but that will cushion my fall.

I push my skis out first, one by one, listening as they tip into the soft snow with a flump. Then my poles. I pull on the borrowed mittens, and grab a helmet at random from the rack. It fits, thank God, because I don't have time to pick and choose. And then I climb up to lie flat along the top of the lockers. They rock precariously — but only for a moment.

I feel sick with nerves. From somewhere in the chalet I hear a cry of surprise — and then a shout of 'Erin? . . . Erin, where are you?'

Liz has discovered that I'm gone.

I slide my legs out first. I am apprehensive about falling onto my bad ankle, but the alternative is dropping face first into the snow, and I don't fancy that either. OK, I'm wearing a helmet, but the fall could still break my neck, or if the drift is deep enough, I might plunge in vertically and suffocate before I could dig myself out. Feet first is safer.

It's a squeeze, but I am managing. One boot, sideways, my good leg first, then the other. The weight of the boot hanging off my bad ankle makes me gasp, but it's bearable, just.

And then the locker-room door opens.

I can't see anything at first, because she's holding a torch — Elliot's phone, I think — and it's shining full in my face. But I can see the shape of a figure in the doorway, and I know who it is before she runs towards me with a snarl of anger that sounds more animal than human.

I feel her hands grappling my arms, snatching,

scratching, but her nails slide off the thick, smooth fabric, and there is nothing for her to catch hold of. I force my bum through the narrow gap, and then my body weight does the rest, dragging me after — until I stick, with a sickening jolt.

For a split second I can't work out what's happened. Has Liz shut the window? Has she grabbed my helmet? Then I realise.

Fuck. The helmet won't fit.

I am hanging from my neck, and I'm beginning to choke, the strap of the helmet is digging into my jaw and throat, and I'm twisting like a fish on a line. My mittened hands are at my neck, desperately trying to relieve the pressure of the strap. My feet are scrambling in the soft snow, frantic to get enough purchase to loosen the strain on my throat.

My foot finds something, loses it again, and then finds it once more, just for a second — just long enough for me to unclip the strap.

And then I fall, gasping and retching, into a heap of soft snow and painful obstructions, that after a minute or two I identify as my own skis and poles.

There is no time to recover.

Liz is yanking furiously at the helmet, stuck in the aperture, trying to pull it free so that she can follow me. I expect her to shout or swear, but she doesn't, and somehow that's more terrifying. She says nothing — all I can hear is her grunting breath as she struggles to get the helmet out of the window. I *have* to get away before she pulls it free.

I manage to stumble to my feet, sinking into the snow as I do, and using my skis as crutches I stagger down the drift to the hard-packed snow.

There, I take a split-second inventory. Mittens — yes. Skis — yes, both. And my poles.

Scarf — gone. It must have got pulled off with the helmet. And no hat of course. I don't wear one now — the helmet is usually warm enough, but with the cold wind scouring my cheeks and face I know I'm going to regret that. Still, there is nothing I can do. I can't turn back. I have to make it down to St Antoine, somehow.

I also have no avalanche pack.

Fuck. *Fuck.* Which way?

Slowly, painfully, I drag myself and my skis round to the side of the chalet, and survey the piste.

The long blue down into St Antoine is a wreck — there is no other way to describe it. I saw the top of the run when Danny and I made our way painfully back from the crushed funicular. The avalanche has dumped everything straight down it — huge boulders — lift poles — tree trunks. It's not just unskiable — it's impassable. And the path through the woods to the green run, Atchoum, is totally inaccessible — the little copse has taken the full force of the avalanche and the trees are crushed and obliterated, buried under a hundred tonnes of snow.

But there is another way.

It's called the Secret Valley, or at least that's what the English skiers call it. I don't think it has an official name — it's not a piste, just an unofficial route that you can *just* about ski if the conditions are right, and if you're very good and you enjoy a challenge. Besides, 'piste' gives completely the wrong impression anyway — it conjures up the image of a flat apron of snow, with skiers criss-crossing each other with elegant turns. This is nothing like that. It's a long couloir between two sheer rock walls, formed by a deep crevasse in the mountains. It needs a lot of snow to blanket the jagged boulders at the bottom, and even when conditions are good, the path at the bottom is so narrow that it can only take a single skier, and in places if you reach out, you can touch both sides with your fingertips.

If I can get down to it, I think it will be passable — surely we've had enough snow to cover the worst of the jagged rocks, and it's out of the path of the main avalanche.

But it's not a run, so much as an obstacle course — a twisting, turning slalom of boulders and tree trunks, hard enough to navigate in daylight, let alone with no light but the moon. It's also very prone to mini avalanches — the snow builds up on the ridges above, and breaks off without warning, deluging the skiers below.

That's not the worst part though. The worst part, the part that is making me hesitate, is that once you're down there — there is no way out. The sides of the crevasse rise higher, and higher, and there is no way of getting a helicopter or a bloodwagon down to someone trapped there. You just have to keep going, until the chute spits you out among the trees at the top of the village.

It is my best chance. And Liz very likely doesn't know about it. There's no way of finding it unless someone shows you the entrance.

It's also my worst nightmare.

But I have no choice.

Holding my skis like a crutch, I begin to walk towards the head of the pass.

LIZ

Snoop ID: ANON101
Listening to: offline
Snoopscribers: 1

Erin is missing.

I almost don't notice. When I first walk into the living room, I am so sure she will be there that it doesn't even occur to me to check. But then something catches at the corner of my vision — something that is not quite as I left it. When I turn round I see what has changed, the sofa is empty.

For a moment I just stand there, too puzzled to be worried. Has she woken up? Stumbled to the toilet?

'Erin?' I shout. I go back into the lobby. I stare around the dark space, shining my torch up the stairs, into the kitchen. 'Erin, where are you?'

She cannot have gone far. She drank enough of those pills to knock her out for a week.

It is only when I go back into the living room that I see the dark spreading stain on the sofa. I touch it and sniff my fingers. It smells of *tea*. That is when I understand. She never drank the tea at all.

I don't often swear, but I do when I see that, and I realise how she tricked me.

I run. First to the door in the lobby, but the snow outside is untouched. She hasn't left the building by that route at any rate.

Then into the kitchen — but she is not there either.

I am halfway upstairs, ready to check the bedrooms, when I hear a noise. It is very faint, but it sounds like something falling onto the snow outside. It is coming from the back of the building, where the ski entrance is.

I make my way back down to the lobby and I open the door to the rear part of the building, where all the ski lockers are. It takes a moment for my eyes to get used to the darkness — and then I see something — or someone — moving at the far side of the room. It is Erin. She has climbed up on top of the ski lockers, and she is almost out of the window.

I hurl myself across the locker room, scramble up the bench she has placed below the window, ignoring the twinges in my knee, and grab hold of her helmet, which is just about to disappear through the window.

Then I realise why she is still there. The helmet won't fit through the gap. She is stuck. She is dangling from the helmet, horrible wheezing noises coming from her throat, kicking and kicking to try and get enough purchase on the snow to twist free.

But before I have had time to figure out what to do, there is a sudden jerk, and the weight on the helmet falls away. The catch has broken — or she has unclipped herself, I am not sure which. For a second she lies, gasping and winded in the snow, and then she staggers to her feet, picks up her skis, and begins to hobble off towards the front of the chalet and the path that leads up to the funicular.

I have to *follow* her, but the helmet is stuck in the frame, blocking it. It is only after a few minutes fruitless tugging that I realise, this is stupid. Erin has her skis and poles. She is clearly intending to ski to St Antoine — and I have to stop her.

I have to ski after her.

Letting go of the helmet, I turn back to the room. I am wearing my jumpsuit already. All I need is boots, skis and mittens. *Fast*, before Erin gets away.

I have two realisations to comfort me — first, in the soft snow, she won't be able to hide her tracks. I will be able to tell exactly which way she has gone.

And second, I can ski faster than her. My wrenched knee is almost recovered, while her ankle has only been getting worse. I saw the way she hobbled back from the kitchen with the tea just a couple of hours ago. She couldn't put any real weight on it at all. I am pretty sure it is broken — and there is no way she can ski aggressively with a broken ankle. She will have to go slowly and carefully, and it will take her a long time to clamber over the broken-up snow at the beginning of the blue piste. I saw what it looked like after the avalanche — a mess of rubble and debris. It will take a while to pick her way through that, even if it clears further down. I will be able to catch her up. *If* I act quickly.

I make up my mind. I ram my feet into my boots, and grab my skis and poles from the rack. My mittens are in the pocket of my jumpsuit. But my helmet — where *is* my helmet? It's missing from the locker, and after a few seconds I realise: it's the one that Erin took, and it is wedged into the window.

I have another go at trying to free it, but it's useless, and I cast around for an alternative before realising that I am wasting time. If Erin gets too much of a head start, even with her ankle, I won't catch her.

Shoving Elliot's phone into my pocket, I hoist my skis onto my shoulder and clack-clack my way back along the corridor to the lobby, where I open the door into the snow, and squeeze into the night.

It is unbelievably cold outside, and I realise that however chilly the chalet was without heating, it was actually doing a pretty good job of protecting us from the elements.

Now, out here, I don't know what the temperature is, but it can't be much over minus 20. Maybe even less. The sky is clear, and the moon has that strange frost halo around it that you only get in extreme cold.

Shivering, even in my warm jumpsuit, I clip my boots into my ski bindings and then straighten up, looking around for Erin's tracks.

There they are — deep slashes of furrowed snow, dark against the moonlit white.

But they are not leading up the track to the smashed-up blue piste. They are going the other way, into the forest.

ERIN

Snoop ID: LITTLEMY
Listening to: offline
Snoopscribers: 10

I had forgotten the beginning. Oh God, the beginning. It's like a sheer wall of thick, soft snow, hemmed in with trees, studded with boulders, narrowing to a steep path just a few feet wide. And taking the first step is basically like jumping off the edge of a cliff and trusting to the snow to hold you.

With two good legs I could do this — probably not elegantly, but I could do this. I'm rusty, but I've done enough off-piste skiing that I am pretty confident in my technique. I know how to manage the deep, dragging snow, how to navigate the heavy turns, how to avoid plunging into drifts and how to keep up momentum.

I know all that in theory. It's just that it's more than three years since I've skied off-piste. And I don't know if I can put any of it into practice with a broken ankle.

My heart is in my mouth. But Liz will have seen my tracks in the snow. She'll be following after me. I *have* to do this.

My downhill leg will be bearing most of my weight. I clip my ski boots into their bindings, and then turn and angle myself so that my good ankle is down the slope. Then, with a sick feeling, I tip off.

At first it goes OK. I schuss sideways in the fresh, fluffy snow, feeling like someone trying to swim with a duvet around their legs. But I'm heading rapidly towards the trees. I'm going to have to turn — onto my bad leg.

I manage an awkward kind of parallel turn, but I'd forgotten the physicality of skiing in thick drifts. The snow drags at my skis, nearly sending me over, but the real problem is the shock as I complete the turn and land on my bad leg. It sends prickles of pain up and down my spine, and I hastily turn back, trying to keep my sound leg down the slope.

But it's no good — I have to turn again to avoid a tree that looms out of the darkness, and this time my trailing ski catches in a drift, twisting my ankle with such excruciating force that I scream, the noise echoing off the steep walls of the valley. I land heavily on my bad leg, try to save myself with a flailing pole, and then — I don't know what happens after that. All I know is that my leg gives way and my pole sinks, and I am falling, tumbling in the soft snow, my arms around my head to try to protect myself from the half-buried boulders that stud the slope.

One ski is ripped off, my poles are wrenching at my wrists, I am upright, and then head down, then sliding bum first, then I somersault — and land with a bone-shaking jolt against a rock, at the bottom of the pass.

For a second I can't do anything except lie there, gasping, winded, trying not to shriek from the pain pulsing through my leg. But I have to move.

My spine makes a sound like crunching glass when I try to sit up, and I think I might throw up from the pain in my ankle — but I can see straight. I'm not concussed. At least, I don't think I am. And when I drag myself to kneeling the pain in my leg is intense, but it's still bearable. Just.

I pull myself to standing using one pole and then I rest for a moment, panting, shivering with shock and pain, forcing myself to breathe long and slow. It works . . . to a point. Then when I'm calm enough, I shake the snow out of my hair and collar and take stock. I have one ski still on, and I'm holding one of my poles. The other is leaning against a rock on the far side of the gully, and I hobble across and grab it with hands that are still shaking with adrenaline. OK. This is good.

The other ski though . . . where is it? I could ski with one pole, but I can't do anything with only one ski. If I can't find the missing ski, I'm screwed.

And then I see it. The tip is sticking out of the snow a few feet up the cliff face I just fell down. I sigh, unclip my remaining ski, and crawl up the soft, shifting side of the crevasse to try to pull it out, but it's too deep, the bindings are stuck against something deep in the snow, and so I begin to dig with my mittened hands. And suddenly, out of nowhere, I am hit with a sickening, jolting flashback — the most vivid I've had since those first, awful days when I woke up sweating every morning, fresh from a relived nightmare.

Digging. Digging through the snow. Will's hair. The end of his ski. His cold, waxen face . . .

Nausea rises in my throat.

I push it away.

I scrabble at the snow with my fingers.

The snow in his eyelashes, the frozen tip of his nose . . .

I want to sob, but I can't. I can't afford to make any more noise than I already have. Liz could be very near.

The torn edge of his scarf His blue lips —

And then I have the ski. The bindings are clear of the snow, and I can pull the rest of it out of the hole.

Every part of me is shaking as I slide back down the slope to where I left my other ski. My teeth are chattering, my hands are trembling so hard that I can't get them through the loops in my poles, and I have to try to force my boots into the bindings six or seven times before I finally hear the answering 'click' and feel the firmness of the clasp.

When it's done I just stand for a moment, resting wearily on my poles, giving my poor, quivering muscles a moment's respite. I'm honestly not sure if it's pain, or exhaustion, or the memory of Will's and Alex's deaths that's getting to me most. Maybe it's all three. But I can't allow myself to rest. I *can't.*

There is a noise from the slope above me. It

might be a marmot, or just the snow I disturbed shifting and falling in my wake, but I can't afford to stay to find out.

I push off with my poles, and begin to ski cautiously into the mouth of the pass.

LIZ

Snoop ID: ANON101
Listening to: offline
Snoopscribers: 1

Have I made a mistake? Erin's tracks stop at the top of what looks like a sheer drop into a gully below. The ravine itself is in deep shadow, and I can't see the bottom. There could be anything down there — jagged rocks, a mountain stream, a thousand-foot drop . . .

And yet, when I peer closer, I can see marks in the snow. Something — or maybe someone — has been down here. I can't believe that anything except for a mountain goat could make it down this slope in one piece, but as my eyes adjust to the shadows, I can see two deep grooves in the snow that look like someone sat back on their skis, catching their breath, before making a turn.

I stand, hesitating, wondering what to do. Surely Erin hasn't skied down here, with a broken ankle? Even for someone experienced in off-piste skiing, it looks like suicide.

But her tracks definitely lead here. And they definitely stop here. Did she climb down? No. Whoever went down there was wearing skis. Did she *fall* down? If she did, my problems may be solved.

Or is it some kind of elaborate trick?

I pause for a moment, looking up and down the valley, but I can't see how it could be a ruse. There are only two sets of tracks leading up to this cliff edge, Erin's and mine, and neither of them leads away. And she didn't have enough time to do anything Sherlock-Holmes-like. If she had retraced her own footprints to lay a false trail, I would have met her coming the other way.

This *must* be a route down to St Antoine. And somehow, Erin has managed to clamber down to it.

Well, if she can do it, so can I.

I am definitely not skiing down there. I don't care whether Erin did — I have not done enough off-piste skiing to trust myself on anything this steep. Instead, I unclip my skis and, holding them in one hand, I sit on the edge of the drop, and lower myself down into the soft snow, to try to walk down the precipice.

I know immediately that it was a mistake. Without skis to spread my weight, I sink deep, deep into the feathery drift. I scramble up, clawing for purchase, using my skis as a support, but as I struggle, the snow begins to shift underneath me. All of a sudden, it gives way, and we slither down the slope with terrifying speed — me, my skis, and a slippery, moving mass of snow. At first it is scary, but OK. I manage to stay upright, I can see where I am heading, and I am able to steer myself away from the trees, slow my descent — but then my boot catches on a rock. I can't stop myself. The weight of snow at my back is too great. I pitch forward. My skis are ripped from my hands. I am falling — falling in a terrifying white blur of snow and rocks and skis.

I have my arms wrapped around my head. I feel something hit my cheek, and my shoulder crunches against something hard. I think I scream. I think I am dying. This isn't how I wanted to die.

And then there is an almighty thump, and I realise I have stopped moving.

I am lying on my back, my head pointing down the slope and there is hot blood coming from my cheek. My shoulder is pulsing with pain. I think I may have broken my collarbone.

I try to pull myself to sitting, but the snow slithers treacherously beneath me, and I suppress a scream as I begin to fall again, but it grinds to a halt after just a few feet, and I lie, panting, sobbing with fear, before I realise that that last slide took me almost to the bottom of the slope. There is a path just a few feet below me. I can see one of my skis lying across it.

Slowly, painfully, I swivel myself around so that my boots are down the slope, and I let myself toboggan the last few feet. Then I am down. I am lying on the valley floor, practically crying with relief.

Everything hurts. I can taste blood in my mouth. But I am down. And now that I am at the shadowy bottom of the ravine, I can see that I was right, and the realisation gives me a little pulse of excitement that helps take my mind off my throbbing shoulder.

Because I can see ski tracks in the snow leading away down the valley, towards St

Antoine. One set, pressed deep into the snow, marked with divots either side where the skier pulled themselves along with their poles.

Erin *was* here. And if I hurry, I can catch her up.

ERIN

Snoop ID: LITTLEMY
Listening to: offline
Snoopscribers: 10

This is harder than I could ever have believed. I remember doing this route in daylight — the sun sparkling from the frosted trees high up above, blazing back at us from the bright snow at our feet. I remember twisting, turning, laughing, leaping over half-buried boulders and dodging moguls.

I cannot see any of those now. Traps loom out of the darkness — tree branches that swipe at my face, jagged projections rearing up without warning so that I have to swerve with sickening force, my ankle screaming with every jolt and twist.

In a way, it helps that the gully is thick with fresh snow. It makes the skiing slow and arduous, and I have no tracks to guide me, but it means I don't have to constantly try to slow myself down. When I came this way last time, the route was hard-packed by skiers who had gone before me. I could see where they had twisted and turned, where they had misjudged an angle and wiped out against an unexpected tree, or ploughed into a drift they didn't see coming. But at the same time, it made the going fast and furious, and with a track far too narrow for proper turns, most of my attention was taken up by trying to slow myself down to a safe pace.

The thick snow makes this much less of an issue. But it gives me an urgent problem. Liz will be coming up behind, skiing in my tracks, where I have already pressed down the snow. She will be going much faster. And she has my tracks to guide her.

I *have* to go faster. But if I do, I could end up killing myself.

I give myself a shove with my poles, ski around a tight turn, my ankle screaming with protest, and then thump over what must be a concealed hummock in the snow. The shock of agony that runs up my leg makes me cry out, and I wobble, and fall with a crash, thumping painfully into the rocky side of the couloir. For a few minutes I just lie there, panting, hot tears running down my face. I cannot believe how much this hurts. I don't dare open up the ski boot to find out what's inside, but I can feel my whole leg throbbing with my pulse. I don't know if I will be able to ski again, after this. I don't know if I will be able to *walk* again.

But Liz has killed three people already. I *have* to keep going.

I take a deep breath, and go to push myself up on my pole. But I can't do it. My muscles are shaking so hard, I can't make myself do it — I can't force myself to put weight on my leg again, it makes my whole body tremble when I think of doing it.

And then, from somewhere up the gully, I hear sounds. There's a cry — the sound of someone who has just been hit in the face by an unexpected branch, maybe — followed by the rough scrape of skis being forced into an emergency snowplough.

Liz is coming. And she is very close.

I have to do this. I *have* to do this.

I force my pole into the snow, and heave myself upright, sweating and shaking.

And then I push off.

LIZ

Snoop ID: ANON101
Listening to: offline
Snoopscribers: 1

Where. Is. She.

Where. *Is*. She.

The words keep repeating inside my head as I twist and turn, doggedly following in Erin's tracks. She cannot have been that far ahead of me, and her ankle is in a much worse state than my knee. I *should* have caught up with her by now. But I haven't. And that fact is making me . . . not worried exactly. I am not at that point yet. But definitely frustrated.

Part of the frustration is because this is difficult skiing, more difficult than I had imagined it would be. Even after my eyes have got used to the moonlit dimness at the bottom of the crevasse, I can't see very much except for Erin's ski tracks, and I have no choice but to follow them blindly, as fast as I can, hoping that if she didn't mess up or wipe out, I won't either.

There is a long straight stretch coming up and I give myself a push with my poles and hunch down, making my body more aerodynamic. I feel the wind in my face, and then I thump into a mini mogul, invisible in the dim light. I feel air

395

for a moment beneath my skis, and then I slam back down, all my weight on my bad knee in a way that makes me catch my breath. I ought to slow down, recover my balance, but before I can do so a tree branch comes out of nowhere, whipping me across the face, so that I cry out.

I go into an instant, reflexive snowplough, the snow shushing beneath my skis, my heart thumping, and grind to a halt.

That was very close. If I hadn't been wearing goggles, that branch could have blinded me. As it is, it has opened the cut on my cheek again. I feel a ticklish trickle of hot blood run down my chin.

I cannot afford to stop, though. I just have to be more careful. I push myself off again, peering into the darkness. I must be catching up. I *must* be.

Then, just a hundred metres further on, I hear it — the hissing sound of skis on snow. Someone up ahead is whisking round a tight turn, throwing up snow with the backs of their skis.

My pulse quickens, and I race to catch up.

ERIN

Snoop ID: LITTLEMY
Listening to: offline
Snoopscribers: 10

It is very dark now, at the bottom of the gully. The rocky walls rise up so high that no moonlight makes it down, and there are tall pines leaning over the top, their canopy blocking out the sky. But I don't dare slow down.

This is the part of the run I remember the best. The part just before it shoots you out into the village. I must be almost there. Here is the long sliding turn that takes you up the side of the couloir, between two scraggly little saplings. I shoot up between them, trying to ignore the scream of my ankle, and the trembling thumps of my heart, flooded with more adrenaline than it knows how to cope with.

Then a swerve to the right.

And then — oh *fuck*.

I'm almost on it before I remember. What looks like a sheer rock wall, and a breakneck left turn, at a point in the path so narrow it's virtually impossible to slow yourself down.

Its blackness looms out of the dark, and I fling myself into a desperate sideways slide, my skis throwing up a glittering, hissing mist of crystals

397

all around me. One ski catches on a rock and I almost lose control. My ankle is on fire with the pain, but I can't stop the frantic attempt to brake — if I hit the turn at this speed I won't just wipe out, without a helmet I will be dead.

I'm turning, I'm turning, my skis almost perpendicular to the slope — and then I'm round, and almost immediately I hit a tree root, my ankle gives way, and this time I do wipe out, in a tumbling flurry of skis and snow.

I have to get up. Liz is very near now. I can hear the hiss of her skis coming closer, the sound growing louder, funnelled by the couloir. I *have* to get up. Only, when I try to push myself to standing, I can't do it. My ankle won't bear my weight. I try — and my knee goes out from under me. I try again, sobbing this time, no longer caring about the noise I'm making, and collapse into the snow, weeping and swearing.

She is almost here. She is coming, she is coming *fast*.

LIZ

Snoop ID: ANON101
Listening to: offline
Snoopscribers: 1

I am very close to Erin now — and then I hear it. A cry from up ahead, and a clatter of skis. Yes. She has fallen!

I feel a surge of triumph, and it quickens my pace. This is going to be OK. I am going to catch her up! I don't think about what will happen when I do. Time for that later.

I crouch down again. I feel the wind in my face. This is it. I can *do* this.

I thump over a hummock, and I feel that same sense of exhilaration I did when I skied the black run, only this is even better. I am skiing by pure instinct now, like a bird, flying in a slipstream, wheeling and turning with effortless skill. It's almost —

And then it happens.

A wall of rock looming out of the darkness, just feet away.

I think I scream, I'm not sure — someone does.

I try, desperately, to snowplough — but the path is too narrow, and I'm not slowing down, I'm not slowing, I'm —

399

ERIN

Snoop ID: LITTLEMY
Listening to: offline
Snoopscribers: 10

The sound when she hits is like nothing else I've ever heard.

It is the sound of skis snapping and bones breaking. It's the sound of flesh hitting rock.

It's wet and yielding, and it's hard as stone all at once.

Was she wearing a helmet? *Was she wearing a helmet?*

There is silence. Total, unbroken silence.

'Liz?' I call shakily, but there is no answer, not even a whimper.

I try to stand, but I can't. Pain roars up and down my leg and my ankle gives way.

I crouch on the snow, hunched on my side, trying not to throw up with the pain.

I know I should leave her, but I can't do that either.

I think of Danny's words before he left. *I know you . . . Don't be starting up with the bleeding heart crap. Put yourself first.*

And I know he's right. But I can't do it. I can't leave her there to die, like Alex, like Will, alone in the snow.

400

I take off my poles. I unclip my ski boots from their bindings, and then I get onto my hands and knees and I begin to crawl, back up the pass, towards the turn.

LIZ

Snoop ID: ANON101
Listening to: offline
Snoopscribers: 1 0

ERIN

Snoop ID: LITTLEMY
Listening to: Offline
Snoopscribers: 10

When I get there, the silence is complete.

Liz is lying on her side at the foot of the cliff, a crumpled heap of red, white and blue. The blue is her jumpsuit, the white is the snow and the red . . . the red is *everywhere*.

She has been bleeding out over the snow, but it has stopped now. In the time it took me to crawl the twenty feet back up the pass, Liz has died. There is no breath coming from between her broken lips. When I put my fingers to the side of her neck, the skin is warm and slick with blood, but there is no pulse, not even a flicker.

For a minute I think about trying the impossible — chest compressions, mouth to mouth . . . but when I turn her very gently onto her back, what I see makes me fall back, choked with horror. The left-hand side of her skull is smashed in like an egg, and there is brain matter on the snow.

I feel faintness wash over me, a great wave of revulsion and nausea that leaves me crouched and rocking on the ground, hugging my own knees, a tearing sound in my ears that I know

403

must be my own sobs, but which sound like they are coming from someone else completely.

I don't know how much time passes. I only know that two things shake me out of my catatonic despair.

The first is that the sun is beginning to come up. The ravine is too deep for the rays to penetrate down here, but faint pink streaks of light are beginning to pattern the clouds above.

And the second . . . the second is that I can hear a buzzing.

For a minute I can't think what it is. It sounds like a phone, but I don't have one — my own phone is miles up in the mountains, back in Chalet Perce-Neige, with a battery as dead and cold as all the bodies Liz has left scattered behind her.

The buzzing stops, and then it starts again — and this time I realise. Liz. It's coming from Liz's pocket.

Her jumpsuit is soaked with frozen blood, but I know I have to do this, and I reach across, my arms stiff with cold, and touch her hip. I pull open the zip, my mittened fingers numb and clumsy, and something slithers out onto the snow, something bright as a jewel, with a jangling sound that makes tears start to my eyes.

It's Elliot's phone.

It is ringing.

And the caller is Danny.

ERIN

Snoop ID: LITTLEMY
Listening to: The Pixies / Where Is My Mind
Snoopers: 8
Snoopscribers: 151

I don't know how long I lay there, side by side with Liz in the slushy puddle of her fast-freezing blood. I only know that when the rescuers finally trekked up the gorge with their stretchers, I was almost hypothermic, and I couldn't answer their questions.

It was Danny who kept me going through those long hours, his voice in my ear, talking, talking, telling me that they were on their way, that I just had to hang on, not to give up. But when the rescue party finally arrived and prised the phone from my frozen mitten, slicked over with a sheen of bloody ice, he couldn't tell them what had happened either.

It wasn't until two days later that I was finally able to piece it together for them — explain the abandoned chalet, the cryptic texts, and headlong flight down the treacherous couloir. But even I couldn't explain everything. Because, how do you explain someone like Liz?

To explain is to assign a reason for something, to make sense of behaviour, to justify it, in a way.

And I cannot, *will* not, justify what Liz did.

I am discharged from hospital after a few days, but I can't go home. Partly because I don't want to — I am twenty-two. I don't want to go back to my childhood bedroom, with its posters of long-forgotten bands, and its photographs, Will and Alex permanent ghosts hovering just out of the corner of my eye.

But partly because I literally *can't*. The police haven't finished processing the crime scene that Perce-Neige has become, and they've asked everyone concerned to remain in the area, at least until their preliminary investigations are complete. We aren't suspects — at least, I don't think we are — so there's nothing legally preventing us from returning to the UK. But it would look very bad to be impeding the investigation, and everyone knows that.

It's clearly impossible to go back to the chalet as long as it's a crime scene, so I accept with some relief the police's offer of accommodation at a hotel in St Antoine le Lac. It is only when I arrive, plastic bag of belongings in my hand, that I realise what this offer means.

It's where they have put *everyone*. Topher. Rik. Miranda. Danny. Carl. Tiger. Even Inigo.

In fact it's Inigo that I see first when I step through the door into the reception area, and my mouth falls open.

'Inigo!'

I pull out my earbuds, and he turns round from where he is inexpertly attempting to sort out Internet access with the French-speaking receptionist. When he sees me, he flushes a deep unflattering red, so dark it's almost purple. The flush doesn't suit him, and it tones down his extraordinary good looks into something approaching normality.

'Um, *excusez-moi*, please,' he says awkwardly to the girl behind the counter. '*Un moment. Je* — I mean — I need to — God, Erin, what must you — let me take your bag.'

He gestures at the crutch I'm using, at my ankle in its surgical boot, and grabs for the plastic bag I'm holding in my free hand.

'It's OK,' I say laughing, though the situation isn't really funny. 'My ankle's fine. I mean — it's not fine, it's broken, but I can walk again now that I've got a cast.'

'No but still,' he says wretchedly. He ushers me over to the 1970s woollen couch in the corner of reception and we sit down, facing each other, like awkward guests on a talk show. For the first time I see that he has a surgical dressing on his forehead, and two black eyes. Has he been in a fight? 'Erin, you must have thought — you must think — I mean, God, I was a total idiot. I'm so sorry. I'm so, so sorry.'

'Sorry for what?' I say, taken aback.

'For going off and leaving you all like that! I had no idea that Liz — that she — '

'Inigo, it wasn't your fault!'

'But it *was*. I mean not Liz — but if I hadn't been such an idiot with the phone call Ani might still, she might still — '

He stops, and I realise that he's very close to crying, and is trying, desperately, to master himself. I also realise that I have no idea what

407

he's talking about. In fact I have no idea what the story is with Inigo at all. What *did* happen in the phone call? Why did he run off?

'Inigo, I have no idea what you're talking about,' I say more gently. 'What happened? *Did* you fake that phone call, after all? Why?'

'What?' It's his turn to look taken aback. 'No! God, no! How could you think such a thing?'

'Then why did you run away?'

'I told you! I left a note — because I made such a stupid mistake.'

I suppress a sigh of irritation and wonder, not for the first time, whether Inigo was ever actually that good as a PA. How did Topher put up with him?

'Yes, but you never said what the mistake was,' I spell out. 'We all thought — ' And then I stop. Inigo flushes again, even deeper this time, but he puts his chin up.

'I know. You all thought it was me. That's why I had to leave — to put things right. The mistake — God, I was so dumb. I told the police we were at Chalet Blanche-Neige.'

For a minute I don't understand. Then my mouth falls open. I have a sudden, vivid flash-back to Inigo on the phone to the police. *Yes . . . OK . . . Chalet Blanche-Neige.*

Blanche-Neige. Snow White. Perce-Neige. Snow-drop. An easy mistake to make for someone who didn't speak French. But one that was fatal for Ani. Oh, Inigo, you *idiot*.

'I know Chalet Blanche-Neige,' I say slowly. 'It's about ten miles away, over the other side of the valley. Of course. Of *course*, that's why the police never came. You told them the wrong place.'

Inigo nods, in miserable assent.

'It was such a stupid fucking mistake. And I realised the next day what I'd done, and I kept trying to get through to explain, but the line was just dead,' he says brokenly. 'So I knew the only thing I could do to try to put it right was ski down to the town, to tell the cops in person what had happened and where we were. So I left. I know it was stupid but I just felt so — so ashamed, and I wanted to put things right. I knew if I told anyone what I was doing they'd try to come and I didn't want them to, I didn't want to put anyone in danger because of my mistake. But instead — ' He gulps, and I see tears brimming in his eyes. I know he is thinking, as I am, of Elliot, and of Ani, both of whom might still be alive if the police had come that afternoon, if they had known where to look. 'Instead I got lost, skied into a *tree*, and woke up in hospital.' He touches his forehead, the surgical bandage I saw when we sat down. For the first time I notice the rawness of the skin on his cheeks and fingers, the blackened tips of his ears, where frostbite must have set in. 'If only I hadn't — ' His voice breaks. 'If I didn't — '

'Inigo, you couldn't have known,' I say softly. 'It was a mistake — just a terrible mistake.' These are words people have been saying to me for months, years now. You couldn't have known what would happen, when you suggested skiing off-piste. It's not your fault. It was just a mistake — just a terrible mistake.

They are phrases that have always seemed meaningless. Now, suddenly, it is vital that Inigo believes them.

'It's *not your fault*,' I say urgently, putting every shred of conviction that I can muster into my words. I put out a hand to touch his, feeling his rough, blistered fingers. Inigo winces, but then looks up at me. He gives a weak smile. I don't know if he believes me. Maybe. Maybe not.

Ani and Elliot might still be alive if Inigo had said the right name. But he didn't.

Maybe he will learn to live with what happened, just as I did. Just as I do.

ERIN

I don't see the others until dinner time, when the hotel serves up a hearty, veggie-unfriendly dinner at 7 p.m. sharp. There is no reservation, no picking and choosing your meal or your time. This is family dining — you come down when the chef tells you and you get the *plat du jour*, or you don't eat. It's quite restful.

I'm in my room, curled up in bed, more than half asleep when I hear the dinner bell ring, and I get up painfully, feeling the aches and pains in my bones from the last few days, and rubbing the side of my cheek where it's imprinted with the wrinkles of the pillowcase. Then I step out into the corridor.

I'm limping along to the stairs when a door opens and another guest comes barrelling out, almost knocking me over, making me drop my crutch. I bend over to retrieve it, feeling my ankle scream in protest, and when I straighten up I'm about to make an irritated remark, but then I see the guest's face. He is standing stock-still, just looking at me.

It's Danny.

'Danny!'

I fling my arms around him, but he just stands, unresponsive, and then, like ice thawing, he seems to melt, and his arms creep around me, holding me in a hug that is at first gentle, then firm, and then crushingly hard, almost as if he's trying to make himself believe I'm here and solid flesh.

'I never believed her,' he says at last, his deep voice coming to me as much through his chest, where my face is pressed. 'I never believed her. That text — I knew something was wrong. I set out straight away — I've never walked so fast in my life — but you were gone. I thought you'd died. I thought — I thought — '

But he can't finish. He just gulps, pressing his face into the top of my hair, and I feel the wetness of his tears on my parting.

'I should never have fucking left!' he says, and his arms tighten. 'I knew you wasn't safe to be left alone. I told you, don't do anything stupid. And what happens? Skiing off-piste with a broken ankle? You ain't Jason effing Bourne.'

I shake my head, and tighten my grip, burying my face in his shoulder, trying to hide my shaking sobs. I love him — I love his attempts to lighten the atmosphere and make a joke of this, but I can't even pretend to laugh. All I can do is hold him and cry, and cry, and cry, for everything.

'Fucking hell,' he is saying, his voice rough and soft in my ear, rocking me back and forth, back and forth. 'You're OK, Erin. You're all right, pet.'

And I want to believe him. But I'm not sure if it's true.

'You look like shit,' he says at last, pulling back to look me up and down. I feel like he wants me to laugh, and part of me wants to. *You should have seen the other guy.* The riposte is on the tip of my tongue. But Liz is dead, and it doesn't feel funny. Instead I just shrug and Danny's lip curls into something close to a snarl.

'Fucking bitch.'

'Don't,' I say. 'Don't — you don't know what she — '

But I'm interrupted by the clanging of the dinner bell for the second time, and Danny rolls his eyes.

'Better go down. You ready?'

'Not really. You?'

'I'm fine, mate. You're the one who pulled off the Bear Grylls stuff.'

I laugh, but my nerves are still jangling as I make my way slowly and awkwardly down the narrow stairs from my room, crutch clamped under one arm, the other supporting my weight with the rickety bannister.

When I enter the dining room, they are all there — all the people who are left, at any rate. Topher, Tiger, Rik, Inigo, Miranda and Carl — they are all seated around the long dining table, and when I come in, unsure of my reception, there is a collective intake of breath and then, to my surprise, Topher breaks the silence with a slow round of applause that is taken up first by Inigo, and then by Rik, Miranda and all the others.

413

'Bloody hell,' Carl says, jumping up from his place to help me with my crutch and my chair. 'You look even worse than Inigo, and that's saying something.'

My seat is next to Tiger, and she puts her arm around me as Carl pushes my chair in, holding me in a warm, one-sided hug.

'Erin,' she says. 'Are you OK? It must have been terrifying. I'm so sorry — we never should have left you.'

'It's OK,' I manage. My eyes are filling with tears. I can't think what to say. My ankle, inside the air cast, is throbbing painfully, and I can feel their eyes on me. It's a welcome distraction when Danny pulls out the chair on my other side and slumps into it with a sigh.

'Smells like that bleeding cassoulet again,' he says morosely. 'It was bad enough last time.' Somehow his irritation breaks the ice, and Inigo is smiling, a watery grin.

'Bit louder, mate,' Carl says, as the young waitress — the same girl from reception — comes into the room carefully carrying three plates of thick pale stew on a tray, breathing heavily with concentration as she navigates round the corner of the table. 'We want to be sure she spits in the right plate.'

'Going by the stuff they served the other night, spit would probably improve it,' Rik says under his breath.

'Shh,' Miranda hisses severely, and Rik grins, and rubs the back of her neck with an easy intimacy that makes me think whatever their situation at home, these two will not be going back to England as just colleagues. Something has changed between them, something irrevocable, and Rik looks stronger, more determined than the person I met just a few days ago.

Topher, by contrast, looks like a pale, deflated version of the charismatic man who stepped off the funicular. It's not surprising in a way — he has lost his co-founder and his best friend, a terrible price to pay for regaining control of his own company, by any standards, and one that seems to have aged him, and scuffed away some of his confidence and sheen. He's still seated at the head of the table, though, and when the cassoulet is served he taps his fork on his glass, and clears his throat as we all look round expectantly.

'Um . . . look, this won't take long,' he says, and then stops, and rubs his forehead wearily, seeming to have lost the thread of what he was about to say. 'But I — well, I've had a couple of bits of news. I thought you deserved to know as soon as possible.'

He takes a long swig from the glass of red wine at his side, and then grimaces, and wipes his mouth. I don't think it's the kind of vintage he's used to drinking.

'The first thing is, well, there's no easy way to say this.' He swallows, his throat working. 'The, er, the buyout offer has been withdrawn.'

There is a murmur from round the table. It's a mixture of shock and concern, but there's not much surprise in people's voices. Rik and Miranda share a glance.

'What does that mean for the company

valuation, if you take Snoop public?' Carl asks, bluntly. Topher doesn't answer. Rik folds his arms, his mouth a thin line of annoyance.

'In the toilet, am I right? You don't need to bullshit here, Toph. You're not wooing investors. It's not surprising, is it? High-profile massacre on company time, one partner dead, arguably the one the investors liked more — '

'Rik!' It's Tiger speaking. She stands up, her chair screeching on the tiled floor, her face twisted, her air of serenity quite gone. 'Rik, for God's sake! Does this matter? Eva is dead. Elliot is dead. Ani is *dead*.' Her voice cracks on the last word. 'How can you give a fuck about share valuation?'

She is right, and Rik knows it. He sinks back in his seat, and shrugs slightly feebly.

'It's a fact,' he says, but not like he's arguing with her, just like he's trying to backtrack on his own insensitivity. 'That's all I was saying.'

And the thing is, he's right. It *is* a fact, and an important one to the people who are losing their money, and the employees who may soon be losing their jobs when Snoop's bubble bursts. But Tiger is right too. It's a fact that pales into nothing compared to the loss of their colleagues.

'What was the second thing?' Miranda says. Her interjection, into the uneasy silence after Tiger's outburst, is unexpected, and Topher looks nonplussed for a moment. 'A couple of bits of news, you said,' she prompts. 'What was the other thing?'

'Oh,' Topher looks . . . I don't know. Sickened, almost. He rubs his face. 'I got a letter. I mean

416

an email. From Arnaud.'

Arnaud? Danny glances at me, frowning, and then I remember. 'Eva's husband,' I whisper, and Danny's expression changes to comprehension and unease.

'Has he heard?' Rik says. He looks a little sick. Topher nods.

'The police told him. They haven't given him the full picture, just the basic facts, that she's been involved in a fatal skiing accident. Anyway, he sent me a file.'

'A file?' Miranda's expression is confused. She's not the only one. 'About Eva?'

'A folder. About lots of people. Letters. Photos. Videos. Eva asked him to send it all to me in the event of her death. Arnaud hasn't seen any of it, it was password protected, but I've been through it and . . . there's this one video . . . ' He runs his hand through his mussed blond hair, tousling it, but it no longer looks like it's sticking up in a way that's been artfully tweaked into place, it just looks like a mess. 'I don't know what the fuck to do with it, you know? Eva's dumped it in my lap, and the rest of it's bad enough but this — this thing — I feel like it's too much for one person.'

He looks . . . the word comes to me. He looks lost.

'You want us to watch it too?' Rik says. 'All of us?'

His glance flickers at me and Danny. He doesn't say it, but the implication is clear — is this private Snoop stuff? But to my surprise, Topher nods.

'All of you. It concerns everyone here.'

Beside me, Danny is frowning, and I know how he feels. Something is about to be dumped onto us — and I don't understand what. Why is this to do with me and Danny? Did Eva send something to her husband before her death?

Topher pulls open his MacBook, clicks a link, and taps in a password. Then he angles the screen towards the rest of the table, and, with a glance at the door to the kitchen to check the waitress isn't hovering, he presses play.

For a minute it's hard to make out what I'm seeing. It seems to be footage from a mobile phone, but it's night-time, and the resolution is grainy and poor. It looks like a garden — or no, a balcony, because I can see rooftops beyond. A man and a woman are standing there, talking, but although I can hear the breathing of the person filming, I can't hear anything from the couple talking on the balcony, which makes me think they are being filmed from inside, through glass.

The woman is leaning against the opposite wall, and her face is in shadow, making it impossible to tell who she is, but there is something about her stance that looks both familiar and more than a little tipsy. She is steadying herself with a hand on the wall, and when the man leans in, offering her more champagne, the glass she holds out is definitely swaying.

The man I don't recognise. I'm sure of that. He is standing with his back to the balcony parapet, so that I can only see his profile, but it's no one I know. He's handsome, in an obvious kind of way, and there is something a little patronising about his expression, like he's enjoying talking down to this young woman in front of him, enjoying her homage. He lifts his glass to his lips and drains his drink, and then says something to the woman.

The woman shakes her head. She makes as if to move away, but the man puts his arm up on the wall over her head, blocking her in. She is hemmed in by his body on one side, and the wall of the house on the other. My heart begins beating faster for her. I know what is happening. I have been this woman. I know her panic. I know how much she will want to escape.

And then, very deliberately, he puts his hand on her breast.

I am screaming at her internally to kick his shins, knee him in the balls, get away.

But I have realised with a sinking feeling that I know this woman. And I know what she is about to do.

She squirms to one side trying to get out from under his grasp, but he blocks her, putting his other hand there to prevent her escape, and now he leans in, too close for me to see what he's doing, though I can imagine, I can imagine all too well. My heart is racing now, sickeningly fast. Why isn't the person holding the phone going to help?

The shove, when it comes, is no surprise to me, even though there is an audible gasp from the person filming, and from a few of the viewers in the dining room.

On-screen, the man staggers back, against the

low barrier of the balcony, winded. And then the next few seconds unfold so fast I can hardly make out what happens.

The woman steps towards him, and for a second I think she is about to help him up. But she doesn't. She pushes him again. And this time his legs go up, his glass slips from his hand, his arms windmill — and he is gone.

It's only when the woman turns to walk away that we see her face.

It's completely calm.

It is, of course, Liz.

ERIN

Snoop ID: LITTLEMY
Listening to: offline
Snoopscribers: 160

There is complete silence around the table as Topher closes his laptop and puts it away. Carl is the first to speak.

'What the fuck did we just watch?'

'I think . . . ' It's Miranda, speaking very slowly, her face drained of colour. 'I think . . . we just watched Liz murder someone.'

'It's why Eva was killed,' Topher says, and his voice is gravelly. 'It must be, surely? Liz must have known she knew.'

'But — that makes no *sense*,' Miranda says, bewildered. 'Why kill Eva when she knew she had footage?'

'I'm guessing she didn't know about the footage,' Topher says. He looks indescribably weary; his face is graven into the lines of a man ten years older than his actual age.

'She didn't,' I say. My words drop into their silence like stones into a well, and they all turn to look at me, astonished.

'You knew about this?' Miranda says, and, very reluctantly, I nod.

'Yes, I knew. Liz confessed to me before — ' I

421

stop, I can't bring myself to say what happened, even though I've already been through it with the police: the endless night, the pills in the kettle, that nightmarish chase in the darkness, the horror of her lonely death. 'Before I ran,' I end lamely.

'She fucking killed a man in cold blood,' Carl says, and his voice is blank with shock.

'He assaulted her,' Miranda says stiffly, but I don't listen to the argument that ensues. I am too busy trying to figure out something else.

Who was filming? And why?

There is only one explanation — it must have been Eva. She was the only other person there that night, by Liz's account. And she had the footage. She *must* have been the person hiding inside the flat, filming through the closed window. It's the only explanation that makes sense, and it ties in with Liz's account of the timings, Eva making an excuse to leave and go to the bathroom, right before it happened.

But . . . I am putting two and two together, as the argument rages around me, Miranda's shrill voice rising over Carl's booming tones. Why would Eva be filming? Unless she knew, or at least had a very good idea, that Liz was going to be assaulted.

And then I remember Liz's words to me, repeating Eva. *Besides, Norland likes her type. He likes them young.*

Did . . . did Eva *send* Liz in there, knowing Norland would likely make a pass, knowing Liz would fight him off and then . . . what?

The pieces click into place, with a horrible finality.

Then, Eva would have video of a man, a

potential investor, sexually assaulting her employee.

She would have him where she wanted him.

Eva is a blackmailer — I knew that already. But somehow, this cruel, calculated set-up is infinitely worse than anything I had imagined.

She sent Liz in there like a lamb to the slaughter. What she didn't know was that Liz was no lamb.

It's like Liz said, everyone at Snoop underestimated her.

Well, that was a mistake. And Eva's mistake killed her. And it killed Norland too. And now it's killed Liz.

'She knew.' I say it quietly, and at first they don't hear me, and the argument carries on over my head, but then Tiger says:

'What did you say, Erin?'

'She knew.' When I repeat it, the others fall quiet, so that my words drop into the sudden silence like little bombs.

'Who? Liz?'

'Eva. She *knew* that guy would probably go for Liz. That's why she was filming. She told you, Rik, do you remember? *Norland likes her type. He likes them young.*'

Rik says nothing, but the expression on his face says more than any speech. He remembers. He remembers perfectly. And he understands. Still, I spell it out for the others.

'She dressed Liz up, and she took her to his flat, knowing that Norland would quite likely make a pass at her and Liz would panic. And she would have it all on film.'

'Fuuuck.' It's Carl who speaks, and his face is

ashen. 'She told me once, when I asked her how she got so good at persuading investors. She said, everyone has a button, you just have to find it, and then you press it as hard as you can, even if they squeal.'

'That film was supposed to be her button,' I say. 'Only it didn't turn out how she planned.'

'And all this time,' Tiger says slowly. 'All this time she was holding it over Liz's head. What do we *do*?'

'What *can* we do?' It's Topher. He stands up, runs his hands through his hair. 'Fuck, this is horrible — that fucking file. And it's not just Liz. She had stuff on all sorts of people. It's like a fucking time bomb.'

'Does Arnaud know?' Rik asks. Topher shakes his head.

'No, I haven't told him what the folder contained. If this gets out, it'll *end* Snoop. What do we do? A company built on blackmailing investors? We might have survived Eva's death, even the revelations about Liz. But if this gets out, we could all be going down.' He looks across the table at Rik. 'I mean *literally* going down. Like, you and me could be looking at prison time. How do we prove we didn't know about this?'

'We can't bury this!' Tiger's voice is horrified. 'Topher, what are you suggesting? That we pretend we never saw this?'

'I'm just saying — ' Topher's voice is desperate. He runs his hands through his tow-coloured hair again, looking half crazed now. 'I'm just saying, what good would it do to drag all of this out? Eva's dead. Liz is dead. Norland is dead. No one can get brought to justice. All we can do is hurt Arnaud and Radisson.'

'And *Snoop*,' Tiger says accusingly. 'That's what you really mean, isn't it? This isn't about Arnaud, this is about protecting your position.' Her usually tranquil voice has grown high with anger and distress. 'What about Liz?'

'Liz is a murderer!' Topher cries.

'She's a victim!'

'She's a fucking psychopath,' Carl puts in, matter-of-factly. 'Was, I mean.'

There is silence, while we all consider this.

Because here's the thing. Liz *was* a victim. And just like she said, she never wanted any of this. She was just a poor, confused kid, in the wrong place at the wrong time. But I can't forget that second, extra push. And I can't forget Ani, little, trusting Ani. Perhaps they are *all* right. Perhaps Liz was both.

ERIN

It's still not resolved, when dinner breaks up, and I climb awkwardly up the steep stairs to my room, leaving the voices of the others still raised in angry discussion and circular argument. It's a relief in fact to stick my headphones in and slump back on the bed with my ankle raised, thinking of nothing but the music in my head.

I barely hear the knock at the door, but something makes me pull out one earbud, and it comes again, a brisk rap-rap.

With a sigh, I swing my legs off the bed and hobble to the door.

It's Danny. And he's holding a crutch.

'You left this, mate.'

'Oh, of course.' I smack my hand to my forehead. 'I'm such an idiot. Thanks.' He hands it over and there's a moment's awkward silence. 'Do you want to come in?' I ask, waving a hand at my slightly meagre room. 'I know it's not exactly the Ritz, but I'm not sure I can face sitting with the others downstairs.'

Slightly to my surprise, Danny shakes his head.

426

'Nah. I'm . . . well, I'm actually gonna go out. For a drink.'

'With who?' I'm surprised. I'm even more surprised when Danny blushes.

'Eric. Landlady's son. He runs the bar up the road, you know, the one with the brass counter on the corner, the Petit Coin? Said . . . you know. Come in for a drink after supper.'

'Danny!' I can't stop a smile spreading across my face. 'That's awesome. Is he . . . ?'

Danny raises one eyebrow, drawing out the silence, making me blush, and then he puts me out of my discomfort.

'If you mean, does he like pina coladas, sources say yes.'

'Ha. Well. Go you.'

'You sure? I mean, you could come . . . ' He trails off, but I'm laughing and shaking my head.

'No. No thanks. No pina coladas for me, I'm going to have an early night.'

'OK. Good plan, Batman.' He pauses, but he still doesn't leave. He just stands there, frowning down at his feet, tracing a pattern on the lurid carpet with his toe. 'Fucking weird, wasn't it?'

'All the stuff with the film? Yeah. What do you think they'll do?'

'Fuck knows. I've been wondering if we should go to the police ourselves, but I dunno if there's much point.'

I've been wondering the same thing, but I don't have any answers either, and in the end I just shrug.

Danny turns as if he's about to go, and I'm just about to close the door, when he swings back as if he's thought better of something. He leans in, and I think he's going to whisper something in my ear, but instead, rather sweetly, and to my surprise, he gives me a kiss. His lips are full and soft against my cheekbone.

'Love you, mate,' he says. I put my arms around him, and squeeze.

'Love you too, Danny. Now go. You've got pina coladas waiting.'

ERIN

Snoop ID: LITTLEMY
Listening to: Carole King / Tapestry
Snoopers: 28
Snoopscribers: 345

It's just over three weeks later, and I'm sitting by the fire in the chalet, staring out of the tall window that overlooks the valley, listening to music and not thinking about anything in particular.

It's still strange being in the chalet without working. Both Danny and I are still employed, technically, but I don't know how much longer that can go on. After Perce-Neige was declared an official crime scene, its photo smeared all over the newspapers in half a dozen countries, it became very clear that even if the avalanche damage was repaired, it wasn't going to be possible to use it for a holiday destination for this season at least.

The remaining bookings for the year have been either cancelled or hastily reallocated to the other properties owned by the skiing company, and now Danny and I are simply waiting to find out what will happen, pacing the empty rooms, looking at the place where Ani last sat, seeing Elliot's ghost, spooning stew into his mouth, hearing the click-click-click of Eva's heels on the parquet, and the slam of Liz's bedroom door.

I can't stay in this place. I know that now. But I can't keep running.

The smells from the kitchen are making my stomach rumble, and I'm just thinking about heaving myself out of my chair and clumping through to ask Danny what time he will be serving up, when my Snoop stream goes dead. For a minute I'm not sure what's happened. I wasn't snooping on anyone else, so the feed shouldn't cut out like that. It was *my* music.

I open up my phone to check on the app, but that's when I notice. There's an email notification. And it's from Kate. The subject line is 'Some difficult news'. My stomach gives a lurching jolt.

'Danny,' I shout, over the sound of pots and pans from the kitchen. There's no reply, and I am about to get up and walk through to show him the notification, when he appears in the doorway, holding his own phone.

'Did you get it too?' he asks, and I nod my head.

'Yeah. I think we're both cc'd in. What does it say?'

'Open it and find out.'

My gut is churning as I open the email and scan down the contents. *Difficult decision . . . not practical to reopen . . . eventual sale . . . sick pay . . . generous redundancy packages . . . four weeks' notice.*

'They're closing the chalet.' I look up at Danny. He nods solemnly.

'Yup. That's about the size of it. Have to say, I'm not exactly surprised, what plonker's gonna want to stay in a place where four guests got killed? I mean, it's not exactly home sweet home, is it, even if you take the banjaxed swimming pool out of the equation. What are you gonna do?'

'What am I going to do?' I stare back at him. It's stupid, because I've had three weeks to figure this out, but I'm no closer to deciding. Would I come back to work? Did I want to? Now it's not even a question.

'I don't know,' I say at last. 'What about you?'

'We could sue, you know,' Danny says conversationally. 'I mean, quote unquote generous redundancy package is all very well, but you were bloody near killed in the line of duty. I reckon that deserves something a bit more than a few weeks' pay and a box of fucking chocs.'

'I don't want to sue,' I say reflexively, without even thinking about it, but as the words leave my mouth I am sure of the rightness of them. I don't want to. It was hard enough going through all this once. I am not putting myself through it all again in a court of law, let alone dragging in Topher, Tiger, Rik and everyone else to give evidence.

'Nah, neither do I really,' Danny says, looking down at the screen, with a little sigh. 'Coulda done with the squids though. Well, as me old ma would say, if wishes were horses and all that.' He sighs again, and then says, 'Shall I serve up? Butternut squash soup with hazelnut gremolata and charred fougasse.'

'Sounds delicious,' I say, trying for a smile. 'I can't wait.'

432

ERIN

Snoop ID: LITTLEMY
Listening to:
Snoopers:
Snoopscribers:

After lunch Danny and I sit down in front of the TV and I get out my phone. I've become slightly addicted to watching my Snoopscribers tick upwards. There's nothing like news getting around that you've been almost killed to send your numbers rocketing. And I like checking up on Topher, Rik and the others too. Rik's username is Rikshaw and he doesn't have nearly as many Snoopers as Topher, but I like his music taste a lot more. He was listening to some amazing Cuban rap the other day.

But when I open up the app, there's nothing there, just a blank home page.

For a second I think I've accidentally logged out, but no — I'm still signed in, and there is my profile picture in the top right, Little My from the Moomins scowling out of the screen. But there is nothing in my recently played list, no suggestions of people to follow, no Snoopscriber list — in fact even my numbers have disappeared. Is the Internet down again? But I remember when that happened before, and it wasn't like this. Have I been *banned?*

'Danny,' I say. Danny is scrolling through Netflix. He speaks, without looking away from the screen.

'That's my name, don't wear it out.'

'Danny, is your Snoop working?'

'Yeah — why?' he says, and then opens up the app to check. 'No, wait, what? I've lost all my subscriptions and all my favourites. What's going on?'

'I don't know. Has this ever happened before? Have we been banned?'

'No . . . ' Danny is scrolling through menus. 'No, I don't think so . . . I mean, there's nothing they can ban you *for*. It's not like Twitter where you can post far-right shit. There's nothing you can do apart from follow people. I think . . . I think this did happen before, ages ago, when they were starting up and they didn't have enough servers. I remember a few days where the whole app just crashed, and it was like this. Just a blank screen. Maybe they're having server problems their end?'

'Maybe.'

I pull up Google, and type in *is snoop down.*

Article after article comes up. *BREAKING* reads the first one. *British tech start-up Snoop files for administration.*

And another one: *Snoop users received a rude shock when they logged into their favourite app today, to be met with a blank screen, after the company shut down servers following a declaration of bankruptcy by founder and CEO Topher St Clair-Bridges.*

'Fuck.' I can see from his face and the way he looks up at me that Danny has just made the same search, and is reading the same article — or one just like it. 'Fuck, they've gone under. Rik was right.'

I let out a long breath, and a tension that I didn't realise I had been holding rolls off me. It's not that I'm glad that Snoop has gone bankrupt — far from it. The thought of Inigo, Tiger, Carl and all the rest of them out of a job, not to mention all the people I never met behind the scenes — that gives me zero pleasure. But it sets my mind at rest over a decision that has been gnawing at the back of my mind for three weeks now. What to do about Eva's video.

Because that was the one question that we never resolved, before the Snoop team left St Antoine. On the one hand, there was Topher's strenuous argument that telling the truth would make no one better off, and would damage Snoop beyond repair, and probably cost hundreds of innocent people their jobs.

But on the other hand, that equation was precisely what made keeping the secret so uncomfortable. We were not doing what was *right*, we were doing what was *profitable*, a fact that Tiger stressed again and again in the increasingly bitter arguments that repeated themselves the last few nights of their stay in the hotel in St Antoine.

'Are you telling me,' Topher raged, 'that if it weren't for Snoop you'd put Eva's family through all that? Would you deliberately add another body to Liz's account, open all those old wounds that poor man's family thought they laid to rest years ago, torment Arnaud with something he never needs to know? Is all of that really worth sacrificing for the truth to come out when everyone concerned is already dead?'

'No!' Tiger cried. 'But that's the point, we're not weighing all that against the truth, we're weighing *Snoop* against the truth, that's what makes this so problematic! Topher, you can't go through life expecting everyone to sacrifice every principle they have for your company's vision — it doesn't *work* like that. It just makes you sound like an arrogant, entitled — '

'Entitled, entitled, fucking entitled!' Topher shouted over her. 'I am so bloody sick of that word! It's become a fucking stick to beat white men with. Do you know what entitled actually *means*, Tiger? It means you *deserve* something, that you are legally *due it*, for whatever reason. Think about that next time you talk about someone being entitled.'

And then he stormed out.

Now, three weeks later, I do think about it. I think about what entitled really means. About the fact that the unknown executive's family are entitled to know the truth about their son and brother. About the fact that Eva's innocent baby daughter is entitled to grow up without the shadow of her mother's actions hanging over her. And I think about the fact that the dead are entitled to be left in peace.

Topher is entitled, and that's the truth. Entitled in the way that Tiger meant. He has gone through life taking, and taking, and taking, just as Eva did. They used people like their own personal

436

chess pieces. Employees, investors, friends, relations — they took and they took from all of them. And they never accepted responsibility for the harm they caused.

I think about what responsibility means.

I think about guilt.

I think about moving on.

ERIN

I am up in my room, packing, when the email comes through. I don't know what I was expecting — Kate, maybe, with some last-minute details about our redundancy packages, or HR with some more legal disclaimers to sign. It's neither of those. And I don't recognise the email address.

But the subject line says 'Sorry' and so I click through.

I scan first to the bottom of the email to see who it's from — and the name there makes me do a double take. Topher. What the hell is he emailing me for?

I frown. Then I scroll back up to read what he's actually sent.

Dear Erin,

I expect by now you'll have seen in the papers that Snoop has gone under. Fucking vulture capitalists. When you're hot they can't get their tongues far enough down your throat — and when you actually need them, you might as well have herpes.

If Eva was here she'd be saying I told you so, I expect, but she's not — and so I can't even give her that small satisfaction.

I got your email off the user database before we got locked out. I know. Don't

438

shop me. But listen, I wanted to say . . . oh fuck it. I don't know. I'm sorry, or some bullshit like that. I'm sorry for everything that happened to you, but mainly, I'm sorry for being such a fucking prick about Alex and Will. I keep thinking back to that afternoon at the chalet when I realised who you were, and — well, look, I can't take the words back, but I never apologised for saying them in the first place, so that's what this is about.

I'm not very good at saying sorry. I haven't had much practice, to tell you the truth, so I'll just come out with it. Sorry. Alex and Will — they were good blokes. They didn't deserve to have that happen to them, and nor did you. And I'm fucking sorry for what I implied — I don't know how much you overheard, you were out of the room at the time, but I said some pretty shitty stuff in the heat of the moment, and I'm not proud of that.

Because here is the thing — now that the dust has settled, and I've had some time to come to terms with stuff, I get it. I get what losing people like that does to you. Eva — Elliot — they weren't blood, but they were the nearest thing to it. Elliot and I came up through the prep school system together, and Eva — I don't know. It's hard to explain. Even after we broke up, we never really severed that connection.

So I get it now. I get why you didn't tell us. I get why you couldn't leave.

I think about them all the time. About Elliot, being postmortemed in some French morgue. About Eva, still up there, frozen in the mountain passes like Sleeping Beauty. And about Ani too, I guess. Fuck.

Anyway — that's all really. I just wanted to say it one last time.

Sorry.

Topher
x

PS I just wanted to tell you, that file — I handed it all to the police. It felt like the right thing to do in the end. And for what it's worth, I did it last week. Before all this happened. It's not why Snoop went under — I'd like to say it was, but it wasn't. But I wanted you to know.

When I look up from the screen, I'm surprised to find my cheeks are wet. And although I don't know what to say, I hit reply and sit, for a long time, my fingers just hovering over the keys. And then I type. Just eight words. And I really, really hope they are true.

Dear Topher, it's going to be all right.

ERIN

'Oh, mate.' Danny's arms are around my neck, his face is buried in my shoulder. 'Gonna miss you, you stupid cow.'

'I'm going to miss you too.' I hug him back, feeling his strong shoulders, hard beneath his down jacket, smelling his permanent scent of French cooking — of simmering wine-rich stews, and melting butter, and sautéed garlic, and all good things.

'You gonna be all right?'

I nod. Because for the first time in a long while . . . I think I am.

'I have to go home,' I say, and I mean it this time. Not home, St Antoine, but home to England, where Will's grieving parents and my own family have been waiting patiently for me to make peace with my ghosts.

I have been alone with them for so long, listening to the Will and Alex in my head, trying to come to terms with what happened, with what I did — trying to come to terms with the responsibility of having said those four little words, *Let's go off-piste*.

Lying there in the snow with Liz, feeling her life ebbing away beneath my fingers, I realised — I can't keep running any more. And maybe that's OK.

'And are *you* going to be all right?' I ask. In the distance the coach is coming, I can hear the sound of its snow tyres against the ploughed road. 'What are you going to do? Try for a job in one of the other chalets?'

'Oh,' Danny says, and to my surprise, he's gone a little pink. The tips of his ears, just visible in spite of his beanie hat, are tinged with rose. 'Oh yeah, well, actually, I've got a place lined up.'

'You have?'

'Yeah,' he coughs, a little awkwardly. 'Um, you remember that B&B the police put us in?'

'The one with the shit cassoulet? Of course I remember!'

'Yeah, well, they've sacked their chef. And, well, um, well, a mate put in a word for me.'

'A mate?' I am grinning broadly now. 'A *mate*? Would that mate by any chance be sexy Eric the landlady's son? Monsieur Pina Colada from le Petit Coin?'

Danny is blushing so furiously that I can't help prodding him in the ribs, making him laugh.

'Oh, Danny! What did you have to do to earn that?'

'Never you mind.' Danny's cheeks are glowing, and he's half glowering, half grinning back, but I can see the happiness radiating out of him. 'Bit of nepotism never did no one any harm.'

'I very much doubt it was nepotism,' I say. 'One taste of your cassoulet and Eric would be mad not to snap you up.'

I want to know more. I want to know

442

everything, but now the coach is nearly here, and there's no time. I kiss Danny on the cheek and he picks up my other bag, and as the coach draws up, he hands it to the guy in charge of loading the luggage.

'Look after her,' he says in French to the driver as I make my way carefully up the steps. I don't need a crutch any more, but my ankle is still in the air cast. 'She's not as tough as she looks.'

'*Bien sur*,' the driver calls back, and winks at me.

I am sliding into my seat, when I hear Danny calling something through the thick window, and I pop open the little vent at the top of the pane and kneel up on the seat to look down at him.

'What is it?'

'I forgot to say — download Choon!'

'Choon?'

'It's the new Snoop, mate. Only better. C, H, double O, N.'

'Choon. Got it,' I call back. And then the coach begins moving and I shut the window. It picks up speed, and I'm waving to Danny, and he's waving to me, and kissing his hand, and I feel a tear tracing down my cheek.

He's calling something through the glass, but I can't hear what.

'I can't hear you!' I shout. My face is crumpling. I swipe at the tears on my cheek, feeling the tight ripple of the fading scar slick beneath my knuckles. 'I love you!' But we're too far up the road, and I know he didn't hear either.

I sink back into my seat, feeling my heart ache

443

for everyone I've lost, everything I'm leaving behind in the mountains. Another tear rolls down my face, and for a minute I think I'm not going to be able to hold it back — the tears are going to come whether I want them to or not, and I'm going to bawl my heart out on the bus. But then my phone gives a single beep.

It's a text message. From Danny.

CHOON, mate. Oh — and my ID, it's DANNYBOI. Luv ya.

ERIN

Choon ID: Little-My
Followers: 1

Acknowledgements

Writing a book is for the most part a selfish, lonesome thing, but I cannot stress enough the extent to which publishing is a team effort — and the tireless teams of editors, publicists, marketeers, designers, sales reps, rights people, production editors and everyone else behind the scenes, are the unsung heroes of the book world, along with the booksellers and librarians who take care of our efforts after they have left the doors of the publishing house. The fact that this book made it from my head into your hands is down to them, and for that I cannot say a large enough thank you.

To Alison, Liz, Jade, Sara, Jen, Maggie, Noor, Meagan, Sydney, Aimee, Bethan, Catherine, Nita, Kevin, Richard, Faye, Jessica, Rachel, Sophie, Mackenzie, Christian, Chloe, Anabel, Abby, Mikaela, Tom, Sarah, David, Christina, Jane, Sophie, Jennifer, Chelsea, Kathy, Carolyn and everyone at Simon & Schuster and PRH, my heartfelt thanks. And to the booksellers, librarians, bloggers, readers and reviewers — I cannot name you all, but you are the reason I keep getting to do this, and I thank you all every day.

While the characters and situations in this book are all my own invention, I was shameless in picking the brains of others to create Snoop — so thank you to Joe, James and James for giving me advice on everything from musical playlists to shareholders' agreements.

To Eve and Ludo, I literally could not do this without you.

To Carmen Sane and my fabulous writer friends, you are funny, wise, wonderful and filthy people and I would get a lot more work done without you but would have much less fun.

To Jilly, Ali and Mark — thank you for being the best skiing support team, media assistants, publicists and drinking companions. And of course for making me ski the Secret Valley (though not at night).

And last and best thanks always to my dear family, for everything.